PRAISE FOR
THE WHITE COAT DIARIES

"Readers looking for thrilling medical-drama goodness should turn to Madi Sinha's *The White Coat Diaries*." —PopSugar

"Move over Meredith and McDreamy, there's a hot new medical couple in town." —E! Online

"Norah Kapadia is among the most lovable and compelling characters in all of medical fiction."
—Kimmery Martin, author of *The Antidote for Everything*

"This authentic, no-holds-barred novel based on a savage intern year is gripping. [Norah's] navigating love—in the hospital and in her traditional Indian family—is touching, funny, and fraught. Welcome, author Madi Sinha, to the club of doctor/writers."
—Samuel Shem, author of
The House of God, *The Spirit of the Place*, and *Man's 4th Best Hospital*

"An engrossing story featuring an endearing protagonist. Madi Sinha offers a compelling glimpse into the world of medicine and desi culture through Norah Kapadia, a witty, fierce, memorable character. As Norah navigates her personal and professional struggles, she may falter, but she's never defeated. Readers will delight in her self-discovery and development—as both a doctor and an individual." —Margarita Montimore, author of *Oona Out of Order*

"Sinha tells a compelling story of self-discovery and blends it beautifully with the chaotic world of medicine and the wrenching nature of love." —Sarah Smith, author of *Faker*

TITLES BY MADI SINHA

The White Coat Diaries
At Least You Have Your Health

AT LEAST YOU HAVE YOUR HEALTH

MADI SINHA

BERKLEY
NEW YORK

BERKLEY
An imprint of Penguin Random House LLC
penguinrandomhouse.com

Library of Congress Cataloging-in-Publication Data

Names: Sinha, Madi, author.
Title: At least you have your health / Madi Sinha.
Description: First edition. | New York: Berkley, 2022.
Identifiers: LCCN 2021053583 (print) | LCCN 2021053584 (ebook) |
ISBN 9780593334256 (trade paperback) | ISBN 9780593334263 (ebook)
Subjects: LCGFT: Novels.
Classification: LCC PS3619.I57624 A93 2022 (print) | LCC PS3619.I57624 (ebook) |
DDC 813/.6—dc23/eng/20211104
LC record available at https://lccn.loc.gov/2021053583
LC ebook record available at https://lccn.loc.gov/2021053584

First Edition: April 2022

Printed in the United States of America
1st Printing

For Nupe

I'd choose you over Mr. Darcy any day.

It is health that is real wealth
and not pieces of gold and silver.
—MAHATMA GANDHI

Diseases of the soul are more dangerous
and more numerous than those of the body.
—CICERO

An appletini a day keeps the doctor away.
—UNKNOWN

AT LEAST YOU HAVE YOUR HEALTH

ONE

When Amelia DeGilles—forty-five, tailored jeans, nude sling-backs with a red sole—caught the arm of Maya Rao—thirty-six, threadbare leggings, brown stain on one off-brand white canvas sneaker—in the parking lot of Hamilton Hall Academy after the October parent council meeting, people noticed.

It wasn't just that Amelia DeGilles was known for keeping the company of a very small and carefully vetted circle of other Hamilton Hall mothers, but that the slightly disheveled young Indian woman with whom she was now engaged in intimate conversation drove a Honda Odyssey with silver duct tape on one side-view mirror and had very recently, only moments earlier in fact, come into some notoriety.

"Isn't that her? The gynecologist?" asked Evelyn Tuttle as she opened the door of her Range Rover, the car she drove on Tuesdays.

Her friend Lainey Smockett, who only owned one car but didn't need to leave the house all that much anymore since discovering that her au pair could be deployed for *so* many tasks besides just child-care, nodded. "Her kid's in Madison's class, I think."

Evelyn pursed her lips thoughtfully. "You know, I could swear I know her from somewhere, but I can't place her."

"I met her once, at back-to-school night," Lainey said, frowning. "She seemed a little standoffish."

"Well, she has nerve, I'll give her that. I came in late, but I heard her little speech. Making a proposal like that, and in front of the whole parent council?" Evelyn shook her head, her long flame-red hair catching the light. "I mean, I know she's new to Hamilton, but for God's sake. I only voted 'yes' out of kindness, but she'll never get that past the school board. They'll be appalled."

"Oh, I voted 'yes' out of kindness, too." Lainey, noticeably younger and less fashionable than her friend, nodded in eager agreement. She adjusted her oversize black sunglasses, the ones she imagined made her look something like Audrey Hepburn but in fact made her look something like a very large hornet. "I wonder if she knows my cardiologist, Dr. Patel. He's standoffish, too. What could Amelia want with her?"

Evelyn shrugged in a way that suggested she didn't care to know when, in fact, she cared very much to know. "Probably to assign her to a committee for the auction. There's still a few openings on Decorations, I think."

"But I'm the head of Decorations!" Lainey's eyelids fluttered in surprise. "Any new volunteer assignments have to go through me first."

Evelyn examined her manicure. "Oh, I'm sure Amelia was going to run it by you. Probably."

Lainey huffed in frustration. "You know, she's always making these unilateral decisions—and what was she thinking with this year's theme? A Night in Marrakesh? What does she want me to do? Rent a camel?"

"I think it could be nice. Tapestries and . . . other Moroccan things . . . earthenware." Evelyn gestured vaguely, as if the tapestries and earthenware were strewn about the parking lot in front of them. "Some Arabian-looking lamps—like the kind the genie pops out of—as centerpieces. And the waiters could wear those cute little hats with the tassels."

"But where am I supposed to get all that stuff?" Lainey crossed her arms petulantly. "I mean, I'm sure Queen Amelia can fly to Marrakesh to go shopping at the bazaar at the drop of a hat, but the rest of us have households to run without the benefit of a butler and chef and whatever else she has." She adjusted her sunglasses again and added hopefully, "Has she invited you over yet?"

Evelyn shook her head. "Carter and Prem broke up last week."

Lainey's face crumpled. "What? No, I'm so sorry."

Evelyn shrugged. "It wouldn't have lasted past graduation anyway. I was hoping they'd go to prom together. I bet I'd at least have gotten an invitation to the house for pictures. I might have gotten a look at the foyer. But now . . ." She sighed dejectedly.

"Oh my God, the foyer." Lainey had a faraway look in her eyes. "I bet it's even more stunning in person than it was in *Architectural Digest*."

"You'd think with a house like that, she'd at least volunteer to host the auction there, instead of making you decorate the gym every year," Evelyn said. "Her philanthropy is a little performative, if you ask me."

Lainey's hand flew to her heart. "Why, whatever would make you think that?" she asked, feigning shock. Then she rolled her eyes in the direction of the far end of the lot, adjacent to the school gymnasium, where a yellow construction crane was parked in front of a gaping hole in the earth. The area was cordoned off with orange and white parking barriers, and a placard proclaimed, in large letters: **FUTURE SITE OF THE DEGILLES MINDFULNESS SPACE**.

Evelyn chortled, and Lainey, encouraged by this reaction, added conspiratorially, "I heard the faculty wanted to use the money to buy new 3D printers and microscopes, but you know Amelia."

Evelyn nodded. "Any real estate she can slap her name on."

A black Aston Martin SUV with red trim glided past them and pulled to a stop next to Amelia and her companion. The driver—a sandy-haired young man in skinny jeans and a sports jacket—jumped out. Amelia nodded at him, a gesture so subtle it could have easily been missed, and he opened both the front and rear passenger side doors. Then, as Lainey, Evelyn, and several other Hamilton Hall parents watched with intense but still discreet interest, the two women climbed into the car—Amelia in the front seat and Maya in the rear—and the driver sped them off.

It was silent for a moment. Finally, Lainey crossed her arms and said, "Well, that woman must be one smooth talker if she's already made friends with Amelia DeGilles."

Evelyn shrugged again, her mouth pinched shut. "Well, she's Indian or Middle Eastern or whatever, right? Maybe Amelia wants her help renting a camel."

Lainey snorted. The merriment, however, was hollow. Both women were surprised to realize how much the gynecologist's coup had unsettled them. Had they misjudged her? That hardly seemed possible. The woman's side-view mirror was literally being held together with duct tape—duct tape, for God's sake! Yet there she was, going somewhere with Amelia DeGilles. *Invited* to go somewhere with Amelia DeGilles, daughter of legendary film composer Rupert DeGilles and model Melinda Spencer DeGilles, philanthropist and entrepreneur, a person named by the *Philadelphia Inquirer* as one of the Main Line's "10 Most Powerful Women Under 50." The same Amelia DeGilles who couldn't be bothered to show up for a single one of the weekly Hamilton Hall Mom Morning Meetups, who never attended nor RSVP'd for birthday parties to which her children had been invited, who'd for years listed her phone number in the Hamilton Hall parent directory as "by request."

Everyone wanted to be invited into Amelia DeGilles's inner circle. It seemed a travesty that the disheveled gynecologist should be, and without so much as even trying. Who did she think she was?

TWO

Two Days Earlier

Maya Rao, cum laude graduate of Temple medical school, dean's list all four years of college, salutatorian of her high school class, should have known better than to take her three children with her to a drive-through car wash. The minute her nine-year-old daughter, Diya, suggested it, warning bells should have sounded in her head. Her motherly instincts should have directed her to drive straight home from school pickup without stopping.

Maybe it was low blood sugar due to her missing lunch, or the fact that Niam, her four-year-old, was beside himself with excitement about the idea, or the blissful silence of the baby, Asha, finally asleep in her car seat after several endless bouts of hysterical, colicky crying. Some combination of factors led to a moment of overconfidence, a split-second lapse in judgment.

The car wash was a treat for the older kids. Their father brought them here in his tiny sedan sometimes when they were starved for entertainment. They would pick up an order of french fries from the drive-through burger place next door and eat them while being ferried through a soapy, aquatic wonderland. Like a very brief, very inexpensive theme park ride.

Maya hadn't taken her Honda Odyssey in for a wash in more than a year. It was a nonessential chore for which she never could find the time. And as dingy as the exterior was, the interior was far worse: ground Cheerios in every crevice, an entire petrified granola bar somehow wedged underneath the floor mat of Niam's seat. She'd been especially aware of the state of the van—which her husband affectionately referred to as the Hotessey—when she pulled up to the curb on the Hamilton Hall campus that morning, along the tree-lined circular driveway designated as the drop-off site for elementary school students, and saw a spotless black Aston Martin SUV with red trim glide past. The woman in the passenger seat was slender, with long, straight golden hair and, though Maya caught only a glimpse of her, seemed to have an almost regal bearing. She was the type of woman whose presence, even from a distance, even inside a car, couldn't be ignored.

Diya noticed the woman, too. Probably more importantly, Diya noticed Maya noticing her. "Maybe we should get a car wash after school," she said, climbing out of the van and tugging on her backpack, which was wedged between Niam's seat and the door.

Maya smiled. She might only be nine, but Diya had the mind of a much older, much more intuitive, and—Maya often worried—much more anxiety-ridden person. "The Hotessey's not looking so hot, huh?" she said, reaching an arm back to help dislodge the backpack.

"No, I mean, it's fine." Diya pulled the backpack straps over her shoulders, then pushed her lavender-framed glasses up the bridge of her nose. "It's just that the other cars are so—"

"Car wash!" Niam pumped his little fist, suddenly more energized than he'd been all morning. He chanted, "Car wash! Car wash!" then added with exuberance, "Can we get french fries, too? Can we go now?"

"Easy there, bud. It's a little early for fries." Maya glanced at the time displayed on the dashboard: 7:58. Eight minutes behind sched-

ule. Her pulse quickened. Morning drop-off was a carefully cali-
brated series of steps that had to be executed perfectly. She had
exactly twelve minutes to drop Niam off at his preschool down the
street before attendance was taken. If they were late, even by a minute, the teacher would make her walk him to the front office to sign
in. That would take another five minutes—or slightly longer, since
she'd be lugging the baby's car seat with her and, therefore, moving
more slowly. She couldn't afford that kind of delay. After dropping
off Niam, she'd have fourteen minutes to drive across town to the
baby's day care and drop her off before making the roughly twenty-
five minute commute into Philadelphia. She knew from experience
that she had to be on the highway by 8:29 a.m. to avoid the worst of
the morning traffic. When everything ran perfectly, she could be
confident she'd pull into the Philadelphia General Hospital parking
deck at 8:54 and walk into her office at 8:59, in time for her first appointment at 9:00 a.m. But the margin for error was dangerously thin.

"We'll talk about this after school. We're late," she said urgently.
"Niam, watch your fingers!"

Diya stepped onto the curb with a feeble wave.

"Bye, honey! Have an awesome day!" Maya called as the van's
door slid shut with a metallic thunk. "Remember to work hard and
try your best!"

Diya was already making her way, feet dragging and shoulders
hunched, across the wide green lawn of the elementary school, join-
ing the stream of other students filing into the building.

"She can't hear you, Mommy," Niam said helpfully. "She's outside the car." He pointed.

"I know." Maya let her gaze linger on Diya for a moment, on her
long, black, slightly frizzy ponytail and floral backpack embellished
with the words *Girl Power!* in pink glitter. She wished she could
telescope her arms out the van window and grab her daughter, hold
her tightly by the shoulders, tell her *this* year was going to be better.

This was where she belonged, and Maya was just sorry—so incredibly sorry—she hadn't realized it sooner.

It shamed her to think of it, but she'd been neglectful, and had slipped unwittingly into complacency when it came to her eldest over the last few years. She'd grown lax in her duty to provide the right environment. To optimize and maximize and capitalize for the benefit of her child. But now, her eyes following Diya as she crossed the verdant expanse toward the ivy-covered buildings, Maya felt a deep and calming satisfaction, like a warm shawl being pulled around her, easing some of the tension she always carried in her neck.

A car horn blared. A Cadillac Escalade was waiting for her parking spot, its driver gesticulating angrily.

"Fucker," Maya mumbled, pulling the van out of its spot and into the traffic inching around the circle driveway. Hunched over the steering wheel, her neck muscles in spasm again, she crept toward the exit and onto bustling, congested Lancaster Avenue.

"That car was a fucker," Niam's voice piped up.

Maya cringed. Glancing at him in the rearview mirror, she said, "Mommy shouldn't have said that. That's not a nice thing to say."

"You should apple pies," he said sagely.

"I should apologize, you're right. Seriously, honey, don't use that word in school, okay? Remember what Mrs. Diaz said?"

"Snookus is licking my toes!" Niam replied, laughing.

"Is he?"

Snookus was Niam's imaginary pet dog. He'd appeared six months earlier and seemed to materialize whenever Niam wanted to change the subject. Niam was fiercely loyal to Snookus and would entertain no suggestions that his beloved invisible pet might not be real. For a four-year-old, he was fairly easygoing—a quality he'd likely inherited from his father—but the question of Snookus's existence, everyone in the family knew, was strictly off-limits.

"That's great, honey, but I just want to remind you about being careful with your words. Remember we talked about that with your teacher?"

"Some words are inappropriate," Niam said.

Maya's shoulders relaxed. "Right." She grinned to herself. He still couldn't pronounce *apologize*, but *inappropriate* rolled off his tongue. Just a year ago she thought he might need speech therapy because he still wasn't speaking in complete sentences and avoided talking at all if he could help it. Something clicked in him a few months later, and ever since then, it felt like he never shut up. More recently, he'd developed a knack for committing impolite words to memory and later working them into casual conversation, usually at the most inopportune times.

"Like *poop*," Niam said.

"Correct."

"And *butthead*."

"Yup."

"And *vagina*."

"Well . . . no, actually . . ." She parked the van in the fire lane in front of the Learning Tree Preschool, a squat red building reminiscent of a barn, and switched on her hazard lights. She twisted around in her seat to face him. "That's just an anatomical—"

"Mommy!" Niam interrupted. "Eight-one-zero! Eight-one-zero!" He pointed urgently at the dashboard.

"Shit! We're late!" Maya sprang out of the driver's seat and over the center console. In one fluid motion, she unbuckled Niam from his car seat, slung his backpack over her shoulder, and unsnapped the baby's car seat from its base. She slid open the van door. "Go, go, go!" she shouted, as if they were infantrymen about to parachute out of a plane.

"*Shit* is inappropriate," Niam said, suddenly in no hurry at all.

"I know! Sorry! Mommy can't be late to work today, Niam, so we have to go fast! Like a superhero!"

Niam liked the sound of that. He put his fists on his hips and jutted out his chin. "I'm superfast! Don't worry, Mommy, I won't let you be late!"

She was late. She arrived at the outpatient offices of the Philadelphia General Hospital department of Obstetrics and Gynecology at 9:12 a.m. and, like a snowball rolling downhill, the day got progressively further away from her. Every patient was more complicated than the one before, and by the time it was 2:00 p.m., despite working through her twenty-minute lunch break, she was running an hour behind schedule.

Staring down a long hallway of examination rooms, each with a chart on the door, each with a patient inside waiting, Maya glanced at her watch and sighed. Diya and Niam would be the last ones picked up from their respective aftercares. Again.

Esther, her medical assistant, appeared at her elbow with a packet of saltine crackers. As usual, she was dressed in fitted pale pink scrubs and her favorite black-and-gold running shoes, her brown waist-length box braids pulled into a low ponytail. "Your patient—not the next one, but the one after her—is pissed, Dr. Rao," Esther whispered. "She's been waiting for over an hour. I told her you were running behind, but—" She shrugged as if to say *same shit, different day*. "Here, you should eat something." She handed Maya the saltines. "This is all we had in the break room. I can totally run to the vending machine for you, though. Also, I ran the urine screen on Mrs. Tremont, and I told her you would call her later today with the results, but not before five, because it's Tuesday and I know you have to pick up the kids today."

Maya smiled gratefully. One of four children, the eldest daughter of Haitian immigrants who both worked long hours—her father nights as a cab driver, her mother days as a nanny to a white family—while she was growing up, Esther could multitask and caretake like no one else. Maya often forgot how young she was. In about a year, she'd have enough college credits to graduate with a degree in biology. Then she planned to apply to medical school and, if everything went according to her plans, to become the second Black female surgeon general of the United States by the time she was thirty-five. She reminded Maya, in many ways, of her younger, premotherhood self: driven, focused, capable. Esther kept a framed photograph of Joycelyn Elders next to her computer and ran two miles every morning before work. She possessed the boundless energy and clear-eyed vision of youth, the type of energy and vision Maya could vaguely recall having once, back when she, too, could comfortably wear fitted scrubs.

"Esther, you're the best. Thank you." Maya dug through the pockets of her white lab coat for loose change. "If you have time, I'd love two packets of Cheez-Its from the vending machine."

"You got it," Esther said. "Oh, and this next patient didn't want to tell me what her complaint is today. You've never seen her before, and she says that whatever's going on is too personal to share with anyone but the doctor." She frowned sympathetically and was gone.

Maya grabbed the chart off the door and leafed through it. In her field of medicine, it was common for patients to be embarrassed about their symptoms: itching of privates, discharges of various sorts, unusual odors. To the layperson, sure, this might be cringe-inducing stuff. But what she felt, overwhelmingly, for her patients was a deep sense of empathy: it was hard being female. Being female meant having a whole set of internal organs that society didn't find important enough to worry or think or care about until a baby was involved and regulations needed to be handed down. A whole set of internal organs that had never, until recent history, been studied in as much exacting detail as the almighty penis. And these were organs that could bleed regularly, rupture unexpectedly, grow painful fibroids or cysts or tumors, become cancerous, scar, or get infected. Even when their internal organs were working perfectly well, women were wracked with anxiety about all the things that might go wrong, might be going wrong at this very moment, without their awareness. Misinformation was everywhere—online, on television, in advertisements for useless vaginal cleansing products—and it was hard to know who or what to believe. It was fear that brought so many patients through the clinic doors.

Tucking the chart under her arm, Maya knocked, entered the room, and apologized for running late.

The woman seated on the exam table was in her midtwenties, but she looked much younger. A paper drape covered her lower half, and she seemed as if she was trying to fold the rest of herself underneath it, too, shoulders curled, head bowed. As if her entire body was cringing. Her chestnut brown hair fell across half her face like a curtain.

"Are you okay?" Maya asked, lowering herself onto a rolling stool so she was looking up at the patient. Hiding your privates under a thin square of paper in a cold examination room was horrible enough without a doctor glaring down at you from above. A few years ago, Maya had tried to convince hospital administration to invest in blanketlike cloth drapes, which would be both more comfortable for the patients and more environmentally friendly, but she was told the department couldn't afford the added expense of laundering drapes.

The woman nodded sheepishly, and Maya asked, smiling kindly, "What brings you in today?"

She diverted her eyes, gazing up at a loose tile in the ceiling. "There's something wrong with my . . . down there."

"Tell me more about that," Maya said.

"I can't . . ." The woman cleared her throat. "I don't have . . . you know."

Maya's brow furrowed. "You don't have . . . ?" She nodded encouragingly.

"*Orgasms,*" the woman replied, her voice a conspiratorial whisper. "I can't have them. I never could, not even when I was a teenager. I mean, I can when I'm . . . you know, alone. But not ever with other people. My boyfriend said it's because my, you know, down there isn't sensitive enough. He said there's a shot you can get in there to fix that? The O-Shot? He read about it online."

"Okay," Maya said slowly, silently mapping the best way to approach the conversation. "So, just to reassure you, a lot of women don't orgasm during sex. It's pretty common."

The woman's eyebrows went up in surprise. "It is?"

"Absolutely," Maya said. "And there can be a lot of different reasons for it. It's treatable, but not with shots. There's no good scientific evidence that having anything injected into your vagina will help you in any way."

The woman's shoulders relaxed. "Oh, okay. Good. It sounded awful anyway." Then she asked, "But is this something I can fix, though?"

"It's treatable, yes," Maya said. "Usually with therapy and medication. But first, let me ask, is it something *you* think needs fixing?"

The woman blinked. "What do you mean?"

"I mean, is not having orgasms during sex something that bothers *you*?"

"I mean . . ." the woman turned the question over like it had never before occurred to her. "I mean, I enjoy sex. The, you know, would be nice, but I don't, like, need it to have a good time, if that's what you mean."

"That's what I mean," Maya said. "The first thing to ask yourself before you try to treat this problem is: Do you think this is a problem?"

The woman grimaced. "I mean, I have a vibrator and it works really well. But it bothers my boyfriend that he can't make me, you know. I guess it makes him feel less like a man or whatever. He's been with tons of women before me, and they've always—you know. I'm the first woman he's been with that he hasn't been able to. And he says if we want to get married and have kids someday, it'll be hard for me to get pregnant if I can't, you know, while he's inside me."

Maya took a breath. "Okay, so there are two issues here. One, he doesn't feel like a man unless he can bring you to climax. That's about him, not you. And about thirty-five percent of straight women don't regularly climax during sex, so statistically your boyfriend's claim seems a little suspect."

The woman chewed the inside of her cheek. "Thirty-five percent is a lot."

"It is," Maya agreed. "And we can discuss sending you both, or just him, to a sex therapist as a first step in treatment, if you want. But the second issue is the idea that climaxing helps you get pregnant. It doesn't. There's no relationship between climaxing and egg fertilization."

"Really?" The woman's eyes widened. "But I thought when you have a—a bunch of eggs get released from your ovaries."

Maya shook her head. "Just one egg gets released every cycle, regardless of whether you have an orgasm or not."

The woman's face clouded with confusion. "Wait, there's an egg in there every month? I thought . . . I thought they sometimes, like, fall out of the ovary by accident, but mostly they get released during sex. Because when you have a, you know, the man's thing hits your ovary and knocks them out."

Maya sighed internally. She opened a drawer and produced a color-coded diagram of the female reproductive system. Then she carefully explained the location and function of the uterus, ovaries, and other pelvic structures, as well as reviewing the phases of the menstrual cycle.

"And the egg comes out during my period?" the woman asked.

"It does."

She raised one eyebrow skeptically. "But . . . I've never seen an egg come out of me."

"They're tiny, the size of a grain of sand," Maya said. "Almost impossible to see."

The woman sat with this information for a moment. "I can't believe I didn't know that."

"You're not alone," Maya said. "There's a lot of misinformation out there about how our bodies work."

"So I don't really need to have orgasms?"

"Not unless you want them." The woman's eyes went glassy then, and Maya asked, alarmed, "Is everything okay?"

"I just thought . . . I thought it was just me. I've had boyfriends, more than one, tell me there was something wrong with me. That all normal women can . . . you know. I never talked about it with anyone because I was too embarrassed." She wiped her eyes with her sleeve and laughed. "I'm not, like, crying because I'm upset. It's just out of relief."

Maya nodded and squeezed her arm reassuringly. "I get it."

Once the visit was over, Maya wished the woman well and sent her back into the world armed with an accurate understanding of her reproductive anatomy, silently hoping the first thing the woman did was dump her idiot boyfriend. Then she found Esther down the hall in the tiny office the two of them shared. "Unbelievable!" Maya said from the doorway, the word bursting from her like air being let out of a balloon. "That poor young woman has gone for years—*years*—with anorgasmia, not knowing how her menstrual cycle works and really misunderstanding where her ovaries are located, and meanwhile her fucking boyfriend has convinced her she's abnormal and what she really needs is an injection of who-even-knows-what into her clitoris."

"It's always the fucking boyfriend," Esther said, nodding solemnly. "Every time."

"Because if you're a young woman and your boyfriend says something about your body, you're probably going to believe it," Maya said.

"When I was sixteen, my boyfriend tried to tell me that women pee out of their vaginas," Esther said. "Like he didn't understand there was a whole separate opening for that. And he was, like, really sure about it. I probably would have believed him, too, if my aunts hadn't already taught me everything."

"See, this is my point," Maya said. "What if you didn't have four aunts that were all nurses? Where would you have learned the truth? Of course you'd believe whatever the Internet and the fucking boyfriend were telling you."

"Once your grant proposal gets approved, Dr. Rao, we'll change all that." Esther smiled hopefully.

Her shoulders relaxing, Maya said, "That's the plan. Although, what we really need to do eventually is get into schools. Educate kids early. But the grant proposal is a good, solid first step."

"Have you heard back from administration yet?"

"Not yet, but it should be any day now. The board was supposed to meet about it last week." She crossed her fingers tightly, and Esther mirrored the gesture.

"Are there any doctors on the board?" Esther asked. "Or just paper pushers?"

"There are a few," Maya said. "But they're all men. I'm not sure how much they're going to support a women's health education program."

"There are no women doctors on the board? Not even one?" Esther frowned. "That seems pretty messed up."

Maya laughed bitterly and said, in a voice like a television announcer, "Women doctors: all the compassion and emotional burnout, none of the power or influence."

Esther chuckled in agreement, then suddenly raised her eyebrows and cocked her head. Maya, caught up in her tristesse, missed the signal entirely. "Seriously, sometimes I wish I'd been born with a dick, because maybe then—"

"Dr. Rao, good afternoon."

Maya whirled around and came nose-to-nose with a silver-haired, grandfatherly man in a long white coat. "Dr. Keating! Good afternoon." Maya nodded stiffly. As one of the most junior doctors in the fifteen-member Obstetrics and Gynecology Department, one of only four women and the only one who, at least for the time being, no longer did deliveries, Maya felt a constant pressure to prove her worth and demonstrate her professionalism. This endeavor had not been going well so far. Earlier in the week, she'd arrived at work with rice cereal in her hair and one of Niam's SpongeBob Band-Aids stuck to the seat of her pants. A few months ago, before she'd given up trying to nurse Asha, she'd forgotten to lock her office door while pumping and Dr. Keating had walked in to an unobstructed view of one of her breasts. You wouldn't think that, for a gynecologist, an exposed breast would be an object of embarrassment—breasts, in their myriad sizes and varieties, being part of the daily, humdrum routine of work—but your elderly boss seeing you topless, as it turned out, was abjectly mortifying no matter your profession.

"I'll just go tell the next patient that you'll be with her in a minute," Esther said, excusing herself and inching past them in the narrow hallway. She shot Maya a sympathetic look over Dr. Keating's shoulder, then fled.

Maya cleared her throat. Smiling sheepishly, she asked, "Was there something you needed, sir?"

Dr. Keating's stern expression softened. Ever since her residency, he'd been something of a mentor to her. He'd never exactly taken her under his wing like he had some of her male colleagues, but she couldn't hold this against him. In her darkest hour, when she'd called him, desperate and afraid, he'd been there for her, extended her a kindness she didn't deserve. That was almost four years ago now, but she still warmed with gratitude every time she saw him.

"Maya, I wish I had better news," Dr. Keating said, "but administration turned down your grant proposal." He shrugged sympathetically. "I know it's disappointing, but that's how these things go sometimes, I'm afraid."

Maya straightened the collar of her white coat. Trying to keep the bitterness out of her voice, she asked, "Did they say why?"

"They thought the idea was good, but they said there's just not enough money in the budget for it this year. And the one day per week you asked to have off to work on the project, well, they couldn't justify the loss in revenue that would cause. Your billing has been on the low side this year, as I'm sure you're aware."

"Well, yes, but I was out for four weeks on maternity leave, so . . ."

Dr. Keating nodded. "Yes, sure, that could account for some loss of revenue. Four weeks is a long time. Not that women shouldn't be able to take as much time as they need for maternity leave, but the truth is, it does affect revenue . . ." He cleared his throat and looked away. Discussing how much money a doctor was bringing into the practice, Maya knew, always made him unhappy. She suspected he felt it was beneath him. But as department head, Dr. Keating acted as liaison between the staff physicians and hospital administration. Middle management, essentially. He reported directly to the VP of hospital operations, a slick-haired thirty-one-year-old business school graduate named Tad, who, Maya was fairly sure, couldn't spell *obstetrics* without help. In his monthly emails to the department, which were always peppered with an unsettling number of exclamation marks, Tad used phrases like "leveraging our strategic partnerships" and wrote excitedly of his plans to target hospital advertising to "capture female patients in the eighteen-to-sixty-five-year-old range." The latter expression always made Maya picture Tad running through a field with a butterfly net, in pursuit of a panicked woman wearing no-slip socks and rolling an IV pole behind her. The point of these emails was always the same: to inform the doctors that their schedules would become increasingly overbooked and to discourage them from complaining or asking for appropriate financial compensation for it. "As we continue to grow the regional market dominance of PGH, we appreciate the commitment and sacrifice of our physicians! Thank you all for being team players!!! Longer-than-usual clinic hours may be necessary in the short or long term!!!!" was how he'd signed off his last message.

"Your proposal, though well thought out, isn't a research project," Dr. Keating continued. "It's more community outreach, this lecture series you came up with."

"Well, yes, that was my intent," Maya said. "I just had a patient who didn't know until today how her ovaries work. I mean, we see this all the time, right? So many women don't understand their own anatomy. We should be helping to educate women about their bodies, not just waiting for them to come to us when things go wrong."

"I agree with you," Dr. Keating said. He shrugged ruefully. "And I admire your charitable spirit, but administration likes to fund research projects that will produce a paper in a peer-reviewed medical journal. That's how we build the reputation of the department, the reputation of the hospital. You understand."

Maya nodded stiffly. She thought she understood perfectly: Tad and his cronies in administration were more interested in the appearance of helping patients than in actually helping them.

Dr. Keating said he was sorry again and took his leave. "I'm late for another meeting," he said, dejectedly smoothing down the few strands of his comb-over, and Maya was struck with despair. Was this what she had to look forward to? Dr. Keating was the highest-ranking member of their department. He'd been practicing gynecology for nearly thirty years, and his career had amounted to nothing more than an endless stream of purposeless administrative meetings. Was this really all there was?

Her phone buzzed in the pocket of her white coat with an incoming call. Her husband, Dean, was his usual buoyant self. "Hey, babe. How's your day going?"

Maya sighed and said, "Do you ever feel like you thought you were moving forward, but it turns out the whole time you were actually just going in circles? Like you're nothing more than a hamster on the endlessly spinning wheel of life?"

There was a brief silence at the other end of the line. Then Dean said, "I drove around campus for, like, twenty minutes after lunch trying to find a parking spot, so I hear you. Those empanadas were worth it, though."

"Very funny."

His voice softening, he asked, "What happened?"

"Grant proposal got rejected," she said.

"What? No way!" Dean's voice was angry but quiet, which told her that he must be in the lab. Several of his coworkers did experiments with mice, and loud voices could scare the animals, potentially ruining valuable data. "That's bullshit!" he whispered.

"Administration said they want to fund research projects, not 'community outreach.'"

"So, it's more important to them that they *study* how to help patients instead of actually helping them," Dean said, and it felt to

Maya like he'd reached through the line and enveloped her in one of his warm bear hugs.

"Just this morning a woman came in with chest pain," Maya said, "and she came to me instead of going to the emergency room because she thought she might have inserted her tampon so far up her vagina that it traveled to her chest cavity and got stuck there. Ninety percent of what I do is educate adult women about how their bodies work. If we could just . . ." she shook her head in frustration. "We could be doing so much more, you know?"

"It's a great idea, Maya," Dean said. "I'm sorry they don't get it. They're idiots."

"Thanks. I'd better go. I'm running an hour behind."

"Want me to get the kids?"

"Don't you have a class to teach?" She looked at her watch. "Like, right now?"

"I could cancel it. It's undergraduate Intro to Biology. Most of the kids don't want to be there anyway. I'm the only thing standing between them and happy hour."

"Aren't there, like, three hundred kids in that class? I'm pretty sure canceling at the last minute would be frowned upon. I'll handle pickup. I'll just be a little late, but"—she sighed again—"I think Diya and Niam are getting used to that."

"The kids will be fine." Dean's voice was like a cup of hot tea. It was one of the first things that had attracted her to him back in college, his deep, soothing baritone. "Cut yourself some slack. You don't have to do everything perfectly, you know."

She snorted. "Perfect? I let go of perfect a long time ago. At this point, I'd be happy if I were doing even one thing sort of well."

"What are you talking about? You're killing it at this Doctor Mom thing."

"I could be doing everything so much better," she said wistfully. "I just need more . . . I don't know."

"Maya—" Dean started, his voice concerned.

"It's fine," she replied, rallying. "I'm fine. I've got the kids. See you at home."

"Are you sure? I'm serious about canceling my class."

"Your adviser will kill you. Go, educate the youth about photosynthesis."

A door at the end of the hallway opened, and an otherwise naked woman wearing a paper gown significantly too small for her emerged, red faced. "Excuse me! I've been waiting for over an hour!" she bellowed to no one and, somehow, everyone.

"Gotta go." Maya hung up the phone as Esther came running with a panicked look in her eyes. The two of them ushered the woman back into the room, though not before several patients in the hallway caught an unobstructed view of her backside.

THREE

The events of the day—the angry patient, the grant proposal rejection, the backside—were still on Maya's mind when, that evening, she screeched to a stop in front of the Hamilton Hall dining commons, the baby howling in her car seat.

"Stop crying, Asha!" Niam wailed. He pressed his palms over his ears. "Mom, make her stop!"

"She's six months old, Niam. I can't make her do anything," Maya said, though she knew he couldn't hear her over Asha's shrieking. The interior of the van seemed to amplify the baby's already deafening volume by several times. Maya fished through her diaper bag and found one clean pacifier, then twisted her body over the seat to deposit it into the baby's mouth. After a few more howls for good measure, Asha settled into contented sucking. Sweet, merciful silence. Sometimes Maya forgot how luxurious that could feel.

Her phone pinged loudly, and she swore under her breath and silenced it. A text reminder about the upcoming Hamilton Hall parent council meeting, the monthly 10:00 a.m. gathering evidently organized by someone under the impression that all Hamilton Hall parents—or at least all those deserving of a say in their children's education—were free at 10:00 a.m. on a weekday morning. Maya had signed up for the text alerts at back-to-school night after noticing all the other mothers in Diya's class enthusiastically doing so. Now she wondered why she'd even bothered. She deleted the message.

Niam pointed out his window. "That lady looks like the Little Mermaid."

"Honey, don't point," Maya said, while noticing the woman on the sidewalk did, indeed, resemble Ariel from *The Little Mermaid*: voluminous flame-red hair that cascaded in waves down her back, tiny waist, pert nose. She wore cigarette pants and a tailored blouse and carried a Fendi bag in the crook of one arm. She was, Maya guessed, probably in her early forties and, with her phone pressed to her ear, had the air of someone at once both tremendously busy and perfectly at ease.

As she flicked on her hazard lights and unfastened her seat belt, Maya was acutely aware of her unmanicured cuticles and the conspicuous coffee stain running the length of one thigh of her elastic-waisted maternity pants. The baby weight seemed progressively harder to lose with every pregnancy, and the baggy pants were the only kind that fit comfortably without irritating her still-sensitive C-section scar. She thought she'd made peace with the idea of perhaps wearing maternity clothes for the rest of her life, but looking at the woman on the sidewalk, she felt sloppy in comparison. Pudgy and lumbering. Frazzled. Tired. She needed to do a better job keeping herself up. When was the last time she'd had a haircut? Had she shaved her legs this week? God, why couldn't she just get herself together? Self-care required self-discipline. She needed to put more effort into herself. To, as ironic as it sounded, work harder to be more relaxed.

She rolled down the windows, then turned off the ignition and tucked the keys into her pocket.

She should probably buy some new clothes. When was the last

time she'd bought new clothes? When was the last time she'd gone shopping for herself? Somewhere other than Target? Certainly not since Asha was born. Probably not since Niam. And a manicure? Well over a year. Nails. She must remember to cut Asha's and Niam's nails.

Ah yes, this was why she couldn't keep herself up. She always allowed her own needs to be superseded by those of her children, because what other choice was there?

"I'll be back in a second, Niam," she said.

"For my birthday, I want a square marble," he replied.

She closed and locked her door, leaving her jacket in the car. The evening was cool, the temperature dropping as sunset approached, but she'd only be outside for a moment. Through the open window she said, "Where am I going to find a square marble?" and rubbed Niam's hair. He giggled.

Aftercare was located just inside the oversize glass double doors of the dining commons. Students sat at large round tables doing homework or chatting quietly, under the watchful eyes of several humorless teacher's aides. It wasn't a bad place to be stuck for a couple of hours after school, but Maya knew Diya hated it, even if she didn't say so. She was always sitting at the table closest to the door, always by herself. "I didn't know anyone else there, and anyway, I can concentrate on my homework better if I'm by myself," she'd explain, and Maya's heart would splinter a little with pain and with pride. Her lonesome, industrious girl.

A short, manicured path, maybe ten feet long, led from the sidewalk to the entrance of the dining commons. Maya jogged to the door and was about to pull it open when a reproachful voice behind her called, "Excuse me!"

She looked over her shoulder. It was the Little Mermaid.

"Can you hold on a second?" the mermaid said to the person at the other end of the line, then tucked her phone against her chest. "Excuse me, you can't park there."

Maya looked around. "Me?"

The mermaid's emerald-green eyes were bright and angry against her pale skin. She craned her neck to look into the van, then back at Maya. "Yes. You," she said pointedly. "You have to drive around to the back of the school and park in the auxiliary lot. There's no parking here. It's school policy."

Maya knew where the auxiliary lot was, but to her knowledge, no parents or teachers ever parked in it. Getting from the distant lot to the main campus buildings required a several-minute walk and multiple steep flights of stairs. She smiled patiently. "Oh, I know. I'm not parking. I'm just picking up from aftercare."

The mermaid glared. "You're not allowed to stop your car here."

"But . . ." Maya shook her head, flummoxed, worried she had missed something obvious. "Aftercare is right here. I'm just going to go grab her and jump right back in my car. All the parents do the same thing."

The mermaid's eyes widened as if she could not believe what she was hearing. "They most certainly do not! Parents are well aware of the parking rules. And you can't just leave your van here with two small children in it, unattended. What kind of caretaker are you?"

Maya had the distinct feeling of being backed into a corner, of being small and afraid and bewildered. When she was Diya's age, she once boarded the after-school bus and tried to take the empty seat next to a popular girl in her class, a straw-haired child named Claire who, everyone knew, owned four pairs of Keds in different colors.

"Can I sit here?" Maya asked.

The girl's face had twisted in revulsion. "No!" She offered no explanation, just that one word, and glared at Maya as if the very question had been an affront. Humiliated, Maya had slinked away, searching for another open seat while the boys at the back of the bus snickered with glee. When she finally found a seat near a window, she had curled against it, wishing she could melt into the glass and become translucent herself. Wishing she could disappear.

"But," she said to the Little Mermaid, tentatively, as if she was unsure as to the location of her own car, "I can see them from the door. They're never out of my sight."

"Is their mother aware that this is what you're doing?"

Maya blinked. "What?"

"Because I bet she wouldn't be very happy to hear about how irresponsible you're being with her kids."

A wave of realization passed over Maya. Diya looked like a miniature version of her, skin a deep brown with red undertones, hair thick and curly and inky black. But Niam and Asha had their father's light eyes and Nordic complexion, their hair fine and straight and coppery brown, their cheeks lightly dusted with freckles.

"What's your employer's name?" the mermaid demanded.

Maya stood unmoving, her mind woolly. She was numb, as if all the blood in her body had suddenly turned cold and sluggish.

The woman shook her head as if to say *do I have to do everything myself?* and approached the window of the van. She stooped a bit to make herself level with Niam's face. "What's your mommy's name, sweetie? Do you know her phone number?"

Maya felt her body come back to life, awaken into rage. It took everything in her not to yank the woman away from the window by her hair. Through gritted teeth she said, her tone measured, "These are my kids."

"Mommy," Niam replied. "She's right there." He pointed to Maya, looking at the mermaid as if she were slow.

"These. Are. My. Kids," Maya said again, louder, the words like tiny sparks of fire, and the woman jumped back suddenly.

"Oh. Okay. I didn't know. Well, regardless, you're not allowed to park here." She crossed her arms, betraying not a flicker of remorse for her error.

Maya regarded the woman. She'd heard stories about mothers leaving their children in a car for a few moments, in absolutely no danger, while they returned a library book or did some other errand that could be completed in less time than it would take to get the children in and out of the car, only to find that some meddlesome, virtue-signaling bystander had taken video of the event and called the police, who subsequently charged the mother with neglect and removed the children from her care. She slid open the van door and unbuckled both Niam and the baby. Asha whined in protest, the cold air sending a shiver through her tiny body. She spit her pacifier onto the sidewalk, opened her mouth, and, after a moment of angry breathlessness, began wailing like an air raid siren. Wordlessly, Maya tossed the dirty pacifier into the passenger seat, tucked the baby against her body with one arm, hoisted Niam with the other, and carried both children, bowing slightly under Niam's weight, to the door of the dining commons.

The mermaid made some vague noises in protest.

"What are we doing?" Niam asked, delighted. He enjoyed being carried. It so rarely happened anymore.

"We're going to get your sister," Maya said.

"Don't we need jackets?"

"It'll just take a second."

"I could call campus security," the mermaid called after them, refusing to abandon her cause now that she was so deeply entrenched in it.

Maya bit back her reply, but her outrage, the searing heat of humiliation, tore into her chest like something wild and clawed. And the old lessons, buried deep in her marrow since childhood, seeped out of her bones, bubbling up to meet the anger, to temper it: don't engage. You don't ever engage, because that only calls more attention to you, gives shape and texture to your otherness, like the rumpling of bedsheets. Leave. Extricate yourself from the situation as quickly as possible. Smooth down the fabric and tuck in the corners as you go. You never really saw us. We were never really here.

She deposited Niam on the sidewalk so she could pull open the door to the dining commons, then ushered him through and followed without a backward glance. She didn't want the mermaid to see that she was on the verge of tears.

The baby's shrieking pierced the silence of the elegant, parquet-floored dining commons, and every head turned toward them. Fortunately, the only students remaining at this hour were a handful of middle schoolers more interested in their phones. At the table closest to the door, Diya's face fell. Embarrassed by the commotion, she quickly gathered her books and papers into her backpack and rushed to join her family. An aide, an older woman with short, bleached hair and bifocals, held out a clipboard, and Maya signed her name next to Diya's on a printed list.

"You could have just left them in the car," the aide said, annoyed, shouting to be heard. She glanced through the tall windows at the van. "You can see them from here, and it's not hot out."

Maya pressed her lips into a line.

"It's what all the other parents do." Catching the flinty look in Maya's eye, the aide added, shrugging, "Just a suggestion."

By the time Maya herded all three children back out to the van, the mermaid had disappeared. Asha was still crying.

"Why don't you give her a pacifier?" Diya shouted from her seat behind Niam and the baby.

"I don't have any clean ones!" Maya shouted back.

"What?"

"I don't have any clean ones!"

"What?"

Maya touched her forehead lightly to the steering wheel and closed her eyes. She meant to either pray silently or take a very brief nap, whichever came easier.

"I'm hungry!" Niam wailed.

Without moving her forehead off the wheel, she reached into her purse and handed him a packet of Cheez-Its over her shoulder. If he knew, Dean would probably have something smart to say about feeding the kids snacks right before dinner. He could be annoying that way.

"I'm hungry, too," Diya said, just as Maya handed Niam a second packet of Cheez-Its to pass back to his sister. There was a crackling of foil.

"Cheez-Its are my favorite," Niam said, crumbs spilling out of his mouth.

Maya started the van. "They're from Miss Esther. She says hi."

"I like Miss Esther," Niam said. "She's the funnest."

Maya smiled at him in the rearview mirror. It had been just over a year since the morning Niam had woken up with a fever, mere hours before Dean had to be at the university to give his first lecture to the undergraduate biology majors. Left with no other choice—the day care had a strict no-fever-for-24-hours policy—Maya had brought Niam to work with her, and he spent the day curled in a sleeping bag on the floor of her office like a sad puppy. She looked in on him in between patients, checking his temperature and coaxing him to eat lunch and take Tylenol, but it was Esther who brought him all the saltine crackers he wanted, played countless rounds of I Spy with him, and, in the afternoon, once he was feeling better, helped him build a four-foot-high tower out of tiny sample bottles of baby formula.

Esther was a natural with children, patient and relaxed in a way Maya both admired and envied. She was always so uptight with her children, the way her parents had been with her. Parenthood, to

Maya, was like walking a tightrope. Even a momentary lapse in vigilance could lead to irreversible consequences. She wasn't sure what lay in the void to her left and right, and the uncertainty frightened her. The rope represented safety, the known universe, and she intended to keep her feet planted firmly on it.

It suddenly became very quiet in the van. Miraculously, Asha had fallen asleep, one cheek of her beatific little face squished against her shoulder. She looked so much like Niam had when he was a baby, the marshmallow cheeks and long eyelashes, the widow's peak hairline that Dean liked to joke made them look like "baby Phil Collins." Maya's chest tightened, her breath catching, as it always did, at the thought of Niam as a baby. The pain was familiar by now. A burning, like a match lit deep inside her lungs, searing them from the inside out. If Dr. Keating had given her a chance she didn't deserve, the universe had given her a son she didn't deserve. The guilt that came with that knowledge had never abated, never even dulled with time, as she'd been assured it would. She still felt it just as intensely every time it crossed her mind.

"Don't make any sudden movements!" Diya hissed urgently, as if the baby were an explosive. She'd recently watched a movie about two children who become government spies and had picked up some catchphrases. Niam laughed loudly, then clamped his hand over his mouth, giggling. Maya smiled at them in the rearview mirror and the pain in her chest quieted, the fire settling into embers. She steered the van down a long driveway lined with hydrangea bushes, past the school gymnasium building and the placard marking the site of the future DeGilles Mindfulness Space at the far end of the parking lot.

The hilly, manicured Hamilton Hall campus, a cluster of stately, historic redbrick buildings just off Lancaster Avenue, was both a short drive and a far cry from the Philadelphia public school Maya had attended when she was Diya's age. She remembered her elementary school as a tall gray concrete box with bars on the lower floor classroom windows. Bare-walled, linoleum-floored hallways where every sound echoed. A cafeteria with long, sterile white tables that smelled overwhelmingly of bleach and lunch meat.

Hamilton Hall was like a small university, with separate buildings for the elementary, middle, and high schools, acres of verdant athletic fields, and an auditorium worthy of a Broadway performance. Diya was one of only twelve students in a spacious, homey classroom decorated with fresh flowers and colorful handwoven rugs, a room deserving of its own Pinterest page.

Maya lowered her window a bit and let the smell of freshly planted mums wash over her as she steered toward the campus exit. She noticed she was scanning the sidewalks and was annoyed with herself when she realized what she was doing: she was looking for the Little Mermaid.

"Where did that mean lady with the red hair go?" Niam asked, as if reading her mind. He had an eerie way of doing that, of sensing the exact thing she didn't want said aloud and then saying it aloud. Like a tiny, spiteful psychic.

"What mean lady?" Diya asked.

"No one, honey." Maya kept her gaze firmly on the road.

Niam crammed a handful of Cheez-Its into his mouth. "A mean lady yelled at Mommy."

Diya sounded wounded. "What? A lady yelled at you, Mommy?"

"No, we just had a disagreement," Maya said.

"About what?"

"A parking spot. It happens."

"But why did she yell at you?"

"She didn't. Sometimes people say mean things, and you can't let it bother you."

"What smells bad?" Niam asked, screwing his face up and making exaggerated gagging noises.

"I think it's poop," Diya said.

"It's mulch," Maya corrected.

"The baby poopied!" Niam cackled gleefully. "Asha, you did a stinky."

"Shh! Don't wake up your sister." Maya put her window back up. "It's not poop. It's outside. It's nature."

"Well, nature smells like poop," Diya said. "Are we going to the car wash?"

"Oooo!" Niam whispered, scissoring his legs, barely able to contain himself. "Yes! Car wash! Please?"

Maya glanced at the time, then at their hopeful faces in the rearview mirror. It was getting late, but they deserved a fun diversion, and she could do with being less tightly wound about the daily schedule. When was the last time she'd done something spontaneous with the kids? Besides, it wasn't an entirely frivolous outing: the van did need to be washed. She glanced over her shoulder at the kids. "Sure," she said, grinning. "That sounds like a good idea."

FOUR

t was not, in fact, a good idea.

At the self-serve kiosk in front of the car wash entrance, Maya swiped her credit card and selected the "Ultra Premium" service, which included an underbelly wash and a wax application. An attendant waved her forward and directed her car onto a track. On his signal, she shifted the car into neutral. Diya and Niam were giddy with anticipation. Maya took her hands off the wheel and leaned her head back. She closed her eyes and breathed in deeply. Maybe, if she tried hard enough, she could convince herself she was at a spa appointment. A four-and-a-half-minute spa appointment.

The beginning of the wash went as expected: the car was sprayed with soap, then with water, then a giant mop-like device swished across the windshield while huge rotating brushes whirled against the sides of the van. The children were silently enthralled, and Maya, soothed by the rhythmic thrum of machinery, felt herself dropping off to sleep.

Then Niam opened his window.

A blast of soapy, frigid water hit him full in the face, then splashed onto Diya and the baby. Diya started screaming first, followed by the baby, followed by Niam, who might have been laughing, but it was hard to tell. Maya twisted around in her seat, also screaming, then reached for the button on her door handle to raise Niam's window. In the confusion, she instead hit the button for Asha's window, which slid open just in time for the drying jets to fire a blast of warm air through the van, followed by several streams of sticky wax.

Seeing wax drip down her screaming baby's front, Maya's first instinct was to prevent the offending nozzles from spraying wax into Asha's mouth. She grabbed the wheel and turned. The van jumped off the track and veered left, and Maya swerved to avoid a steel support pole. There was a loud bang, followed by the high-pitched shattering of plastic as a portion of the side-view mirror—not the glass itself, but the casing surrounding it—was knocked off. Maya slammed her foot on the brake, and the whirling and spraying came to a grinding halt.

"Is everyone okay? Is anyone hurt?" She climbed into the back and unstrapped Asha from her car seat. Red-faced and shrieking, the baby was angry and waxy and damp, but otherwise unhurt.

"I'm wet!" Diya wailed.

"Hoooly fuck!" An attendant, a pimpled boy of no more than sixteen, ran to them. This was clearly the worst thing he'd seen thus far in his brief life. He raked both hands through his hair. "Are you guys okay?"

"Niam!" Maya whirled around, apoplectic, the baby in her arms. "What were you thinking? Why would you open your window?"

Niam, who had been having the time of his life up until this moment, pouted. "It wasn't me! It was Snookus! Snookus likes to stick his head out the window."

For a moment it looked like he might be crying, but it was, Maya realized, just water dripping off his hair and onto his round cheeks. For some reason, this heightened her rage. Before she could stop herself, she shouted, "Snookus isn't real! Snookus is an imaginary dog!"

Which is how Maya found herself standing on the curb with three wet, crying children, the broken-off piece of the side-view mirror in her hand, as the attendant and his associate maneuvered the van out of the car wash. After doing his best to dry the interior, the attendant pulled up beside them. Then he used a roll of duct tape to secure the broken piece of the side-view mirror back in place.

"There you go, ma'am," he said, handing her the keys.

Maya couldn't meet his gaze. "Thanks. I'm really sorry, again."

"It happens," the young man said, even though they both knew it didn't.

Wet and cold, the older children were quietly sullen on the drive home. Asha, of course, cried. Maya noticed the earthy smell of nature from Hamilton Hall seemed to have followed them and permeated the van, which was odd, considering the interior of the van had just undergone a vigorous wash and waxing, and made her wonder if the smell really was poop, but she was too tired to pull over and check the baby's diaper.

Wynnewood, where they lived, was at the southernmost tip of Lancaster Avenue, just outside the Philadelphia city limits. Real estate became progressively more expensive the farther north on Lancaster one went, through Ardmore, Haverford, and Bryn Mawr (where Hamilton Hall was located), culminating finally in the capstone of the Main Line, Villanova, with its multimillion-dollar estates and exclusive country clubs.

It was past seven by the time Maya parked the van in the driveway of their split-level, midcentury house tucked into the side of a hill. The neighborhood was full of quaint houses like theirs, packed close together on small lots, the twisted roots of old oak and birch trees pushing up through the sidewalks. She and Dean had fallen in love with the house at first sight. She was still a resident at the time, pregnant with Diya, and imagined rocking the baby to sleep in front of the bay window that overlooked the street, sledding down the steep front yard in the snow when Diya was old enough. All of that had come to pass, yet her love for the house had faded. Now what she noticed when she looked at the facade was not the beautiful bay window, but the impossibly long flight of stairs from the driveway to the front door. She shooed Diya and Niam out of the van, hooked Asha's car seat in the crook of her elbow and the diaper bag over her shoulder, and followed the kids as they trudged up the steps.

Dean was defrosting Swedish meatballs from Ikea on the stove, combining them with sour cream and a random array of spices to create one of his signature weekly dinners. Swedish Meatball Tuesdays. "There you are! I was about to call you. Was getting worried." He wore an apron with a red-and-pink-paisley pattern over a T-shirt and gym shorts, a baseball cap backward on his head. Diya and Niam squealed when they spotted him, dropping their book bags in the tiny, already-cluttered front hall and running full speed and open armed into his legs.

"Daddy! Are you wearing my apron?" Diya asked, giggling.

"I'm borrowing it," Dean said, squatting down to wrap one arm around each child, pulling them in for a hug. "Hey there, kiddos," he said, before slowly releasing them and patting Niam's damp hair. "Why are you wet?" He looked up in confusion at Maya, who was busy unzipping the book bags and removing their contents. There was a moment of quiet, which was as long as the children could contain themselves.

"Niam opened his window in the car wash!"

"Mom drove the van into a pole!"

"Um . . . okay?" Dean tried again to catch Maya's eye, but she was consumed with emptying the remnants of the kids' lunches from their lunch boxes.

"Can we buy pumpkins and paint them?" Niam climbed onto one of the high stools at the kitchen island, ready to put the whole ordeal behind him. "Is dinner ready, Daddy?"

Asha, who had quieted when they came into the house, began fussing again. Dean turned the flame down on the burner, then lifted her out of her car seat. "Hello, Miss Asha," he said. He wrinkled his nose. "You need a new diaper." Turning to Maya, he asked, "How was your day, hon? What's this about the car wash and driving into a pole?"

His tone was nonchalant. Dean was unflappable, always had been. Maya couldn't remember the last time she'd seen him really angry. Other than a particularly gut-wrenching war movie, the only thing that stirred any genuine passion in Dean these days was the success or failure of the Philadelphia Eagles. Still, he asked the question with an edge of anticipation. This was probably a good story, and he wanted to hear it.

Maya, however, had no interest in telling it. "That's pretty much it," she said, soaping the lunch containers and running them under the tap, too spent and irritated with herself to elaborate. "Went to a car wash. Drove into a pole. How was your day?"

Dean gave her a skeptical look, one that wordlessly communicated that he understood there was more to the story, but that this was not the time to press for details. "Probably not as exciting as yours," he said. He lay Asha on the changing table in the corner of the dining room—they'd never bothered to buy a dining table and, over the years, the room had morphed from a formal dining room into a combined playroom-office-storage area—and opened her diaper. "Hon?" he called, concerned. "How long has Asha been in this diaper?"

Poop had dried to the baby's bottom, adherent as cement. Dean held Asha's legs at arm's length and tossed four diaper wipes onto her rump, trying to somehow clean her without actually making contact with her.

Maya poked her head into the dining room. "Here, let me do that," she said, rolling her eyes. "It's just poop. It can't hurt you, Dean."

She took over wiping the baby while Dean leaned against the doorjamb. "She must have been in that diaper for a while," he said, his mouth twisted with disgust. "Do you think they gave her to you with a dirty diaper at pickup?"

Maya did not think that. In fact, she was certain the baby had just been changed when she picked her up from day care. Asha had probably pooped at Hamilton Hall, during or shortly after Maya's encounter with the Little Mermaid. She did not, however, say this to Dean. What she said was, "It's possible. They always bundle her up so much in her coat and blanket that I might not have smelled it."

"And she's the first one of the kids you pick up, so she could have just been sitting in it in her car seat for . . ."

"An hour? Over an hour?"

Dean grunted with displeasure, and Maya tried to steady herself against a wave of self-doubt. Asha cried all the time, regardless of the state of her diaper or how tired she was or if she'd been fed or burped. That's what colic was. Inconsolable crying for absolutely no reason, for hours and hours a day. Medically harmless, but it made it impossible to tell what her needs were. This wasn't the first missed dirty diaper they'd ever experienced, but every time made Maya feel like a failure as a parent.

The baby cooed up at her now, big-eyed and adorable and forgiving, as if she hadn't spent the better part of the afternoon hysterically shrieking in a manner most consistent with being attacked by falcons. Like a reflex, the tightness in Maya's chest dissolved and she beamed at Asha, her whole being alight. It was like this with all her children: periodic swells of love, rousing crescendos of emotion so overwhelming she almost couldn't breathe that shortly thereafter receded into the ever-present low background hum of fatigue and annoyance. Riding the swell now, reenergized, she carried the baby back to the kitchen, kissed the top of her head twice, and strapped her into her high chair. "Maybe we should reconsider sending her to Radnor Park," she said, as if the idea had just now occurred to her.

"Have you seen the tongs?" Dean asked, rifling through the kitchen drawers.

"Thongs," Niam said, unable to stop himself from giggling. "Thongs thongs thongs!" He grinned with impish delight. There was something naughty about that word, he was almost certain of it. There was a song about it.

Diya, seated next to him at the island and reading a Percy Jackson book, rolled her eyes. "You don't even know what that is."

Niam glared at her. "Yes, I do."

Dean gave up and used two forks to lift egg noodles out of a colander and onto plates, dropping a few on the floor as he went.

Diya closed her book over one finger to mark her page and met Niam's gaze. "Fine then, what is it?"

"It's . . . a bra," Niam said, his confidence wavering only slightly.

Diya laughed scornfully and flipped her book open again. "It's underwear." She looked at Maya uncertainly. "Right?"

"Underwear!" Niam laughed. That was one of his favorites. An oldie but goodie. He tried out the word with different inflections— "UnDERwear! UNderWEAR!"—and, in his merriment, nearly fell off his stool.

"Dinner!" Dean said. He ladled meatballs over the noodles and slid the plates across the island to Diya and Niam, like a barkeep in an old Western. "Dee, put your book away, okay? No books during dinner."

"Dee, why are you reading that again?" Maya asked, frowning at the book. "Don't you have something nonfiction to read? Something educational? Where's that *1001 Fun Science Facts* book I got you?"

"This is educational," Diya countered feebly. "There's Greek mythology in it."

Maya gave her a skeptical look and, reluctantly, Diya pushed the book aside.

"I don't want Swedish meatballs!" Niam complained.

"Sorry, bud. That's what we're having," Dean said, shrugging. "Take it or leave it."

Diya looked at her parents expectantly, still awaiting an answer to her question. "Well? Is it?"

"Yes, a thong is a kind of underwear," Maya said. Dean handed her a bowl of pureed peas for the baby and a plate of noodles and meatballs for her. As usual, he and Maya ate their dinners standing up at the island. Sometimes Maya felt guilty about this—didn't experts say it was important to sit down and eat together as a family? But then, the experts were probably all men whose wives or mothers had prepared all their meals, fed all their children, washed all their dishes, and cleaned all their counters for their entire lives so, honestly, the experts could go fuck themselves. She and Dean still had bath and homework time to contend with, plus the fact that Asha still woke up crying every four hours at night. They were eating only to sustain themselves for all the rest of it.

"Radnor Park has a much better reputation," Maya said. Their conversations were a scramble, too, spliced in between interjections and changes of topic from the kids.

"But why do they call it a thong?" Diya urgently wanted to know.

"Because," Maya said as she spooned liquefied peas into the baby's reluctant mouth, "the part that's supposed to cover your butt sits in between your cheeks. Like flip-flops in between your toes." She turned to Dean. "I could call and see if they have any openings."

"Isn't Radnor Park twice as much as what we're paying for day care now?" he asked.

Niam had been trying valiantly to contain himself, but to no avail. He sputtered, sending bits of pasta and meatball spraying from his mouth. "Butt cheeks!" he said, and keeled over laughing.

"But it's twice as good," Maya said. "Remember when we went on the tour? How beautiful the garden was? How the staff wore uniforms? The koi pond in the lobby? The kids all looked so happy."

"Asha's happy," Dean said, then shook his head. "Scratch that. Asha's not happy, but that has nothing to do with her day care."

Diya's face was twisted in horror and confusion. "But doesn't that feel like having a wedgie?"

Maya nodded. "I mean . . . in a way, it *is* a wedgie."

Another man might have objected to his wife and daughter discussing female undergarments in such detail during a family meal, but after a decade of marriage, Dean was not in the least affected. In the early years of their courtship, after it became clear that—like most men—Dean's breadth of knowledge about female anatomy and physiology was just wide enough to cover the basics, Maya would haul her multivolume medical school anatomy textbooks to his apartment and lay them open on his coffee table. At the time he hadn't yet started working toward his PhD in Immunology, but he was a scientist with a lifelong love of random facts. So while he mixed drinks, Maya taught him about the biology of reproduction and the difference between the vulva, the labia, and the vagina, the endometrium, and the myometrium. He'd kept her company while she was studying for her board exams, listening as she read aloud about ectopic pregnancy and ovarian cancer and menopause and birth control. Dean understood the hormonal changes that occurred throughout the menstrual cycle and could competently discuss the four most common types of menstrual protection products and the pros and cons of each. A discussion about underwear was nothing.

"But isn't that uncomfortable?" Diya asked. She still hadn't touched her dinner, psychically wounded as she was by the existence of thong underwear.

"Some people don't mind them," Maya said. She returned her attention to Dean. "How do you know it has nothing to do with her day care? Maybe if we switched to a different place, she'd stop crying so much and would start sleeping through the night."

"Niam, eat, please," Dean said, placing Niam's fork, which had somehow migrated all the way across the island, back into his hand. "You really think uniforms and a koi pond are going to get her to sleep through the night?"

"All I'm saying is that environment makes a difference."

"Enough of a difference to be worth twice as much money?"

She looked at Diya, who was back to reading her book. "Yes." Dean raised his eyebrows skeptically, so she added, "But you're right. We should probably put the money toward Niam's tuition next year for Hamilton Hall."

"I want to go to kindergarten with Jake," Niam said, mouth full. His best friend, to whom he was ardently devoted, lived two houses down and attended the same preschool as him.

"Jake's going to Little Creek next year," Dean said, more to Maya than to Niam. All the kids in their neighborhood went to Little Creek. The local public elementary school was well reputed and walking distance from their house. But, of course, Diya had gone to Little Creek, with disastrous results.

"I want to go to Little Creek, too," Niam said.

"We can't spend our lives following Jake around," Maya said, more to Dean than to Niam. "The McConnells are sending Poppy to Hamilton Hall."

"So we're following Poppy around instead?" Dean asked.

Better Poppy than Jake. The boy next door could be sweet, but also gave Maya the impression that he'd one day set his high school on fire. When he wasn't playing with Niam—games involving a lot of primal shouting and the imaginary exploding of things—his favorite way to pass the time was throwing rocks at the stray cat that frequented their neighborhood, an activity his parents only weakly discouraged.

Poppy McConnell, at four and a half, took Suzuki violin lessons, studied conversational Chinese, and displayed a clear love of wildlife and a sense of environmental stewardship. The upward trajectory of Poppy's life was indisputable.

"I don't like Poppy," Niam said. "She never plays what I want to play. She's bossy."

"Poppy is assertive and a natural leader." Maya gave Dean a pointed look, and he laughed and shook his head.

Dean thought tuition at Hamilton Hall was astronomical. It was thievery. But to Maya, sending their children to the best K-through-twelfth-grade private school in southeastern Pennsylvania was as essential as outfitting them with a reliable winter coat. Wasn't a quality education priceless? Isn't that what her parents—and the entire Indian immigrant community—had taught her, that education was the only sure path to success for people like them?

Great Kids, Going Places was Hamilton Hall's motto. It was printed in bold type across the front of the leather-bound recruitment brochure distributed to prospective students and their parents. Inside were pages of glossy photographs of smiling former students in graduation regalia underneath the names of the Ivy League universities to which they'd recently matriculated. Each the picture of professionalism and promise. Not a cat tormentor among them. You couldn't put a price on being around the right kind of people. The student body at Hamilton Hall was like a hot-air balloon rising toward a glittery collective future, a mass with its own upward momentum, and a prospective parent couldn't help but want to tether her child to it, so they, too, would be buoyed to greatness.

Maya smiled at her three children around the kitchen island. As their mother, she would accept nothing less for them than greatness.

FIVE

Her own mother had expected nothing less from her. She had named her Mahalakshmi, after the Hindu goddess of wealth and power, setting the bar for achievement high from the start.

Maya's mother, Lalita Rao, was the youngest of eight children, nine if you counted the sister who had died of jaundice at six days old, her parents able to afford neither the long journey from their rural village on the western coast of India to the closest town to see a doctor, nor the fee for a doctor to come to them. "At least it was only a girl," the neighbors had said, comforting the grieving couple. "Think how much worse it would have been to lose a son!"

Lalita's oldest sister was ten years her senior, and it was universally agreed that she was a beauty. Sushmita had thick black silken hair that reached her ankles—hair she wore in two long braids down her back—and bright green eyes that earned her the nickname Billoo, little cat. She married well: an educated man, an engineer—at least he claimed to be; her parents had never asked to see a diploma—who promised his young bride a life of glamour and luxury in America. Not just in America, but in the crown jewel of the United States: Jackson Heights, Queens.

All the ambitious young men were emigrating to America in those days. Billoo sent Lalita long letters detailing the wonders of the grocery store—aisles that went on forever! So many kinds of yogurt!—the spotless public restrooms, the machine that washed their dishes for them. Billoo's husband found work as an engineer, but his salary was lower than he'd anticipated, so he borrowed money and purchased a small business—a fifteen-room motel on Route 1 in Bensalem, Pennsylvania, called the Jarrett, an excellent investment as the area was a burgeoning corporate epicenter—but he had no intention of moving to Pennsylvania and so needed a reliable motel manager. Someone to work nights and weekends. Someone to reside in the little apartment behind the main office. Someone who would be grateful for this opportunity and ask for minimal financial compensation. This was how Lalita and her new husband, Suresh, had emigrated to the United States in 1980 and became the proprietors of a motel they didn't own.

At first, they were content, maybe even happy. They befriended the other moteliers and hoteliers in the area—they were all Indian immigrants back then. The Shastris owned the Bensalem Motor Inn on Street Road. The Patels owned the Best Western off the turnpike. Lalita and Suresh's apartment was too small to entertain in, but they went to their new friends' homes on Saturday evenings so they could laugh and reminisce about the old country, so they could complain about how expensive the long-distance phone calls back home were, so the women could gather in the kitchen to cook daal and rice and listen to the latest Bollywood records while the men in the living room debated whether or not Reagan should have fired the striking air traffic controllers. They were young, the future stretching out before them heavy with possibility, like fruit ripening on the vine.

The years passed. Lalita and Suresh had a first child, Mahalakshmi, and then a second, Dakshesh. Real estate prices in Bensalem soared in the mid-eighties, and many of their friends sold their small hotels and bought or built bigger ones, ones with ballrooms or swimming pools where they hosted their children's birthday parties. Lalita and Suresh were still at the Jarrett, still in the cramped two-bedroom apartment they'd started in over half a decade before, while their friends—who'd started at the same place they had—rose to success around them. The American Dream, once-removed.

Lalita, Suresh, and their children still attended the Saturday evening gatherings at their friends' homes, but now the homes were lavish ones with elaborately landscaped front yards, and the food was catered from one of the many local Indian restaurants. Other new immigrants from India joined their social circle, many of them doctors. The US government, desperate for physicians in those days, practically laid out a red carpet for foreign doctors to immigrate and become citizens. Lalita watched quietly as the doctors' wives, after only a few years in the country, bought themselves BMWs and Jaguars, moved their families into more desirable neighborhoods, and began sending their children to private schools, presumably so that they, too, could become doctors and continue the upward spiral of family achievement. To Lalita, the path to success for people who looked like them could not have been more clear: it was all right there, laid out in front of them like a blueprint.

Neither she nor Suresh had finished college; there hadn't been the money for it. Her English was just passable, but Suresh's was good. "Why don't you take night courses and at least finish your degree?" she'd suggested, showing him the brochure for the local community college. "I'm thirty-two!" Suresh said from in front of the television, half his attention still fixed firmly on *Knight Rider*. "I'm too old to work that hard. Study *and* run the motel? No, that's for a younger man." They had a home, an income that covered their expenses, a community of friends. What more could they want? Compared to how they had grown up, in a tiny village in India, their children were living like royalty. Never mind that the dishwasher was broken and they couldn't afford to buy a new one, or that Mahalakshmi and Dakshesh shared a room big enough only for bunk beds and one desk, or the fact they were fairly sure the yellow-haired, blue–eye shadowed woman who checked into the motel alone every weekend was a prostitute. Their children were fed, educated, loved, and safe. Suresh was still content.

It was little surprise, then, that he balked when Lalita started looking for work. She already had a job, he argued. She looked after the children and oversaw the cleaning of the motel rooms. They were forever hiring and losing cleaning women, and Lalita often pulled on yellow rubber gloves and took up a toilet wand herself when they were short-staffed, dragging Mahalakshmi and Dakshesh along with her, barking orders. Before they'd learned to read, both children knew how to make up a bed perfectly.

Despite her other duties and over her husband's objections, Lalita found a part-time job as a cashier at Macy's. She took the bus from the motel to the mall and back three times a week while the children were at school and every Saturday morning. Though Suresh had taught her how to drive, she was never confident in her ability and, regardless, the bus was less expensive than paying for gas.

At first, Lalita dreamt of saving up enough of her earnings to buy the motel from her brother-in-law. That dream died quickly after she saw her first pay stub and Billoo told her how much the motel was worth. Then came the Saturday morning when, with the children still asleep in their beds and Lalita at work, two men with guns walked into the motel office and forced Suresh to open the safe under the counter. They took $2,000 and Lalita's gold necklace, the one she'd just brought home from the safety-deposit box at the bank to wear to a friend's anniversary party that weekend. It had been a wedding gift from her in-laws and was the single most valuable thing they owned. The thieves bound Suresh's hands and feet, debated shooting him, and finally taped his mouth shut with duct tape and left. Mahalakshmi, ten years old, found him an hour later when she stumbled out of her room, bleary eyed and asking for breakfast.

That was when Lalita started working full-time at Macy's. She saw no other way to improve her family's situation. Her coworkers mocked her accent when they thought she wasn't listening, and sometimes when they knew she was. They turned up their noses when she heated up biryani in the break room microwave. But she ignored them and ate alone. She had no interest in being one of them.

In contrast to the drudgery of cleaning motel rooms—something she still did several nights a week—Lalita's job at the department store was easy, almost pleasant. Her primary role was selling accessories: cuff links, shoes, belts, and silk ties. She unboxed and arranged displays of beautiful designer handbags made in Europe, running her fingers over their butter-smooth leather, admiring their precise stitching and gaping at their price tags. These were the things her friends could easily afford, the trappings of respectability she felt her family both needed and deserved but was well aware they couldn't have. At least, not until her children became doctors, too.

The trouble was that, as they grew older, neither of her children wanted to become a doctor. This was the greatest frustration of Lalita's life, the abject stupidity of her children. This wasn't their fault, of course. It was a distinctly American phenomenon, having stupid children. The entire country was filled with self-absorbed young people bent on squandering the opportunities right in front of them in favor of following their whims. This was even encouraged in public school. *Follow your dreams! Shoot for the stars! You can do anything!* When children said they wanted to become actors or painters or baseball players, their American (and by "American" she specifically meant "white American") parents and teachers applauded this nonsense. They watched passively as their children left home in pursuit of goals they were obviously not capable of achieving. But what else could you expect from a populace that had never seen true poverty? Americans had never had to dodge sunken-eyed orphans begging for coins on the street or witness blind, broken-backed lepers desperately scrabbling like birds for the scraps of food dropped from a street vendor's cart. This was the stuff of storybooks to them. They lacked the imagination required to be truly frightened for their children, so they indulged them. They overwatered their sons and daughters and then wondered why they wouldn't grow.

Lalita wished she could afford to take her children back to India for a visit, so they might understand the brutality of life. Life was about survival and power. And achievement was the best guarantee of both. So, when Dakshesh asked for guitar lessons and Mahalakshmi asked for piano lessons, Lalita refused. They were too expensive, she told them. In truth, the family could have afforded them—not without some difficulty, but they could have managed—but that would have been a foolish waste of their limited resources.

There was a time, as a child, when Mahalakshmi wanted to be an elementary school teacher. When she was seven, her aunt Billoo gave her a tiny blackboard and a box of chalk, and young Mahalakshmi spent hours pretending to teach her stuffed animals math problems and grammar. This went on for almost a year, until Lalita had had enough and threw out the toy one afternoon before Mahalakshmi came home from school. She told her daughter the blackboard had fallen and broken into pieces, too many to put back together, and then held her while she cried. "When you're a doctor, you'll be able to afford ten blackboards," she promised. Lalita had never seen or even heard of an Indian teacher in America. She didn't know how much elementary school teachers earned, but she imagined it wasn't much, and, at any rate, she wouldn't send her daughter down an untrodden path to an uncertain future. That was far too risky. The sure path to success and security for people like them was as follows: four years of college, followed by four years of medical school, followed by four more years of residency in a prestigious specialty and, ideally, a marriage to a like-minded Indian spouse. Simple.

The education of her children—especially Mahalakshmi, who showed the most academic promise and the least defiance of the two siblings—became Lalita's obsession. She was merciless in her expectations. A report card without straight A's sent her into a rage. "Idiot girl! Do you want me to send you back to India to marry a man who herds goats? Your father and I left everything behind in India, and for what? For you to be lazy? For you to sleep instead of studying?" Her love and approval, it was clear to her children from an early age, were entirely conditional. She would adore and support them as long as they did and became and achieved exactly what she told them to. "No one gets ahead in this world by doing less," she liked to admonish whenever their motivation flagged. When Dakshesh, in high school, tentatively revealed to his parents that he didn't plan to attend college, Lalita threatened to kill herself. "Fine. Go be a musician instead. I'll just die, if that's what you want." Dakshesh enrolled at Penn State the following year and majored in biology, just as Mahalakshmi had five years earlier.

Both of her children, as it turned out, disappointed her, though Dakshesh far more so than his sister. After college, he'd started going by Dak—she could never figure out why on earth—and joined a band. Now he lived in a tiny two-bedroom apartment with four roommates in San Francisco and worked at an Apple store while he waited for his music career to materialize from nowhere. He was thirty-one years old and had nothing to show for it.

Mahalakshmi did well until her last year of medical school. It was around that time that she asked her family to start calling her Maya, which at least was an actual Indian name, though not one that Lalita particularly liked or ever got used to. That was also when she chose the most family-unfriendly and unprestigious specialty, obstetrics and gynecology. She had spent years and hundreds of thousands of dollars in borrowed tuition to become not something respectable like a heart specialist or an eye doctor, but a doctor of ladies' private areas. Lalita couldn't even talk about her daughter's work in mixed company. Not that she wasn't proud of how well Mahalakshmi had done for herself—that wasn't it at all. The trouble was that Lalita could so easily imagine her having done better.

Then, as if to prove that she was incapable of making prudent decisions regarding her future, Mahalakshmi refused to even meet the handsome Punjabi surgeon Lalita had found for her—a family friend's son who was already established in a successful practice in California—and married a white man from a poor family who was "thinking about getting a PhD at some point."

The wedding, a small, no-frills affair, was officiated by a justice of the peace on a Friday at the local VFW hall. Mahalakshmi wore a white strapless gown she'd found on the clearance rack at Saks, one that she said she'd immediately fallen in love with, despite the fact it was several hundred dollars over budget. Suresh took the money out of his retirement account. "Don't tell your mother," he'd told Mahalakshmi, though he was never any good at keeping secrets from his wife.

When Mahalakshmi greeted her mother in front of the hall the morning of the wedding and asked what she thought of the dress, Lalita looked her daughter up and down and said, the disappointment in her voice sharp even to her own ears, "You look like an American."

SIX

"Madison Smockett told everyone at the playground today that if a boy kisses you while touching your boob, you get pregnant," Diya said, mouth full of toothpaste.

The house had two bathrooms upstairs, but Diya was afraid to go down the hall by herself, and Niam—in that adorable, annoyingly compulsive way universal to four-year-olds—insisted on being wherever his older sister was, so every evening before bedtime the two of them crammed into the tiny master bathroom with their parents and Asha. This forced Maya to climb into the tub with the baby to give her a bath and forced Dean out of the bathroom entirely, into the doorway.

"Well, that's ridiculous," Maya said. She called to Dean, who she couldn't see because the older kids were blocking him from view. "See? This is exactly my point. Fourth grade. They're in fourth grade and most of them still don't know anything, not even the basics."

Dean, who'd noticed the Hotessey's broken side-view mirror after dinner while taking out the trash, had laughed with his head thrown back for entirely too long when Maya finally recounted what had happened at the car wash. Since she was already tired and annoyed, his reaction—especially the reproachful way he'd raised his eyebrows when she admitted she'd called Snookus imaginary—had only further aggravated her. Like a smoldering fire, she felt primed now to erupt into rage.

"At no point in your life does anyone teach you about your own anatomy," she continued, wrapping Asha in a towel and handing her off to Dean. "It's not part of the public school science curriculum. You can get through twelve years of primary school and four years of college, and you'll probably have dissected a frog, but you won't know where your own kidneys are, let alone how they work. And, in health class—which is probably taught by a gym teacher, not a science teacher—they will spend six months a year telling kids not to use drugs, and maybe if you're lucky they'll spend fifteen minutes covering pregnancy and condoms in high school, but that's the extent of it."

"What are condoms again?" Niam asked, a neon flosser hanging out of his mouth. Diya shushed him.

"And of course if you're a girl," Maya said, "there's all this shame around talking about your body, so women go through life not knowing where their parts are, what they're called, or how they're supposed to take care of them. And how are you supposed to teach your daughter about her body if no one ever taught you? You know what that's about, don't you?"

"It's about the—" Dean started.

"It's about the patriarchy!" Maya said, wringing out a washcloth with vicious force. "It's the way men have kept women oppressed for hundreds of years, by making sure we were ignorant about our own bodies. By making it taboo and shameful to talk about totally normal, natural things like periods and menopause and—"

"And pregnancy hemorrhoids and yeast infections," Dean said, stifling a yawn. "You're right, hon."

"You know, I ran the idea for my proposal past Tad a full year ago, before I started working on it, and he was totally supportive," Maya continued. "He was in love with the idea back then. Now suddenly he's decided that educating women about their bodies isn't worth the investment, it's not profitable enough. It makes me sick."

"Why is mommy sick?" Niam asked. He had successfully inserted the grip of the flosser up one nostril and was grinning at himself in the mirror.

"She's not sick," Dean said, pulling the flosser out of his nose and tossing it into the trash. "That's enough flossing." To Maya, he said, "Maybe they think there won't be enough interest? That people won't come to the classes?"

Maya shook her head. "No way. Gastroenterology did a lecture series about digestive health, and every session was packed. They had a waiting list to get in. People want to be educated about their bodies."

"I told Madison she was wrong," Diya said, a bit smugly. "I told her she needs to ask a grown-up for the facts instead of spreading false information."

"That's my girl." Maya smiled approvingly at her firstborn, this child on the cusp of tweendom, so full of precocious wisdom.

"She also said that your dad has to earn more money than your mom, because otherwise your mom will leave him for a man who makes more."

"What?" Dean asked, incredulous. "She said that?"

"But I told her she was wrong because you guys have been married for a long time and Daddy makes way, way less money than Mommy."

Dean rubbed his forehead. "You told her that, huh?"

Maya grinned. "Did you use the words, 'way, way less'?"

"Did you tell her that I'm still a student and Sallie Mae takes a good portion of my money?" Dean asked, shaking his head slowly at Maya while trying to suppress a smile. Kids these days. "What did Madison have to say about that?"

"Who's Sally Mays?" Niam wanted to know.

Diya shrugged. Then she asked, "You used to deliver babies, right, Mommy? Madison says all gynecologists deliver babies."

Maya busied herself mopping water from around the tub with a bath towel. "Yup. I used to."

"How come you don't anymore?"

"Because babies come at any time, even in the middle of the night, and I got tired of leaving you two squirts to go to the hospital."

"It was because Niam didn't sleep at night," Diya said knowingly.

"No, it wasn't!" Niam glared at her, affronted.

"Yes, it was," Diya said coolly. It was like this between them, the two siblings. Once one of them noticed a weak spot in the other, they went after it like a shark to blood. "You were supercute but you never slept, so Mommy had to quit her job delivering babies. You ruined her career."

"Diya!" Maya and Dean exclaimed at the same time, while Niam made a noise like a wounded animal.

"Diya, that's a mean thing to say and it's not true." Maya squeezed Niam's shoulders reassuringly. "You need to apologize to your brother."

"Sorry, Niam," Diya muttered, arms crossed.

Niam, knowing he'd been wronged and never one to let an opportunity for melodrama slip by, cried bitterly while asking "What's a career?" as Dean ushered the three children out of the bathroom, insisting it was well past bedtime.

Maya sat on the edge of the tub, suddenly very tired. She tried not to think about what had happened the year Niam was born, because this is what it did to her. It winded her, made her weak and

frail and useless, and she didn't have time for it. She had patients to
attend to, children to raise. Three whole human beings who were, for
all intents and purposes, entirely dependent on her. She was the
breadwinner. She was the linchpin.

She thought of families with four or five children and wondered
how the mothers survived. Maybe those mothers were hyper-
competent, hyper-organized, genetically superior beings? Or did
they all have help?

The bathroom looked as if a tornado had recently come through
it. What they really needed was an au pair, but the house was too
small for one. A night nurse for Asha and a daytime babysitter for
drop-off and pickup would be ideal, but a reliable sitter was expensive and, maybe more than that, Maya had never quite recovered
from the Linda Episode.

Linda was Diya's babysitter when she had been Niam's age, hired
at the very reasonable rate of eighteen dollars an hour. She was a
cheerful woman in her midfifties with yellowing teeth that almost
exactly matched the color of her hair and a faint, not unpleasant
scent of spearmint and tobacco smoke about her. Things went fine
until the day, four months after hiring her, that Linda fell asleep
while driving Diya home from preschool. Stopped at a red light not
far from the house, she simply closed her eyes and drifted to sleep.
Her foot slipped off the brake and the car rolled, mercifully very
slowly, backward down a hill and bumped into someone's front yard,
narrowly missing their dog, but denting their mailbox. It wasn't until the homeowner banged angrily on her window that Linda finally
awoke. A police officer waited on the front lawn with Diya until
Dean and Maya, both beside themselves with panic, arrived from
their respective workplaces to collect her.

Linda, groggy and slurring her words, was arrested and spent
the night in the municipal police station, where she admitted to the
regular nonprescription use of Vicodin. Dean and Maya told Diya

that her beloved Miss Linda had taken a lot of pills she shouldn't have and needed to go to a hospital so she could stop taking them. Diya asked if they could visit. Maya told her maybe. They never saw Linda again.

Dean had quickly shrugged off the Linda Episode as bad luck, but Maya was never able to shake the thought that if she'd just checked Linda's references more carefully, done *something* differently, their child's scrape with death could have been avoided. She felt this way, too, about Diya's troubles at Little Creek last year. If she'd been paying closer attention, if she hadn't been distracted by work and potty-training Niam and her pregnancy with Asha, she might have recognized that Diya's friends and classmates were bad influences, that her child was surrounded by cat-tormenting Jakes, not Mandarin-fluent Poppy McConnells, and she might have acted sooner, before the fated year-end math test.

Diya had copied the answer to a tricky word problem—something about how many kids were on what baseball team that required a tedious amount of long division to solve—from the paper of the girl sitting next to her. It was so easy to do, she copied the rest of the girl's answers, too. When her teacher caught her, Diya couldn't explain why she'd done it. She'd never cheated before, Maya was sure of it, and she admitted she'd known it was wrong even while she was writing down the numbers. The incident was followed by tears and a great deal of remorse from Diya, then by meetings—which Maya and Dean attended with a mixture of solemn parental concern and cringing embarrassment—with the principal and guidance counselor.

It was no secret that Diya had no interest in science or math, that her ambition was not to become a scientist like her parents but to follow in her uncle Dak's footsteps and become a musician, maybe a novelist, but that was clearly the school's fault. Little Creek failed to teach the important subjects in an engaging way, failed to prime its students for future success. Dean hadn't been overly concerned—"It's a good learning experience for Diya," he'd said. "What kid hasn't cheated at least once?"—but to Maya it was clear that public school was a breeding ground for mediocrity and criminal behavior. Before the week was out, she'd called Hamilton Hall and arranged a tour.

Diya hated to switch schools, to leave her friends behind, but Maya knew they needed to take drastic action to regain the ground that had been lost. Dean thought Maya was overreacting, but he hadn't grown up the way she had. Her upbringing had taught her that in life, the only way to keep from falling behind was to be constantly trying to get ahead.

SEVEN

Maya usually put Niam to bed. He liked to listen to a bedtime story while kneading the loose skin around her elbow between his fingers, a compulsion that seemed to soothe him, and just about the only thing that made Maya feel better about her sagging triceps. She had been reading to him from *Alice in Wonderland*, a red fabric-bound copy she'd found at a flea market one lazy Sunday afternoon in Philadelphia back when she and Dean were first married and did things like spend entire weekend afternoons at flea markets. There was an intricate, gold-embossed print of the Cheshire Cat on the front cover that Maya had loved from the moment she laid eyes on it.

To that point in her life, the only books she'd ever owned were college and medical school textbooks. Her mother had taught her that novels were a frivolous expense, that fiction itself was a waste of time. Why read if she wasn't going to learn something from the effort? Why spend money on something that wasn't even real? On a fantasy? If she wanted to read a storybook that badly, her mother suggested, she could always take the A bus from the motel to the bus depot, transfer to the C bus, and walk to the public library. It had never seemed worth the effort.

After some bargaining, Maya had convinced the seller at the flea market to accept $10 for the beautiful book, which was all the cash she and Dean had left after spending $50 earlier in the day on a slightly damaged coffee table for their apartment. Buying the book had felt like a small rebellion, a tiny victory against her upbringing.

She traced her finger now over the glinting Cheshire Cat, smiling at the memory. Dean was probably asleep on the floor of Diya's room next door. He usually lay on the rug next to her bed until she fell asleep, because even with twinkling fairy lights over the windows, a *Moana* night-light plugged into the wall, and the hallway lights on, her bedroom, she insisted, was creepy. While Diya lay awake for hours, her mind making monsters of the shadows that fell across the furniture and walls, Dean would fall asleep immediately, then reliably wake around 1:00 a.m. and stagger to bed, complaining his lower back bothered him.

Maya hadn't told Dean about her encounter with the Little Mermaid earlier that day. She knew he'd be appropriately angered by what happened, but he'd be angered because he knew he was supposed to be, because he was an empathetic person who could imagine her feelings, not because he had ever himself felt what it was to be mistaken for their children's babysitter. What it was to be talked down to, dismissed, and underestimated for your entire life. To feel like you'd worked for years trying to earn the respect, or at least the acknowledgment, of people like the mermaid, only to find in your midthirties that you were still viewed as the same collection of adjectives: overweight, brown, female. No one of consequence, in other words. She'd done everything people like her were supposed to do, all the things she was told as a child would secure her place in society. She'd been educated, she'd become a professional. She had the beginnings of a respectable 401(k) and paid her taxes early. She was neither too loud nor too brash, nor did she call undue attention to herself. She'd made herself milquetoast so there'd be nothing to object to.

But she'd never be one of them. She'd never be a mermaid, not even if she offered up her voice to a sea witch and asked for a tail fin in place of legs.

EIGHT

Maya had never heard of Bertrand and Bunny Foster. She would have had no reason, under normal circumstances, to be familiar with either the husband or the wife. But at 4:30 p.m. the following afternoon, while she was trying desperately to wrap up her clinic hours before 5:00 p.m. so she could pick up her children from aftercare at a decent time, Esther received a phone call from Dr. Keating.

"Tell Maya there's a VIP patient coming in to see her today at 4:45," he said.

"But she has to leave at five, and she's already running behind, and she already has another patient booked at 4:45," Esther said.

"Bunny Foster is the name," Dr. Keating said.

"She has to pick up her kids," Esther said.

"It's a medication refill, I was told," Dr. Keating said. "On her hormone replacement therapy. No big deal."

"It's a brand-new patient," Esther said. "She doesn't have time for that."

"It's a VIP," Dr. Keating repeated, ending the conversation.

"A VIP?" Maya asked incredulously when Esther relayed the news. "What does that even mean?"

Esther shrugged. "I guess all our other patients are, you know, just regular people, people who have to wait for an available appointment, but this lady, *this* lady is *very important*." She rolled her eyes. "Get this, all she wants is a refill on her hormone replacement therapy."

Maya rubbed her forehead. As simple as it was to refill the medication, because she'd never seen the patient before there would be ten solid minutes of documentation to fill out so her insurance would cover the cost of the visit and her medication. Maya was going to get stuck in the height of rush-hour traffic. There was no telling what time she'd finally pick up all three kids. Asha would fall asleep on the way home and then be up half the night, and then tomorrow—

"Mrs. Hailey can't give you a urine specimen today," Esther said, interrupting her downward spiral of thoughts. "She already peed right before she got here. And Mrs. Tremont said you never called her yesterday?"

"Oh my God, I totally forgot," Maya said, cringing. Mrs. Tremont had a psychological condition that caused her to believe, several times a year, that she was pregnant, despite the fact that she was sixty-five and had undergone a hysterectomy a decade earlier. She was seeing a psychiatrist, but she came in once every two or three months for a urine pregnancy test and a consultation during which Maya would gently break the news that a pregnancy wasn't possible. Mrs. Tremont was devastated every time, and every time Maya would sit with her and hold her hand while she wept. Her heart broke again and again for Mrs. Tremont—for her dashed hopes, for her inability to comprehend or accept her situation, for the fact that she seemed so out of touch with the reality of her own body—but the interactions took at least twenty minutes and, when it came down to it, there just wasn't time enough in the schedule for all that.

There were too many patients with real medical problems to see. So earlier that week, Maya asked Mrs. Tremont to leave her urine sample and promised to call her later with the results. In all the chaos of the car wash, Mrs. Tremont had been washed from her mind. She felt shot through with guilt. "I had this accident with my car yesterday night and—"

"You were in a car accident?" Esther's hand flew to her mouth. "Are you okay? Are the kids okay?"

Maya waved her hand. "It wasn't a car accident, it was just . . . anyway, I forgot about Mrs. Tremont."

"She left a message. She was pretty upset," Esther said. "Do you want me to call her?"

Maya shook her head. "No. It should be me. I promised her I would call her myself. I'll do it right now."

"I don't get why you don't just refuse to see her. Like, why even bother with the pregnancy test?"

"Because if I don't see her, she'll end up at another practice and they'll think she's crazy," Maya said.

"She *is* crazy. Girlfriend is, like, totally delusional."

"But her delusions are triggered by stress. And coming in to talk to me and get a pregnancy test, it calms her down, brings her some comfort. After she grieves, she's good for a few months. If another doctor just dismissed her, I'm afraid she'd spiral and end up . . . I don't know, trying to steal someone's baby or something."

Esther laughed and shook her head. "I don't want to see Mrs. Tremont on *Dateline* or whatever, so I guess you'd better call her."

Maya dialed the number and paced the hallway as she spoke quietly to her patient. "It's okay. It's going to be okay," she soothed, while Mrs. Tremont wept bitterly at the other end of the line.

At 5:05 p.m., Maya knocked and entered Bunny Foster's exam room.

"Hi!" She said brightly. Over the years, she'd grown adept at concealing her exhaustion from patients. "How are you today?"

"I've been better, obviously," Bunny Foster replied, without looking up from her phone. A meticulously preened woman in her early sixties, she wore a Chanel pantsuit in pink linen and was sitting not on the exam table on which she had rested her Louis Vuitton signature handbag, but on the rolling stool, in Maya's seat. She pushed a lock of blond-white hair from her forehead and sighed.

Maya leaned awkwardly against the sink and smiled. "What brings you in today?"

Bunny glanced up at Maya. Her eyebrows drew together. "I just need a refill on my estrogen tablets. I've been taking them forever. My naturopath in Phoenix, Dr. Vince, has been prescribing them, but my husband and I just moved to Philadelphia, and apparently naturopaths aren't allowed to prescribe medication in your state for some reason, so here I am." She handed Maya an empty translucent orange prescription bottle and glanced at her watch pointedly.

"What are you taking the estrogen for?" Maya asked.

"They're my Fountain of Youth pills," Bunny said, smiling wryly. Her milky skin, even around her eyes, was enviably taut and wrinkle-free. "They keep everything hydrated. I'd shrivel up into an old lady without them."

Maya examined the bottle's label. "This is a very high dose," she said, concerned.

"Dr. Vince gives me the strongest dose," Bunny said, a hint of pride in her voice, as if Dr. Vince did this special favor for only his most cherished patients.

Maya cleared her throat. "Ms. Foster, I have to tell you, this dose of estrogen is dangerous. It's way too high."

"Dangerous?" Bunny raised her eyebrows skeptically.

"This much estrogen could cause blood clots, strokes, even a heart attack."

"Well, Dr. Vince assured me it was perfectly safe."

"I have to disagree."

Bunny squinted, annoyed. "Dr. Vince is very reputable. He's been in practice for years."

"I'm sure that's true, but there's no question that this dose is—"

Bunny waved her hands impatiently. "I don't have time for this! I have dinner reservations at Zahav at 6:00. Can you just send the doctor in? The other girl who showed me in here, the one with all the crazy braids, she said the doctor would be right in. My appointment was at 4:45 and I've been waiting for him now for"—she glanced at her watch again—"over twenty minutes."

Maya stared at her. She looked down at the lapel of her white coat, where her name tag clearly read, in large letters, MAYA RAO, MD, STAFF PHYSICIAN. There was a clawing in her chest, an angry, desperate scrabbling. This time, nothing rose up in her to quell it.

Excuse me, you can't park here.

What's your mommy's name, sweetie?

"I'm the doctor," she said.

"*You're* the doctor?" Bunny's eyes flicked from Maya's hair, to her name tag, to her maternity slacks. Her expression rearranged itself from one of surprise to one of withering indignation. "Well, are you always this late?"

Under normal circumstances, Maya's immediate instinct would have been to apologize profusely. Instead she said, "Are you always this rude to your doctors, or only to the ones who aren't white men?"

Maya didn't try to stop Bunny Foster from storming out of the exam room. In fact, she held the door open and pointed her toward the clinic exit.

"You will regret speaking to me like this, I can promise you that!" Bunny called over her shoulder. She left a cloying trail of perfume in her wake.

Esther's eyes went wide. "What happened?"

"She asked me if I was always this late," Maya said.

Esther gasped. "No, she didn't."

"So I asked her if she would be asking a white male doctor the same question." Maya said it matter-of-factly, though her heart pounded in her chest. "And then she said, 'Do you know who I am?' and I said I didn't give two shits who she is, she's not any more important than my other patients, and she got mad and left."

"Well, wow," Esther said, grinning and folding her arms across her chest. "I'm impressed, Doc. I really am. I've never seen you tell off anyone, let alone a patient."

Maya smiled, tight-lipped. "Any idea who she was?"

Esther shook her head. "Want me to google her?" Without waiting for an answer, she typed the name into her phone. Her face fell. "Oh shit. She's married to the new CFO of the hospital, Bertrand Foster. He just started a month ago."

Maya and Esther stared at the screen together for a long, horrified moment. "I mean, it's probably fine," Esther offered weakly.

Maya clenched and unclenched her hands, which had gone ice-cold. "I meant what I said. I'm not sorry."

"Yeah!" Esther said righteously. "Good for you. She can get her estrogen pills elsewhere." She handed Maya a chart. "So listen, bad news. This next patient's cervical biopsy came back positive for cancer. It's stage two. Want me to call the kids' schools and tell them you'll be extra late?"

Maya nodded gratefully and handed Esther her phone. She leafed through the chart and paused at the door of the next exam room to take a deep breath. As she emptied her lungs, she tried to brace herself for everything that was coming next.

Maya was zipping Asha into her footed pajamas later that evening when Tad called her cell phone. She recognized the hospital administrative office's number flashing on her lock screen and was nearly bowled over by a wave of nausea. She managed to clutch the phone against one shoulder and the baby against the other, gently bouncing Asha to keep her from fussing.

Tad was very concerned, *very* concerned, he repeated, about the treatment the wife of their new CFO had received earlier that day. "She says you swore at her and ejected her from the examination room. As you know, if her account is accurate, that type of behavior is in direct conflict with the standard of professionalism that Philadelphia General Hospital represents."

"I wouldn't say I swore *at* her," Maya said, when she was sure Tad was finished speaking. "I swore. And then she left, saying that I didn't know who she was and that I'd be sorry."

"Using profanity during a patient encounter is unprofessional, Dr. Rao. I shouldn't have to tell you that." Maya felt something twist in the middle of her stomach at Tad's patronizing tone. He continued, "Can I ask why you did that, Maya? Were you feeling overly emotional? Stressed out? I understand you were running behind schedule—"

Had Tad been in the room with her, she might have thrown her phone at him. For a moment, she considered telling him she was on her period and thus unable to control her actions. He'd probably believe her and, disgusted, end the conversation there. "She was overtly disrespectful to me."

"She asked if you frequently run behind schedule," Tad corrected. "That doesn't sound disrespectful."

Maya breathed in through her nose. "She asked it in a very disrespectful way. In a tone she never would have used with a"—the words felt dry and brittle in her mouth—"person of another race or gender. A white man. In other words." There was silence on the other end. A too-long silence. Maya added, "And she was sitting on my stool." She immediately regretted it; it sounded petty even to her.

"Okaaay." Tad's breath was a loud whooshing in her ear. "Since this seems like a . . . diversity and inclusion thing now, I'll have to bring in our HR diversity committee to review the facts. You'll need to email me a formal statement by tomorrow morning. The committee will meet tomorrow and we'll let you know."

"Let me know what?"

"Emotions are running high right now, Maya, I understand that. Mr. and Mrs. Foster are very hurt and upset."

"I'm very hurt and upset."

"And we want to deal in facts, not emotions. Take the day off tomorrow. We'll see you in my office on Friday morning at six."

"I can't take the day off tomorrow. I have a tubal ligation scheduled in the morning. And I can't come in Friday morning at six. I take my kids to school."

"Dr. Keating can do the surgery for you and cover your patients," Tad said, clearly unconcerned that Dr. Keating's schedule was already overbooked. "And I'm sure you can figure something out for Friday."

"I can't figure something out. I have three children. I've tried figuring things out and I've figured out that I can't come in before 9:00 a.m." She was starting to hyperventilate, and the baby was starting to get bored and fussy. Asha yawned, plucked her pacifier from her mouth, and thumped it against Maya's chest with her tiny fist, demanding her mother's attention.

"Before 9:00 a.m.? Sure, let's meet at eight on Friday, then," Tad said distractedly.

"But I can't— Wait, could I lose my job over this?"

"We'll talk further Friday morning. Good night, Maya." Tad hung up.

Dean had poked his head into the room moments earlier and now walked in, brow furrowed with concern. "What's going on? Why are you hurt and upset?"

Maya laid Asha in her crib, but Asha was having none of it. She wailed until Maya sat in the glider and cradled her against her chest. Staring at the pink floral wallpaper, Maya said, "I need you to take the kids to school Friday morning so I can get to work by eight." Her voice sounded hollow, as if it wasn't her own.

"This Friday? I can't. I'm lecturing at eight."

"You'll have to. I might be getting fired."

Dean slowly sank to his knees so that he was level with Maya's face. "Babe? What's going on?"

Maya told him. As she did, tears fell from her cheeks onto Asha's. The baby blinked in surprise, then gurgled with delight.

Dean raked a hand through his hair. "You told her you didn't give two shits? You said those words exactly?"

Maya nodded.

"Good for you," Dean said. "She deserved it. I bet no one has ever called her out on her behavior before."

"Tad is talking to HR about me tomorrow."

Dean shrugged. "Fine. Let him talk to them. You've been at PGH for years. They know you. They're not going to fire you because of some entitled rich white lady. Look around, they're literally everywhere. If they went around firing doctors every time one of them got mad, the health care system would collapse."

"Do you think I should get an employment lawyer?"

"Let's see what happens Friday," Dean said. He kissed her temple and took Asha from her arms. "I'll put her to sleep. You should get a glass of wine. You have a day off tomorrow. Might as well take advantage of it."

Maya gave a mirthless laugh and went down to the kitchen. She poured herself a glass of wine and, before she knew it, had downed half the bottle and was quite drunk.

She'd been this drunk, maybe slightly more, for the duration of her wedding to Dean. Her memories of that day were so fraught that, even ten years later, she couldn't bring herself to look at her own wedding pictures. Her mother had hated her dress—though she'd never said the words, Maya could tell instantly from the way her face fell at the sight of it—and both her parents, whom she thought would eventually come around to the idea of her marrying Dean, had been so viscerally unhappy the entire day.

"We look different from everyone else in this country," her father was fond of reminding her. "So there are different rules for us." He never acknowledged the fact that the rules were mostly self-imposed. That her parents and their fellow immigrants had created an almost comically narrow path for their daughters to traverse in the name of safety and success. Marrying a non-Indian was against the rules. But so was practically everything else: wearing a bikini in public, eating meat, liking sex, owning cats, being anything other than grateful, obedient, chaste, religious, and good-natured. Also frowned upon: drinking.

One of Dean's groomsmen had had a flask of tequila in his jacket pocket that he generously gave up to Maya when it was clear she needed it more than he did. Dean had five groomsmen, which was ridiculous. Six if you counted Maya's brother. Maya's maid of honor was her intolerable cousin Preeti, sixteen years old and a wannabe social media star obsessed with her own appearance—"Maya didi, do you have lip gloss I can borrow? What about eyeliner? I mean, eyeliner that's not a drugstore brand?"—and she had no bridesmaids. Her two best (and only) girlfriends from medical school were in residency across the country and couldn't get time off to attend the wedding.

Maya's parents hadn't seen the point in paying for a traditional Indian wedding—a "real" wedding, as they called it—when half the guests wouldn't even be Indian. "We'd have to hire a translator," her mother had remarked. Really, though, it was a punishment. They all knew that, even her brother, Dak, who was—as a rule—so clueless about anything related to Indian culture it was embarrassing. It was her penance, the crappy wedding. The VFW and the justice of the peace and the cheap plastic tablecloths. All that she and Dean could afford at the time. "You marry an American who comes from no money and has no career, this is what happens," her mother said in the bathroom after the reception, as if Maya herself were now a cautionary tale. Maya didn't bother pointing out that Dean was Canadian. Instead, locked in the stall, she hugged the toilet bowl full of tequila and catered lasagna and wept drunken tears. She loved Dean, but she felt like a failure. All she'd had to do was stay on the path, and she couldn't even manage that.

Dean could make neither heads nor tails of her unhappiness. Not then, not now. But, of course, she never expected him to understand. All she'd had to do was keep her mouth shut, swallow Bunny Foster's impertinence the way she'd swallowed the Little Mermaid's. The way she'd swallowed so many other slights and insults over the course of her life. But she couldn't even manage that.

NINE

The next morning's school drop-off routine was made more challenging by the hangover.

As Maya signed Niam's name into the register in the front office of his preschool—and she was taking her time with it, as she had nowhere to rush off to this morning and her head was pounding—the school secretary, a peevish woman with chronic sinusitis and a wooden plank sign above her desk that read SHOWING UP ON TIME IS HOW I SHOW I CARE, looked pointedly at the clock on the wall and clucked her tongue in disapproval. Then she glared at them while loudly blowing her nose.

Niam considered the stout, short-haired woman behind the desk. "You need tissues?" he asked helpfully. "My mommy has tissues in her purse." The woman, busying herself with some papers on her desk, didn't reply and, for a few moments, Niam wrestled silently with another question. Then, as Maya hoisted Asha's car seat off the floor and reached for his hand, Niam smiled at the secretary and asked conversationally, "Do you have a vagina?"

Maya sighed quietly. The secretary's eyes widened and her mouth made little twitching movements like a rabbit's. She produced a collection of offended sounds of varying pitch. "I'm so sorry," Maya said to her. "Niam, that's private."

"But you said I can say 'vagina.'"

"You can say it, but you can't ask other people about things that are private."

"But she's sick," Niam argued. "She needs to go to a doctor." He turned to the secretary. "My mommy's a doctor. But only for people with a vagina." He nodded, satisfied that he'd explained everything, then added by way of further clarification, "I have a penis. And two testicles. So does my dad. But my mom and my sisters have a vagina. Sometimes boys can have a vagina, and girls can have a penis. It's either or."

The secretary's facial expression, in a subtle but noticeable shift, morphed from offended to appalled. Behind her, the school director, a kind, older lady with white hair called Mrs. Pugh, was standing in the doorway to her office, arms crossed, trying not to laugh. "You certainly know a lot about anatomy, young Mr. Anders. Who taught you all of that?"

Niam smiled and said with pride, "My mommy. Because she's a doctor."

Mrs. Pugh smiled at Maya. "A doctor and, I can see, a great teacher, too. Well done, Mom." She nodded her approval.

Maya could have hugged her. Or cried. She took Niam by the hand, mouthed *thank you* to Mrs. Pugh, and suddenly knew how she would spend the rest of her morning.

After dropping Asha off at day care, she turned the car around and headed back to Hamilton Hall.

S he was late, but it was just as well. The mothers who attended the parent council meetings weren't sticklers for punctuality. They were still milling about the dining commons, about thirty of them, refilling their coffee cups at a long buffet table filled with breakfast foods in the center of the room and chatting in tight little groups. Maya recognized many of their faces from drop-off and pickup, including one mother she'd spoken with briefly at back-to-school night. The woman was dark haired, her harsh bob held back by the most enormous pair of black sunglasses Maya had ever seen. She approached the woman, who was picking the seeds off a poppy seed muffin, and smiled. "Hi, I'm Maya, Diya's mom?"

The woman briefly looked Maya up and down, then said warily, "Lainey Smockett. Madison's mom."

Maya nodded. "I remember from back-to-school night. Our girls are in the same class. Diya's new to Hamilton Hall this year and I was hoping she'd make fr—" She trailed off as an exuberant woman with icy pink lipstick and a forehead frozen smooth with Botox caught Lainey's eye from the other end of the buffet table and called, in a voice so loud and piercing it could have been a smoke alarm, "How's Xander's arm?"

"Getting better!" Lainey called back. "Thanks for recommending that physical therapist. He seems great. He's been coming over to the house twice a week, and Xander is definitely getting more movement back in his shoulder. They're doing aquatic therapy in our pool, which is helping."

"I heard what happened," Icy Pink said. "He was tackled at a backyard soccer game? By some public school kid?" The woman shook her head. "That's why I never let my Dawson play on the fields over at the park. You never know what kind of kids are going to be there."

Lainey nodded in agreement. "It was at our neighbor's house. The kid just jumped on him. It was ridiculous. Xander said he never saw him coming. The kid claimed it was an accident, but"—she shrugged—"who knows? And I never heard from the mom or anything. No apology, nothing. Anyway, the ambulance wanted to take him to Mercy, can you imagine?" Mercy was the closest trauma center to the Main Line. It was within the city limits and, Maya had always thought, a good hospital despite the run-down neighborhood in which it was located.

"Oh my God." The other woman's face fell. "I hope you said something!"

"You bet I did!" Lainey was full of righteous maternal fury now. "I said 'You're taking him there over my dead body.' I mean, I've heard stories about Mercy. Dirty, no private rooms. I told the paramedic, I said, 'I want him taken to Lankenau Hospital, nowhere else, and don't you dare argue with me.' Dirk made a few phone calls and someone he plays golf with knows someone in administration at Lankenau, so we had Xander seen immediately after he got to the emergency room by the chief of Pediatric Orthopedic Surgery, and he had the surgery that night. We were NOT messing around."

Icy Pink's face, after some effort, rearranged itself into a look of relief. "Well, thank goodness! I've heard horror stories of kids having their fractures set by an emergency room doctor or, even worse, an assistant, and having to wait days to see a specialist, and by then it's too late for it to heal properly."

Lainey raised her eyebrows in agreement. "Exactly. I've heard those stories, too. No way was I letting that happen. You have to advocate for your child."

"Absolutely!"

They nodded together, a pair of bobbing swans.

You have to advocate for your child and have a husband who's well-connected enough to pull strings with a busy surgeon so your kid can jump the line, Maya thought. It was like Icy Pink hadn't even seen her standing there, right in front of Lainey, mid-conversation. And it was like Lainey had forgotten she existed at all. For a moment she was back at Bensalem High School, sitting at a lunch table alone, one of only a handful of poor, brown faces in a sea of middle-class whiteness. At least once every few weeks, she was mistaken for the other Indian girl in her grade, Rani Srinivasan, who, with her pin-straight hair and petite stature, looked nothing like Maya. It should have been a compliment—Rani was far prettier and more popular than Maya. It should have been like being mistaken for a supermodel. But it wasn't.

She shifted her green canvas Coach handbag, an extravagant gift from Dean for their tenth wedding anniversary earlier that year, from one shoulder to the other, holding it in front of her chest like a placard. *I'm just like you. I belong here. Look at me, I'm standing* right here. Lainey walked away to join Icy Pink at the other end of the table.

There was a woman holding court near the front of the room, vaguely familiar and impossible not to notice. She was tall and lithe with smooth pearly skin and sleek golden hair almost to her waist. She wore a smart cream blazer over dark tailored jeans and red-soled sling-backs. She made the other women who surrounded her seem, in comparison, like poorly executed replicas of her. One real flower in a bouquet of silk imitations. Maya looked away to stop herself from staring, and as she did, a frisson of something familiar shot through her. Envy. What would it be like to command a room like that? To be instantly admired and respected the moment you set foot in a place? Maya had never in her life wielded that kind of power, but she yearned for it, felt the ache for it like a twisting in her core. As if she were starving for it.

A towering, mustachioed man in track pants and a Villanova T-shirt, the only man in the room, materialized next to her. He held a bagel clenched between his teeth, a cup of coffee in his left hand, and a bottle of water in his right. "Excuse me, would you pass the cream cheese?" he mumbled, the bagel flapping precariously. Maya handed him a packet of cream cheese, and he tucked the water bottle under one arm to receive it.

"Here, let me." Maya held his coffee for him so he could take the bagel from his mouth.

"Thanks!" He smiled gratefully. "Have you tried the bagels here? They're amazing. I'm Gill, by the way. Gill Newall. Two daughters here at Hamilton. One in the elementary school, one in the middle school. You?" His face was pleasantly weathered, his voice softly accented with a southern drawl. With his strong jaw and congenial folksiness, he could have been a cowboy.

"One daughter," Maya said. "Fourth grade. I'm Maya Rao."

"Have you been to parent council before? I've never seen you."

"First time. Our family is new to Hamilton."

Gill nodded. He squirted a generous amount of cream cheese onto his bagel, then opened his cavernous mouth and bit it clear in half.

"Parent council is great," he said, his mouth full. "If you want to have a say in what your kids are learning, this is the place. Don't get me wrong, they'll try to get you to volunteer on an auction committee, which is a total time suck and one hundred percent thankless, by the way, but just remember not to look directly into their eyes and you'll be okay." He winked.

Maya laughed. "Are you volunteering on an auction committee?"

"Oh, yeah. I'm on Decorations again this year with Lainey." He tossed his head in the direction of the far end of the buffet table and lowered his voice. "Not gonna lie, it's miserable. It almost makes me wish I never quit working. And I was a divorce attorney, so you can imagine how much fun that wasn't." He took another bite, finishing off the bagel, and answered the question Maya was silently pondering but would have never asked aloud. "Yes, I'm a house husband. Stay-at-home dad. Male domestic worker engineer guy. Yes, I braid hair like nobody's business. Fishtail, waterfall, reverse, French. If it's a braid, I can do it. No, I'm not gay—but you should probably examine why you wanted to know if I was—and I'm also not ashamed to say I think Chris Pine is the best-looking dude I've ever seen. And yes, my wife knows how lucky she is. Anything else you wanna know?"

Maya liked Gill. In fact, she wished more of the world were like Gill. Straightforward, unfussy, covered in cream cheese. She handed him a napkin, though he hadn't asked for one.

"No, I think you covered it," she said. "Let me ask you, though—how receptive do you think the council would be about a science assembly for the elementary schoolers?"

Gill wiped cream cheese from his mustache and took his coffee back. "You kidding? STEM? They love that stuff. The Franklin Institute comes in every year and does this whole show about the solar system. And the kids eat that stuff up like chocolate on a stick."

Maya shook her head. "No, I mean, what if I were to give an assembly or, like, a classroom presentation?"

"About what?"

"About sex."

Gill, to his credit, only spit out a tiny bit of coffee. "What now?"

"It would be age-appropriate information, of course," Maya added quickly. "I'm a gynecologist."

"You're a doctor!" Gill looked relieved, as if he'd been starting to wonder if Maya were some sort of pervert. He squinted thoughtfully. "A doctor comes in to teach the kids about sex." He nodded, then squinted, then nodded again. It was like she was watching the actual operation of his brain play out on his face. Finally he announced, "I support that idea. Hell of a lot better than them learning about it on the Internet."

"That's what I think, too," Maya said.

"Not gonna lie, though. It'll be a tough sell to this room."

"Why?"

"Well, you gotta understand. What you have here at Hamilton is a group of very opinionated, very uptight parents who are trying to relive their childhoods through their kids. If they didn't learn about sex in elementary school, they're sure as heck not going to want their kids to learn about sex in elementary school. They want their kids' days to be filled with unicorns and rainbows and the occasional diorama made out of a Jimmy Choo shoebox. Not woke liberal science. Is that how you use the word 'woke'? I'll be honest, I'm not really sure what 'woke' means, but my daughter uses it all the time, so I've been trying it out."

"What is liberal science?" Maya wanted to know.

Gill gave this some thought. "Basically science after 1975, I think."

"You don't seem uptight, though."

"That's because my wife's a teacher here. My kids are going here tuition-free. I don't have cause to have a stick up my rear like the rest of the parents."

"I have no problem with unicorns and dioramas," Maya said, returning to the point. "I just want to suggest adding some anatomy lessons."

Gill held up his palms. "You won't hear me arguing. I don't want to have to talk to my girls about the birds and the bees, so if you want to do it for me, be my guest. You just have to get it past the Stepford Wives first."

The meeting was finally called to order. Chairs were arranged near the front of the room in rows, and Maya and Gill sat together in the back. Icy Pink, whose name was Patricia Grace, stood before them and, with great verve, reviewed the morning's agenda. The first thing needed was a vote on whether to spend the $3,000 raised from the summer Boat-A-Thon in Avalon to hire a feng shui consultant to rearrange the furniture in the elementary school classrooms as a way to promote better concentration. To Maya's horror, the measure passed nearly unanimously, with one woman remarking, "I can't believe we've never thought of this before!"

Patricia Grace checked off the item on her leather-bound legal pad. "The second order of business is the prom limo fundraiser for the high school. I'll be frank, I didn't get much of a response to my email." She frowned, then said, impassioned, "I know we can do better than that. Open those wallets, people! Remember that this money will go toward a very good cause. We're going to make it possible for one of our less-advantaged students to go to the prom who, otherwise, without our help, wouldn't be able to go to prom"— she paused to collect herself—"in a limo."

"Hold on," Maya whispered to Gill. "We're raising money for a *limo* to the prom?"

"The kids need limos, Maya," Gill whispered back with mock sincerity. "They're human beings. It's basic decency that they go to prom in a luxury vehicle."

The final item on the agenda was the annual school auction. "We are going to start aggressively selling tickets next week," Patricia Grace announced. "Remember, we like to have ninety percent of parents or more attend the auction. So buy your tickets early or you'll be hearing from me!" It was more a threat than a joke, but everyone laughed.

Amelia DeGilles could have sworn she knew the plump, slightly disheveled, out of breath Indian woman who appeared, unexpectedly and fifteen minutes late, at the October parent council meeting. She'd never met the woman before, at least not in this life, but Amelia could feel their connection—a slight but unmistakable vibration in the air, not unlike a voice singing—from the moment the woman set foot in the dining hall commons to the moment she rose from her chair to address the council about updating the elementary school's health curriculum.

The woman was sitting with Gill Newall, whom Amelia always thought of as a Shetland pony. She often did this, matched people with their spirit animals. It had nothing to do with appearance or personality; people often misunderstood that. It was based on the other party's energy, their unique aura. Amelia was particularly good at sensing auras. She always had been, even in childhood. This was why she herself was a giraffe. The giraffe was the spirit animal of intuition, of knowing.

Patricia Grace, who was a peahen, asked for an update on the annual auction. Amelia announced the Night in Marrakesh theme, and there were audible gasps of delight from the other women.

"That's brilliant," Patricia Grace said with reverence. "How do you do it? How do you just come up with these amazing ideas, Amelia?" Patricia Grace had always laid it on a bit thick for Amelia's taste.

There was some discussion about the Autumn Harvest Concert and then, just as the meeting was about to adjourn, Gill Newall raised his hand and said, "One more item, Patricia Grace. Got a parent of a new student here, Dr. Rao, with a curriculum idea. I think we should hear her out."

Patricia Grace, who disliked nothing more than last-minute additions to the agenda, sighed and reluctantly gave over the floor. "We only have this room for another five minutes," she said. "Then it's time for second grade to have their lunch."

The Indian woman, who was a porcupine, smiled—her teeth white and straight and shiny against the muted brown of her skin—said she only needed a moment of their time, and introduced herself as Maya Rao, mother of a fourth grader, and a practicing gynecologist. She wasn't striking or even particularly pretty. She didn't have the almond-shaped eyes or the long narrow nose or the straight, thick hair Amelia found so beautiful on other Indian women. But there was something about her. She looked like the young women at the ashram in Allahabad, the ones who wore their saris tied around their waists so that their sturdy, unshaven legs were showing almost up to the knees and carried the day's wash balanced on their heads in woven baskets. Plain, unadorned, natural. And her name. Amelia wanted to say it aloud. Maya Rao. It was rounded the way a mantra was. It stretched the mouth, flooding the lungs with light and air. Rao. It was both familiar and fey. There was one other Indian family at Hamilton, the Dhruvas, real estate brokers who owned half the Lehigh Valley. Amelia had met Mrs. Dhruva on several occasions, but that woman—soft voiced and wafer thin—had nowhere near the spiritual energy of this one.

In a confident but pleasing tone, Maya Rao explained that she'd like to propose a course on anatomy and sexual education for the Hamilton Hall elementary students. She, a gynecologist, was happy to volunteer as course director.

There was a long silence. "You're suggesting we teach sex ed to *elementary* students?" someone finally asked.

Amelia, seated at the front of the room, twisted around in her seat to see the speaker, but it didn't matter. The women had all assumed the same mortified expression. "Absolutely not!" someone else muttered.

"It'd be taught in an age-appropriate way, of course," Maya Rao said reassuringly. "With a formal curriculum—there are several to choose from, all endorsed by the American Academy of Pediatrics. They cover reproductive anatomy and physiology, the menstrual cycle, interpersonal relationships, sexual identity and orientation, and body image. Teaching sexual education early has been shown in studies to lead to healthier sexual choices in teens, especially girls, and lower teen pregnancy rates."

A woman in the front row scoffed. "I don't know what school you came from, but we don't have teen pregnancy at Hamilton Hall."

The other women nodded. "We really don't," Patricia Grace murmured.

Maya Rao arched one eyebrow. "So then you're saying the teens here either aren't having sex at all or are practicing perfect contraception. Which one do you think it is?"

An uncomfortable murmur rippled through the group.

"But don't the middle schoolers already get sex ed?" Someone asked.

Maya Rao had done her homework. "They get three days in sixth grade. And most of it is focused on abstinence and STIs. There's so much more we could be teaching them, basic things they should be learning *before* they get to middle school."

The woman who'd asked the question shifted uncomfortably in her seat.

Maya Rao continued, "Pretending the issues don't exist won't make them go away. But if we educate our kids early—"

"My first grader needs to learn how to read. She doesn't need to learn about sex," someone said.

"The curriculum would teach her about female and male *anatomy*," the doctor said. "Not about sex. That would be for the third or fourth graders. For the younger kids, we'd be making them comfortable talking about their bodies and giving them the correct anatomical terms."

"I don't want my kid going around calling his wee-wee a . . . you know!" A woman in the back row said, scandalized.

Maya Rao blinked. "Penis? Okay, but that's actually what it's called, so . . ."

"No, no," several of the women started to say, shuddering as if they'd all caught the same chill. A flock of flamingos ruffling their feathers in unison.

"Do you use another term for their elbows or knees or earlobes?" Maya Rao asked. "There's no need to give their genitals special names. You don't want to send the message that their private parts are something shameful. We have a lot of cultural discomfort around talking about our bodies and sex, but it's not like that in other countries. In Scandinavia, it's really normal for parents and teachers to talk to elementary school kids about sex so that, when they're older, it's not this mysterious thing they're embarrassed to ask questions about. Educating kids at an early age takes the weirdness out of it and leads to teenagers who make better decisions about their bodies and relationships."

The ruffling of feathers grew louder.

"I think it's a fantastic idea," Amelia said. A hush fell over the room. Thirty pairs of eyes blinked at her in surprise. "We have the most antiquated sex ed curriculum. Jesus, they still separate the boys and the girls into different classrooms in the middle school. Personally, I want my son to learn about the menstrual cycle, and in great detail, too. Why the hell not? Maybe if we educate our boys, they won't grow up to be such assholes as men. No offense, Gill."

"None taken!" Gill's voice echoed from the back of the room.

Amelia continued, "I think we've needed to revamp our Health curriculum for a long time, and I'm glad Dr. Rao brought it up." She turned to Patricia Grace. "Can we vote to take this amazing idea to the school board?"

Patricia Grace looked momentarily stunned, then said, "Of course! Certainly. Let's vote. All those in favor of taking this proposal for a new elementary school health curriculum to the school board for approval, raise your hand."

Amelia stretched the fingers of one hand toward the ceiling. There was an uncertain rustling. Then, one by one, the other women followed suit.

The motion passed unanimously.

TEN

Amelia waited for Maya Rao to come to her.

She made several minutes of tedious small talk with Lainey Smockett, the mother in charge of the Decorations committee—or was it the Food and Beverage Committee?—outside the dining hall commons until, finally, they were interrupted by the grateful doctor, who thanked Amelia profusely. Amelia dismissed Lainey with a nod and took Maya by the arm, leading her toward the parking lot.

"There's no need to thank me!" Amelia said. "Truly, I think your idea was long overdue. In a lot of ways, Hamilton Hall seems stuck in another era." They stopped at the edge of the parking lot. "A lot of the students here are third-generation Hamiltonians. It's hard to break old habits, but that's why it's great when new families come in and shake things up, like you did. I'm Amelia, by the way. Amelia DeGilles. I have one in the high school and one in middle." They shook hands.

"Maya Rao. One fourth grader and two littles."

"I have to say, not many women would be brave enough to drop the word 'penis' at their first parent council meeting," Amelia said, smiling. "You have my respect, Doctor."

Maya Rao laughed. "I was nervous about it, to be perfectly honest. That's why I was rambling."

Amelia cocked her head, puzzled at the comment. "I didn't think you were rambling. Not at all. You commanded the room."

"You think so?" The doctor's cheeks went pink at the compliment.

"Absolutely. Do you have experience as a public speaker? Because you'd be great at it. Or a lecturer."

"I've always wanted to be a teacher," Maya Rao said. She looked suddenly sheepish, as if this was information she was not used to admitting aloud. "But, I mean, I love what I do, of course."

"Where do you work?" Amelia asked.

"Philadelphia General."

"Have you been there long?"

"About four years. And I did my residency there, too."

"And you're an ob-gyn?" She wanted to make absolutely sure.

The doctor shook her head. "Just a gynecologist. I don't do much obstetrics anymore."

Amelia nodded. She couldn't help but feel that the universe, in all its mysterious generosity, had conspired to bring this person into her life today. At just the moment Amelia needed her, Maya Rao had been provided, like a gift. She smiled at the doctor and said, "Would you like to grab lunch?"

There was something vaguely mesmerizing about Amelia, as if her presence was making Maya a little high. At this proximity, it was impossible not to stare at her bright blue-gray eyes and the gentle slope of her perfect pink lips.

Maybe Amelia had that effect on everyone, though, judging from the way the women on the parent council seemed to flock around her and follow her lead, like an orchestra following the minute hand gestures of a conductor. Maya knew nothing about this woman, yet she gratefully accepted her lunch invitation. Declining didn't cross her mind, not even for a moment.

"Let's take my car," Amelia said. She tapped a quick text message into her phone, and a moment later a black Aston Martin SUV glided into the parking lot, as if it had been idling somewhere close by but just out of sight. A young man in a sports jacket and skinny jeans jumped out and opened both the front and rear passenger-side doors. "Maya, this is Blake," Amelia said. "Blake, Dr. Maya Rao."

"A pleasure." Blake nodded politely and extended his hand. After a moment's hesitation, Maya took it, and Blake helped her into the back seat. The very act of sinking into the soft, buttery leather felt luxurious. And it was so spotless! So remarkably free of food debris it made Maya ache a little at the thought of having to drive home later that day in the rolling garbage disposal that was the Hotessey.

"I promise to have you back before one o'clock," Amelia said, fastening her seat belt as Blake pulled the car out of the parking lot.

There was a strip of popular restaurants not far away, but today the traffic on Lancaster Avenue was at a standstill. It could be like that in the afternoons, just gridlock for miles. Blake checked the GPS, then frowned. "It's not looking good, ADG."

That was the second time he'd called her that, *ADG*. The first time, Maya had heard "Aidy," but this time it was clear: A. D. G. Amelia DeGilles. Maya suppressed a smile. It was a little ridiculous. A wealthy, starched white woman with a moniker that could have belonged to a K-pop band or a rapper. The Notorious ADG.

Amelia sighed. "I hate this fucking town sometimes." She looked at Maya over her shoulder. "What if we just had lunch at my house? Would that be okay with you? I'm not far."

"Oh . . ." Maya fumbled for a response. "Sure, I guess. I hate to be an imposition . . ." The interior of the car was so spacious, she felt as if Amelia and Blake were very far away. She wondered if she should speak more loudly.

Amelia waved away her concern. "Not at all. I'm the imposition. I'm imposing my cooking on you. Do you like scallops?"

"I love them," Maya said, though she'd only eaten scallops once before in her life and she hadn't particularly enjoyed them.

Blake turned the car onto a side street. As they wove through the hilly, tree-lined neighborhoods of Villanova, the houses became progressively larger and spaced farther apart. Then the houses disappeared entirely, hidden behind walls of mature trees and lush flowering bushes. Leaves and branches knotted together into a dense, impenetrable curtain that stretched for miles, concealing behind it generations of wealth. Every driveway was gated and vanished into an invisible distance.

"You know, what you said about educating kids about their bodies really spoke to me," Amelia said. "And I'm so glad to meet a gynecologist, because I'm in the women's health space, too."

"Oh?" Maya tried not to sound too eager for information. "What do you do?"

"I own Eunoia Women's Health. It's a boutique medical practice."

Boutique practices were all the rage on the West Coast and catered to the well-heeled patient: exclusive, high end, and they didn't accept insurance. "Are you a doctor?"

Amelia laughed. "Oh God, no. But I've been involved in women's health for a long time. We do a whole range of holistic health maintenance: checkups, nutrition counseling, physical therapy, herbal medications, that sort of thing."

Just then, the car turned through a pair of tall wrought iron gates. A long gravel driveway underneath a canopy of stately oaks led to a colonial Georgian estate with a gray-and-black brick facade, its dozens of leaded windows encased in thick white molding. The house sat on a wide expanse of perfectly manicured lawn and was ringed with flower beds in verdant autumnal bloom. Black-eyed Susans and zinnias in shades of yellow and orange. Roses in coral and carmine. A monarch butterfly flitted past the windshield, its delicate black-and-orange wings catching the light, as the car came to a stop in front of the columned portico.

"Wow. Your house is beautiful." Maya knew there were people who lived in houses like this but, to her knowledge, she'd never met any. She'd certainly never been invited to lunch at a house like this. She felt acutely out of place and blurted jokingly, before she could stop herself, "Someone call *Architectural Digest*!"

Amelia smiled as Blake opened her door, then Maya's. "Oh, do you read *AD*?" she asked. "They did a story on the house last June. The photos were great, but the article was shit. Their articles are always shit. Let's go in through the side door."

Amelia led her up a flight of flagstone steps and through a teeming English garden, from which vantage point Maya caught a glimpse of a structure that looked like a pool house in the distance. They passed underneath an ivy-covered trellis to the side door of the house. Blake held it open for her, and Maya caught her breath as she stepped into Amelia's kitchen.

The floor was herringbone hardwood, the countertops white-and-gray marble slab. Open shelves displaying labeled mason jars in neat rows lined one wall, interrupted by French doors that led to a little paved courtyard where herbs grew in elevated containers. The island was the size of a luxury car and, as if the kitchen was always ready for a photo shoot, a white porcelain bowl of persimmons was the only item on it.

"Is it too early for wine?" Amelia asked Blake with a chuckle. "That commute was stressful."

Blake smiled. "Only five more hours until happy hour."

Amelia shook her head. "I'll never make it." Then she turned to Maya. "Mint tea?"

Maya nodded, trying to take in the kitchen without gawking. "Sure. Thank you."

Blake pulled a tall glass pitcher from a beverage chiller and poured two glasses of iced mint tea while Amelia retrieved scallops from the refrigerator, lemon from the walk-in pantry, and rosemary from the herb garden. They moved about the kitchen together comfortably, the way a couple who'd been together for years might. Blake was, however, far younger than Amelia, and the deference he showed her was obvious. After the drinks were poured, Amelia nodded to him, and Blake smiled and disappeared through a doorway.

Harp music wafted in from somewhere, beautiful and melancholy. Amelia put a pan to heat on one of the eight burners of the stove and began slicing the lemons. "Can I help with that?" Maya offered. She felt awkward, standing there watching this elegant woman she'd just met make her lunch.

"No, thank you, I've got it. Would you like more tea?"

Maya looked down at the glass. She'd drained it without realizing. It had been delicious. "No, thank you," she said, noticing that Amelia had barely touched hers. Three silver dog bowls—two large, one tiny—sat near the door. "What kind of dogs do you have?"

"Two sheepdogs and a Boston terrier," Amelia replied. "All rescues. They're out for a walk right now with their trainer, or I'd introduce you." She motioned toward the counter stools with a spatula. "Please, sit. Make yourself at home."

Maya sat down and cleared her throat. "Can I ask . . . is Blake . . ." She hesitated. ". . . your partner? Or . . ."

Amelia dropped the scallops into the pan. She looked over her shoulder at Maya, her forehead furrowed. "Partner?" Then she threw her head back and laughed. "You mean, like, my boyfriend? Oh my God, no."

Maya felt her face flush. "I'm sorry, I just wasn't sure—"

Amelia waved off her apology. "Don't be sorry. I guess we do give off an old-married-couple vibe." She grinned, still amused. "But, no. I've been uncoupled ever since the kids were little. Their dad is still very much in their lives, but we're not together."

"So Blake is, like, your butler?" Maya asked.

"House manager," Amelia replied. "I've had him for years. Don't know what I'd do without him. I never learned to drive, do you believe that? I grew up in LA, and everyone had drivers." She shrugged. "Meanwhile, on the East Coast, I'm the odd one out." She plated the scallops and garnished them with rosemary, then joined Maya at the island, taking the seat across from her. "It's simple, I know, but I like to have a high-protein lunch without frills. Is this okay?"

"Are you kidding?" Maya laughed. "I had pepperoni Bagel Bites for lunch yesterday. This is amazing."

"What are Bagel Bites?" Amelia asked, tucking into a scallop. Her expression was one of earnest curiosity.

"Oh." Maya was suddenly self-conscious. "They're like little frozen pizzas for kids."

Amelia shook her head. "Ugh, I would die before I let my kids eat processed foods. It's disgusting what the food industry wants us to feed our kids, right?"

Maya wasn't sure why, but the thought that came to mind at that precise moment was the day, about a year ago, when Diya and Niam together mindlessly polished off an entire party-size bag of nacho-flavored Cheez Doodles while on a family road trip, then both had bouts of explosive diarrhea within ten minutes of each other, necessitating panicked stops at two different rest areas. As disgusting as that was, they still had a pantry full of Cheez Doodles and similar snacks at home; though, to be fair, she'd stopped buying anything nacho flavored. She smiled wanly. "Right." She popped a scallop into her mouth. It tasted, she thought wistfully, like the sun-kissed sea. "How long have you owned your practice?"

"Three years," Amelia said. "I started Eunoia after I went through a health scare of my own, and I was just done with the health care system and how it treats patients, especially women, you know? Like a number. Like you're just a body on a conveyor belt."

Maya nodded and leaned forward with a degree of disbelief. Amelia was the exact inverse of business school Tad. "Yes. I know exactly what you mean."

"Did you know it takes the average woman with an autoimmune condition four years before she's diagnosed? It took me five. I saw eight different specialists before I finally got my diagnosis."

"That's awful. I'm so sorry."

"I was sorry, too. But more than that, I was pissed." Though her tone was one of righteous anger, Amelia had a detached look in her eyes, as if she wasn't quite talking to Maya as much as trying to re-member the exact wording of her origin story. "And I decided to do something about it. So I started Eunoia to uplift and empower women. To take care of the whole woman. A client can make an ap-pointment with us and see a general practitioner who specializes in women's health, a nutritionist to talk about her diet, a physical therapist for exercise tips, and a life coach, all in the same morning. I also have a neurologist on staff, and we have a yoga and meditation instructor."

It was impossible not to be impressed. "That sounds amazing," Maya said.

"It really is. The best part, though, is that we go to the patients."

"You make house calls?"

Amelia nodded proudly. "We do. That's our entire practice, in-home consultation and treatment. We're a disruptor in the health space, because we're the only practice in the region that offers that. And we're incredibly discreet, so clients who value their privacy know they can rely on us."

"Does insurance reimburse for that?" Maya had once tried to arrange for in-home IV antibiotic infusions for one of her wheelchair-bound patients and, after three weeks of daily, circular telephone conversations with the woman's insurance company, had finally given up. In-home care was astronomically expensive and, in Maya's experience, insurance companies did everything in their power to avoid having to pay for it.

"Oh, definitely not," Amelia said. "You can't run a practice like ours, with the quality of care we provide, and also be a slave to insurance companies. That's why we don't have anything to do with them. Aetna approached me last year to set up a partnership, and I literally gave them the finger and kicked them out of my office. They don't care about women, they care about profiting off our bodies."

Maya speared another scallop with her fork and imagined, for a brief ecstatic moment, giving Tad the finger and kicking him out of her office. The fantasy was almost as delicious as the scallop. "So patients pay out of pocket?"

Amelia nodded. "We have a subscription model. Clients pay a yearly fee to use our services, and a premium for certain specialty treatments. They schedule through our Eunoia app. Clients love the convenience. We have a few hundred on the Main Line and in Philadelphia, and we're growing every month. We don't even advertise; it's all word of mouth." She smiled, then added, "We treat every woman like a VIP."

Maya smiled back. She wondered what Bunny Foster would think of being just one of several hundred VIPs.

Amelia continued, "The only thing I don't have, and desperately need, is a gynecologist on staff."

Maya looked up in surprise, and Amelia raised her eyebrows pointedly. The harp music became suddenly erratic, one dissonant note after the other, then stopped abruptly. "Fuck me!" an exasperated, high-pitched voice somewhere distant exclaimed. This was followed by the sound of stomping feet approaching. Amelia sighed and gazed into the middle distance, as if praying silently for patience.

A gamine girl of about seventeen appeared, her hair golden like Amelia's, but cut short to her ears. She was barefoot, and her crop top and cargo pants hung loosely on her skinny frame. Maya felt a pang of maternal concern. *Somebody needs to feed this kid.* Clearly preoccupied, the angry young woman wordlessly stomped over to the freezer, yanked open the door, and rooted around inside until she found an ice pack. She held this against one of her wrists while using her elbow to pry open the refrigerator. "Where's the fucking hummus?" she muttered under her breath.

"Prem," Amelia said, sighing.

The girl continued to move things to and fro in the refrigerator, becoming increasingly agitated. "I'm going to fucking kill whoever ate all the hummus."

Amelia brought her open palm down onto the countertop. "Prem!"

"What?" the girl whirled around, her face full of rage.

Amelia took a long, measured breath. Then she said calmly, tilting her head toward Maya, "We have a guest."

Maya watched the anger recede from the girl's face, mortification dawning in its place. "I'm sorry," she said sheepishly. "Hi. I'm Premrose. I'd shake your hand, but . . ." she indicated the ice on her wrist.

Maya waved off the formality. "I'm Maya. Was that you playing the harp? It was beautiful. I thought it was a recording."

The girl shrugged as if this was a compliment she received all the time. "Thank you." She turned back to the refrigerator.

"Prem is auditioning for scholarships in a few months. That's why she's not at school today. She needs to practice."

"And senior year is a waste of time anyway." Prem located a glass container with a chalkboard label on which *hummus* was written in decorative script, and her mood brightened. Maya watched with fascination as Prem next pulled open one of the tall kitchen cabinets to reveal several steel racks on which different varieties of fresh bread were neatly arranged. She grabbed a giant round of pita bread.

"Have the pita with spirulina, too," Amelia instructed. "Paloma made a fresh batch yesterday."

"I hate spirulina," Prem protested, pouting.

"You're so spoiled! Stop complaining. It's delicious." Amelia turned to Maya. "We grow our own spirulina. Would you like some?"

Maya shook her head. "I'm sorry, what is that?"

"Spirulina?" Amelia's eyebrows shot up in surprise.

"I've never heard of it," Maya admitted.

"It's the most nutrient-dense food on the planet," Amelia's voice was tinged with pity. How shocking and sad that Maya didn't know this. "It's a type of algae. I swear, the ocean holds the keys to all of our health problems."

"It tastes disgusting," Prem said as she spooned a pungent, forest-green paste onto her plate from a glass mason jar.

"Sorry, babe," Amelia said. "You're basically an elite athlete. You have to eat like one."

"The harp must be hard on your wrists," Maya said sympathetically.

"Carpal tunnel syndrome," Amelia answered for her daughter. "Occupational hazard. Her hands hurt and go numb."

"Do you play, too?" Maya asked her.

Amelia shook her head. "I play the piano, of course. Like everyone else. But Prem is in the top 1 percent of high school harp players. We're looking at scholarships to Yale and Stanford, though I'd prefer she go to Princeton and stay closer to home."

Prem, her mouth full of pita, slid onto the counter stool next to her mother, and Amelia wrapped an arm around her shoulders. "Princeton is so boring," Prem said. "It's hours from the closest city."

"But it's the cutest little town, and they have the most adorable little houses. I'll get you a place right off campus if you go there," Amelia said.

"She's afraid of Yale," Prem said to Maya. "She thinks I'm going to get murdered there."

"Because it's in the ghetto!" Amelia said.

"It's in Connecticut," Prem corrected, rolling her eyes. She shrugged off her mother's arm.

"It's in New Haven, which is a ghetto," Amelia said. "Remember all the homeless people walking around at our campus tour?"

"No," Prem said. "I didn't see any homeless people."

Amelia turned to Maya. "You'd think for sixty thousand a year they could do a better job of keeping vagrants off the campus."

"What vagrants?" Prem asked, annoyed. "The Black people?"

"Prem!" Amelia half-laughed, then gave her daughter an admonishing look. "Not funny, young lady." She turned to Maya. "You know what I mean. You don't want people who look like thugs wandering around your child's college campus."

Maya, suddenly acutely aware of the color of her own skin, felt a line of sweat beginning to form above her upper lip. She looked down at her plate, her heart thudding in her ears, and swallowed. Then she looked up again and forced her mouth into a smile. "Of course. As mothers, we worry."

Amelia reached across the island and squeezed her hand. "*Ex-*

actly. Thank you." She raised her eyebrows at her daughter. "See? You have to be a mom to understand."

Prem rolled her eyes again. "Whatever you say, Mom."

Amelia opened a drawer in the island to reveal a neat line of little glass pill bottles. She retrieved one and placed it in front of her daughter. "Don't forget to take your fish oil." To Maya, she explained, "For a musician, fish oil is good for their nervous system. It helps keep their nerves coated in fatty acids, which increases their reaction time and finger dexterity."

Maya only vaguely remembered neurophysiology from medical school, but this claim seemed scientifically suspect at best. It was, though, a harmless belief. It's not as if fish oil was bad for you. Prem crammed three of the pills into her mouth and swallowed them without water.

"What brand is that?" Maya asked. She'd been thinking of getting Dean started on some supplements for his high cholesterol.

"Pureganic Ancient Naturals. It's a small, family-owned nutraceutical company out of Alaska," Amelia said, handing Maya the bottle to inspect more closely. "It took me forever to find an organic, high-quality brand. This fish oil is made in small batches from freshly caught North Sea mackerel. Most commercial fish oil is made from tuna and is lower quality and can have toxins. Fishing for North Sea mackerel is controversial, because they're supposedly overfished, but this company has responsible sourcing." Seeing Maya's surprised expression, she laughed. "I do my research. On literally everything. You can ask Prem."

Prem nodded. "Literally everything. She's online all the time."

"Not *all* the time, but yes, I like to keep up to date on everything health-and-wellness related. It's my line of work, after all. I can text you the website for Pureganic Ancient Naturals if you want, Maya."

Maya accepted the offer, and she and Amelia exchanged phone

numbers. Then Amelia glanced at her watch and turned back to Prem. "Do me a favor. Pick up your brother from lacrosse practice today? You have a break between your yoga class at 4:00 and the tutor at 5:15."

Prem frowned. "Why can't Blake?"

"He's off at 3:30 today."

Prem grunted. "Fine. I'll do it, for you."

"Thank you, sweet girl." Amelia kissed Prem's hair.

Maya smiled at their interaction and imagined a teenage Diya, self-assured and full of endearing attitude, having lunch with her at their tiny kitchen counter.

"Bodhi will be eternally grateful," Amelia said.

Prem guffawed. "Yeah, right."

"Bodie?" Maya said. "Those are great names. Primrose and Bodie."

"Prem," Amelia corrected. "*Prem*rose and *Bodhi*. I traveled around Tibet in my senior year at USC, and I was really inspired by the culture." She said this, Maya couldn't help but notice, as if her interest in Tibetan culture was a gift she had bestowed upon it. "And I always wanted to name my kids something evocative of that experience. So first I came up with Bodhi—like the bodhisattva, the ultimate enlightened being—but then when it turned out my first child was going to be a girl"—she frowned playfully at her daughter—"I loved the name Primrose, but I said, you know, I want something more meaningful, so let me change it to Premrose, because Prem means 'love' in Indian."

In Hindi, Maya silently corrected her. She smiled. "They're great names. Very unique." Maya had given her own children easily pronounceable, two-syllable names to spare them the humiliating awkwardness that had been part of every introduction, every first day of school, of her youth. "Ma . . . halakeemee? Molokai? Ma-hala-kimi?" the teacher would try, their eyebrows drawn together with the effort of reading aloud a name they'd never seen before. The discomfort of forcing a foreign collection of syllables through their English-speaking lips. Always, the other children would laugh, and Maya, her face burning with shame, would give the correct pronunciation—usually not more than once—of Mahalakshmi before muttering, "You can just call me Maya." Her teachers never objected, never insisted on learning how to properly pronounce her name. They always seemed relieved there was an easier alternative to call her by, and she was always happy to provide it, happy to make things easier for them. Something told Maya that Premrose and Bodhi DeGilles were never laughed at for their Indian-sounding names. On the contrary, their names—their unusual, exotic names—made them cool.

Prem scooped a heaping mound of spirulina onto her last bite of pita and popped the whole thing into her mouth. "Gotta get back to practicing," she said, mouth full. "Nice meeting you." She smiled, and her teeth were coated in green algae. She disappeared through a doorway and, a few moments later, the harp music resumed.

"She seems like a terrific kid," Maya told Amelia. "You must be very proud."

"I am." Amelia smiled. "But she has her moments, believe me. She's been so moody lately, which I've been chalking up to stress over her auditions coming up, but I'm wondering if she's out of alignment somehow. Something's off, I know it. I think I need to take her to the chiro again."

"She sees a chiropractor?"

"Oh, she has since she was four. It works wonders. We just hired a prenatal chiropractor at Eunoia, and clients love her."

Maya reflexively quirked an eyebrow. Back at PGH, her colleagues would have laughed at the idea of having a chiropractor on staff.

"I know it's unconventional," Amelia said, "but we're offering our clients something that no other practice is. We're listening to their symptoms and giving them options. We're not pandering."

Maya nodded. "Women have been talked down to by Medicine for long enough."

"Exactly!" Amelia said. "I knew you'd get it. And I agree with what you were trying to do at the parent council today. Education is key. That's what I'm trying to do at Eunoia, empower women and educate them about their choices. All of their choices." She took a breath and asked searchingly, "Would you ever consider leaving Philadelphia General?" In response to Maya's stunned expression, she pressed on. "I've been trying to hire a gynecologist for over a year, but no one I've interviewed has been the right fit for us. You seem perfect. You seem like exactly what we're looking for."

Sitting in this sprawling kitchen in this gorgeous house, Maya had the dawning feeling of stumbling headfirst into good fortune.

"You'd basically be an independent contractor. Patients would schedule with you through the app, and you'd keep 50 percent of your fees," Amelia continued. "You could make your own schedule, have total control. Any interest?"

Maya blinked. "I mean, it sounds amazing and . . . I mean, thank you. For offering. That's a surprise."

"What?" Amelia said casually. "You didn't think you were going to lunch with a fellow mom and would end up with a job offer?" She laughed.

Maya shook her head, then said vaguely, "I've been at PGH for a long time."

Amelia leaned her elbows on the counter. "Fifty-five percent, then."

"Oh," Maya said, shifting uncomfortably in her seat. "No, I mean, I don't think I could just leave PGH. Not at this point in my career. But thank you for offering."

Amelia shrugged, as if the matter were far from settled. "Well, think it over. You have my phone number. Call me if you have any questions, okay?"

"Okay . . ." Maya knew she should have dozens of questions, but her mind had gone blank.

Amelia said, "You know, I don't believe in fate, Maya, but I do believe in karma. Cause"—she pointed to herself—"and effect." She pointed to Maya. "I think that's what this is. Inevitable. Part of the balance of the universe." She smiled and raised her glass of mint tea. "To karma."

Maya hesitated, then raised her empty glass. "To karma."

ELEVEN

Our entire first floor would fit in her kitchen," Maya told Dean that evening. She was still awash in a mixture of disbelief and awe.

"So you've mentioned," Dean said, amused. They were having leftover Ikea Swedish meatballs. He held out a plate to her, but she waved it away.

"You should have seen the size of her pantry. Like a giant walk-in closet." She tossed the bag of meatballs back into the freezer. "I think maybe we should stop going grocery shopping at a furniture store," she said, then added, "Oh! And there was a little garden with all these fresh herbs."

"We could start an herb garden," Dean said gamely.

Maya snorted. "Sure. Where?" She motioned to their cluttered countertops. Among the random items strewn over every inch of their limited space were a decapitated Barbie doll and one of Niam's art projects involving several foam cups linked together with pipe cleaners. "Can we throw some of this stuff out?"

"No!" Niam said desperately as Maya picked up his art project. "I need that, Mommy!"

"What do you need this for?"

Diya looked up from her book. "It's his telephone. He calls people on it," she said.

Maya sighed. "Diya, are you reading a novel again? Have you finished your homework?"

"No," Diya grumbled, pushing the book aside.

"No books during dinner," Niam admonished, and Diya stuck her tongue out at him.

While Maya straightened up the counters, Dean took off his oven mitt and searched for the Eunoia website on his phone. The home page was sleek and modern, a white background with elegant black script: "Eunoia, the evolution of women's health," he read aloud. "There's a menu of services. Whoa."

Maya looked up. "Whoa what?"

"The yearly fee to sign up to be a patient—wait, sorry, a *client*—is twenty thousand."

"Dollars?" Maya's jaw dropped.

Dean continued reading. "Services include biophoton therapy."

"What's biophoton therapy?" Maya asked. "I've never heard of that."

Dean scanned the website. "Basically, it looks like you sit in front of this glowing trash-can device and it's supposed to emit some sort of healing energy. According to this, it 'recalibrates the body's cha- otic light into coherent light, restoring the foundation of the client's health by clearing her luminous energy field.'" He laughed. "Yeah, that doesn't actually mean anything. It's like they just strung to- gether a bunch of words that all sounded good. Luminous. Energy. Health." He continued scrolling, then said, "Wait, they also offer 'sacred crystal healing,' whatever that is . . . 'colonic cleansing'— which looks like . . . yeah, it's just laxatives—'Himalayan salt treat- ments, and bee venom therapy.' Bee venom!" Dean laughed again. "Holy snake oil, Batman. Oh wait, they also do in-home intravenous vitamin infusions for only '$250 per session, recommended number of sessions: eight.' Is that on top of the twenty grand? Jesus Christ. Your friend's a scammer."

Maya shook her head, confused. "But . . . she said she had an internist on staff, and a neurologist."

Dean clicked on the Meet Our Staff tab and said, "Oh, here's the neurologist." Up popped a photograph of a smiling man in a Grateful Dead T-shirt who could not have been less than seventy-five years old, standing in a jungle holding what appeared to be a live python. Dean read the man's bio: "'Dr. Tripp is a nerve specialist with a particular interest in the healing secrets of tropical rain forests. He holds a BS degree in biology from Villanova University and a doctorate in herpetology from the University of Florida. He specializes in using medicinal herbs from the Amazon for the treatment of various nerve disorders, such as restless legs and anxiety.'"

"Herpetology?" Maya was sure she hadn't heard correctly. "The study of snakes?"

"The neurologist is a Deadhead who specializes in rain forest snakes!" Dean was so overcome with mirth he was gasping for breath. "Oh, it says he's currently on sabbatical in Costa Rica!"

"I want to see a picture of a snake!" Niam said, bouncing in his seat.

"That can't be right," Maya said, annoyed at Dean's merriment. "Some of it has to be legitimate health care." She took the phone from him. "See? The internist is an actual doctor. Gretchen Stiles, MD. She's also the practice manager." She showed Dean the photograph of a stout blond woman wearing a white coat and sitting at a desk, her expression serious and thoughtful.

"Does she specialize in arachnids?" Dean asked.

Diya looked up. "What are arachnids?"

"Spiders. Maybe Gretchen Stiles, MD, is a spider doctor!" Dean said to the kids, waggling his fingers at them like insect legs, which sent the two of them into stitches.

"Okay, come on," Maya complained. "Lots of private practices offer alternative treatment options. See here? They do Botox and acupuncture, and there's a chiropractor on staff, too."

"Who heals you with his mind powers, sure," Dean said. He quirked an eyebrow, put two fingers to his temple, and stared intently at Maya.

Maya swatted his arm. "Will you stop? Amelia is a successful businesswoman. She's very impressive."

"Is she?" Dean thought about it for a moment. "She came from money, and she took that money and started this business to make more money. That's not that impressive to me. She doesn't even manage the practice herself. You know who I'm impressed by?"

"Who?" Standing over the sink, Maya spooned some of the baby's leftover pea puree into her mouth before rinsing out the bowl.

"You," Dean said. "You grew up in a motel on Route 1, and now you're a doctor—a real one—and a mom of three. You impress me, not Amelia DeGilles the third or whatever her name is."

Maya considered telling Dean about Amelia's comment that New Haven was a "ghetto" filled with "thugs." The way Amelia reached across the island and squeezed her arm in what felt like solidarity after Maya agreed with her. Was that what she'd done, agreed with Amelia? Agreed that the Yale campus was overrun with vagrants? Maya hadn't said those words, but she certainly hadn't voiced her disagreement either, hadn't pointed out that Yale was located in a city with a large Black population, and that Amelia's discomfort likely had less to do with actual crime statistics and more to do with skin color. She was ashamed of her cowardice, her impotence. "You know what I mean," Amelia had said, the phrase like an invitation that couldn't be refused.

"She offered me a job," Maya said.

Dean shook his head. "No way."

"She did. She made me take her phone number in case I changed my mind."

"Oh, I bet she'd love to have a gynecologist on staff. These are the type of people who eat their own placentas. Please promise me you're never going to work for this woman."

Maya laughed. "Maybe. Depending on what happens at this meeting with Tad tomorrow."

"Nothing's going to happen at the meeting with Tad. I canceled my class, by the way, so I'll take the kids to school in the morning. At worst, they'll reprimand you or something, but just roll with it and it'll be fine."

Maya turned away and began washing the dinner dishes. *Just take your punishment, whatever it is, and it'll be fine* was what Dean was saying. She felt something small and angry cry out in her chest, like a trapped animal struggling to get free, rattling the cage of her ribs. She'd felt it before, so many times in her life, and knew that if she ignored it for long enough, it would eventually subside. This time, however, though she tried to put it out of her mind, the thing wouldn't quiet. It grew stronger and louder until the next morning at eight, when it finally escaped.

TWELVE

T he CFO of the hospital, Bertrand Foster, wanted you termi-
nated, of course," Tad said from behind his desk, an enormous,
intricately carved mahogany creation more suited to an Edwardian
sea captain than someone in upper-middle management. "His wife
was traumatized, frankly, by her interaction with you."

Dr. Keating, seated next to Maya, looked carefully at his own
shoes. In a corner of the office, a member of the hospital legal team,
a slight, older woman with bifocals named Janet, took notes on a legal pad.

Maya knew Tad had a stay-at-home wife and two young children. She wondered if any of them genuinely liked him, or if they
tolerated him only because he paid for things.

"But he was willing to compromise," Tad continued. "We agreed
on a three-month unpaid suspension and a written apology to Bunny
Foster."

Maya blinked. "An . . . apology?"

Tad looked pleased with himself. "It took a lot of negotiating,
but I went to bat for you on this, Maya. Me and Dr. Keating."

Dr. Keating was now studying his cuff links. He cleared his throat.

"But the diversity team . . ." Maya began, then faltered.

Tad adjusted his tie. "The diversity team determined there was nothing discriminatory about Mrs. Foster's comment to you. She asked if you were the doctor, and she wanted to know if you were always late to your appointments. Which, to be fair, you often are, although I'm not faulting you for that. The gyno clinic is busy, I know."

"Gynecology," Maya said.

"What?"

"*Gynecology* clinic," Maya said, more loudly. "Or G-Y-N clinic. Not 'gyno' clinic. No one calls it that."

"I think the three months off will be good for you," Tad said after a moment. "Sometimes it's good to pause and reflect. Maybe look into meditation or some sort of stress management. The hospital has a great mindfulness program."

"Dr. Keating?" Maya asked. She wasn't quite sure what her question was.

Dr. Keating picked at a spot on the hem of his white coat. He sighed. "This is an unfortunate situation. But it's only three months. Three months out of a long career. Given the alternative . . . it's the best we could have expected, I suppose."

The room went quiet. Maya was aware of the sound of her blood pulsing in her ears. She looked at Tad. "I see. And will Mrs. Foster be sending *me* a written apology?"

Tad made some noises of confusion.

"Because I know what she meant," Maya continued. "She meant to belittle me."

Tad began, "Like I said, the diversity committee—"

"Wasn't there, were they?" Maya said. "They weren't in the room. I was. I've been on staff at PGH for four years, and you're taking

Bunny Foster's word over mine? Just because of her husband? He's only worked here a month!"

"This isn't about taking sides, Maya," Tad said.

"That's absolutely what it's about," Maya said. "It's karma," she added softly to herself, her gaze drifting.

"It's what?" Tad cupped a hand to his ear.

"Cause and effect," Maya said, too loudly. She cleared her throat. "Okay, so. I quit, I guess." The words fell effortlessly from her mouth.

Dr. Keating looked up. "What?"

Maya glanced around the room at the two men and one small, silent woman. "I quit," she said again. "I'll just . . . get my things and go. Thanks."

Then, to her own astonishment, she rose and left, walking out of Tad's office while squinting to hold in her tears. She willed herself to keep moving. One foot in front of the other. When she'd gone into labor with Diya, in the midst of the most blinding, unspeakable pain she'd ever experienced, that was how Dean had coaxed her from the house. "No screaming until we get to the car. One foot in front of the other until we get to the car. Then you can scream your head off all the way to the hospital." He'd been so calm, though later he admitted he'd been terrified, too.

She imagined Dean here with her now, his arm around her waist, leading her down the hall toward the elevator. She returned to the gynecology clinic, told Esther what had happened, and cleaned out her desk. She felt the eyes of her coworkers on her, but she ignored them and piled the few textbooks and personal items from her tiny cubicle into a plastic emesis basin (she and Esther had tried and failed to find a suitably large cardboard box) and focused on breathing. In 2, 3, 4, out 2, 3, 4. Just like labor. On top of the basin she laid her stethoscope and a copy of her grant proposal, bound, a clear plastic cover over the title page: "A proposal for a pilot series of community lectures to increase education regarding women's health and anatomy in our patient population, submitted by Maya Rao, MD, Clinical Assistant Professor, Philadelphia General Hospital, Department of Obstetrics and Gynecology."

Saying goodbye to Esther was the hardest part, but still, she didn't cry. Bill, the kindly security guard with the hangdog face and the bum knee, was summoned to walk her to her car, as per hospital protocol when an employee quit or was fired. Ostensibly, this was a courtesy, but really it was to prevent the slighted party from stealing or destroying hospital property on their way out the door. When they reached the parking deck, Maya thanked Bill, placed the basin carefully in the rear of the van, and slid behind the wheel. Bill rapped on the window, and she rolled it down.

"Sorry, Doc. Security badge."

She unclipped her PGH staff ID badge from her blouse and handed it to him. He smiled sympathetically. "Good luck to you, ma'am. God bless."

Maya rolled her window up again. In the rearview mirror, she watched Bill hobble into the elevator and waited until the doors slid shut. Then she dropped her head into her hands and wailed with abandon. What had she done?

She was rooting through her purse for a Kleenex when the passenger-side door opened and Esther slid into the front seat beside her, holding a smaller emesis basin that contained her personal items from her two years at PGH. She'd been running and was out of breath. She fastened her seat belt while Maya stared at her.

"Hey, Dr. Rao!" Esther said, as if it hadn't been mere minutes since they'd mournfully bid each other farewell. "Can I get a ride to the train station?"

Maya felt as if her tears had waterlogged her brain. She shook her head to clear it. "But . . . it's 8:30 in the morning. You have clinic."

Esther indicated the basin in her lap. "I quit, too."

"You did what?"

"Yeah, it took me a minute to find the nursing supervisor and let her know, but I'm glad I caught you. I can make the 8:45 back home if you drop me off."

Maya was still not following. "You quit?"

Esther waved her hand. "Oh, yeah. PGH pays medical assistants crap. Did you not know this?" Maya did not know this. "I could have quit a year ago and worked somewhere else for way more money, but I stayed at PGH because I liked working with you and I felt like I was learning. Plus, you were going to write me that killer letter of recommendation for med school, so you know, I figured I'd stick it out. But now?" She shook her head. "I just texted my aunt who works at Temple, and"—her phone buzzed—"yup. Her supervisor said he'll interview me today and I can start next week. The commute will be much shorter for me, too." Esther looked up and then out the windows, as if wondering why they weren't moving yet. She glanced back at Maya, who was still staring at her.

"Esther, I don't know what to say."

Esther shrugged. "Medical assistants are crazy in demand, I guess."

"You stayed at PGH out of loyalty? To me?"

Esther smiled. "Sure, I did. We made a good team."

Maya smiled and wiped the tears from her face. "Esther, can I hug you?"

Esther quirked an eyebrow. "We just hugged inside not five minutes ago."

"That was before you quit for me."

Esther shook her head. "I quit for *me*. Just like you quit for you. And I don't blame you. They had no right to try to suspend you after what that woman did." She glanced at her watch. "Oooh, train."

"Right!" Maya backed the van out of its parking spot.

"What will you do?" Esther asked. "Spend some time at home with the kids, or look for another job right away?"

"I haven't even thought about it," Maya said. "I still can't believe I did that. I've never quit a job before. I've resigned, but I've never just walked out like that."

"Feels pretty good, though, right?" Esther said. "I've only done it once before. And it didn't really count, because it was just a part-time job at Forever 21 when I was sixteen."

"Why did you quit?"

"A drunk lady pooped in one of the dressing rooms and the manager was like, 'Hey, Esther . . . somebody has to clean that up,' and I was like, 'Yeah, I gotta go.'"

"Gross!" Maya shuddered. "How does someone poop in a dressing room?"

"Oh, you have no idea what goes on at Forever 21," Esther said cryptically. "No. Idea."

Maya pulled the van into an emergency lane in front of the Market Street station, and Esther hopped out. After exchanging a few words of incredulity—had they both just quit their jobs today?—they parted ways. "Let me know what you decide, okay?" Esther called, waving.

As she pulled away from the curb, Maya suddenly hit the brake. She had no idea where to go next. Home? To sit in the empty house all day until it was time to pick up the kids? That didn't sound right. Dean's office?

She'd only visited Dean at work once before, years ago when Diya was two months old and she was still on maternity leave. She'd shown up at the lab one hot afternoon sweaty, unshowered, tearful, and with the baby strapped to her chest in a carrier. "I can't do it," she'd whispered, standing before him at his workstation, a line of colorful petri dishes on the lab bench in front of them. "I can't be a mother. It's too much for me." Dean had wrapped her and the baby in his arms and silently rocked the three of them back and forth, his forehead pressed against Maya's, while his colleagues pretended not to watch them. "We will figure this out," he said finally. "But first, ice cream." He'd strapped the baby to his own chest, and they'd gone for a walk to the gelato shop a few blocks away. He'd bought her the biggest ice cream cone she'd ever seen (she couldn't remember what flavor anymore), and as he'd helped her finish it, they sat on a low wall in front of one of the university buildings and watched the cars go past. It had reminded Maya of the early days of their relationship, well before they'd had children or she'd started her residency, when time seemed expendable, as plentiful and never-ending as water from a tap. She'd felt at ease that afternoon, sitting on the wall with the fingers of one hand intertwined with Dean's, for the first time in weeks. Two days after that summer walk to the gelato shop, Dean cut his course load in half, turning his two-year master's degree program into a four-year program, and they'd hired their first baby-sitter.

But the hormone-fueled emotional breakdown of a flustered new mother was nothing compared to this, the devastation of losing their primary source of income with three children to support.

A police cruiser flashed its lights behind her in warning, and she pulled back into traffic, pointing the car toward the only other place she could think to go.

Lalita deposited a plate of crunchy, fried Indian snacks of various types and shapes in front of Maya. She'd already laid out a selection of samosas and chutneys. A slight woman, she'd always coped with life's stressors not by eating, but by feeding everyone else. Her brow furrowed with worry. "What are you going to do now? I've never heard of a doctor being fired. Not for something like this." She was trying hard to be supportive of her daughter, but couldn't quite keep the sharp edge of reprimand out of her voice.

"I didn't get fired. I quit." Maya shifted her weight, and the cushion beneath her squeaked. The dining set had been purchased in 1986 and, thanks to Suresh's refusal to remove the clear plastic packaging from around the seat cushions, was still in pristine condition. Similarly, the television remote control was wrapped in plastic, and the carpeted stairs were covered with a protective plastic runner.

Suresh had retired several years ago, when his health had started to fail and Billoo and her husband finally sold the Jarrett. After that, he and Lalita had moved into a small town house in Bensalem, on a street full of Indian-owned businesses. There was a threading salon next door, a halal meat purveyor across the street, and a Patel Brothers grocery one block down. It was the first home they'd ever owned, and since moving in, Suresh's compulsion to preserve all of his and Lalita's worldly possessions under a layer of industrial-grade plastic had only worsened. With only Lalita's income and his social security to sustain them, he felt it his duty to not waste their limited income on replacing household items due to "wear and tear." Wear and tear was for Americans. Indians knew how to take care of their possessions, how to make them last. The secret was plastic.

"We will get a lawyer," Suresh said with fiery resolve. "This is discrimination! We can fight this. Ashok bhai at the immigration office across the street is very good—"

"I can't fight it, Dad," Maya said, waving off the idea. "I can't fight an entire hospital. And I don't want to."

"Can you tell them you don't quit?" Lalita asked. "Tell them you made a hasty decision and see if they will take you back."

"I'm not doing that, Ma."

Lalita shook her head, as if her daughter's reasons were beyond her understanding. "So you'll look for another job, then," she said matter-of-factly. "There must be plenty of other jobs for gynecologists. There are many other hospitals."

Maya hesitated. "I'd have to go back to delivering babies. I doubt another hospital would hire me and let me do just gynecology without the obstetrics part. The reason I was able to at PGH was because I did my residency there and the department head, Dr. Keating, knew me."

"So you'll deliver babies again." Lalita shrugged. "Isn't that why you became a lady doctor in the first place?"

"But all those night calls, rushing to the hospital at any hour," Suresh said, wringing his hands. "She has three children at home, Lalita. The girl is only human."

"Yes, and she's a girl who chose to do a residency in obstetrics and gynecology," Lalita said. "A girl who chose to marry a man who earns less than her and can't support his family by himself. She has to do whatever she has to do."

The barbs, so casually delivered, were all the more painful for it. But they weren't unfamiliar. "Really, Ma? We're going to have this conversation about my choice of specialty *and* my choice of husband again, right now?" Maya said, raking her hands through her hair in frustration. "Because what a terrific way for you to kick me when I'm already down."

"I'm not kicking you, beti, I'm being honest with you," Lalita said evenly. "You have to live in reality."

"Let's not talk about this now—" Suresh began.

"What is that supposed to mean?" Maya demanded, pushing the plate of snacks away from herself.

Lalita pushed the plate back toward her. "You have so much. You're smart, you're beautiful, you're educated, but you make these decisions . . ." She turned away, her eyes pained. "I don't know how you make these decisions. You girls raised in America, you think you're so modern, but really, you're selfish. Always thinking what's going to make you happy, never thinking what's best for your future. You can't eat happiness, Mahalakshmi. You can't feed your children your happiness."

Maya made an affronted sound at the back of her throat and was about to reply when Suresh silenced her by holding up his open palm. To her mother, he said, "It's almost 3:00. You should go catch your bus, or you'll be late for work."

Lalita glanced at her watch, then nodded, sighed, and went to the front hall to put on her shoes. She hobbled a bit—those first few steps after getting up from sitting were always the hardest. She needed a knee replacement, but she'd never go through with it. She was too stubborn.

Maya called after her, "I can drive you, Ma."

"That won't be necessary," Lalita replied. "I always take the bus." She fastened a red-and-white name tag, one that identified her as a SENIOR EVENING SHIFT MANAGER at Target, to her shirt. Her name was spelled incorrectly—LALIDA—but she'd never bothered to correct it because, somehow, people had less trouble pronouncing Lalida.

"It's not a bother, Ma. I'm happy to drive you," Maya said, holding up her car keys.

Lalita waved her off. She shrugged on her jacket, then took off her shoes and came back into the kitchen to kiss the top of Maya's head. "Stay here. Talk to your father." As she turned to go, she added fondly, their near-argument temporarily put aside as if slipped back into a desk drawer, "Next time you come, beti, bring the kids. Promise me."

"I promise," Maya said.

"Don't worry about the job. You'll find something else. And if you need me and Dad to watch the kids, just bring them over here, okay?" It was like this with her mother, an emotional seesaw. Cutting insults and remarks that brought Maya to her knees, interspersed with words of love and support that lifted her back up.

"There're three of them. You wouldn't survive."

Lalita scoffed as she headed toward the door. She put on her shoes again, sensible black sneakers shaped like loaves of bread. "Don't be ridiculous. I used to watch you, your brother, and the neighbor's two kids all day by myself."

"You were a lot younger then, Ma."

Her mother rolled her eyes in response.

Once she had gone, Maya said, "I still think she should retire."

Suresh shrugged. "She likes to get out of the house. She's more social than I am."

"She's moving slower than she used to."

"We're all moving slower than we used to, beti." He smiled wanly.

Though her parents hated to talk about it, Lalita still worked because she and Suresh needed her health insurance benefits. Medicare alone wouldn't cover their prescriptions, and Suresh took several expensive medications. He had a nervous system disorder, peripheral neuropathy, that caused painful burning sensations in his hands and feet, probably the result of years of exposure to the industrial cleaning products they'd used at the Jarrett. It wasn't something provable, just a hunch, since two maintenance men who'd worked with her father at the motel had also developed the rare disorder.

Her father had kept working for years after the other men were diagnosed and he started to develop similar symptoms. He only allowed Maya to take him to a neurologist when his symptoms became so severe, he could no longer walk down a flight of stairs without stopping midway to rest. Maya wondered if his condition could have been prevented had he acted sooner, sought treatment earlier, and heeded the warnings from his coworkers. The decisions he had made had negative consequences for him, yes, but also for her mother, whose life was inextricably tied to his. The way Dean and the kids were tied to her.

"Dad, do you think I make bad decisions?"

Suresh considered her over his teacup. A moment passed.

"Your silence isn't reassuring me, Dad."

"You want reassurance, or you want advice?"

She hesitated. "Advice. I think."

He stretched and tucked his hands behind his head, scratching at the few wisps of hair that still remained there. "You remember when you were young, one time you and Dakshesh were in the car with me and we went to the gas station?"

"I remember."

"And there was a man behind us, waiting for me to be done filling the gas tank so he could use the pump, and I guess he thought I was moving too slowly, and he started shouting?"

"Yeah."

"He was saying 'Go back to your country' and all that nonsense. I thought he might have a gun, did I ever tell you that? He said 'I'll shoot you if you don't move your car.' I don't know if he had a gun or not, but I was scared."

Maya didn't like this story from her childhood. It was one she tried never to think of. "Where is the advice here?"

Suresh held up his hand. "Wait, I'm explaining. You know, I could have punched that man. I wanted to. I could have walked over and punched him right in the nose, you know? Or at least I could have yelled at him, 'Hey, you racist American, shut up.' It would have been my right, hundred percent. But then he might have shot me, and who would have taken care of you and your brother and your mother? I would have been dead."

"Your point being?"

Suresh sighed. "You would have punched that man. If you were me. And you would be dead. And look what you would have missed. Your whole life. Your kids."

"You think I should have taken the three-month suspension," Maya said, irritated. "I should have apologized and groveled for forgiveness."

"What is groveled?"

"Like begging."

Suresh shrugged. "In India, some people make a good living by begging."

"I'm serious, Dad."

"Beti, your generation, you're so angry that things aren't fair. But people like me who came to this country . . . listen, life in India wasn't fair either, okay? You think it's fair that most people are dirt poor while some lucky few live in a mansion? You walk out of the Taj Mahal Palace in Mumbai, a five-star hotel, and there are blind children wearing rags right outside the gate. There is nothing fair in this life. That woman was rude to you because you're Indian and a female?" He shrugged again. "Beti, so what?"

"So what?"

"So what."

"So, I can't just allow people to treat me that way."

"You don't have to allow it. They will do it anyway."

"And I just let them? What kind of advice is that?"

Suresh shook his head. "You don't allow or let or give permission. You accept. This is a fact of life. Some people are prejudiced in this country. We have to live with that."

"I don't want to have to live with that."

"You'll change the whole country, then? While you're at it, you can give those blind children in India homes, too." He shook his head. "Take care of your family, beti. By whatever means necessary. That's all you can do."

Maya was quiet for a moment. "A woman offered me a job yesterday."

Suresh's eyes narrowed. "What kind of job?"

"Gynecology for crazy rich people."

Suresh gave her a look that suggested he hadn't heard anything objectionable so far.

"It's house calls, which is unheard of for gynecology, first of all. And I'm not sure how I feel about being a doctor for a bunch of rich white ladies on the Main Line."

"What's wrong with rich white ladies?"

Maya raised her eyebrows. "Um. I just had a run-in with one that cost me my job."

Suresh shook his head. "*You* cost you your job. You quit. This time, don't quit."

"I could make my own hours."

"That sounds good, beti."

"I'm not even sure how it would work. I guess I would carry all my equipment around with me in my car?"

"That's how doctors do it in India," Suresh said. "Would you have an assistant? It's not safe to go into a stranger's house by yourself."

"I hadn't thought about it. I guess I could ask them to hire me one."

Suresh nodded. "You could. This sounds like a good opportunity. What does Dean think?"

Of course her father, ever the Indian man, would want to know what her husband thought of her job offer. He recognized how patronizing it was, but he couldn't help himself. She rolled her eyes. "I didn't tell him I quit PGH yet."

Suresh's eyes widened in mock surprise. "Then why are you asking me for advice? You should always ask your husband first."

"You didn't even want me to marry Dean, and now you're afraid of stepping on his toes?"

"I didn't want you to marry him?" Suresh had conveniently forgotten the drama leading up to Maya and Dean's wedding, as if it had all been a fever dream he'd once had, years ago. He shrugged. "Well, if that's the case, see? I accepted it." He smiled, raising his palms up to the ceiling as if to say, *Wasn't that easy?* and Maya shook her head and sighed.

Before she left to pick the kids up from school, she called Amelia.

THIRTEEN

Amelia answered on the first ring, as if she'd been waiting for Maya to call. Maya asked if she'd been serious about her job offer the previous afternoon, and Amelia replied, laughing with delight, "When can you start?"

"Probably next week, actually," Maya said, still not entirely sure if Amelia was joking.

"This is amazing news. You've just made me very happy," Amelia said. "Are you excited?"

Maya hesitated. It wasn't excitement she was feeling as much as vague trepidation and a sense that her career was veering dangerously off course. "Yes. Yes! Very excited," she said, trying to match Amelia's enthusiasm. "So, I'm guessing I'll have to go through a credentialing process, background check, that sort of thing?"

"Oh, it's much easier to work with us than it is to work for a hospital," Amelia said. "We have no red tape. My practice manager, Gretchen, will call you to iron out the details, but it'll be easy peasy, I promise."

"I'll need supplies. And if I wanted to bring on an assistant?"

"Gretchen will get you outfitted with whatever you need in terms of equipment. She's a whiz at that," Amelia said. "And let's see how busy you are—and you're going to be busy, I have no doubt about that—but we can definitely bring on an assistant if you feel like you need one. We want to do whatever we can to support you doing your best work. "

The feeling Maya had in Amelia's kitchen, of stumbling into good fortune, returned to her now like a warm glow. "You're right," she said. "It's a lot easier to work with you than it is to work for the hospital."

Amelia laughed again, a bright tinkling sound, and said, "Welcome to Eunoia."

There was still the matter of telling Dean. He'd texted earlier in the day to ask how the meeting with Tad had gone, and she'd replied *Tell you about it later. Can you get milk on your way home?*

She'd decided to wait until they could speak in person, but he was late getting home—the Friday night traffic was unusually bad—and in the scramble of dinner and bath time, the window of opportunity to tell her husband she had just quit her job and joined a medical practice of questionable legitimacy was prohibitively narrow.

When she finally did tell him, while the two of them were crammed into the bathroom with the children, Dean had to sit down on the edge of the tub. "You did what?"

"They were going to suspend me for three months!" Maya said, focusing all her attention on getting the baby's bathwater to the exact right temperature. "I had to quit."

"Mommy doesn't have a job?" Diya's face went white and she nearly dropped her toothbrush. "Isn't that bad?"

"If Mommy's not going to her job, do I still have to go to aftercare?" Niam wanted to know.

"I have a job. Like I said, I'm going to be working for Eunoia." She smiled at Niam. "But I can make my own hours, so no, you probably don't have to go to aftercare."

Niam cheered, sending toothpaste spraying all over the mirror above the sink.

"I thought you promised never to work for that woman," Dean said, sounding a little like a spoiled child.

"I need a job, Dean. We can't afford our mortgage if I'm not working."

"I know that," Dean said, bristling only slightly. "But why not just apply at a different hospital? Mercy or Temple or somewhere like that?"

"They'd want me to do obstetrics." A look passed between them.

"There are other job options," Dean said.

"Maybe. But they'd all be the same as PGH. And my career was a dead end at PGH. I want to do something different. I could grow a practice on the Main Line. Do something bigger and more meaningful."

Dean looked at her skeptically. A long silence followed, during which not even the baby moved.

"I want to try this, Dean, okay?" she said in exasperation. "I have an opportunity, and I want to take it. Do you have a problem with that?"

Dean shook his head slowly. "No. I have no problem with that," he said, in a way that made it clear that he did indeed have a problem with that, but he would let this play out and was confident that, in the end, he would be proven correct.

Maya ignored his tone, smiled, and said, "Good. Thank you. For your support."

Then she handed him the baby with daggers in her eyes.

———

Gretchen Stiles, MD, lived nearby in Radnor and preferred to meet face-to-face to discuss Maya's employment at Eunoia, so at noon the following Monday, Maya met her at a coffee shop on the Main Line.

Gretchen was a raspy-voiced, ruddy-cheeked woman with a pixie haircut and the energy of a cocker spaniel. She was dressed in a blazer and skinny trousers and wore a pair of red Converse sneakers. In her navy skirt suit and sensible heels, Maya felt overdressed, dowdy despite the fact the other woman was clearly at least a decade older than her.

"Maya? Hi! I'm Gretchen!" She sprang to her feet and pumped Maya's arm in greeting, her smile wide and bright white. "So excited to have you on board." She motioned to the empty chair across from her. "Can I get you a coffee?"

Maya declined, and Gretchen leaned back in her chair. "Well! Look at you. You are not what I was expecting, but here you are!"

Maya's brow furrowed slightly. "What were you expecting?"

Gretchen leaned forward and clasped both of Maya's hands in hers. "A bitch!" she said, then burst out laughing in a way that attracted all the attention in the room.

"I'm sorry?"

Gretchen collected herself. "God help me, I was expecting you to be a bitch. Every female gynecologist I've ever had has been a stone-cold bitch. I don't know what it is about your specialty. But look at you! You seem so nice and polite and sweet."

Maya found this assessment of her perplexing, as she'd only said three sentences to Gretchen since she'd arrived, but she smiled collegially. "How long have you been with Eunoia?"

"Three years. Ever since ADG started it. Let me tell you, you make a lot of money in this job. Do you like money, Maya?"

Maya struggled to formulate a response and finally settled on "I don't think anyone's ever asked me that before."

"I have a condo in Boca," Gretchen said, waggling her eyebrows as if she'd gotten away with something. "*Three* bedrooms. Do you believe that?"

"That's . . . Wow," Maya said. She gathered she was supposed to be impressed.

"'Wow' is right," Gretchen said. "Do you know how many bedrooms I could afford in Boca if I was working as a hospitalist or in one of those tiny mom-and-pop internal medicine practices? None! I couldn't get anywhere near Boca. Believe me, I spent the first ten years of my career trying. Luxury medicine is the hidden secret of health care. You're smart to be getting in now, because in a few years it's going to be huge."

"Luxury medicine?"

"That's what we like to call it. Any boutique practice can call themselves *concierge*, but we take client service to the next level. We offer things no one else does."

"Like bee venom?" Maya said.

"Someone's been on our website. Good girl, doing your research." Gretchen nodded approvingly. "Honey, not only will we sell you bee venom and inject it into your cellulite or blend it into a cream to slather on your face, if you want to stand naked in a field full of bees and let them sting the *beejeesus*—see what I did there?—out of you, we can make that happen."

Maya recoiled. "Why? Why would anyone want that to happen?"

Gretchen shrugged, as if this question was unimportant. "People swear by bee venom. People swear by all sorts of things. That's the point. Out there"—she motioned to the parking lot—"if a woman wants to try a treatment she read about, she hears 'No, it's not covered by insurance' or 'No, there's not enough research' or 'No, it's not practical.' Well, the hell with that. The hell with doctors telling women what we can and can't do with our bodies, right?"

Maya squinted. "I mean . . ."

"Look, would I want to get stung by a thousand bees? Of course not. But am I going to judge another woman for wanting that?" She shook her head. "Not I."

"What kind of doctor did you say you were again?" Maya asked, her concern growing exponentially. Sitting in front of a harmless glowing trash can was one thing, but actively tempting death by being stung by bees was an entirely different level of unhinged.

"Internal medicine," Gretchen said. "I trained at the Mayo Clinic."

Maya let out the breath she'd been holding. "So you agree that getting stung by bees on purpose is . . ."

"A batshit crazy idea, absolutely," Gretchen said, nodding. "It'll take some getting used to, this way of practicing medicine, Maya. Our clients tend to be especially clear on what they want from their personal physicians. It's vital to respect that. They are, when it comes down to it, our employers."

"And our patients," Maya said, her tone somewhere between a question and a statement.

"The traditional doctor-patient relationship"—Gretchen pursed her lips—"well, you probably want to let that idea go. It just doesn't apply to luxury health care." She seized Maya's hands again. "But you're going to love it! No insurance companies to deal with, no mindless paperwork—"

"But we keep charts, right?"

Gretchen nodded. "Oh, of course. You definitely want to keep some sort of medical record, but you decide what works for you. Voice memo, notebook, whatever."

"But . . . what if you get sued? And all you have is a voice memo? Is that legal?"

Gretchen laughed, then looked at Maya as if she were precious. "Oh, you poor sweet thing. Maya, what do patients sue for?"

Maya blinked. "I mean . . . money?"

"Money! And what do our clients already have loads of?"

"Money?"

"Money! Do you know what they don't have enough of? Our clients don't have enough time or privacy. And what does a lawsuit cost you?"

"Time and privacy?"

"Time and privacy!" Gretchen said, smacking the table with her open palm three times in quick succession. "So. If there are no more questions, young lady, tell me what you need, and let's get you examining some hoo-has!"

Maya produced a printed list from her purse. "These are the supplies I'll need."

"This doesn't look too bad," Gretchen said, holding her bifocals, which she wore on a chain around her neck in place at the end of her nose. "The ultrasound machine is the big-ticket item."

"It's to check for ovarian cysts or masses, fibroids, that sort of thing. Although I can always refer the patient to a radiology center if I don't have my own machine."

Gretchen shook her head. "We like to do as much in the privacy of the client's home as possible. We will get you a portable ultrasound. But I'm going to need you to do some prenatal care, too, to offset the cost. ADG said she wasn't sure you did obstetrics."

"I don't," Maya said, and Gretchen frowned. "But I can do prenatal care," she added quickly. "That's simple enough. I just, obviously, can't deliver anyone. I'd need a hospital for that." This was mostly true. More accurately, she'd need a hospital and a very large dose of antianxiety medication for the inevitable panic attack that would ensue but, as a rule, she never mentioned the part about the panic attacks aloud.

"But you could, say, tell a woman she was pregnant and when her due date would be and if it was a boy or a girl? That sort of thing would be okay?"

Maya nodded. "That's fine."

Gretchen looked pleased. She promised to have everything on the list delivered to Maya's house and showed her how to use the scheduling app to keep track of her appointments and find the client's address. Most of Eunoia's clients, she explained, lived on the Main Line, but a few were in Philadelphia. "I'll send out an email blast to our clients this afternoon, to introduce you and let them know they can schedule with you. Fees are paid through the app. You'll charge our standard physician consultation fee." She handed Maya a printed list from a manila folder on the table. "This is our fee schedule."

Maya's eyes went wide. Eunoia charged over four times what PGH did for a consultation with a physician. "Wow."

"I know, right?" Gretchen grinned and sat back in her chair. "I think you're going to do great here, Maya. Just remember what I said about the type of practice this is. Don't go putting your two cents into someone else's vagina, okay?" She howled at her own joke while Maya pressed her lips into something that approximated a smile, trying desperately to push the creeping doubts from her mind.

FOURTEEN

Amelia knew the way. She knew to pass the hyacinths on her left and walk to the far side of the burbling stone fountain. She knew to leave the garden and step through the trees there, just there where the saplings clustered with their heads together like a group of whispering schoolchildren, and to step carefully over the moss-slick rocks. Fourteen steps forward, always exactly fourteen, and then she fell. She expected it, and yet it always surprised her, knocked the breath out of her, sent her heart shooting up into her mouth. The descent itself, however, was slow and meandering. A feather finding its way to earth. She always landed on her feet, her heart safely back behind her ribs.

As usual, the cave was damp and cold. But today she didn't have to wait for Evette, didn't have to call for her. The giraffe's big brown eyes glowed high in the darkness.

"I don't have much time," Amelia told the creature.

Evette nodded, a slight movement of her long, curving neck.

Panic began to creep over Amelia's skin, prickly and slick. "Please help me," she pleaded.

"If you ask me a question, I will answer it," Evette replied. Her eyes were kind.

"I want to know," Amelia said urgently. As it always did, fine white powder began to drift down from the emptiness above them. It fell like snow, but felt like granules of sugar against her skin. It came down slowly at first, then faster and faster, building into a storm, a thundering noise like rain on a tin roof echoing around her as she was buried up to her knees, her chest, her chin. Buried alive. "I want to know!" she screamed.

"What do you want to know?" Evette's tone was calm, steady, loving, even as Amelia opened her mouth again and the powder rushed in to fill her nose and lungs.

It was only when she opened her eyes that she realized she was sobbing, gagging. Someone helped her sit up and put an empty basin in her lap. The drums and chanting had stopped. The night sounds of the jungle were louder now. Her empty teacup had turned onto its side.

The moonfaced woman with the brown, weatherworn skin who'd served her the tea murmured softly to her in Spanish and used the hem of her dress to wipe Amelia's face.

Amelia shook her head, then vomited into the basin and fainted, the fall into empty space coming as a relief, something like a precious gift.

FIFTEEN

Two weeks after her meeting with Gretchen Stiles, MD, Maya tried in vain to convince the heir to the Hauser's of Manchester potato chip empire that she did not, in fact, want to get into the pool.

"Just jump in in your underwear! What's the matter? Are you not wearing any? I don't care if you're naked. Don't be ashamed of your body!"

Skye Hauser fluttered her hands in the water, trying to steer the giant inflatable pink flamingo over which she was helplessly draped, her body folded into a V, her backside wedged into the center of the inner tube that constituted the waterfowl's body. She managed only to set herself spinning. The flamingo's cartoonish, air-filled head towered several feet above her, supported by a thick neck that intermittently blocked her from view. Skye was a young woman, twenty-two maybe, with blond hair that was dyed lavender and pulled into a messy bun, and an intricate Polynesian-style tattoo of a sea turtle covering one shoulder. She wore a bikini crocheted from thick yarn in multiple bright colors.

Upon her arrival at the Hauser estate in Villanova, a friendly guard at the gate had handed Maya a small welcome gift bag containing two packets of Hauser's of Manchester potato chips—original and buffalo sauce variety—and a note that read, "Welcome to the Hausers' place! We hope you enjoy your visit!" He found her name on a list and waved her through. At the end of the long driveway, a massive bronze statue of a rearing horse mounted on a marble pedestal stood sentry. Just beyond it, a redbrick mansion winked from behind a row of tall trees, like a debutante hiding behind a fan. After she'd parked—the stallion, nostrils flared, glaring down at the Hotessey as if in distaste—a security guard appeared at her window and informed her that her client was in the pool house. He'd walked her to the perimeter of a manicured garden, where they'd been met by a sharply dressed East Asian woman who introduced herself as the estate manager. The woman held out a clipboard. "Nondisclosure agreement. Sign by the X, please." Maya signed her name and the woman showed her to the door of the pool house, which was not, as it turned out, a small shed used for showering and changing, as Maya had expected, but a massive Greco-Roman-columned white stucco structure that housed an Olympic-size pool under a vaulted glass roof. All of this splendor, all from potato chips, Maya marveled. She'd entered the pool house through a set of French doors to find Skye afloat and full of cheerful familiarity.

"I'm really okay, thanks," Maya called to her now from the far end of the pool, her voice echoing in the cavernous space. The polished concrete floor was surprisingly hot against her bare feet. Her shoes, sensible flats that she'd paired with equally sensible dress pants, sat at the base of a towering palm tree that grew not in a pot, but out of a decorative mulch bed in the floor. She dipped her toe in the water. "You're right. It's very warm."

"Right? It's some geothermal heating system thing that makes the floor warm, too." Skye's voice had a pleasantly nasal quality. "Totally green and good for the planet. Isn't that so amazing?"

Maya nodded and agreed that it was.

"And this is salt water with, like, minerals," Skye continued. "It's the same composition as the springs in Iceland. It's very therapeutic."

"Sounds great," Maya said, anxious to steer the conversation back to where it had started several minutes ago. "So you said this is your first pregnancy?"

Skye was having none of it. "I'll have someone grab you a bathing suit. I just have to call the house. Hand me your phone." She began to paddle fruitlessly again, pointing her toes and flicking at the water with their tips. She threw her head back and laughed at herself.

"Really, that's not necessary," Maya replied.

Sometimes, regularly in fact, a chatty patient at PGH would take up more of Maya's time than she could afford to give. She had a standard script for dealing with these situations: *Unfortunately, we have limited time together. I have other patients waiting for me. We'll have to schedule another visit if you have multiple concerns to discuss.* The lines were always, out of necessity, delivered with one foot already out the door. Here, Maya felt trapped. Skye was a client, Eunoia's client, and she had paid for as much of Maya's time as she wanted to consume. An all-you-can-eat buffet of minutes.

"We can't bond if we're each standing in a different element," Skye said, exasperated. "Fine. You take the float!" She wriggled vigorously, and the flamingo bobbed wildly from side to side. "Oh my God, my fat ass is stuck. Just totally stuck!" She was laughing so hard now, she'd given herself the hiccups.

"Oh, don't do that," Maya said, trailing the float around the pool. "I can just put my feet in, if that would help."

Skye waved her off. "No, no. You have to be fully in or on the water, so our energies can intersect. If I'm in water, you're in water." Hiccup. "If I'm on earth, you're on earth." Hiccup. "If I'm in air, you're in—" she screamed as the flamingo tipped precariously, sending her tumbling into the water. She resurfaced a few seconds later, overcome with merriment, her hiccups cured. Dragging the flamingo to the side of the pool, she said, "So, come on. Just try it. It's super relaxing floating around out here, under the sky and the sun. Don't be all uptight and doctor-y."

Maya hesitated, and Skye sighed impatiently. "Oh for fuck's sake, don't worry about your clothes. I have pants and underwear. You'll have a change of clothes in case you get wet."

Maya knelt and reached for the float to steady herself, then clambered awkwardly aboard, straddling the flamingo's neck. "I doubt I'd fit into your clothes," she said, relieved to have avoided falling into the pool.

Skye floated on her back, resting her hands on her toned, flat stomach. She sighed blissfully. "Isn't water amazing? It's my favorite element. What's yours?"

"What's my . . ." Maya shook her head, confused, and Skye looked at her expectantly.

"Favorite element."

"Oh. I guess . . ." All she could think of was the band Earth Wind & Fire. "Wind, I guess. Air?"

Skye looked disappointed. "Huh." She turned onto her stomach and began a slow, contemplative breaststroke away from the float.

"So how far along are you?" Maya called after her, fluttering her feet in the water, trying to paddle after her.

Skye flipped onto her back again. "A few weeks? Maybe a couple of months? I'm not totally sure."

"When was your last period?"

Skye shrugged. "No idea. I don't keep track. I trust my body to do what it needs to do when it needs to do it."

"But have you had an ultrasound yet?"

Skye shook her head and smiled. "No ultrasounds."

Maya steadied herself on the float. "What do you mean? You haven't been able to get one?"

"I don't want any ultrasounds," Skye said. "I don't want that artificial energy being blasted through my baby's body, you know?"

Maya blinked. "But . . . ultrasounds are perfectly safe."

"But are they really? Like, do we *really* know that?" Skye asked.

There was a long beat. "Yes. We really know that," Maya answered.

Skye shrugged, unconvinced. "Women have been having babies without ultrasounds since the beginning of time," she said. "Anyway, the baby told me she doesn't need one."

"The baby told you?"

"Mm-hmm." Skye rubbed her palms over her belly. "I can hear her thoughts. I think she's the spirit of my grandmother."

She was batshit crazy, this woman.

"Do you believe in reincarnation?" Skye asked.

Maya wasn't sure how to answer. She was raised Hindu and, therefore, was supposed to believe in rebirth and an upward spiraling of the soul, the Atman, lifetime after lifetime, ascending toward enlightenment. But since starting medical school in her twenties, she'd been firmly rooted in the secular, and religion barely crossed her mind anymore except when she felt guilty about not passing on her cultural heritage to her children. Dean had been a staunch atheist for as long as she'd known him and, at heart, Maya was a scientist like him. She didn't believe in spirits or ghosts or souls or anything similarly intangible or immeasurable. And she certainly didn't believe that this woman was carrying her dead grandmother in her uterus.

"It's a nice thought," she said. "I'm sorry you lost your grandmother."

Skye stood, looking up at Maya on the float, the water just under her chin. She smiled gratefully. "I know it's unconventional to not have ultrasounds and to just let nature do its thing, but it's what I believe. I'm also thinking of having a home birth."

Maya groaned internally. She'd met women like this before. Women who seemed to think childbirth was akin to baking a pie from scratch, something pioneer women did routinely and without difficulty but that the modern woman, because she'd been made lazy and ignorant by time and the rise of the industrial complex, felt incapable of attempting without various unnatural aids and crutches. Frozen pie dough and frozen embryos.

"I have to advise against that. Home births are inherently risky. But you can have as natural a birth as you'd like in a hospital."

Skye rolled her eyes. "You sound like my stepmom. She says midwives are all kooks. Could you deliver my baby?"

"I'm afraid not. But I could recommend you to someone at one of the local OB practices. Lankenau Hospital is excellent for obstetrics."

"But you could be my doctor until I deliver, right?"

Maya hesitated. "Sure. Yes. I mean, I strongly suggest having routine ultrasounds and testing—all of which I can do for you, and—"

"I can tell you care," Skye said, thoughtfully waving her arms about under the water. "You have very positive vibrations. The vibrations are magnified by the water, you know." She clapped her hands in delight. "That settles it, then. You're my OB. You're the best out of all the ones I've interviewed. I'm so excited!"

Maya shook her head in confusion, having not understood until that moment that this was an interview, an audition to be Skye's doctor.

Skye waded to the side of the pool and hoisted herself out. A stone-faced, uniformed maid appeared—had she been there the whole time? Where?—and handed her a towel. Then the maid, who moved with the hunched stiffness of someone who suffered from sciatica, shuffled around the pool, seized the flamingo's tail, pulled the float in, and offered Maya both of her hands to help her back to solid ground. Maya thanked her, and the woman nodded wordlessly and shuffled away. "It was so nice meeting you," Skye said, and suddenly she seemed older, more mature out of the water. "I think this is going to work out great."

"I should see you every month until we get closer to your due date," Maya said.

"Let's make it every two months," Skye said, smiling. "We can meet downstairs—I have a space for medical exams. But in the meantime, I promise I'll call you if I have any problems." She turned and walked away, leaving a trail of sopping wet footprints behind her. Before disappearing around a corner trailed by the hobbling maid, she turned around, gave Maya a small wave, and called, "The baby really likes you, too!"

The estate manager reappeared at the pool house door. "I'll walk you back to your car, Doctor," she said.

Maya slipped her shoes back on. "I get the feeling she doesn't actually want an OB," Maya said, looking in the direction Skye had gone.

"Ms. Skye would have preferred a doula," the estate manager said impassively, betraying none of her own feelings in a way Maya found admirable, with the professional detachment of a surgeon, "but her father, Congressman Hauser, insisted she have traditional medical care."

"Congressman?"

"Republican congressman," the estate manager said, and this time her eyebrows rose a bit. "The family appreciates your discretion, doctor."

"Of course," Maya said quickly. As they walked across the garden, she felt her way forward in the conversation gingerly. "So . . . is Skye married?"

The estate manager shook her head. "She is not."

"And her father the congressman is probably up for reelection next year?"

"He is."

"He probably has a pretty conservative base of supporters, given the area we're in."

"Very conservative."

"So his daughter's pregnancy is a secret."

They had reached the Hotessey. The estate manager eyed the duct-taped side-view mirror. "The family appreciates your discretion, like I said. Have a nice day, Doctor."

SIXTEEN

W elcome back." Gretchen knew to keep her voice down the morning after one of Amelia's getaways. She didn't know exactly where her employer went for four days every two months, but she strongly suspected it wasn't St. Barts. "How was St. Barts?"

"Beautiful." Amelia turned her desk chair away from the view of the grounds of her estate. "As always." She adjusted her dark sunglasses and nodded at the extra cup of coffee in Gretchen's hand. "For me? You're a doll."

Gretchen handed over the chai latte. The Cadillac of all espresso machines was only steps away in the kitchen, but ADG still preferred Starbucks. It was the only thing that seemed to help with her post-vacation migraines.

Amelia clutched the cup between her hands. "Everything's going well with the gynecologist?"

Gretchen's smile was triumphant. "It is. Clients love her. And she's busy. It's only been a month, but she already has a full schedule, and she's bringing on an assistant, someone she used to work with at Philadelphia General. We can finally put the midwife fiasco behind us. We have a board-certified ob-gyn on staff."

The steam rising from the latte fogged Amelia's sunglasses. "She doesn't do deliveries, though."

"But she *could* do one if she had to. She could even do a C-section, if she had to. That's the important thing."

Amelia breathed in the steam and breathed out gratitude. The universe had found a way to help them move past what happened two years ago, when the inexperienced midwife they'd hired choked in the middle of a home birth. The baby's shoulder became lodged in the mother's birth canal, and the midwife had bolted out of the room, hyperventilating. 911 was called, and a nineteen-year-old pimpled EMT twisted the shoulder free and delivered the baby—not in the candle-and-incense-filled suite specially prepared in the client's home—but in the back of the ambulance, its doors wide open to the neighborhood. The client had been livid enough to ruin them, but a generous refund of her subscription fee, plus payment commensurate with her emotional suffering, plus a legal mediation in which Amelia promised that Eunoia would never employ another midwife, convinced the woman to sign a nondisclosure agreement that ensured the reputation of the clinic remained unscathed. Improved, even, as it turned out. Midwives were a dime a dozen, but how many wellness clinics could say they offered an ob-gyn who made house calls?

"Skye Hauser is officially a client now," Gretchen said. "She's expecting."

Amelia's eyebrows shot up. "The congressman can't be happy about that."

"He's frantic," Gretchen said. "So much so, he paid for the whole year up front." She grinned. "If we're lucky and Dr. Rao does a good job, we might get his wife on board as a patient, too."

Amelia nodded. "The wife is well connected. That could be good for us."

"How's Prem feeling?"

Amelia sighed. "The same, I think. I'm telling you, there's something wrong with her. She's acting so strangely. Whatever it is, it's getting worse."

"All her labs were normal. I checked everything," Gretchen said, a little defensively.

Amelia nodded. "I know you did. But call it mother's intuition. I finally got that acupuncture guy—the one from New York—to agree to come up this Saturday to work on her. He wants her to try a bone broth diet for a few days in the meantime, cut out all carbs, all legumes, all sugar. Poor Paloma doesn't know what to feed her."

Gretchen sighed. "I know you don't want to hear this, ADG, but a lot of teenage girls get like this when there are boyfriend troubles." Amelia gave her a tired look. "I'm just saying," Gretchen continued, "this all started around the time Carter broke up with her."

Amelia rubbed her forehead. "This has nothing to do with Carter. Prem is focused on college. Should we try the bee venom again?"

"She didn't love it the last time."

"No. I guess she didn't. I just want to do something to help her, Gretchen. What can I do to help her?"

"You've done everything you can," Gretchen said. "I'm not a mother, so I'm not going to tell you not to trust your intuition, but I've checked, and there's nothing medically wrong with the girl. She's probably just stressed out. What does she do to relax?"

"She paints."

Gretchen shrugged. "Have her do more of that, then. And try to be patient. This is probably just some phase she's going through."

"I was sick as a child," Amelia said. "Did I ever tell you that?"

Gretchen shook her head. "You didn't."

"I spent my childhood in and out of hospitals. Poked and prodded. I had something like seven spinal taps in two years."

Gretchen sank into the closest chair. "Holy Jesus, Amelia. I'm so sorry. What was wrong?"

Amelia looked out the window again. "They could never figure it out. One test just led to the next test, which just led to the next test, for years."

"Was it the autoimmune disorder?"

Amelia shook her head. "No, I didn't start with that until I was forty. The symptoms all went away when I was sixteen. After I left home and went to live with my father. All the pain, the fevers, they just stopped. At least that's how I remember it. But my memories of the time are . . . murky."

"The body heals itself," Gretchen suggested. "It's like we always say."

Amelia gave her a tight-lipped smile. "I guess so." She sat at her desk for a long time after Gretchen left, trying to pull the past back to her, to dredge up the memories that had receded into the dark waters of her mind.

She closed her eyes but saw only the falling of white powder.

SEVENTEEN

The silk-robed woman seated on the sofa across from Maya adjusted her glittering peacock blue head wrap and tucked her bare feet underneath her. "So," she said expectantly. Her gaze was unblinking, even as she took a sip of the green liquid in her martini glass. "You're the gynecologist?"

Maya tried to keep her attention fixed on the woman's face, on the way her pale foundation had settled into the lines around her small eyes and angular nose, and away from the furry, claw-toed creature that had draped itself across the woman's shoulders. "Yes," Maya said and cleared her throat. "Yes, Mrs. Cunningham, I'm the gynecologist. May I say, that is a lovely animal. Is it a ferret?"

Mrs. Cunningham turned up her nose, offended. "No."

"It's a kinkajou," Esther, seated next to Maya on a brocade couch that matched the one Mrs. Cunningham occupied, said helpfully. Maya raised her eyebrows, and Esther shrugged and whispered, "Paris Hilton had one."

"Correct," the woman said, not smiling, but raising one bejeweled finger in a way that somehow communicated her pleasure. "This is Ambrosia, and she is indeed a kinkajou. And you are?"

"Esther. Dr. Rao's medical assistant."

It had taken a fair amount of convincing to coax Esther into accepting this per diem role. "House calls? I don't know how I feel about that," Esther had said when Maya called her about the job offer. "I'd have to cut back my hours at Temple. They're not going to like that."

"They'll pay you thirty an hour," Maya said. "That's more than Temple. Plus, we'd get to work together again. I miss you, Esther."

"Aww, I miss you, too, Doc," Esther said. "Look, I'd do it for thirty-five, and they'd have to cover my train fare to the Main Line."

Maya convinced Gretchen to agree to the terms, and Esther began accompanying Maya on client visits the following week. Maya picked her up at the train station, and while navigating to their appointments, Esther managed their daily schedule and returned client phone calls.

"You can't be serious with this," Esther said the first time she saw the trunk of the Hotessey, boxes of gauze and test tubes and microscope slides strewn about among the kids' sports equipment. "Just no," she declared, and then set about organizing and securing the supplies and equipment into bins with labels so that, when she was finished, the back of the Hotessey looked like a sleek mobile clinic. "Now we can work," she said proudly, and Maya could have cried with gratitude.

They had a portable, folding examination table that weighed as much as the two of them put together, but that they nevertheless rolled into each appointment so that Maya could perform examinations without the clients having to lie awkwardly on their beds or sofas. In the van were the ultrasound machine, a microscope for looking at culture slides, a stash of medication samples that Esther had acquired from a pharmaceutical sales rep she was friendly with, and enough disposable gloves and speculums to last them six months.

They'd developed a routine. They would sit with the client for a consultation, then set up their equipment and perform whatever examination and testing were needed. Then Maya would counsel the patient while Esther entered the information into a Word document on a laptop that served as their medical records library.

They were several minutes into Mrs. Cunningham's consultation, and still they had no idea why they'd been summoned. Some clients needed routine checkups: a Pap smear, breast examination, and referral for a mammogram. Others had specific complaints or symptoms that required attention. Mrs. Cunningham had, thus far, shown Maya and Esther through the labyrinthine hallways of her palatial, dimly lit home in Gladwyne, waving her drink at the bust of one dead relative after another as if she were a boozy museum tour guide, then settled them in the library, where she opened a silver cage in the corner and retrieved the kinkajou that now gnawed on one of her dangling earrings.

"I noticed you speak very well," the woman said, her gaze unfocused, not quite looking at either of them. "You express yourself well. I'm impressed." The kinkajou yawned and bared its razor-sharp teeth.

"I can read, too," Esther said curtly. She gave Mrs. Cunningham a steely smile. "And this is a dream library. You have quite the collection—all the classics, I see."

"Those are all first editions," Mrs. Cunningham said, nodding at the towering bookshelves that lined the walls all around them. Behind her was an antique Louis XV–style writing desk with an ivory inlay and, beyond that, a wrought iron spiral staircase that led to a second level of books. "Can I offer either of you a drink?"

Maya and Esther shook their heads. Maya glanced at her watch. It was eleven.

"It's probably a little early for alcohol, I know," Mrs. Cunningham said, shrugging as if she didn't care, but obviously a little annoyed by their unwillingness to partake. "But my great grandmother lived to be a hundred and two years old, and she swore by two drinks before noon every day. As they say, an appletini a day keeps the doctor away!" She picked up the smallest of three silver handbells that sat on a wooden pedestal on the coffee table and rang it sharply. Maya and Esther flinched in surprise. Almost immediately, the door to the library flew open and a uniformed maid whisked in carrying a silver tray of ripe green grapes and something black and shiny, like chocolate-covered espresso beans, in a small ceramic bowl. The young woman placed the tray on the coffee table between Mrs. Cunningham and her guests, bowed, and retreated from the room as swiftly and silently as she had arrived. Maya and Esther smiled after her gratefully.

Maya, who had skipped breakfast, reached for a grape but froze, hand outstretched, when she identified the contents of the ceramic bowl. Beetles. A small pile of black beetles. She cleared her throat again and redirected her hand, using it to push her hair behind one ear. Esther shifted to the far corner of the sofa, visibly repulsed. The kinkajou, however, seemed ecstatic. It made a barking sound and scrambled off Mrs. Cunningham's shoulder and onto the table, where it tucked into its lunch with rabid delight. Its small paws were remarkably dexterous, and it bit into a beetle the way a human might negotiate a sandwich. There was a splintering sound as its sharp teeth pierced the insect's carapace.

Maya watched the creature with a mixture of disgust and fascination, thinking that Niam, who delighted in watching nature documentaries where small animals were eaten by large animals, would have loved to witness this. Esther piped up, "So, Mrs. Cunningham, what can we help you with today?"

"I seem to have misplaced something," Mrs. Cunningham said, her tone somewhere between annoyed and anxious. Her hand went to the string of pearls around her neck. Her skin was paper-thin and her nail beds startlingly blue.

Maya shook her head in confusion. "Misplaced something?"

"Something quite expensive," Mrs. Cunningham said. She shifted her position slightly and winced, and Maya understood.

"How long ago did it . . . go missing?" she asked.

Mrs. Cunningham considered this. "Probably three or four days."

Next to her, Esther sighed almost inaudibly and began to unfold the examination table on the plush Persian rug. "That's quite a long time," Maya said, concerned.

Mrs. Cunningham stood and dropped her robe. "I suppose you'll just have to go after it," she said, ignoring the exam table and laying her now entirely naked body across the sofa, knees splayed. "Just be quick about it, please."

Back at PGH, Maya and Esther had a running joke about some of their patients having exhibitionist tendencies, women eager to undress even before Esther had left the room or who refused the paper privacy drape. They tried not to look at each other now, knowing that making eye contact would send them both into hysterics.

"Let's just cover you a little," Esther said, her face a mask of professional insouciance. She picked up the gown and draped it over Mrs. Cunningham.

"If you must," the woman sighed impatiently.

"Why don't you tell us what we're looking for," Maya said.

"It'll be obvious, I'm sure," Mrs. Cunningham snapped. Then she sighed again and leaned her head back, closing her eyes at the exhaustion of it all.

The missing item was a pale green, Washington Monument–shaped crystal the size of a fountain pen. Esther had received it from Maya into a hand towel provided by the hapless maid, who had entered the room to a full, unobstructed view of her employer's genitalia after being summoned again by the ringing bell.

The towel and crystal now sat in the middle of the coffee table, next to the tray of grapes and beetles. The kinkajou had slinked off under the desk to curl into a ball and nap, its belly full of insects.

"Well." Esther, who could not escape the library of Mrs. Cunningham quickly enough, folded the exam table, put the used speculum in a small red biohazard bag, and prepared for their exit. Maya, however, was in no hurry to leave.

"May I ask . . . why?"

Mrs. Cunningham waved her hand defensively. "The instructions said to use the crystal wherever balance was needed."

Maya nodded. "And is there a reason—a symptom you had—that made you feel that your vagina was out of balance?"

The woman considered this. "I've been very distracted lately. And tired. It's been difficult to concentrate on anything because I've been so tired. At my last rotary club dinner, I fell asleep at the table! I woke up when I tried to rest my head on the shoulder of the woman next to me—I barely know her! It was so embarrassing."

Maya nodded sympathetically.

"Anyway," Mrs. Cunningham continued, "I had my monthly biophoton session last week, and it just didn't work as well as it usually does. I didn't feel like my energy was flowing any better, and the nurse said it could be because my yoni is out of balance. So I bought the crystal from the website and—"

"Wait, you bought that off the Eunoia website?" Maya asked.

Esther had already brought it up on her phone. "Yup. The Towering Heights Mayan Meditative Crystal. Guaranteed to realign your karmic energy and restore balance." She showed Maya the screen. The crystal contained 3 percent jadeite and cost $2,000. "It does say to 'use it wherever you need balance restored.'"

"See?" Mrs. Cunningham said. "Honestly, for that much money I expected better results."

Maya looked the woman in the eye and said, "Mrs. Cunningham, an object like this with a sharp point is dangerous. You're lucky it didn't damage your cervix or puncture the wall of your vagina. Your . . ." Despite herself, she stumbled over the word. ". . . yoni isn't out of balance. That's not really a thing. The vagina is self regulating. It doesn't need balancing or restoring or cleaning or anything. It's fine just the way it is."

The woman looked at her skeptically.

"I promise you," Maya said. "But your nails. Have they always been blue?"

Mrs. Cunningham held her hands up to the light. "My nails? What does that have to do with anything? You know, I usually have a manicure, but my esthetician is out on maternity leave and I refuse to go to anyone else. No one else does a gel manicure like Conchetta."

"Blue nail beds can be a sign of anemia," Maya said. "When's the last time you had blood work?"

"Blood work?" Mrs. Cunningham looked surprised. "I can't even remember. But I get regular intravenous vitamin infusions and my diet is extremely healthy. What on earth would I need blood tests for?"

"Fatigue can be caused by a lot of different things," Esther said. "Thyroid problems, low iron, early diabetes. You need to get your yearly blood test to check for that."

"Do you see a primary care doctor?" Maya asked.

Mrs. Cunningham shook her head vehemently. "I saw all kinds of doctors before I joined Eunoia two years ago. None of them ever did anything for me. They sent me for mammograms and X-rays, and oh! All of that radiation. It made me so sick." She wrung her hands. "Mind you, they never spent more than five minutes talking to me, those doctors. I've finally restored my body through my treatments with Eunoia. Up until a few weeks ago, I felt better than I ever have."

"It's important to see your primary care doctor every year, though," Esther said.

Mrs. Cunningham shrugged. "Sometimes I see Gretchen, but she never orders any tests. She says if I'm keeping up with my treatments, that's all I need to do."

Esther's mouth dropped open, and Maya, having once listened to several minutes of a podcast about the benefits of meditation, tried inhaling a calming breath through her nose. "We have test tubes. And we can mail your sample to the lab overnight. Why don't I draw the blood for your tests right now?"

Mrs. Cunningham shook her head. "I'm sure that won't be necessary," she said. "I just bought a new type of coffee. A special Peruvian blend, very rare. It's specially formulated to detoxify the liver. I'll try that first."

"Respectfully, ma'am, your liver doesn't need detoxifying, and drinking coffee wouldn't do that anyway," Maya said.

Mrs. Cunningham raised her eyebrows. "Oh, I don't drink the coffee."

Maya and Esther exchanged a glance. "What do you do with it?" Esther asked.

"I give myself an enema with it," Mrs. Cunningham said, surprised at the question. "Surely you're familiar with the health benefits of coffee enemas."

Maya shook her head, feeling traumatized.

Mrs. Cunningham said haughtily, "It's been used for centuries in South America."

For what felt like a long time, the only sound in the room was the soft snoring of the animal under the desk. Then Mrs. Cunningham nodded curtly. "Well, I thank you ladies for your services. I'll have someone show you out."

She rang one of the silver bells again, loudly, and Maya and Esther sprang to their feet and took their leave.

Back in the van, they fastened their seat belts and stared straight ahead in silence for a solid thirty seconds without moving. "Well, that was the fucking weirdest experience of my life," Esther said finally.

"What's her squirrel monkey's name again?"

"Ambrosia. And it's not a squirrel monkey."

They looked at each other and burst into laughter.

"I love how she thought we 'expressed ourselves well,'" Maya said, trying to collect herself. "Like that was a compliment."

Esther glanced at her with a bemused expression. "You think that comment was directed at you?"

Maya squinted in confusion. "At both of us, yeah." Esther raised her eyebrows and laughed. "What?" Maya asked.

Esther waved her hand, as if the conversation wasn't worth having.

"Seriously, what?" Maya had the feeling she was missing something vital. Like the punch line of the joke had somehow escaped her.

"I mean, I'm pretty sure that was for me," Esther said. "I don't think she was surprised *you* expressed yourself well."

"Maybe the only other Indians she's ever met couldn't speak English or something," Maya said, shrugging. "But, either way, it was offensive."

"Yeah, but . . . not in the same way," Esther said.

Maya glanced at her, perplexed. She shrugged. "It's not a contest."

Esther was quiet for a moment. Then, pointing to the duct-taped side-view mirror, she said, "Your mirror is still broken."

"I keep forgetting to make an appointment to get it fixed," Maya said with a regretful grimace. "It's been hectic with the kids and the new schedule." As if to prove her point, her phone pinged with a text from Dean. "He wants to know if I'll be able to take Niam to soccer."

Esther scrolled through their schedule. "Yeah, you're good. We only have two more for today, and they're both close by."

Maya looked up at the facade of Mrs. Cunningham's mansion and said with reverence, "Can you imagine living in a place like this?"

Esther shook her head. "Seems creepy. You think she lives here alone? That's sad."

They pulled out of the driveway and made their way back toward Lancaster Avenue.

"Should we grab Starbucks?" Maya asked, straight-faced. Esther had always shared her dry sense of humor. It was part of the reason they worked together so well. But now there was a too-long silence, and tension played across Esther's face. Maya wondered if she'd spoiled something with her earlier attempt to commiserate about Mrs. Cunningham's ignorant comment. The truth was, Maya had been offended. So had Esther. So why did it feel like the two of them were suddenly at odds?

The discomfort was too much to bear, and she turned toward Esther to say something just as Esther asked, her delivery as flat as Maya's, "You think Starbucks has any Peruvian blends?"

They were still laughing when they pulled up to the next appointment.

EIGHTEEN

t was widely agreed among the parents of Hamilton Hall Academy
that the annual Harvest Concert was, by far, the most tolerable
student recital of the school year. Vastly superior to the spring's Junior Opera Night or the more recently added Winter Holiday Poetry
Marathon, the fall Harvest Concert featured mercifully short group
performances from every grade and spotlight performances from a
handful of particularly gifted student musicians. Though lengthy,
the program always ran on time, and there was a bar set up outside
the auditorium that dispensed locally brewed alcoholic apple cider in
chunky ceramic Hamilton Hall mugs to parents whose autumnal
spirits needed boosting.

By the time Dean pulled the van into the school parking lot at
7:00 p.m., every space was filled and the assistant principal was waving cars onto the grass in front of the gym. "Are we late?" Maya
wondered, checking the time. "The concert doesn't start for another
thirty minutes." Dean squeezed in between two luxury cars—a
BMW and a Bentley—and Maya, who never noticed the make of
cars, noticed.

Inside the auditorium, all of the orchestra seats and most of the first mezzanine seats were taken. "My legs are tired!" Niam announced, clutching Maya's hand with both of his and letting his legs give way, nearly yanking her shoulder out of its socket.

"Ow! Niam!" Maya yelped, more loudly than she'd intended.

"Maya?"

Amelia stood behind them dressed in dark jeans, a pale pink blazer, and matching heels, her hair loose around her shoulders as usual. She carried a mug of cider.

Maya was surprised to see her here. A student concert seemed somehow beneath Amelia DeGilles. "Hi! Is Prem performing?"

Amelia nodded proudly. "It's her last Hamilton Hall concert. It's bittersweet. Did you guys just get here? You'll never find a seat."

Maya introduced Dean and the children, and Amelia cooed down at the baby in her car seat. Then, as the house lights flashed twice in warning—five minutes to showtime—Diya dragged herself off in the direction of backstage, reluctantly clutching her violin case to her chest. "Good luck, Dee!" Maya and Dean called after her, brimming over with parental pride and enthusiasm. Diya rounded the corner without looking back.

"Why don't you sit with me?" Amelia said. "I saved seats for Greg, my ex, and for Bodhi, but I don't think they're coming. Bodhi had a fencing tournament in New York and they're driving back now, but there's no way they'll make it in time."

"Are you sure?" Maya asked.

Amelia smiled warmly. "Of course! I'd love the company."

As her family followed Amelia down the center aisle to the front of the auditorium, Maya considered when the right time was to broach the question of why Eunoia was selling $2,000 crystals on its website and claiming they had sanative properties. She hadn't shared this information with Dean. She suspected she already knew what he would say: that he had warned her, that he'd told her Eunoia wasn't a true medical practice, that if something sounded too good to be true, it probably was. Dean hadn't even been impressed with her first paycheck from Eunoia, even though it was significantly more than what she'd been making at PGH. Gretchen hadn't been wrong about the money.

Every few aisles, another parent stood from their seat and stopped Amelia to say hello. Usually it was a woman, sometimes a couple. They were, to a person, impeccably dressed and delighted to see her. They greeted her with a quick kiss on each cheek, asked how Bodhi and Prem were doing, confirmed that Prem would indeed be performing tonight, and shared some personal anecdote. After each encounter, Amelia turned and introduced Maya, Dean, and the children. "They're new to Hamilton this year," she explained to the other party, who leaned in to pay particular attention. "And Maya's just joined us at Eunoia as our gynecologist." At this, eyebrows were invariably raised in approval, and several women promised they would be making appointments. Maya's hand was pumped enthusiastically, and she felt a bit like a celebrity working a red carpet.

When they were finally seated, Dean on the aisle with Asha's car seat near his feet, Maya with Niam on her lap next to Amelia, Maya couldn't help but notice that Amelia smelled pleasantly like coconut and something floral. It wasn't perfume exactly, but more like a tropical breeze had recently washed over her. Maya discreetly sniffed Niam's hair. It was due for a shampooing.

The preschoolers were first to perform and were, as expected, achingly adorable. "My ovaries hurt," Amelia whispered to Maya as the children filed offstage after their rendition of "This Little Light of Mine."

Maya laughed. "It's never too late, you know."

Amelia shuddered and sipped her cider. "Oh, it's definitely too late. For me, anyway. I'll stick to adopting dogs."

"That seems easier," Maya agreed. "And less expensive."

Amelia shook her head. "Boarding and training for them costs me an arm and a leg. And their specialty dog food and vet and therapist. But at least none of them will ever call me a bitch to my face."

Maya winced. "No! Not Prem?"

Amelia nodded conspiratorially. "Yup. This morning. Just wait until Diya's a teenager. They change. It's like a backwards metamorphosis. They start out as these sweet butterflies and they just mutate into these awful little . . ." She shook her head, looking embarrassed, as if she'd said too much. "Never mind. Just ignore me. It's the cider talking."

The kindergartners had made their way onstage and were preparing to play recorders. Maya turned back to Amelia to continue their conversation, but Amelia was now smiling beatifically again, the picture of calm perfection, gazing adoringly at the children nervously fidgeting onstage. The moment had passed. Reluctantly, Maya settled back into her seat, and Niam rested his head against her shoulder. She suspected she'd just gotten a glimpse of the real Amelia DeGilles, the woman beneath the polished veneer, and she was desperate to find out more. If Amelia struggled with her children, maybe she and Maya had more in common than it had, at first glance, appeared. Maybe Maya had misjudged the span between herself and Amelia, between their achievements, between the tiny house at one end of the Main Line and the sprawling estate at the other. The conversation about crystals, she decided, could wait for another time.

The evening went on at a steady, efficient pace. Diya's class performed a lively rendition of what, at least according to the program, was *Dance of the Sugarplum Fairy* from the *Nutcracker Suite*. Niam fell asleep, and though one of Maya's legs was throbbing from lack of blood circulation, she didn't dare move and risk waking him. Then Asha started fussing, and Dean leaned over to Maya and whispered, "Should we just grab Diya and get out of here?"

Maya shook her head. "We can't just walk out in front of all these people. It'd be rude. And Amelia's daughter is performing later."

Dean flipped through the thick program, its pages filled with loving messages from parents and advertisements from local businesses, including four cosmetic dentists. "There's another hour to go."

Maya shrugged helplessly. Dean sighed and stood, lifting Asha's car seat. "Okay, then. We'll be in the lobby. Look for us near the spiked cider." He made his way up the aisle, toward the exit.

"Do you guys have to go?" Amelia asked. "It must be late for your littles."

Maya waved her hand. "Not at all. I'm looking forward to hearing Prem play again."

Amelia smiled. "She's been working so hard for her auditions. The piece she's playing tonight is her signature. It's by a Russian composer and it's so challenging, but she played it perfectly this afternoon, so fingers crossed."

When Prem finally took the stage, an anticipatory hush fell over the audience. She wore a knee-length powder blue dress, flared at the waist with white lace around the hem, and her hair was held back by a simple pewter headband. The emcee, a sweaty music teacher who had the glazed look of someone who was coming to the end of a marathon, introduced her as the senior spotlight performer of the evening. After a brief round of applause, Prem lay her fingers atop the strings of a gleaming black harp and began to play.

The piece was melancholy, the notes low and full of despair, and Maya couldn't help but smile to herself. What did Premrose De-Gilles, she of bespoke spirulina and chauffeured SUV, know of despair? Of Russian-level suffering and toil? Yet she played it so beautifully, so convincingly.

Maya had always wanted to play the piano as a child, but her family couldn't afford lessons, let alone an instrument. One Christmas, when she was eleven, a $48 miniature Casio keyboard appeared under the miniature tree on their living room coffee table, white and plastic and tinny, boasting thirty-one keys and a catchy, preprogrammed demo tune that showed off the device's various electronic sounds and features. The gift came with a thin "Learn to play piano!" booklet. If she were really serious about learning to play, her parents strongly implied, she could start by teaching herself. Ravi Shankar had taught himself how to play the sitar at age seven, and, like all Indian instruments, the sitar was much more complicated and demanding than the piano. But, though Maya spent hours every day that winter trying to make sense of the notes and symbols in the booklet, she was only able to learn a few melodies—"Hot Cross Buns," "Mary Had a Little Lamb"—and tap them out with one finger on the tiny keys. She had no talent for music, she concluded, and, come spring, put the Casio away under her bed.

Prem struck what sounded, to Maya's untrained ear, like a false note. Next to her, Amelia flinched slightly. A few seconds later, another discordant note. Then another. Prem's face reddened. She lifted her hands off the strings, shook out her fingers, took a breath, and started again. Amelia shifted in her seat. Another false note followed, then another. Prem's jaw quivered. The music trickled to a stop, then she abruptly pushed back her chair, stood, and walked offstage, disappearing into the wings.

Several people in the audience gasped, then the auditorium fell silent. It was as if there had been a collective drawing of breath that no one dared release. Amelia stared straight ahead for a long moment, then she blinked. "Oh my God," she whispered to herself. She stood, and Maya, with Niam clutched to her chest, slid out into the aisle to let her pass. Amelia vanished up the aisle without a word.

The harried music teacher appeared onstage looking confused and said, "Premrose DeGilles," and applauded. The audience politely followed suit. A few minutes into the next performance, a jaunty cello duet by two sixth graders, Niam stirred and announced with urgency, "Mommy, I have to go potty!"

"Shh!" Maya's cheeks reddened as she looked around at the other small children in the audience, all of whom were sitting quietly and seemed to have no immediate needs whatsoever. "Can you hold it for a few minutes?" she whispered.

Niam shook his head vigorously. "No no no." He slid off her lap and danced about in the aisle. A man recording the cellists on his cell phone glanced at them in annoyance.

Sorry! Maya mouthed. She put a hand on the back of Niam's head and gently steered him up the aisle and back out into the theater lobby. Dean had disappeared, probably back to the car with Asha to wait out the rest of the concert while listening to the Eagles game on the radio. Maya asked a waistcoated bartender for directions to the closest ladies room and, when he pointed, Niam took off running. "I really have to go!" His voice echoed down the empty school hallways.

By the time Maya caught up with him, Niam was pushing past a woman exiting the girls' room. "'Scuse me, lady! 'Scuse me!"

"I'm so sorry—" Maya started to say, then realized Niam had almost knocked over her employer. "Amelia! Hi! Sorry, my son has a heightened sense of drama when it comes to his bladder."

Amelia smiled wanly and shrugged. She looked exhausted. "Oh, believe me, I get it. My daughter has a heightened sense of drama when it comes to everything."

Maya hesitated, wondering what the most tactful way to approach the subject was. "Is Prem okay? I saw her . . . leave the stage. She seemed upset."

Amelia shook her head and motioned to the door. "She's in there. It was a disaster, her performance." Her exasperated tone barely masked the worry underneath. "She just wasn't focused. She was making simple, stupid mistakes—I'm sure you heard them—that were unacceptable for someone at her level. If I could just figure out—" she stopped herself and shook her head again. "Anyway, if you hear crying, that's her." She sighed and waved her hand. "I'm just going to wait out here until she's done."

Maya nodded sympathetically and followed the sound of Niam's voice. He was already on a toilet in one of the stalls, swinging his legs and loudly reciting the Pledge of Allegiance. "And through the red sticks forest stands, a nation, and the frogs, invisible, with liberty and justice for all."

"You done, bud?" Maya asked.

"Mommy, listen." He pointed one finger to the ceiling.

"Yup, echo," Maya said, helping him off the toilet. The sound of someone blowing their nose reverberated from several stalls away.

Niam shook his head gravely and squinted one eye. "Somebody's crying." He crouched down to look under the stalls. "I see feet! Hey! Why are you crying? Don't be sad, okay?"

"Shh!" Maya hissed urgently. "Let's go wash hands." She dragged him toward the sinks, but Niam was undeterred. Pressing his face into the gap in the stall door, he shouted, "You need tissues? My mommy has tissues in her purse."

Maya was mortified, but Prem's voice from the other side of the door was sweetly amused. "No thank you, bud."

Niam's face lit up. "My mommy calls me bud, too!"

The door unlatched and Prem emerged, her face tearstained, mascara smeared.

"What's on your face?" Niam asked, leaning toward her with interest.

"Give her some room, Niam," Maya said, pulling him back by the arm.

Prem smiled at them, then said, "Oh, hey. We've met. You're the gynecologist. Dr. Rao, right?" She had none of the twitchy self-consciousness, none of the faux apathy teenagers were so famous for. Prem met her eye with a quiet, assured confidence.

"Maya," Maya said, impressed the young woman had remembered her name. "Are you okay?"

Prem shrugged, as if the answer didn't matter. "Yeah."

"For what it's worth," Maya said, "I thought your performance was lovely."

Prem gave a mirthless laugh. She ran a paper towel under the tap and wiped the smeared makeup from her face. "It wasn't my best, but thanks." She stopped to shake her wrists out, then resumed wiping.

Maya shrugged. "Well then, you're so good that even when you're not at your best, you're still amazing. It sounded great to me."

Prem's face brightened a bit. "Thank you."

"How long have you been playing the harp?" Maya asked.

"Since I was five."

"Hey! I'm almost five!" Niam said, as Maya held his hands under the water. "Mommy, when's my birthday again?"

"Not for a few months," Maya said. "It's April 16."

"Hey, my birthday is in April, too," Prem said, shaking her hands out again. She and Niam exchanged grins.

It occurred to Maya that Prem might make a great babysitter, at the same time it also occurred to her that Amelia's daughter would have no need to babysit for extra money. "Are your hands still bothering you?" she asked.

Prem nodded. "My fingers go numb. Sometimes, like tonight, they just won't do what I want them to. It's really annoying." She sighed. "I probably shouldn't have just walked offstage. But it's frustrating, you know?"

Maya frowned sympathetically. "Have you seen a doctor for it?"

"My parents took me to a hand specialist last month. He said I don't actually have carpal tunnel syndrome, but he didn't know what was wrong either. I'm going to try acupuncture with someone my mom knows."

Maya nodded. "I've heard good things about acupuncture," she said.

Prem shuddered. "I don't like neebles," she said, then laughed. "I mean, neebles." She looked at herself in the mirror and carefully worked her lips, watching her mouth move. "Nee-dles. My mouth doesn't work either. Needles. Not neebles."

Niam snorted in merriment.

"Hey! Are you laughing at me?" Prem asked, feigning offense.

Niam tucked in his lower lip, trying not to laugh, until Prem fixed him with an intense gaze and declared, "neebles!" and they both erupted in hysterics. Prem took a step toward the trash can and listed to one side, her shoulder colliding with the paper towel dispenser attached to the wall. "Oh, ouch!" she gasped, still laughing. Niam, who couldn't remember the last time he'd been so entertained, doubled over at the waist. Then Prem turned toward the wall, and her expression momentarily clouded. She looked confused, as if she couldn't work out where the paper towel dispenser had come from. She stared at it for a beat too long.

"Be careful there," Maya said lightly, wrapping an arm around Prem's shoulders and gently steering her toward the door. *Has she been drinking?* Maya thought back to her lunch at Amelia's house: *Is it too early for wine?* No doubt there was an impressive wine cellar somewhere on the property. The idea that Prem DeGilles, moody teenager and overscheduled harp prodigy, was a budding alcoholic who would show up inebriated to a school recital didn't seem particularly far-fetched. "I think we'd better get out of here before one of you two hurts yourselves. Come on, Niam."

In the hallway, Amelia met them with a bemused expression. "What was going on in there? It sounded like a comedy routine."

"Neebles!" Niam said, and he and Prem dissolved into laughter again.

"Nibbles? I don't get it," Amelia said. "I see you're feeling better, at least." She wrapped both arms around Prem's waist, her expression relieved.

Prem nodded and tucked her head against her mother's shoulder. "Can we go home now?" Her voice reminded Maya of her own children on long car rides.

"Yes, my love." Amelia sighed. "Oh shoot. I forgot our coats." She considered her predicament silently. It did not need to be said aloud that neither Amelia nor Prem DeGilles would humiliate herself by walking back into the theater, past all the other Hamilton Hall parents, after Prem's disastrous performance.

"Just ask Blake to grab them," Prem suggested.

"I can grab them," Maya offered. "We're heading out, too, and I have to get Niam's."

"Oh, are you sure you wouldn't mind?" Amelia asked gratefully.

"No, it's no problem at all."

"Blake is already out front, so we're off. But maybe you can hold on to them for me? You know, why don't you come over on Sunday? You can meet Bodhi and my ex. Bring your husband and kids. We'll do brunch. Around ten. Are you free?"

"Sure, that sounds nice," Maya said. She felt a frisson of excitement at being invited.

"Perfect. See you then. I'll text you our address." Amelia waved, and Prem said, "Bye, Maya! Bye, Niam! See you Sunday!" She pointed at Niam. "Neebles!"

Niam keeled over in merriment.

"I still don't get it," Amelia said to Prem as they walked off down the hallway.

Maya leaned back against a locker, clasping her hands in front of her. As she waited for Niam to get it out of his system, she watched

Prem and Amelia go. After so many years of practicing medicine, she'd developed what doctors call clinical intuition, a kind of sixth sense for other people's ailments. She often felt in her gut when something was wrong with a patient before her conscious mind realized it. Prem swayed slightly on her mother's arm, and Maya felt her stomach twist with trepidation. Something was off.

The thought nagged at her on the ride home and through bath and bedtime. When she opened *Alice in Wonderland* to read to Niam, she noticed how much the illustrations of young Alice resembled Prem. The straight blond hair held back with a headband, the girlish blue-and-white dress. The facial expressions alternately dazed and pensive, angry and laughing. As she read in the dim light, Alice wandered through Wonderland, Niam drifted off to sleep, and Maya's disquiet about Premrose DeGilles grew steadily stronger.

NINETEEN

A melia DeGilles spent her tenth birthday, and the two months preceding it, in a bed at Children's Hospital Los Angeles, in a private room in a wing named after her father. This was how the mysterious illness, the one that would leave her intermittently bedbound for years, began. A sudden, violent fall from perfect health into sickness. One day she was swimming and riding her horse at her family's lake house, the next it was all she could do to brush her own teeth.

Upon her return home, back to the house in the Hollywood Hills where she'd lived all her life, back to her sweet-smelling, pinkwallpapered bedroom just above the garden, she found a commode beside her bed and a new doll nestled underneath her covers. As much rest as possible with as little stimulation as possible, the doctors had ordered. There was no clear diagnosis, and her parents were left frustrated and frayed, their questions hanging limply in the air while the white-coated doctors, all men, avoided eye contact and muttered things like "challenging case" and "unusual symptoms." Perhaps it was some rare genetic disorder, they suggested, as if to transfer responsibility back to Amelia's parents. They even went so far as to suggest that perhaps Amelia's symptoms were psychological, a result of her parents' recent divorce. But that was ridiculous; there was no way to somatize life-threatening anemia or sky-high fevers into existence. Something was physically, palpably very wrong with the girl, that much was obvious. Her mother rarely left her bedside, and her parents were forever arguing about her medical care. Amelia could hear them downstairs in the evenings, when her father would stop by after work to visit her. Should they call another specialist? Should they let her doctors do yet another spinal tap?

The new doll, a gift from her father, was beautiful. Straight and yellow hair, brown and ever-alert eyes, a permanently charmed expression. Amelia hated it. When she swung her legs over the side of the four-poster bed and set her feet on the hardwood floor; when she felt the pain splinter up her shin and thigh bones as if they were glass on the verge of shattering; when she lay on the floor next to the toilet, her knees having buckled beneath her, the wind knocked out of her from the fall, from the agony, she hated the doll. The small, inanimate girl felt no pain. She just smiled vacantly down at Amelia from the bed, oblivious to her suffering.

Her mother, though, adored the toy. Turning it over in her hands, she marveled, "She looks just like you! Except the eyes. The eyes should be blue." She asked Amelia what she thought the doll's name should be. "Claribel," Amelia suggested, but her mother shook her head disapprovingly. "That's a name for a cow or a sheep, not for a beautiful little girl."

Her mother named the doll Evette. "She'll watch over you and keep you safe," she said, tucking the toy into bed beside Amelia. She placed a silver tray on the duvet. Two pills and a cup of applesauce. She kissed Amelia's forehead. She kissed Evette's forehead.

A few weeks later, when she was feeling a bit better, Amelia struggled out of bed and put the doll on the highest shelf she could reach in the bookcase across the room. From then on and for years afterward, as night fell and Amelia drifted into fitful sleep, her parents' angry voices from below punctuating the silence like fireworks, the last thing she saw were Evette's two glowing brown eyes high in the darkness.

TWENTY

On Sunday morning, the Anders-Rao family stood at attention at the front door of the DeGilles estate, Amelia's and Prem's coats folded over one of Maya's arms. Maya, Diya, and the baby wore velour dresses, and Dean and Niam wore dress pants and vests. They looked a bit too much like they were arriving for an appointment at a JCPenney portrait studio, Maya thought regretfully. She'd made the kids and Dean change their clothes twice before she was satisfied that they all looked presentable, but there was no dressing up the Hotessey. The old van looked clunky and conspicuous parked in front of the elegant landscaping.

Blake swung open the door and, smiling widely, waved them into the foyer, and collected their coats. "Dr. Rao, nice to see you," he said. "And it's a pleasure to meet your family." Maya introduced Dean and the kids, and Blake solemnly shook hands with Niam and Diya while saying with exaggerated seriousness, "Delighted to make your acquaintance," which made the two children giggle. From the corner of her eye, Maya noticed Dean taking in the massive house, his eyes widening.

The foyer was a soaring, light-filled affair with black-and-white Venetian marble flooring and a spherical crystal chandelier overhead that looked big enough to have its own gravitational pull. On one wall hung a massive framed oil painting of a European countryside, and in front of that stood a black grand piano on a white sheepskin rug. Across the room, a sweeping staircase with a gracefully curving wrought iron banister hugged the wall. And the centerpiece: an ornate fountain, a dancing Ganesh in white marble with water burbling out of its trunk and into a matching, flower-shaped basin below. Maya had seen the tiny silver cross Amelia wore around her neck. She was not Hindu, yet here was a Hindu god decorating her foyer. The presence of the deity was jarring and reminded Maya of the sprawling Ganesh mural on the wall of the trendy yoga studio she'd frequented during medical school. *Why?* she'd always wanted to ask the proprietor, an aging hippie whose given name was Doris, but who preferred to go by Saffron. *Why is this not weird to you? What is God doing here? Ganesh has as much to do with yoga as Christ has to do with stationary cycling. And no one wants to work out at SoulCycle while staring at a mural of Jesus.* Though she'd come close several times, she'd never quite summoned the nerve to confront Saffron about the mural, nor about the culturally appropriative "Namaste All Day" T-shirts they sold at the front desk. Instead, she swallowed her discomfort and leaned into her downward-facing dog.

A pair of Australian shepherds bounded in and began sniffing them all in turn. Diya and Niam were delighted. "Kona, Java, down," Blake said sternly, and the dogs reluctantly backed away. "Recent additions to the household," Blake said apologetically. "They're still working on their manners. Please, follow me." The dogs trailed them past the kitchen and into a sunny conservatory, where the DeGilles family was gathered around a farmhouse table near a window overlooking the back lawn, all of them still in their pajamas.

"Guests!" A tall, chiseled man in his early fifties with a goatee and a British accent jumped up from the table to greet them. "Bodhi, get your feet off the table, you animal." He swatted at the legs of the skinny boy in flannel pajama pants seated to his left. The boy looked up from his phone, startled. Prem sat next to him, her long legs tucked up so that her teacup rested on her kneecaps. She waved at Niam, and he enthusiastically waved back.

"You must be Amelia's friends," the man said, pumping Dean's arm jovially and then kissing Maya once on each cheek. He smelled pleasantly of maple syrup. "I'm Greg, Prem and Bodhi's dad. Come, sit! Hope you're hungry!" As he waved them toward the table, he shouted over their heads, "Babe! Your friends are here! They've brought adorable children!"

Amelia glided in from another room wearing joggers and a long cardigan, a beady-eyed Boston terrier tucked in the crook of one elbow. "You made it!" she said, as if Maya's family was late and the ones who looked like they'd just rolled out of bed. She held the dog out for Diya and Niam to pet and nodded toward her family. "This is Greg, my ex-husband. You know Prem. And that's Bodhi, who has soccer practice in forty minutes and needs to go get dressed." She raised her eyebrows at her son, and he rolled his eyes and said, "Okay, okay." As they took seats at the table, Amelia said to Maya, "This is the thanks I get for letting him try out for travel soccer."

"I play soccer, too," Niam, who saw the age difference between himself and twelve-year-old Bodhi as being only minimal, offered proudly. Bodhi smiled approvingly at him, and Niam beamed.

"Every kid plays soccer, that's the problem," Greg said. "It's useless for college admissions. Too competitive. That's why Bodhi here plays lacrosse and golf, too. And we just got him started with fencing."

"I hate fencing," Bodhi said sullenly, mouth full.

"But Harvard loves it, my boy," Greg said, clapping his son on the shoulder. "Just look at what your sister's done with the harp. Princeton loves the harp, so she does, too."

"Greg!" Amelia said. She was laughing, but her tone was reproachful. "That's not the only reason Prem plays harp. It's a beautiful instrument. Right, honey?" She glanced at Prem, who was staring dispassionately into her teacup.

"Unlike you, my dear, I'm not ashamed of angling to get my kids into the ivy league," Greg said. "It's competitive as hell out there. You have to be savage to ensure the survival of your offspring, am I right?" He lightly elbowed Dean, who looked at him in bewilderment. Turning to Maya, he said, "Speaking of which, Amelia tells me you're her new gynecologist, but you don't deliver offspring?"

Maya smiled and shook her head. "No. No offspring."

"But you were trained as an ob-gyn, right?" Greg pressed. "You did a— What's it called in America? A residency?"

"I did."

"But you don't deliver babies anymore?"

Maya felt her throat tightening. "No."

"Why not?" Greg leaned one elbow on the table and peered at her in a way that made Maya feel he was trying to look straight through her skull and into her mind. "Because the home birth market is exploding, and—"

"Greg, please," Amelia said. She turned to Maya. "Just ignore him. He sometimes forgets that Eunoia is *my* company."

"I'm a partner," Greg said defensively. "I think I should get to ask some questions."

"*Silent* partner," Amelia said, giving him a pointed look.

"I helped her start Eunoia when we were married. I'm in finance," Greg said to Dean, as though he'd asked. "We still work together, even though we're divorced. People are always surprised by that, but . . ." He shrugged and looked at Amelia, who smiled.

"But it works for us," she said.

Greg nodded and sipped his coffee. "The only thing that didn't work for us was the institution of marriage." He laughed hollowly, and an uncomfortable silence followed.

A pleasant-faced Hispanic woman wearing an apron—Paloma the housekeeper, as she introduced herself—asked what they'd like for breakfast. Diya and Niam looked at each other in confusion, then at their father. Breakfast at their house never involved choices, unless it was between two different types of cereal.

"Whatever everyone else is having," Dean said.

"Oh, Paloma can make you anything," Greg said. "Pancakes, waffles, oatmeal, eggs, you name it. She's the best."

"I'll have pancakes," Diya said happily, at the same time Niam exclaimed, "Waffles!"

"Pancakes and waffles, Paloma," Greg said, at the same time that Dean admonished the kids, "Pick one, guys. You don't need two separate things."

"Oh, it's no trouble," Amelia said. She turned to Paloma. "Waffles and pancakes, Paloma. And for the adults?"

"We'll all just have pancakes, thanks," Dean said, his tone—to Maya's ear—a little clipped.

"Are you sure?" Amelia asked, and Maya nodded in agreement.

"Yes, that's perfect. Thanks."

Amelia shrugged and nodded at Paloma, and the woman smiled obligingly and disappeared into the kitchen.

"Is that your mommy?" Niam asked Amelia.

"Paloma?" Amelia laughed. "No, but sometimes she acts like she is."

The adults all chuckled, but Niam was not satisfied. "Then who is she?"

"She's the housekeeper," Maya said quietly and with finality, hoping he would drop the subject.

"What's a housekeeper?" Niam asked, but the adults were determined to move on to another topic of conversation.

"So, Dean, what do you do, mate?" Greg asked.

"I'm working on my PhD in Immunology," Dean said. "At UPenn."

Greg raised his eyebrows, impressed. "Immunity is big right now. Lot of money to be made in immunity."

Dean smiled politely. "I guess so."

"What's your take on immune supplements? You know, Eunoia as a medical practice is all fine and good, but the real market is in nutraceuticals. I keep telling Amelia we should start a line of Eunoia supplements. B vitamins, that sort of thing."

Dean shifted Asha from one shoulder to the other while glancing across the table at Maya. He seemed to be considering his reply carefully. "That's a little outside my field," he said.

"What's a housekeeper?" Niam still wanted to know. His voice had taken on an urgency that indicated he would continue asking the question until it was answered to his satisfaction.

"She does things around the house," Diya said, matching her mother's quiet tone. "Like cook and clean. Nancy Drew has a housekeeper."

"Because her mommy has to work?" Niam asked.

"No, because her mom died," Diya said.

Niam's face fell. He turned, wide-eyed, to Amelia, who was pouring herself a cup of coffee. "Did your mommy died?"

Amelia looked up, startled, and the coffee spilled from the carafe onto the white tablecloth.

"Niam!" Maya shot a barbed look at her son while dabbing the spill with her napkin. "Enough questions." She glanced at Amelia apologetically. "I'm so sorry." It was as if she were begging forgiveness for her son's remark, the coffee spill, and her family's obvious lack of breeding all at once. She was sorry her children didn't know what it meant to be waited on.

"Oh, it's okay." Amelia waved her off.

"Her mom actually did die," Prem said matter-of-factly, to no one in particular. "Recently."

Amelia stiffened, and Greg said, "Though accurate, a little more sympathy, Premie, would be appreciated."

"Why?" Prem asked pointedly, in that way children do when they're hungry for conflict. "Mom didn't even like Meemaw."

Greg's expression was stern. "Hey. That's enough, Prem." Paloma returned, balancing plates on her forearms. She served Amelia what looked like Cream of Wheat with blackberries. "Syrup?" Paloma asked Maya, before dispensing a generous pour over her stack of pancakes.

"I liked her," Amelia said defensively. "I loved her. She was my mother. We just had a difficult relationship."

Prem snorted. "*That's* an understatement."

"Prem, you're being rude," Greg said, his tone cautionary.

Bodhi's eyes had gone wide. Prem muttered, "Shut up, Greg. You don't even live here."

Amelia, whose expression had been distant, snapped to attention. "What did you say?"

Maya and Dean exchanged a glance of regret and guilt. It was Niam's question about Amelia's mother that had launched their hosts into this fraught conversational terrain.

Amelia's face crumpled. "What is wrong with you?" she asked her daughter, her voice wounded.

"Nothing!" Prem cried, suddenly on the verge of angry tears. "Why are you always criticizing me?"

"Okay, then," Greg said, sliding back his chair and standing up. "This is far too much estrogen for 10:00 a.m. on a Sunday. Bodhi and I are off to change clothes and go to soccer. Nice meeting you, Maya and Dean, and your lovely children." Bodhi, who had been eating an English muffin, crammed the rest of it into his mouth and followed his father out of the conservatory. "Prem," Greg called over his shoulder, "do consider taking a walk, won't you?"

At this, Prem wordlessly stood up from the table and went out the closest door, letting it slam shut behind her. They watched her stomp off across the back lawn and disappear behind a hedgerow.

The Anders-Rao family stared helplessly at each other. Maya and Dean attempted to communicate silently with their panicked eyes: *We should leave now. You say something. No,* you *say something.* Diya looked frightened. Asha began to fuss. Only Niam was unperturbed, tucking into his pancakes with delight, syrup dripping down his chin. He tried to feed a bit of his breakfast to the terrier, which was now padding about under the table.

Amelia stopped rubbing her temples and looked up. "I'm so sorry about all of that," she said. "Greg is a good co-parent, but you can see why we're divorced. And Prem," she said, sighing and rubbing her temples again. "I swear I don't know. I thought we'd gotten through the worst of the teenage years with her, but lately . . . she's just so volatile."

"We should go . . ." Dean half stood, but Amelia didn't notice.

"I really think it's something out of alignment, or her energies not flowing correctly. Maybe her womb being toxic." She looked at Maya. "That's what her chiropractor thinks. She always gets worse around her period."

Maya, who wasn't quite sure what energies or alignment Amelia was referring to, was silent for a beat. "Her womb being toxic?"

Amelia continued. "I hate how men attribute everything to a woman's hormones. But maybe her hormones *are* out of whack because of toxins. I've been telling her to steam, but she never listens to me."

Maya blinked. "Steam?"

"Her womb, you know." Amelia waved her hand toward her pelvis distractedly. "With chamomile and myrrh. It always helps me."

"Oh," Maya said. "The thing about vaginal steaming is that the steam doesn't actually reach the uterus, and—"

"A uterus is where the baby grows in," Niam announced, always proud to show off his vast fund of knowledge.

"Could you see her?" Amelia asked suddenly. "As a patient?"

"Me?" Maya felt foolish as the word left her mouth. Obviously, Amelia wasn't suggesting the children or Dean see Prem as a patient.

"She's seen Gretchen a few times and had a ton of blood tests, but nothing's shown up so far," Amelia explained. "And she said you were so understanding after her Harvest Recital disaster. She likes you, and she usually doesn't like doctors. Maybe you can make some recommendations about how she can detox and balance her hormones? She'll listen to you, certainly more than she listens to me."

Maya nodded sympathetically while wondering where on the Internet Amelia had heard such nonsense. Toxins and balancing? From the corner of her eye, she caught the baffled expression on Dean's face. "Oh. Sure, of course," she said. "I'd be happy to speak to her. It couldn't hurt to ask some questions and see if she could have something gynecological going on."

Amelia smiled gratefully. "Thank you! I'm telling you, she wasn't like this until just recently. There has to be a reason." She stood up and motioned to the door. "She's probably in her art studio. That's where she goes when she's upset. I can take you over."

"Right now?" Dean asked, his fork frozen over his plate.

Amelia's cheeks flushed with embarrassment. "Oh my gosh, what was I thinking? It's Sunday, you're probably busy. Please, enjoy your breakfast. I can schedule her an appointment with you this week—"

Amelia's frazzled vulnerability struck a chord in Maya. She knew what it was to be worried for your daughter. Perhaps more than that, there was something about Amelia's discomfort that made Maya feel obligated to allay it. "No, no, don't be silly," she said gamely, avoiding Dean's eyes and turning toward the door. "Of course I can see her now. Lead the way."

The grounds of the DeGilles estate were extensive. Manicured paths led off into the unseen distance in every direction, branching through the garden and beyond. Prem's art studio, nestled among a cluster of hydrangea bushes, was a converted shed designed to look like a miniature version of the main house. A Petit Trianon, Maya thought wryly. Prem was like Marie Antoinette, her life of privilege so burdensome she needed a smaller house to escape from her larger house.

Amelia left her at the door with a grateful smile. "Thank you again for doing this," she said. "Her first college audition is in four weeks. The sooner we figure out what's going on with her, the better." She turned back toward the house. "Take as much time as you need. I'll keep your lovely family entertained."

There was no way around the awkwardness of the situation. Maya felt acutely embarrassed for Prem—first the humiliation of her recital performance, then her behavior at brunch, now her mother was sending a doctor to her sanctuary to ask personal questions. Maya thought back on her own angry teenage years. Her parents had been too busy, too overwhelmed with basic survival, to notice or acknowledge her unhappiness, so, after an outburst, she was left to stew alone in the tiny bedroom she'd shared with Dak. Her brother steered clear of her as well, avoidance being the time-honored family strategy for dealing with difficult emotions, probably dating back several generations. "Ungrateful," her mother would mutter into the steam rising off the stove, then launch into a story about her own, far more difficult, childhood in India.

Prem, meanwhile, was a product of the hyper-parenting revolution, her life adjusted and tweaked, analyzed and controlled, right down to the fish oil and the spirulina. For a moment, Maya wasn't sure who'd had it worse. Then, on second thought, she decided she would've very much liked to have a Petit Trianon of her own when she had been eighteen. If she was being honest, she'd like to have one now, at thirty-six.

She knocked.

"Who is it?"

Maya had expected Prem's voice to be sulky or affronted, but instead she sounded sweetly surprised, as if she wasn't expecting visitors and was delighted to have one.

"Hi, Prem. It's Maya."

The door swung open immediately. Prem, in a decidedly better mood than she had been in ten minutes earlier, said, "Hey, come in. Did my mom send you?" She rolled her eyes. "Of course my mom sent you." She held the door open, and Maya stepped into the cheerful, sunlit space.

The studio was pleasantly cluttered, but tidy. The wood floor was covered with paint-splattered rugs, and several large easels held canvases of different sizes, each with a work in progress. An assortment of paints and brushes and palettes was neatly arranged on a long table against one wall, and a tiny desk piled with art books was tucked into the far corner. Leaning against all four walls, stacked three or four deep, were Prem's completed artworks: landscapes, fruit in bowls, a portrait of the Boston terrier.

"Wow. Did you paint all of these?"

Prem wiped her hands on her smock. "Yeah." She shrugged. "It's just a hobby."

"They're beautiful," Maya said. "Have you given them titles?"

Prem shook her head. "Nah, I'm not that serious about it."

Maya motioned to a rendering of a young man, his face turned toward the distant horizon, eyes in a half squint, the wind whipping back his dark hair. Though she'd used mostly cool blues and grays, Prem's treatment of the subject was warm, almost reverential, the light giving the young man's face a halo-like glow. "Is this someone you know?"

"My boyfriend." She hesitated. "Kind-of boyfriend."

"Kind-of boyfriend?" Maya frowned sympathetically. "Sounds complicated."

Prem gave a half laugh and looked away. "You could say that." She began mixing paints on a palette, then made a careful emerald green stroke on her work in progress. This appeared to be a portrait, too.

Maya looked for a place to sit down, but the two wooden chairs in the studio were piled high with canvases. Without the pockets of her white coat to bury her hands in, she didn't know what to do with her arms. She crossed them awkwardly over her stomach, holding her elbows. "So, Prem, your mom asked if I would talk to you to see if there's anything I can help you with. She said you haven't been feeling well?"

Prem smiled and shook her head. "I'm really sorry. You haven't been working for her very long, so you probably don't know this yet, but my mom's a hypochondriac."

Maya suppressed a laugh. "What makes you say that?"

"She always thinks something's wrong with me or Bodhi. Our cosmic energy isn't vibrating at the right frequency or something. She's been doing this since I was a little kid."

"Doing what?"

"Making me see healers and get Reiki and wear crystals and magnets and stuff. This one time, she literally made me sleep with peacock feathers in my bra to help detoxify my lungs or something. She's a little nuts."

"Why peacock feathers?"

"Peacocks are my spirit animal." Prem dipped a tiny paintbrush into a dollop of cerulean blue and twirled it between her fingers. "Apparently."

"When's the last time you had a checkup with your pediatrician?"

Prem considered this. "I don't know. I don't go to the doctor for checkups. My mom says it's not necessary. I've seen Gretchen, though. She gave me some blood tests."

Maya shook her head, not following. "But . . . what about getting your vaccinations?"

Prem shrugged. "I don't know. You'd have to ask my mom if I ever got them as a baby. She doesn't believe in the flu shot or anything."

Maya's stomach sank. That Amelia believed in the medicinal power of bird feathers over vaccines wasn't entirely surprising, but it was still hard to hear. "Really?"

Prem squinted at the canvas, debating her next brushstroke. "Yeah. My mom doesn't believe in doctors and, like, pharmaceuticals and stuff. She says the body will heal itself, if we let nature do its thing. If we eat healthy and clear out our toxins or whatever. I've never even been to a dentist." She paused to smile widely at Maya over her shoulder, her bright white teeth perfectly aligned. "But my teeth are great."

This was the fundamental flaw in logic, Maya knew, that drove alternative health fanatics and women with elaborate birth plans: the idea that if you were spared bad health, it proved that Medicine was unnecessary instead of suggesting that you'd been dealt a lucky hand. People like Amelia, for all their talk of respecting Mother Nature, were quick to take her mercy for granted.

There seemed to be, among the proponents of alternative medicine, a belief that nature was always good and gentle and kind. That the natural order of things was to heal and renew and rejuvenate. Yet nature was also responsible for arsenic and scorpion venom. Aneurysms were natural, as were polio and rabies. Bleeding to death during childbirth was particularly natural. Man's manipulation of nature was necessary for the survival of our species because nature, it seemed obvious to Maya, has forever been trying to kill us.

"So you feel okay?"

"Except for my hands going numb, yeah." Prem put down the brush to stretch and roll her wrists. "I feel fine." She hesitated, then added, "And sometimes my feet go numb, too. Is that weird?"

Maya shook her head. "No. I mean, it could be a hint about what's going on. Any other symptoms?"

"I've been super tired lately. And just . . . foggy, mentally. It's hard to concentrate on anything anymore."

Maya ran down a list of other worrisome symptoms, but Prem denied having any of them. "Do you take any medications?"

"Just vitamins and fish oil and stuff. My mom wanted me to try collagen, so I started taking that a couple of weeks ago."

"What about alcohol or recreational drugs?" Prem raised an eyebrow, and Maya added quickly, "No judgment, I'm just trying to think of anything that might cause those symptoms."

Prem shook her head. "No. And I don't smoke either. Honestly, I think it's just stress."

"Tell me more about that," Maya said, concerned.

Prem sighed. She used a pair of heavy, steel-tipped scissors, the blades covered in splatters of paint, to snip the top off a tube of cadmium red. "It's really just stupid drama. I've been seeing this guy, and his mom doesn't want him hanging out with me."

"The kind-of boyfriend?"

"Yeah." Prem nodded wearily, mixing the paint. "Carter. His mom hates me and it's this whole thing. It's exhausting."

"Why doesn't his mom like you?"

Prem looked over her shoulder at Maya and said matter-of-factly, "It probably has something to do with the fact that he's thirty-five and married."

"Oh." Maya blinked, her vision going momentarily spotty with panic.

Prem laughed. "I'm kidding. He's eighteen and goes to my school, and his mom and my mom don't like each other. Something about them both bidding on the same VIP Bon Jovi tickets at the Hamilton Hall auction three years ago. My mom thought she'd made the winning bid, then Carter's mom somehow snuck *her* bid in after the deadline, then they each thought they'd won and it was super awkward and Carter's mom—who has never liked my mom and is a terrible person, by the way—low-key caused a scene and she ended up with the tickets but, basically, she forbade Carter from ever going out with me because she's just petty." Prem, who had finally used all the air in her lungs, took a deep breath. "So, Carter and I see each other in secret when we can."

"Wow," Maya said. "That's very Romeo and Juliet."

"It's very Bon Jovi and Juliet," Prem corrected.

Maya grinned. It was impossible not to like Prem. "Have you talked to your mom about all of this?"

"Oh, my mom's impossible to talk to," Prem said. "If I say I'm stressed or anxious, she thinks it's my diet or that I need to have my meridians realigned. And she was never a fan of Carter, or any boy-friend, actually. She wants me totally focused on harp and Prince-ton. As far as she knows, Carter and I haven't seen each other in three months and I've forgotten all about him."

"That's what you've told her?"

"If she knew I was still seeing him, she'd never let me leave the house. She says he's too much of a distraction."

Maya recalled the way Amelia dictated what Prem should eat, organized her regimen of supplements, scheduled her down to the minute. Suddenly Prem's easy confidence didn't seem innate, it seemed manufactured, the product of years of her mother's meticulous control and purposeful training. Underneath it all, Prem was likely depressed, given her symptoms of lethargy and mental fog. Maya fought the urge to hug her protectively.

"She's just doing what she thinks is best for you," Maya said. She added apologetically, "It's a mom thing."

"Oh, I get it, believe me. But there's just so much she doesn't know." At this, Prem turned back toward the canvas. She was avoiding eye contact, keeping her gaze firmly on her work.

Maya waited for her to elaborate, then prodded, "So much she doesn't know . . . about what?"

"It's just a lot of pressure. She doesn't understand."

Maya wanted to tread carefully. "Is it not what you want? Princeton?"

Prem waved a hand, dismissing the thought. "Oh, it's definitely what I want. It's what I've wanted since forever, to go to an Ivy. It's my dream." She made a few more brushstrokes on the canvas. Then she said, talking fast, "It's just Carter's mom. She knows about me and Carter—at least, she suspects something's going on—and she's trying to use me to get back at my mom."

Maya shook her head, nonplussed. "To get back at your mom about the Bon Jovi thing?"

Prem shrugged, squinting with agitation. "I guess? I mean, I don't know. She clearly hates me and is trying to break us up. She follows me—I've seen her car in my rearview a bunch of times—and she takes Carter's phone when he's not looking and deletes my text messages to him. She's even started rumors on social media about me."

"Wow. She sounds—"

"Horrible, I know. She is. She's basically the devil. Carter and I sometimes argue about her—he doesn't think she's that bad, but of course he doesn't, he's her son—and the worst part is that I can't talk to my mom about any of this because—" She shook her head in frustration.

"Because you don't want your mom to know you're still dating Carter," Maya said.

Prem sighed. "Exactly."

"That does sound stressful," Maya conceded. She felt out of her depth. She was used to counseling teenagers about reproductive health, not how to contend with the unhinged mothers of their romantic partners. Thank goodness Diya was still too young to be interested in any relationship that didn't revolve around building Legos or discussing Percy Jackson. "For what it's worth, I think your mother would understand."

Prem smiled ruefully. "You don't know her." Then she added, "You won't tell her, right? We have doctor-patient confidentiality?"

Maya nodded. "We do. I can't tell her anything you don't want me to." Then she added, "Prem, could you be pregnant?"

Prem laughed. "You sound like Gretchen. She's constantly asking me to pee in a cup so she can test it. At least twice a month. Like if I was pregnant, she could just blame all my symptoms on that. There would finally be an explanation. But no, sorry, I'm definitely not."

"Okay, but while we're on the topic, do you have any questions about safe sex? Do you and Carter use condoms?"

"We do," Prem said. "I mean, we did. We haven't had sex in a while, just because of everything going on. But I'm always careful."

"Smart girl." Maya nodded approvingly.

"So will you tell my mom to calm down?"

Maya laughed. "Sure. On one condition. You let me program my number into your phone, and you promise to call me if you need someone to talk to. Deal?"

Prem grinned and handed over her phone. "Deal."

Amelia was relieved to hear that Maya didn't think Prem had a gynecologic or hormonal issue that required treatment. She nodded thoughtfully as she paced around the kitchen. "Did she tell you anything else?"

Maya hesitated. Keeping Prem's confidence felt like betraying Amelia. She'd been in this position before, between a young patient and her mother, and though it was part of her job, it always made her uneasy. "She's a bit stressed about some things. Maybe talking to a therapist would help?"

Amelia looked taken aback. "No, no. It's not all in her head."

"Oh, that's not what I meant—" Maya started to say apologetically, but Amelia turned away, tapping her chin with one finger.

"If nothing else is wrong, there must be something in her record," she said, mostly to herself. Asha, who had been asleep in her car seat, awoke and started crying before Maya could ask what record Amelia was referring to. A few seconds later, Dean appeared with their coats, and he rushed her and the children out of the house. "Very nice time. Thank you! Nice meeting you!"

"Oh! Blake would have fetched your coats for you," Amelia said, trailing them to the front door with a confused expression, as if she couldn't understand how Dean had managed to find the coats on his own.

"Thank you so much for having us, Amelia," Maya said.

Amelia extended her hand in a way that made Maya feel vaguely like she ought to kiss it and curtsy. "Of course! It was so nice to meet your family. Thank you for your help with Prem."

Once they had all piled into the van, Dean rolled down the windows. "Wave bye-bye to Auntie Amelia!" he said, his eyes slightly crazed. Diya and Niam waved without enthusiasm. They were sad to be leaving; they'd wanted to play with the dogs.

As the DeGilles estate disappeared in the rearview mirror, Maya turned to Dean. "Auntie Amelia? Really?"

Dean shook his head, his eyes on the road. "I don't know. Kids, don't call her Auntie. That lady is not your Auntie."

"Auntie Amelia is pretty," Diya said.

Niam nodded in agreement. "And she makes good pancakes."

"She doesn't make the pancakes, buddy," Dean said over his shoulder.

Maya raised her eyebrows at him, bristling. "She was perfectly nice. What's the matter with you?"

"With me?" Dean's grip on the steering wheel tightened. "That woman is . . . She is not someone you should be working for."

"Why not?"

"Why not?" Dean's nostrils flared. "Maybe because she wanted to know if her daughter's pelvic organs being out of alignment—whatever that means—is the reason she's an entitled brat instead of, I don't know, the fact that they have a butler and a maid waiting hand and foot on their kids."

Maya felt compelled to fly to Prem's defense. "She's not a brat. And don't be mad at them just because they have money."

"There's a difference between having money and being normal and having money and being a scourge on society. Maya, she literally thinks her kid's uterus—no, sorry, her *womb*"—Dean shuddered with disgust at the loathsome word—"is filled with toxins. First of all, what toxins? You should ask her to name one of these toxins. Like, what's the chemical compound she's referring to? And you—" He shook his head, too angry to finish his thought.

"You, what?" Maya demanded. "What do I have to do with this?"

"You didn't say anything!" The words exploded out of Dean, more impassioned than any Eagles game had ever made him. "You just sat there and smiled, like it's totally reasonable and not misogynistic at all to believe that the female pelvic organs are a radioactive waste depository! You're a doctor, Maya!"

Maya's jaw clenched. "And she's my boss!"

"Diya was sitting right there!"

The suggestion that Maya had not only failed women everywhere by not correcting her employer's misconceptions about the female reproductive system, but also failed her own daughter by not speaking up, crossed the line. "Diya knows that's not true!" Maya looked over her shoulder for confirmation. "Don't you, Dee?"

Diya flinched, startled by the sudden appearance of her mother's ravening face in the gap between the two front seats. "What?" she squeaked.

Dean slammed the brakes at a stop sign. "Why are you working for someone who knows less than a fourth grader?"

"Oh, I guarantee you, Tad from PGH knew way less than a fourth grader," Maya said. She adjusted her seat belt. She and Dean had had many arguments over their years of marriage—all couples did, of course—but she sensed something different this time. Something dangerous. Something with teeth.

They crossed the intersection, and Dean's grip on the wheel loosened. "Maya, this isn't who you are."

Maya tucked in her chin, getting a wider view of him. "Excuse me? Who are you to tell me who I am?"

"You're better than this. You don't need to be the hired help for this ridiculous woman."

Maya's voice was low and tight in her throat. "In case you haven't noticed, I'm putting food on our table. I'm paying our mortgage."

"You could easily get a job somewhere else. You could always go back to delivering. It's been years and—"

"I don't want a job somewhere else, and I don't want to go back to delivering babies. I *like* working for Eunoia. I have a flexible schedule. I can pick up the kids from school—"

"*That's* the price of your integrity? A flexible schedule and school pickup?"

Well, yes, Maya thought. If Dean were a mother he would understand the value of a flexible schedule and school pickup. But there was more to it than that, if she was being honest with herself. She'd liked being introduced to Amelia's friends at the Harvest Concert. They'd all looked at her with genuine interest and respect. Every one of them had leaned in to hear what she had to say. But Dean wouldn't understand why that was so important to her, why it meant anything to her at all. He'd think her shallow and desperate for validation. So she said, "At least I'm willing to make sacrifices for our family."

"What does that mean?" Dean shook his head. "Maya, she steams her vagina. As if it were a vegetable."

"Dean, unlike you, I think women have the right to do what they want with their bodies."

"Even if it's not based in science and could lead to burn injuries? Come on. At PGH, you were all about educating women. What happened?" Maya was silent for a moment, then Dean muttered, "Doesn't apply to rich women, I guess. It's enough that they have money."

Maya turned away and said, just loud enough that she was very sure he could hear it and moderately sure the kids behind them couldn't, "Fuck you, Dean."

TWENTY-ONE

The last weeks of autumn passed in a blur of "Why I am grateful" essays for school, apple picking in the crisp weather at a local farm, and a nine-hour trip in the Hotessey to visit Dean's parents in Montreal for Thanksgiving, during which Asha had not one but two massive diaper blowouts, Niam demanded the *Frozen* soundtrack on repeat and would cry if it wasn't restarted immediately after it ended, and Diya's nose bled. Maya, for the first time, signed up to be the Mystery Reader at preschool. She read *Dragons Love Tacos* to twenty rapt four-year-olds while Niam, seated near her feet, bounced with excitement, whispering every so often to his classmates, "That's my mom!" She attended a Coffee with the Headmaster event at Hamilton Hall Academy, where she was assured that the school board would be voting on her proposal to update the Health curriculum very soon. Probably after the holiday. Definitely by the spring, at the latest. She also signed up, with great enthusiasm, to be a volunteer judge at the Hamilton Hall science fair in the spring. "You should enter!" she urged Diya. "I'm only judging the high schoolers, so I can help you with your project!" Despite Diya's obvious lack of interest, Maya was heady with the possibilities. "We could do the classic tornado-in-a-box experiment, or we could grow plants in different types of soil . . . whatever you want." Diya said she would think about it and returned to her Percy Jackson novel.

They weren't nearly as busy as they had been in their clinic at PGH, but Maya and Esther's list of clients was expanding rapidly. They treated patients in wealthy alcoves of the city, like Chestnut Hill and Rittenhouse Square, as well as on the Main Line. They met the women at their homes but also, if requested, at their offices, at their country clubs, and, on one occasion, at baggage claim at the Philadelphia airport where the client, a forty-four-year-old executive, urgently needed to be tested for a urinary tract infection before embarking on a seven-day corporate retreat in a remote part of Switzerland. The woman handed her urine sample to Maya underneath a stall door in the public restroom, and Maya discreetly slipped the container into a specimen bag and ran it outside to where Esther was idling the van in the short-term parking lot, waiting with testing strips and the microscope. Setting up the microscope in the back of the van was awkward—they had to open the hatch and stand outside in the freezing cold, passersby regarding them suspiciously as Maya squinted through the eyepiece. After diagnosing the infection, they searched online for a pharmacy near the airport in Geneva. A few phone calls and some very rudimentary German later, it was all arranged.

Esther called the client. "There's a pharmacy in the Geneva airport, and your prescription will be ready by the time you land. All you have to do is go pick it up. Terminal D."

The woman was relieved and grateful—"I don't care if you guys don't take tips, I'm paying you extra"—and headed off to catch her flight after promising to refer all her friends to Eunoia.

Two weeks before Christmas, they visited the Hauser estate for Skye's first prenatal checkup. This time, the estate manager led them down a flight of stairs in the pool house to a lower level, where they made their way past a birchwood sauna, a softly lit yoga studio, and a brightly lit squash court. The hallway smelled pleasantly of lavender. Esther carried their bag of supplies and the ultrasound machine, and Maya dragged their folding exam table. At the end of a long hallway, they were shown through a frosted-glass door. Maya blinked, stopping short in the doorway.

In the center of the bright white room was an examination table, a sleek, adjustable brown leather plinth with hydraulic controls. The walls of the room were lined with medical equipment: an EKG machine, ultrasound, portable X-ray machine, microscope, scale, otoscope and ophthalmoscope for checking eyes and ears, all top of the line. A set of matching glass apothecary bottles filled with tongue depressors, bandages, gauze, and cotton balls was arranged neatly on a gleaming quartz countertop, next to a stainless steel sink.

Esther's eyes went wide as saucers. "So . . . you've seen *Get Out*, right?" she whispered.

"I think this is where they harvest the brains, yeah," Maya replied under her breath.

The estate manager said, "Miss Skye will join you shortly. Can I bring either of you a beverage while you wait?"

Maya and Esther shook their heads, and the estate manager left them.

Esther gave a low whistle that echoed off the vaulted ceiling. "These people have a doctor's office in their basement?"

"In the basement of their pool house," Maya corrected.

"Right, right," Esther said. "The basement of the main house is where they store their bars of gold."

Their eyes met, and the two of them burst into laughter. It was all too ridiculous, too over the top, too . . . *sad*, Maya thought as she pulled herself together, wiping tears from the corners of her eyes. How many people outside the gates of this estate couldn't afford even routine health care, and here an entire suite of state-of-the-art medical equipment was being reserved for the exclusive use of one small family.

The door burst open, and Skye bounded in, ruddy-cheeked and dressed in jeans and a white peasant top with puffy sleeves, her now-blond hair—the lavender having faded completely—in two braids down her back. She looked uncannily like a Scandinavian milkmaid, the kind pictured on containers of yogurt or cheese. "Sorry I'm late!" she said breathlessly. "Have you been waiting long?"

Maya and Esther assured her they had only just arrived, and Esther introduced herself.

"Nice to meet you, hon!" Skye enthused, grabbing one of Esther's hands in both of hers. "What's your favorite element?"

"Magnesium," Esther said.

"Huh," Skye's smile faltered for only a moment. Then she howled with delight. "Right on, sister!"

Esther raised one eyebrow.

"How are you feeling, Skye?" Maya asked.

"Amazing!" Skye beamed. "I feel fantastic, and the baby says she's doing great, just growing and thriving."

Esther smiled skeptically. "The baby says that, huh?"

Skye nodded. "I believe she's the spirit of my grandmother." She turned to Maya. "Let me tell you, this is the most amazing experience, feeling life blossoming inside me." Her eyes were hooded, as if she might slip into meditation, and she drew in a deep, long breath and let it go with a sigh.

Maya resisted the urge to roll her eyes. She cleared her throat and said, "When you told me you had a space for medical exams, I didn't think you meant . . ." She gestured to their surroundings.

Skye's brow furrowed. "Oh! Is this okay? Is there any other equipment you need?"

"It's perfect," Maya said. "It's just more . . ."

"More than we expected," Esther completed the sentence while helping Skye onto the exam table. "So much more."

"My dad gets his medical checkups here," Skye explained. "He and his wife, my stepmom, are big on privacy, especially since my dad first ran for office."

Maya and Esther exchanged glances. Maya had filled her assistant in on what the estate manager had told her the first time she'd visited.

As she checked Skye's blood pressure, Esther said conversationally, "That must be amazing, having a dad who's in Congress. Is that something you want to do, too?"

Maya raised her eyebrows discreetly at Esther—*really?*—and Esther gave her a pointed look as if to say, *What? I'm just asking.*

Skye lay back on the table and lifted her shirt to expose her stomach. She shook her head and said, "No. No, I don't believe in government. I don't believe in rules. I think that people should be free to follow their spiritual path wherever it may take them."

"Hmm. Where's your spiritual path taking you?" Maya asked, feigning interest as she stretched a tape measure across Skye's small belly bump.

"Belize."

"Really? I've never been," Esther said.

Maya wrapped a tourniquet around Skye's arm. "Me neither. I'm just going to draw some blood. You'll feel a stick."

"Oh, you have to go!" Skye said. "It's the most magical place. The sea, the wildlife, the people. It's beyond words. Ouch!" Skye watched her blood flow into the test tube, mesmerized. "Blood is so amazing, right?"

Esther held up the ultrasound probe. "Are you sure you don't want to do an ultrasound? See the baby?"

Skye shook her head firmly. "No ultrasounds."

Maya placed the bell of her stethoscope on Skye's belly. "It might be too early to hear the baby's heartbeat this way, but we can try." A faint flutter of sound was audible beneath the gurgling of Skye's intestines. "Do you want to hear? You have to listen carefully, but you can just make it out." Maya plucked the eartips from her own ears and fitted them into Skye's. At the sound of her child's heart, a sound as fast and fragile and steady as the beat of a hummingbird's wings, Skye's face broke into a wide, teary-eyed grin. She seized Esther's hand. No matter how many times Maya had done this in her career, let a mother hear her baby for the first time, it never lost its wonder. Every time, she remembered why she'd chosen Ob-Gyn as a specialty.

"Oh my God! There she is!" Skye said. Then she whispered, "Hi, Nan." She placed Esther's palm on her belly. "I want you two to really connect with the baby. Doc, give me your hand." Maya hesitated, and Skye reached over and placed her palm next to Esther's. Then she put one of her own hands over each of theirs. She held them there, two dark hands firmly pressed into the soft ivory flesh of her stomach, for a long moment, looking from Maya's face to Esther's and back again, beaming. Esther gave Maya a pleading look. *Do something!* Maya returned it with a slight shrug and shake of her head. *Like what?*

Skye looked at her belly. In a whisper, she addressed the bump. "Should we tell them?"

Esther tried to pull her hand away, but Skye's grip was determined. "Tell us what?" Maya asked.

Skye turned her glowing, golden-haloed face toward them and said, "The baby says she wants to be born in Belize."

Maya's eyebrows shot up. She laughed, assuming this was a joke.

"And she wants you two to come with us." Skye squeezed their hands.

"To Belize?" Esther asked, and Skye nodded.

"To a hospital in Belize?" Maya asked, her voice hopeful.

"To the beach in Belize," Skye corrected. "She wants to be born of the sea."

Maya and Esther stared down at her, agape. Born of the sea? This was worse, far worse, than the home birth Skye had been considering.

"Asher and I have discussed it, and we think water is the baby's element. And she was Belizean in a past life."

Esther stared at her. "Wait, I thought she was your grandma."

Skye nodded. "In her most recent past life, she was my Nan. But before that, way before that, she was a fisherman's wife in Belize, living her life on the sea. That's where she needs to enter this life. That's where her energy is. That's how her cosmic chakra circle will be completed." She made intense eye contact with Maya, who felt sweat start to bead between her shoulder blades.

"I don't do deliveries," Maya said.

Skye nodded again. "Oh, I know. I've already taken care of the delivery part. But my dad won't let me take his plane to Belize unless I'm accompanied by a doctor. He's afraid I'll go into labor in the air and create some sort of international incident, which is ridiculous." She scoffed. "The baby would never enter this world into air. That's completely the wrong element for her."

Maya and Esther each placed a hand on Skye's back and helped her sit up. Behind her, Esther widened her eyes at Maya and gave a barely perceptible shake of her head. *Say no.*

"So, you'll come with us, right?" Skye's expression was buoyant, as if the three of them were planning a girls' weekend getaway together.

"Who'll do the delivery?" Maya asked.

"I've already spoken to a doctor there. Well, she's actually a midwife, but she has tons of experience. It's all arranged. I even found the perfect house. I just have to wait for it to go on sale in a couple of weeks."

"You're buying a house?" Maya squawked, as Esther shook her head slowly in disbelief. Remembering herself, Maya said, "Skye, a home birth, especially in a foreign country, is risky. Esther and I have both seen things go very wrong."

"I once saw a baby in the ER who'd suffocated while being delivered at home," Esther said. "Believe me, it's not worth it."

Skye smiled at them patiently. "The baby spoke to me. She told me everything will be fine. Better than fine. She said it'll be perfect. And I believe her." There was such conviction in her face, Maya was torn between wanting to hug Skye and resisting the urge to slap her.

"The baby is a non-sentient collection of cells," Esther said. "It can't speak to you."

"Of course she can!" Skye said. Then she asked, a little sanctimoniously, "Are you a mother, hon?"

Esther bristled. "No."

"Then you wouldn't understand," Skye said with a shrug. She turned to Maya. "Doc understands what I'm saying. Right? Mothers just know."

Maya forced her mouth into something like a smile. She was vaguely aware of feeling as if she couldn't disappoint Skye, as if some vital principle would be violated if she verbalized her disagreement. The customer is always right.

Her father used to wear a gold Om on a chain around his neck, always tucked into his white undershirt. When Maya once asked him why he hid the necklace—which she'd loved to play with as a child, turning the charm with the curling Hindu symbol through her fingers as she sat on his lap—under his collar instead of letting it show, he'd replied, "Americans won't understand what it means." This was the only explanation he gave, yet she understood, almost instinctively, what he meant: they could be themselves around other Indi-ans, but in front of Americans, they were required to shape-shift into something more palatable, something less foreign and mysterious. You didn't want to put off the customers. The motel, their livelihood, depended on it. It was a particular kind of learned obsequiousness, practiced over a lifetime, that now came naturally to her.

"Mothers just know," she said, and was rewarded with a beaming smile of approval from Skye.

"You'd only be my medical team for the seven-hour flight to Be-lize," Skye explained. "That's it. Just an insurance policy. Then you two can go off to the hotel—Oh! I'd put you guys up at the nicest place. It has the world's most amazing spa!—and you could enjoy a little vacation time before you fly home. It'd be perfect. And I'd pay double whatever your rate is."

Esther shook her head. "That's very generous, but—"

"I'm sure we can work out the details closer to your due date," Maya said. In her peripheral vision, Esther's eyes doubled in size.

Skye clapped her hands and seized both of their arms. "Oh my gosh, you guys! I've literally never been happier." She squeezed, and Maya watched the blood drain from Esther's face.

The house manager showed them back to the van, asked if they needed any bottled water for their drive, and then bid them farewell. As they loaded their gear back into the trunk, Esther said, "Doc, I know you didn't just sign us up to fly to Belize with that crazy woman."

"Esther, look—"

"Because I'm sure neither one of us wants to be in the position to have to deliver her baby—sorry, her Belizean grandmother—*on a plane.*"

They climbed into the van, and Maya steered them past the

towering bronze horse and down the long driveway, saying, "I don't think she's really going to go through with it, Esther. She's so flaky, she's bound to change her mind before her due date."

Esther folded her arms. "But what if she doesn't?"

"She will. She'll be huge and uncomfortable, and who wants to take a seven-hour plane ride while nine months pregnant? She'll realize soon enough what a dumb idea that is, and she'll cancel the whole thing and deliver in the closest hospital, like a normal person. I've seen this before."

Esther raised her eyebrows skeptically. "You've seen *this* before?"

"Sure. When I used to do OB, women would come in for their first few prenatal visits with their five-page birth plans—no drugs, no epidural, Mozart playing in the delivery room, all that nonsense—and then, by the time they hit the third trimester, they were all, like, 'Just get this baby out of me! I don't care what you have to do!' and the stupid birth plan went out the window. Skye will come to her senses."

Esther was unconvinced. "Skye doesn't seem like the type to ever come to her senses. Why didn't you just tell her no?"

"We're a concierge practice," Maya said. "We have to try to keep our clients happy if we're going to grow. We need the word-of-mouth referrals."

"Patients," Esther corrected under her breath, staring out her window. "Not clients." Maya pretended not to hear her and kept her eyes on the road. After a moment, Esther said, "Worst-case scenario, if Skye goes into labor and we can't get her to a hospital—"

"That's not going to happen," Maya said.

"But *if* it did," Esther pressed. "It's been a long time since you've done a delivery, right? I mean, I just think maybe we should consider all the possibilities, think them through."

"I know how to deliver a baby," Maya said, her tone more defensive than she'd intended it to be. "It's not really something you can forget how to do. *If* it came to that. Which it won't because Skye will be in a hospital."

Esther was quiet for a moment. "You've never told me the reason you stopped delivering babies."

"I needed a more predictable schedule after Niam was born."

"Yeah, I know. But I mean, you never told me the real reason."

It was silent as the van rolled through an intersection. Then Maya said, "That is the real reason."

Esther pursed her lips, thinking. Finally she said, "Back at PGH, there were rumors."

Maya's eyes didn't stray from the road ahead. "What did you hear?"

Treading carefully, Esther replied, "That there was a case. In the ER at another hospital. And that it didn't end well."

Maya breathed in sharply. She struggled to keep her voice even. "Well, you can't believe everything you hear," she said.

Esther turned back to the window. "Your side-view mirror is still broken," she pointed out.

Maya nodded tersely. "Yeah. I keep forgetting. I'll get to it." She switched on the radio.

They rode to their next appointment without speaking, the Christmas carols in the background, to Maya's ear, joyless and grating.

TWENTY-TWO

t was her second year in practice, and Niam was three months old and wouldn't sleep. She'd taken the job right after graduating from residency at PGH, choosing it because she thought it would challenge her and help her grow as a physician. All of her mentors, including Dr. Keating, had told her that was what she should want for her career, to grow. "Never stop learning," they'd said and, smiling encouragingly, sent her off into the world.

She was one of four ob-gyns at a small community hospital in the northwest corner of Philadelphia. They cared for the most vulnerable: the poor, the working class, the Medicaid recipients. She'd loved it at first, despite the one-in-every-four-nights call schedule. Diya had been four years old then, too old to wake up throughout the night, too young to question or protest her mother coming and going at odd hours—it was all she'd ever known.

After Niam was born—via C-section after nineteen hours of labor—she'd pushed herself to return to work as quickly as possible. She'd planned to take the three months of unpaid maternity leave offered by her employer, but there was the mortgage on their house to consider, as well as her and Dean's student loans to repay, not to mention the guilt over the fact that her other three colleagues were selflessly covering her shifts while she was away on leave. There was also the discovery, the shameful dawning realization, that she did not enjoy being home with her two children as much as she'd thought she would. She loved her children, but she longed for work. Work that gave her life structure and purpose, work that didn't involve the endless, mindless washing and sterilizing of bottles and recitation of the alphabet.

She started work again when Niam was eight weeks old and, while he had been a good sleeper, he began to wake several times a night, inconsolable unless Maya nursed him. "The baby misses you. You went back to work too soon," her mother said, which only deepened Maya's shame and guilt. She nursed Niam three to four times a night, night after night, never getting more than two to three hours' sleep at a time. At the end of six weeks of this, a dark-skinned young woman walked into the emergency department late one night, screaming, blood coursing down her legs in bright red rivulets. She was rail thin, her arms and legs barely wider around than a broom handle, and it seemed to defy physics that her body was supporting the weight of her eight-months-pregnant belly. The woman spoke a language no one in the ED understood or recognized. She had no identification and no cell phone. The emergency room physician—a young man fresh out of residency—performed a quick examination and found the woman's cervix to be completely dilated. He felt certain he could feel the baby's head against his fingertips. He called to the nurses to page the obstetrician and the neonatologist on call. "Tell them to get here ten minutes ago!" he cried, his voice shaking.

Dean had always been a sound sleeper. He didn't hear Maya's pager going off on the bedside table next to her pillow. Maya had stumbled into Niam's room in a stupor several minutes earlier and had fallen asleep in the glider next to the crib, holding the baby to her breast. She usually took her pager with her, but in her exhausted, addled state, she'd forgotten. When, ten minutes later, Maya's cell phone started ringing in their bedroom, Dean slept through that, too. It was a full thirty minutes after the first page that Maya awoke with a start, placed the sleeping baby back in his crib, and ran to her room to get her pager. To her horror, she'd missed eight pages and twice as many phone calls.

By the time she reached the ED, the patient was unconscious. Her blood had soaked the bed linens and pooled on the floor. It wasn't the baby's head the young ED doctor had felt; it was a foot. The baby was breech, faced the wrong way, and now stuck firmly in the birth canal, one foot protruding out of the vagina, while the mother hemorrhaged. Maya called for nitroglycerin to relax the cervix and tried to maneuver the baby free. When the child would not budge, she performed a C-section right there in the ED, opening the woman's uterus and pulling the child out of a pool of its mother's blood. The baby emerged blue and limp. The neonatologist worked on the little boy for an hour before, in a voice scarcely more than a whisper, pronouncing the child dead.

The mother survived, though barely, and Maya sat at her bedside in the intensive care unit several days later with a translator—the woman, a recent immigrant from India, spoke only Bengali—and slowly explained what had happened to her and her child. She took responsibility and apologized, but the words sounded meaningless, even to her own ears, in the face of what had been lost. The woman's grief was unbearable. She hadn't been able to afford prenatal care, but she had dreamt of this baby, of holding him in her arms, of a family. Of things Maya already had and, she was shamefully aware, took for granted.

The months that followed were dark. Hospital administration, after a brief investigation, determined that Maya had been negligent in her duty to the patient. It was impossible to say whether the child would have survived had she arrived at the ED sooner, but it didn't matter in the end. She was asked to resign.

She began having flashbacks to that night in the ED, waking nightmares in which she reached her gloved hand into an abdominal cavity full of blood and pulled out a tiny, dusky arm or leg. For a time, it happened whenever she saw a pregnant woman, a flash before her eyes that knocked the breath out of her and set her heart racing. At night, she often dreamt of a little boy's body floating facedown in a swimming pool. She would dive in after him, and her arms and legs would suddenly go limp and useless, like lead weights dragging her under the surface. Sometimes the boy would drift farther away from her the more she tried to reach him. Sometimes she would reach him and, when she turned him faceup, would see Niam there, blue and unbreathing. She would wake from these nightmares screaming, and in doing so wake the whole house, wake the real Niam, who was asleep in his crib down the hall.

She started medication for depression and counseling for PTSD. The bills kept coming, however, and she finally called Dr. Keating and told him what had happened. He was kind and sympathetic, so much so that she was moved to tears and had to pull the phone away from her ear so he wouldn't hear her sobbing. He offered her a job in the hospital gynecology clinic where she'd trained as a resident. She wouldn't have to return to obstetrics until she was ready, he said. That was nearly four years ago.

Every time she thought of returning to obstetrics, the reason she had chosen her specialty to begin with, all those years ago back in medical school when she'd delivered her first baby under the watchful eye of her supervising resident, she was seized by panic. The world would fall away, replaced by the frenzied galloping of her heart and a deafening ringing in her ears. Once, just overhearing one of her colleagues in the clinic discussing a difficult labor-and-delivery case sent Maya into an attack. She'd felt her way along the wall to the bathroom and crouched in one of the stalls until it was over.

"Wounds heal in their own time," her therapist had said, and at a co-pay of $65 per session, she couldn't afford to keep going just to pass the time. She never spoke of that horrific night, or of returning to obstetrics, and Dean knew not to bring it up. Even Dr. Keating avoided the topic. For a long time, Maya couldn't look directly at Niam without feeling her heart race and her fingers and toes go icy and numb. But the more years that passed, the less she caught herself thinking of the blue little boy she'd once gripped in her hands. That, she told herself, was progress. That, she was almost sure, was healing.

TWENTY-THREE

Parent-teacher conferences at Hamilton Hall were always held on the first evening of the winter recess and were, as a rule, attended by both parents, sometimes also by grandparents and nannies, and occasionally by the child's private sports coach or therapist. In fact, it was not unusual for a student to have three to five adult representatives at each end-of-semester conference, especially as college application season approached. Maya and Dean did not know this. In the public school, they'd felt the full, enveloping warmth of the teacher's relief that one designated guardian had showed up to the conference at all. If they arrived on time, they were treated like paragons of child-rearing, the teacher heaping praise and gratitude on them as if they were visiting dignitaries from a far-off land.

When Maya arrived alone for her conference with Diya's teacher at Hamilton Hall, the pleasant-faced woman poured her a cup of tea, offered her a freshly baked scone and one of several seats across from her desk, glanced at her watch, and said, "Is everyone else stuck in traffic?" Maya replied that, no, it was only she who would be attending, as her husband was home watching the kids, and the teacher's eyelids fluttered in surprise. "Well! Okay, then." It only took her a moment to recover. "Well, Diya is such a delight to have in class, and she's done a wonderful job this first semester. I know she transferred in from the local public school district this year, but she's fluent in all of her multiplication and division facts, which is great, and she reads well above her grade level."

Maya exhaled in relief. "That's good to hear. Is she making friends? Who does she sit with at lunch?"

"She does have some friends. She does." The woman pursed her thin lips and nodded, as if trying to convince herself of the accuracy of her own words. "She prefers to sit by herself at lunch. She's always got her nose in a book, as you know! Which is great. It's great to see a child enjoying reading so much."

Maya shook her head. "I'm a bit worried about her. She left a lot of old friends behind when she switched schools. She left her comfort zone. She needed the change, but I worry that reading is her way of hiding, of avoiding having to try to make new friends."

The teacher nodded, understanding but, at the same time, missing the point entirely. "True, true. But some children are just introverts. There's nothing wrong with being quiet and loving books. I mean, I wish I had a classroom full of Diyas! She's really just delightful."

It occurred to Maya, as the teacher went on about recycled art collages and the classroom hydroponic garden, that Diya's delightfulness was directly related to her silence, to her unwillingness to complain or speak up for herself. Maya had done the same for years, all through her schooling, swallowing her objections, tamping down the words before they could escape her mouth, never wanting to disturb or vex or rile—wanting to remain ever *delightful*—and look what had happened. The rage, pushed down and bottled up for all that time, had become pressurized. Now she was a detonation risk.

Are you always this rude to your doctors, or only to the ones who aren't white men?

Her conference with Diya's main teacher was followed by brief meetings with her special area teachers for art, music, history, and media. Each of them also commented on how delightful, how perfectly well-behaved and quiet a student Diya was. Maya knew she should be grateful—who wouldn't want an agreeable, well-behaved child, especially after last year's mortifying cheating incident?—but every compliment about Diya's docility made her skin crawl, made her fists clench until her fingernails left angry red marks in her palms.

Her final meeting of the evening was with Diya's science teacher, a lanky, fidgety young man called Mr. Grove whose preferred work uniform consisted of skinny jeans, a sports jacket, and a T-shirt featuring a science-related pun. Today he wore a shirt that read NEVER TRUST AN ATOM. THEY MAKE UP EVERYTHING.

"Diya is super bright," Mr. Grove said. He absentmindedly spun the dials on a microscope as he spoke. It struck Maya as endearing. "She's curious, but more than that, she's logical, and she asks good questions. I'm not sure science is her favorite subject, but she's doing well with it regardless, and I was happy to see she signed up for the science fair. I'm looking forward to seeing what she comes up with for her project."

"Me, too," Maya said gratefully. Finally, a teacher who didn't feel the need to praise Diya's ability to not draw attention to herself. And she knew Diya didn't enjoy math or science, but that fact seemed irrelevant. Doing unenjoyable things was just a part of life, a necessary step on the path to success. Though Diya didn't understand it now, she'd eventually realize the path to success was lined with math problems, not with Percy Jackson novels.

His brow furrowed with regret, Mr. Grove continued, "She mentioned she might want to use the 3D printer for her project, but we only have one of those right now, and it's only for use by the high school kids, unfortunately."

"They need to get you another 3D printer," Maya said, smiling sympathetically.

"I've asked, believe me," the man said. "We also need another mass spectrometer and about fifteen more microscopes, but we got a meditation building instead." He paled, and his hand froze mid dial-twist. "Sorry, I shouldn't have said that."

Maya waved a hand. "Don't worry about it. I'd feel the same way."

"I shouldn't complain," Mr. Grove said. "Most schools don't even have one mass spectrometer, let alone two."

"Most schools don't have a meditation building."

Mr. Grove grinned. "Also a fair point."

"What do you use the mass spectrometer for?" Maya wanted to know.

"Chemistry experiments. For the fifth and sixth graders. I give them a bunch of mystery formulations, and they try to identify what they're made of by using the mass spec machine. They have fun, but it also teaches them that each element has its own distinct mass."

They discussed the periodic table and Diya's ideas for her science fair project, and Maya left the meeting thinking she might have liked to be a science teacher. But Maya, as a student, had been like Diya: delightful. Her parents had expected her to go to medical school, that most exalted of immigrant parent dreams, and she had delightfully obliged. To do otherwise would have never occurred to her, not at that age. It wasn't until she'd reached adulthood and started making her own decisions, she thought ruefully, that she'd become truly difficult and problematic.

In the hallway outside the science lab, she heard someone call her name.

"Maya!" A woman wearing a pink trench coat and Hunter rain boots, her hair in a short, dark bob, waved to her from the doorway of the music room, smiling widely. She seemed surprised Maya didn't recognize her. "Lainey Smockett," she said. "My daughter Madison is in Diya's class."

Maya suddenly placed the woman with the enormous sunglasses who had ignored her at the parent council meeting two months ago. She mirrored Lainey's smile, an involuntary reflex. "Hi! Nice to see you again."

Lainey approached, weaving through groups of chattering parents. "Maddy wants to invite Diya to her birthday party!" she exclaimed, seizing Maya's arm. The contact was unexpected, and Maya flinched. She forced herself not to pull her arm away. Lainey continued, "She's been desperate for me to call you, but I couldn't find your number. Sorry this is so last minute, but it's tomorrow. Are you free? What's your number? I'll text you the address. It's at Sugar and Spice in Bryn Mawr, the kids' salon? Two o'clock. Cauliflower pizza and gluten-free cake, don't worry. Moms can have wine while the girls get their makeovers—so fun, right? Oh, I hope you guys can make it!" She squeezed Maya's arm. "It'd be so nice to spend some time getting to know you."

The force of the woman's bonhomie crashed over Maya like a tidal wave. "Oh! Um . . . sure. We'd love to." Her heart leapt. Diya had a friend at school? She gave the woman her phone number, thanked her, and, as they parted, called to her over her shoulder, "See you then! Diya will be so excited!"

Diya was not, in fact, excited.

"You didn't ask me if I wanted to go!" she wailed, the depth of her distress surprising both her parents.

"I thought you'd have fun!" Maya said. "Aren't you friends with Madison?"

"No, I'm not friends with Madison!" Diya stamped her foot, indignant. "She barely ever talks to me!"

"Okay, so it'll be a chance for you to get to know her," Maya said. "And there will be other girls from school there, too."

"An opportunity to make new friends," Dean agreed. He slid a tray of roasted turnips out of the oven. Maya had signed them up for a meal kit service that delivered a box of raw, organic ingredients and an "easy-to-follow" recipe for dinners twice a week. Tonight's selection was a warm turnip and farro salad with sheep's milk cheese. Plated, the dish looked nothing like the photograph on the laminated recipe card, and its fusty smell was unexpected. "Huh," Dean said. "Did I miss a step?"

Niam, from his perch at the kitchen island, cried, "That smells like feet!" and pinched his nose shut. Asha, in her high chair next to him, made the decision to throw her teething ring to the floor and immediately regretted it. She wailed loudly.

"I don't want to make new friends," Diya insisted. "I don't want to go."

"Is it supposed to smell like this?" Dean wondered aloud.

"It's just an hour-long birthday party, Diya," Maya said impatiently while on her hands and knees, searching in vain for the teething ring as Asha's fussing escalated.

"Can't you just cancel?" Diya pressed.

Maya looked up at her. "They were nice enough to invite you. It'd be rude to cancel now."

"I'm not eating that," Niam said, crossing his arms.

"It's what's for dinner, bud," Dean said, shrugging. "It's this or a banana and milk."

"Banana and milk!" Niam yelled, as if the choice were obvious.

"He can't just eat a banana and milk for dinner," Maya said. She washed and returned Asha's teething ring, and the baby immediately threw it to the floor again and, once more, Maya had second thoughts.

"I mean, I'm not exactly surprised that he doesn't want to eat this," Dean said, poking at the salad with a fork. "How much is this meal kit service costing us?"

"It's worth the extra money to give them healthier food," Maya said.

"It doesn't matter if the food's healthy if they won't eat it," Dean replied.

"Well, I'm not going," Diya said petulantly.

"What's the big deal, Dee?" Dean asked. "You love birthday parties."

"They need to expand their palates." Maya put a hand on her hip, standing her ground. "We can't just keep feeding them processed foods!"

"I'm just saying, I don't think you needed to throw out all of their snacks at once," Dean, who had earlier that week wanted nothing more than a handful of Goldfish crackers but discovered the pantry all but empty save for some mealy wheat-free chickpea wafers, shot back. "You could have phased us into this new food philosophy gradually instead of dropping it on us without warning."

"Well, excuse me for wanting our family to be healthier!"

"Look, I agree with getting rid of the soda and chips, but no one is going to drink that much kombucha. Why is our fridge full of kombucha?"

"You don't understand! You never understand anything!" Diya cried, running from the room. They heard her stomp up the stairs and slam her bedroom door.

Niam took one bite of the turnip salad and gagged loudly.

TWENTY-FOUR

Fun. She was having fun. That was the unfamiliar warm feeling spreading through Maya's chest. It had been so long, she'd almost forgotten.

There had always been joy, of course. Parenting was filled with moments of joy; even through the exhaustion there was richness, there was gratitude, there were moments of unrivaled bliss. But fun was an entirely different kind of delight, one whose absence she hadn't noticed until, like an unexpected old friend, it turned up at this fourth-grade birthday party.

Sugar and Spice was located in a renovated two-story Colonial decorated for the season with holly and red-berry wreaths in the windows and a rustic twig-and-pinecone garland wrapped around the banister of the staircase. The first floor was a neon and glitter wonderland. A row of pink salon chairs, sized slightly smaller than normal for the salon's younger clientele, stretched across the main room in front of a wall of mirrors framed with light bulbs so that the space resembled a dressing room for Hollywood starlets. In an adjacent room, a low catwalk was flanked by chairs for spectators, and pastel-colored posters on the wall proclaimed things like "Work it, girl!" and "Fierce and sassy!"

Maya had dressed for the party, wearing a cowl-neck sweater and fitted jeans that had cost far more than she'd ever paid for a pair of pants in her life. She'd straightened her hair, put on lipstick, and filled in her eyebrows with pencil. "You look so different, Mommy!" Niam had exclaimed when she'd emerged from the bathroom. When she asked how so, he'd replied, with all the innocence and earnestness of youth, "You look *pretty*!" Diya, who refused to wear anything that wasn't comfortable, had tried to slip past her mother wearing her favorite sweatshirt, the one with a dime-size hole in the left sleeve, but was sent straight back upstairs to change into something more presentable. Her mother was anxious to make a good impression.

Dean had been right: this was an opportunity to make new friends, for Maya as well as for Diya. As a woman with young children, opportunities for socializing were scarce and limited to playdates or, like this, a venue where your child would be otherwise entertained for a specified length of time and, therefore, unable to bother you. Everyone knew that the hour during a birthday party was precious time, so the mothers of Madeline Smockett's friends had wasted no time depositing their daughters into salon chairs and proceeding upstairs to the parents' lounge, where a well-stocked wine bar and an array of comfortable seating awaited.

"So, is Amelia DeGilles a friend of yours?" Lainey had asked, the reverence in her voice clear, as she poured a generous amount of chardonnay into Maya's glass. "I couldn't help but notice the two of you sitting together at the Harvest Concert."

Maya hesitated. Did Amelia consider her a friend? Is that what they were? They were more than just work colleagues, certainly, but friends? No, that didn't fit either. "I recently started working at Eunoia," Maya replied, because that, at least, was accurate.

Lainey nodded. "Oh . . ." she said, as if finally understanding a difficult riddle that had been eluding her. "You're a gynecologist, right? I was at the parent council meeting. I thought—"

A tiny woman with a hulking baby asleep in a fabric sling strapped to her chest turned around suddenly. "You're a gynecologist?"

Once the other mothers—eleven of them in total—had discovered there was a specialist in women's health among them, they converged, pulling over chairs and gathering in front of Maya in a way that reminded her of Niam's classmates encircling her for story time and, clutching their wine in one hand and their pearls in the other, they leaned forward in rapt attention.

"So, Kendra thinks if you have sex while you're on your period, you're more likely to get pregnant. Is that true?" The woman with the baby demanded to know, her voice low and conspiratorial.

"Not get pregnant," Kendra, who was dressed in a smart pantsuit, like she'd just arrived from a campaign event, corrected, her face reddening to the roots of her platinum-blond hair. "More likely to have a boy. Like *if* you get pregnant, you're like 80 percent more likely to have a male child."

The woman with the baby rolled her eyes. "I call bullshit on that." She turned to Maya. "Is that true?"

Maya blinked. "No. Neither of those things is true."

"Hah!" The woman with the baby, vindicated, pointed at Kendra. "Told you."

Kendra adjusted the high collar of her shirt, shrugging. "Okay, well maybe not 80 percent, but you're a little more likely to have a boy, right?"

Maya shook her head, a slight, barely noticeable movement. "Um. No. Unfortunately, there's no way to control if you'll have a boy or a girl. It depends entirely on whether the sperm that fertilizes your egg is carrying an X or a Y chromosome. That's it."

Kendra's brow furrowed. "But doesn't it have something to do with the pH in there"—she pointed discreetly to her pelvis—"or something like that?"

"Meaning, are the X and Y sperm different somehow?" Maya asked, trying to clarify where the confusion was.

"Does one or the other swim better depending on what else is in the pool—that's what she wants to know," the woman with the baby said, sipping her wine.

The other women tittered.

"Nope," Maya answered lightly. "All the little guys have the same shot at success. There's no way to rig the game. Sorry."

Kendra looked disappointed, but nodded her acceptance.

"What about if you have sex while you're breastfeeding?" a different woman, one with severe eyebrows and an Eastern European accent, asked. "You can't get pregnant, right?"

"It's less likely, but definitely not impossible," Maya said. The other women seemed to have inched closer to her. "You should make sure to use birth control, even while you're nursing."

"What about avocados?" a woman with short silver hair and a red leather jacket wanted to know.

"What about them?"

"If you put one in before sex, it works like a diaphragm. No?"

Maya stared at the woman. "No. Please don't do that."

"Oh my God, Heather," the woman with the baby said, her hand on her forehead. "Your vag is not for serving guacamole!"

The group burst into laughter as Heather tried to explain. "I heard about it from my yoga teacher! She swears by it!"

"No food in any opening except your mouth," Maya had said, grinning. "Good rule of thumb." It was then that she'd noticed the warm feeling. The fun. She relaxed into her chair.

The questions continued to come at her now, lobbed like tennis balls, from one woman after another.

"Does drinking wine lower your fertility?"

"No, not in moderation."

"Can you get pregnant if you're on the pill?"

"Yes."

"Can you get pregnant with an IUD?"

"Yes."

"Is it true there's no such thing as a G-spot?"

"There isn't one magical spot, no," Maya said.

"Well, good." Heather crossed and uncrossed her legs. "I can tell my husband he can stop looking for it." The women laughed, and she added, "After fifteen years you'd think he'd have given up by now," which made them all positively lose their minds.

Lainey pursed her lips. "Oooh, you know what would be incredible? If you could donate some sort of women's health treatment for the auction." The other women murmured in agreement.

"I've heard a lot about this auction," Maya said. For almost two months, she'd been avoiding the aggressive phone calls from Patricia Grace, who left peppy, vaguely desperate messages on her voice mail saying that she hoped for her and Dean's support for the fundraiser and that tickets were "only $750 per couple until March 1, then they'll be $1,500, so snap them up now!" When Maya had played one of the messages for Dean, he'd laughed and said, "Seven fifty? They realize we're barely affording their tuition, right?"

"I'm on the planning committee," Lainey said. "Have you gotten your tickets yet?"

Maya shook her head. "Not yet. Do most parents attend?"

"Oh, everyone attends," Lainey said, surprised by the question.

Heather nodded in agreement. "Everyone. And everyone donates something to auction off."

Maya looked from one woman to the other. "Oh?"

"Goods or services. It could be anything, really," Lainey said. "One of the sixth-grade moms is M. Night Shyamalan's accountant—

he still lives in Wayne. I mean, he also lives in LA, but he keeps a house in Wayne for his wife and kids—and she got him to donate an experience where he comes to your house and films a creepy movie trailer starring you and your kids. It's so outside the box and so perfect."

"People love that sort of thing," another woman chimed in. "I can't wait to see the bidding war for that one. Can you imagine putting a video directed by the guy who made *The Sixth Sense* on your Instagram for Halloween?"

They all agreed such a thing would be unimaginably wonderful, far superior to the tired custom of posting a picture of your family in coordinating costumes.

"Evelyn, tell them what you scored for the auction," Lainey said. A striking woman with waist-length red hair had entered and gone directly to the bar on the far side of the room for a glass of wine. She approached them now, and Maya placed her instantly. The Little Mermaid. "A tennis lesson with Venus Williams!" the woman said triumphantly, taking a seat on an empty chair at the periphery of the group, where she looked vaguely unhappy to be. She seemed like the kind of woman who was unused to being at the periphery of any gathering. "Hello, ladies. Sorry I'm late. Paisley had a golf lesson and it ran overtime. Who's the new girl?"

"Maya, this is Evelyn. She has a fifth grader at Hamilton, one in the high school, and one at Dartmouth," Lainey said. "Ev, this is Maya Rao. She's a gynecologist with Eunoia. Her daughter Diya is in Maddy's class."

Evelyn looked her up and down, and Maya waited for the moment of recognition. It didn't come. "A gyno?" Evelyn raised her eyebrows. "Oh, that's right. I remember from the parent council meeting." She chuckled, though it wasn't clear what about, and sipped her wine.

"Evelyn is the head of auction donations this year," Lainey explained. She turned to her friend. "We were trying to get Maya to donate something related to women's health. She's been so educational this afternoon." The other women giggled.

"Oooh, we could do a whole women's health basket!" Evelyn clapped her hands in delight, like a child being presented with a birthday cake.

"We could call it a Vag Bag," the woman with the baby suggested.

The other women laughed. "Oh my God, that's brilliant," Lainey said. "It's edgy and funny."

"A Vag Bag of Swag?" Maya suggested, grinning. The other women doubled over in hysterics.

"You're funny!" Evelyn said, eyes shiny with approval.

"Okay, okay," Lainey said excitedly. "What would go in it?"

"Maybe a nice agenda?" Maya suggested. "So women could write down when their Pap smear and mammogram appointments are?"

"Ugh, boring," Evelyn said, waving a hand in dismissal. "Something outside the box, please, ladies."

"Okay, how about this." Lainey drew one hand through the air as if she were drafting a sign. "'Perk up your tired vag with this bag of swag!' And we put in some high-end probiotics and like, a luxury douche."

Evelyn squealed with mirth. "That's hysterical! And some feminine deodorant spray!"

"And lube! We put in lube!" Someone else said.

"The fancy kind! And a vibrator!" They were all shouting out ideas now.

"And detoxifying pearls!"

"And that vagina-scented candle!"

The women were nearly breathless with laughter now, gasping for air. "Can you imagine the headmaster's face? He'll have a stroke!" Lainey said.

"I bet you his wife bids on it, though!" Evelyn said. "The old biddies will fall over themselves trying to win it!"

Maya's face was fixed in a tight-lipped smile, and she clutched the wineglass in her lap with both hands. There was something obliquely mean-spirited about the turn their conversation had taken, like they had crossed a line from promoting women's health to mocking it. As if the work of her career was a joke.

"And what if we throw in some estrogen suppositories and a voucher for a Brazilian wax?" Evelyn turned to Maya. "And oh! The centerpiece of the basket could be a lift. Would you be willing to contribute that?"

"A . . . lift?" Maya shook her head, confused.

"You know, the laser surgery to tighten it up. The rejuvenation procedure. Is that something you do?"

"There's laser surgery for that?" Lainey asked, suddenly serious and interested in learning more.

"Well, there is, but it's not something I do or recommend doing," Maya said.

Evelyn cocked her head, disappointed, as if Maya was spoiling their fun. "Why not?"

"It's basically plastic surgery for your vagina," Maya said. "And it can be dangerous. There's no reason anyone needs a laser fired around down there. We don't shoot lasers at men's penises for cosmetic reasons. There's no such thing as a testicle lift to rejuvenate men's balls."

The women looked sheepish, like schoolgirls caught passing notes in class.

"And douches and feminine deodorant and detoxifying pearls are bad for your vaginal health, too. Not to mention they support the patriarchal idea that vaginas are dirty and smell bad."

"Well, they don't smell *good*," Lainey mumbled peevishly.

"I mean . . . but we could definitely come up with something else fun," Maya offered, a bit too feebly and a beat too late. The enthusiasm had left the group like air escaping a tire.

"Well." Evelyn crossed her legs and regarded her wine. "It was just an idea. We have plenty of other items to auction off."

"How did you manage to score Venus Williams?" Lainey asked, trying to steer the conversation to less awkward ground.

"When all three of your children play tennis, you make connections," Evelyn said, shrugging. "It's too bad it wasn't Serena, but I think Venus will still go for at least five grand."

Heather laughed. "Be careful, Evelyn."

Evelyn gave her a quizzical look. "What?"

"You can't go around talking about auctioning off a Black person. You could get arrested for that sort of thing these days. Or even worse, *canceled*!"

"Oh my God, Heather, stop," Evelyn said lightly, though the look she gave Heather was anything but. "The *tennis lesson* with her will go for five thousand. There. Better?" She rolled her eyes.

Heather shrugged, as if it wasn't up to her, and glanced at Maya. There was a palpable shift in the air, as if every woman in the group was silently working out a complex math equation. Having felt, just a moment earlier, like a part of this gaggle of women, Maya sensed her honorary membership status being quietly reconsidered.

Lainey asked, her smile forced, "So. What's Diya's sport?"

"Oh, she doesn't have one yet," Maya replied.

Lainey's eyebrows shot up. "Really? But she's nine, right?"

Maya nodded.

"Well, does she play an instrument?"

"Violin. She just started this year."

Lainey put a hand on her arm. "Oh, I'll give you the number for our teacher. He's wonderful." She arched an eyebrow reproachfully. "You're cutting it close! College application season will be here before we know it. Right, Ev?"

Evelyn sighed dramatically. "It feels like just yesterday I was setting up playdates for my sons, now I have one about to go to Stanford on early admission and one at Dartmouth." She smiled, showing her straight, white teeth. "You know, I don't think I've seen you around, Maya. Did you just move to town?"

Maya shook her head. "We live in Wynnewood. Diya transferred in from the public school at the beginning of this year." Even as the words passed her lips, she regretted sharing this information. Evelyn's emerald green eyes bore into her, as if she were assessing the quality of a piece of clothing, rubbing the fabric between her two fingers. *This isn't real cashmere.*

"Wynnewood?" Lainey said, and Maya could feel the other women take in her slightly split ends, her off-brand sweater and boots. "Wynnewood is so cute." She excused herself to refill her wineglass.

"Diya is such a pretty name," Evelyn said. "Does it mean something? In your language?"

"Diya means light in Hindi," Maya said.

"And your name?"

"Maya means illusion in Sanskrit." She didn't explain that she was actually named after a Hindu goddess. It seemed irrelevant. It had been a long time since she'd thought of herself as Mahalakshmi, and she had no desire to engage in a question-and-answer session about why Hindu deities have multiple arms and heads and if cows are indeed sacred. Instead, returning Evelyn's intense stare, she asked, "Does Evelyn mean anything?"

"No," Evelyn said. "It's biblical. Is your husband a doctor, too?"

"No, he's getting his PhD."

"Impressive," Evelyn said, though she didn't look impressed. She continued her interrogation. "You have other children?"

"Two. An eight-month-old and a preschooler."

"And your preschooler is at Hamilton, too?"

"No. He goes to a different school. One closer to home."

Lainey returned from the bar with another glass of wine and said, horrified, "Two drop-offs?"

"Three, actually," Maya replied. "The baby goes to day care."

"That's brutal. Do you have help?"

Maya shook her head. "No, not right now."

"Well," Lainey said magnanimously, "Madison says Diya is the smartest one in their class. She says Diya always has a book in her hands."

Maya smiled. "She's always been a reader."

"Is she on scholarship?" Evelyn asked casually.

Veiled though it was, the implication that her family couldn't afford tuition at Hamilton Hall Academy was impossible to miss. Maya's face burned. "No, she's not on scholarship," she replied. "But she's doing great in school this year. I think the small class size suits her. And I have more time to help with homework ever since I left my old job and partnered with Amelia." The name hung in the air for a long moment, then wrapped itself around Maya like a cloak. *I'm with Amelia.*

"How's that been?" Evelyn asked. "Working for Amelia?"

Maya bristled. "I'm not working *for* her. I'm more of an independent contractor under the Eunoia umbrella. It's been really great so far." She considered stopping there, but added, "And ADG—that's what everyone calls her—is so easy to work with. And Greg, too. The whole family has been so warm and welcoming to us. Prem's my patient now." She hated herself for doing this, for name-dropping Amelia and for mentioning Prem at all, but she couldn't help it. She felt like a small trapped animal, scrabbling for leverage. "We were just over at their house for brunch."

"You've seen the inside of her house?" Lainey asked, leaning so far forward she nearly slid off her seat.

"What's it like?" Heather wanted to know. "I saw pictures in *Architectural Digest* last year, and oh my God."

"It really is gorgeous," Maya said, smiling. She pushed the image of the Ganesh fountain from her mind.

Evelyn pressed her lips together. "So, is it true she has a personal chef?"

Maya glanced at her coolly. "She's very private, and I'm not sure she'd want me to say. You could ask her, though."

Evelyn's smile faded as Lainey piped up, "Oh, we don't know her like that! We just, you know, know *of* her."

Evelyn glared at her, and Lainey, looking ashamed, averted her eyes.

"I know she can be intimidating," Maya said sympathetically, "but she's actually very easy to talk to." Based on Evelyn's humiliated expression, she knew she'd delivered the kill shot, though it wasn't nearly as satisfying as she would have expected.

A girl of about fifteen wearing an apron that read "Sugar and Spice girls are NAUGHTY, not NICE!" appeared in the doorway. "Time for the fashion show, moms!" she chirped. "Please join us downstairs at the catwalk!"

The mothers all turned to look, but only Evelyn rose and followed the girl out of the room, without a word to the rest of them, her heels clicking loudly on the wooden floor. For a moment, they listened to her clomp down the stairs. Then they all dutifully followed.

Megan Thee Stallion's song "Savage" blasted from somewhere, and the curtain at the top of the catwalk flew open to reveal Madison Smockett dressed in a sparkly silver lamé catsuit one size too big, her hair in two elaborate French braids, her face made up with Japanese-beetle-green eye shadow and a bright red lipstick. "Please give it up for our birthday girl, Ma-di-sooooon!" one of the several teenage girls manning the event shouted into a microphone.

The mothers all whooped and cheered, and Lainey held up her phone to record the moment. Madison pouted, rested one hand nonchalantly on her hip, and strutted down the catwalk, pausing at the end to blow her mother a kiss and perform some sort of gyrating dance move. She returned to the curtain, and out popped the next party guest, wearing a similarly glamorous but ill-fitting outfit and doing the same dance move.

"What is this dance?" Maya asked the woman next to her.

"It's from TikTok!" the woman replied, shouting over the music.

Through the gap in the curtain, Maya could see the teenagers helping the little girls layer the outfits, chosen from several hanging on a garment rack, over their clothes. It occurred to her that this seemed like the exact type of activity Diya would hate, donning and doffing scratchy costumes, the application of makeup.

She was right. When it was Diya's turn to walk the catwalk, she emerged from behind the curtain wearing no special outfit, just the sweatshirt and leggings in which she'd arrived, and a lime-green feather boa around her shoulders. Her hair was pulled into a too-tight formal bun, and she'd smeared her lipstick onto one cheek, presumably while trying to wipe it off. She dragged her feet down the catwalk, glaring resentfully at her mother. Maya dutifully recorded it on her phone. Diya didn't bother to pause at the end of the catwalk or to dance. She simply walked back to the curtain and disappeared, without having smiled once.

"Guess somebody is NOT in the mood," the woman next to Maya said, chuckling.

Diya, to Maya's great embarrassment, moped through the cauliflower pizza and gluten-free cake, too. Finally, Maya had had enough. She approached the long table where the girls were seated, still in their costumes, licking frosting off forks. "Dee!" she hissed into her daughter's ear. "What's with you? It's a birthday party!"

Diya burst into tears.

"Oh my goodness!" Evelyn exclaimed from across the table, more incredulous than concerned.

Maya kneeled in front of her daughter. "Diya! What's the matter?"

In between sobs, Diya managed to gasp out, "I . . . want . . . to . . . go . . . home!"

"What happened?" Lainey appeared with a pack of tissues.

Maya held Diya's face between her hands. "What happened?"

"I just want to go," Diya pleaded, her voice a whisper.

"Diya, we can't just walk out of a party. It's rude. Just tell me what happened."

"She said I had fat thighs."

"What?"

"She said none of the costumes fit me because my thighs were too fat."

"Who?"

"Madison."

Lainey, her face frozen in an expression somewhere between mortification and fury, said, "Did Madison say that? Madison Maria Teresa Smockett, you get your hiney over here this instant! Your friend is crying!"

Madison, after exchanging an exasperated glance with the girls seated next to her, arose from her chair at the head of the table and made her way over to Diya, her arms crossed. "Sorry."

"What are you sorry for?" Lainey demanded. "And look at the person when you're apologizing to them."

"I'm sorry for saying your thighs are fat," Madison said dispassionately to the space above Diya's head. "They're not."

Diya bit her lip and stared at her shoes.

"Oh, that's okay. Right, Dee?" Maya rubbed her daughter's back as if trying to rub away the insult. "I'm sure it was just a misunderstanding."

The party had gone silent, the quiet broken only by the sound of Diya's sniffling. *Please just stop crying*, Maya pleaded silently to her daughter, to no avail. Then, another plea crossed her mind: *Please just fit in. Please, can we just fit in?* It jarred her as soon as it emerged into her consciousness from somewhere deep and hidden. She felt the urgent need to escape.

"Well, it's getting late," she said suddenly, standing up. "We should get going. Thank you for inviting us."

Lainey didn't try to stop them, but trailed Maya and Diya to the door with a goodie bag, saying, "I'm so sorry about that. I have no idea where that came from. We talk all the time about body positivity and I don't even know where she would have gotten the idea that some people's thighs are fat or skinny. I—"

"Oh, don't worry about it," Maya said, waving her off, desperate to flee but still desperate to please. "Diya can be . . . sensitive, I guess."

"Well, I hope we can get together again. This was fun!"

"It really was. Thanks again. Will you text me the number for your violin teacher?"

Lainey smiled in relief, sensing all was forgiven. "Absolutely. I'll do it right now. You'll love him. He's toured with Yo-Yo Ma!"

In the van, Maya turned around in her seat. Diya was still staring at her shoes, her arms crossed angrily. "I'm so sorry, Dee. That was a crappy thing for Madison to say," Maya said. "You know that's not true, right? You are perfect and beautiful. You know that, right?"

Diya shrugged. "Yeah. I guess."

"I mean it! You are," Maya said, tightening her grip on the steering wheel. "Don't let anyone else's insecurities get to you." Diya didn't reply, and after a moment she added, "So . . . Madison kind of sucks, huh?"

"I tried to tell you."

"Yeah, you did. I'm sorry I didn't get it before."

Diya stared out the window and said quietly to her reflection, "I'm not sensitive."

Maya's mouth opened, then closed. "You're right. You're not."

"Then why did you say I was?"

She sighed. "I shouldn't have. I'm sorry for that, too."

"Is it because you didn't want Madison's mom to feel bad?"

"Yeah, but it's not like I care about Madison's mom's feelings more than I care about yours. You're the most important person in the world to me, Dee."

"And Niam and Asha. And Dad."

"Right. The four of you. Madison's mom is just someone I'm trying to get to know."

"Why?"

"Well, it might be good for my practice, for one. Madison's mom is a lady, and she's friends with lots of other ladies, and those ladies may need a doctor."

"So, for work."

"For work, yes, but also now that you're going to Hamilton, we want to get to know other Hamilton families."

"Why?"

"It's good to know people. To be connected."

"What for?"

Maya considered it for a moment before saying, "They say you can tell a lot about a person by the company they keep. Have you ever heard that?" In the rearview mirror, Diya shook her head. "It means that who you spend time with matters. It says something to the rest of the world about you, it sends a message. And we want to make sure we're sending the right message. Does that make sense?"

"Is that why you won't let Niam play with Jake next door anymore?"

Maya sighed, suddenly tired. "Dee, you know how you're half Indian? And remember how we talked about how some people are about people with darker skin?"

"Like how some people are racist?"

"Yeah, like that."

"Jake is racist?"

"No, no," Maya shook her head. "Not at all. But no one in his family has dark skin like yours or mine, right?"

"So?"

"So Jake is going to be able to get away with things—with doing things and being things—that you and I are not going to be able to get away with. If Jake and Niam do something naughty, like throw rocks at cats, it's going to look worse for our family than it will for Jake's."

"Why?"

"Because that's just how it is."

"But daddy's skin isn't dark. And Niam looks like daddy."

"Yeah, but you and I don't. And it's not fair, but it means that our family needs to be more particular than Jake's family about who we spend time with. We want to hang out with people who aren't stoning cats. You know what I mean?"

Diya shrugged. "I guess."

"We can talk about it later. It's been kind of a long day, right?" They passed a green-and-white sign, and suddenly she knew exactly how to cheer up Diya. Starbucks, a treat saved only for special occasions, never failed. "How about a Frappuccino?"

Diya asked how many calories were in a Frappuccino. Maya met her eyes in the rearview mirror. "You're nine. You don't need to worry about calories." She bought them both a decaf Frappuccino at the drive-through window. When they got home, Diya jumped out of the van and ran inside, and Maya found her frozen drink in the cupholder in the back seat, untouched and melting.

TWENTY-FIVE

Christmas passed, then Valentine's Day. Maya and Esther's roster of patients grew exponentially, Niam mastered basic addition, and Diya reluctantly learned to play "Hot Cross Buns" on the violin. Esther called on a Sunday morning in late March while Maya, in a robe and slippers, was making her children pancakes.

"Remember Mrs. Cunningham? The one with the $2,000 crystal? Well, we've never seen her granddaughter, but apparently the granddaughter is a high school freshman, and she wants a doctor's note to get out of gym class."

"For what reason?" Maya asked, pouring herself a cup of coffee.

"For no reason," Esther said. "I asked if she had medical problems, and Mrs. Cunningham was like, 'No, she just doesn't want to have to do gym, so could Dr. Rao write her a doctor's note with some excuse? Can you believe that? She had the gall to just ask that like it wasn't totally unethical for you to make up a medical problem for this girl you've never even met."

Maya laughed. "Do I believe Mrs. Cunningham had the gall? Yeah, actually, I do. You can just put down 'Irregular painful periods' as the reason and sign my name. That should work." Esther was silent on the other end of the line. "Or maybe we should get some Eunoia letterhead and type it up on that?" Maya wondered.

"I just . . . You're going to give her the note?" Esther said.

"Well, yes. It's just gym class." Maya stretched her arms above her head. Esther started to reply, but Maya's call waiting beeped. "Hold on a second, Esther. It's Gretchen. I'll ask about the letterhead."

Gretchen's voice was frantic. "Maya? Prem is in the ER at Philadelphia General."

"What? Why?" Maya asked. "What happened?"

Gretchen sounded out of breath, as if she'd been jogging. A lone seagull cawed plaintively in the background. "Apparently she was in Philadelphia for some sort of march—women's rights or free the immigrants or whatever. Anyway, she took the train in with her friends this morning—and she fell and hit her head. Amelia called me, but I'm at my place in Boca this weekend. She's freaking out. She's in the ER and they won't let her see Prem. You used to work there, right? I thought maybe you could help."

"Oh, of course," Maya said. "I'll call her right—"

"I think it'd be better if you went to the hospital, actually," Gretchen interrupted. "Amelia doesn't . . ." She paused, searching for the words. "She doesn't do well in hospitals, around doctors. It'll help if someone she knows is there. Could you go over?"

Maya glanced at her three children around the kitchen island. If one of them was in the ER, she'd be frantic, too. "Yes, of course," she said.

She clicked back to Esther. "Amelia's daughter is in the ER at PGH. I'm going over there to help."

"I'd meet you there, but I have a shift at Temple," Esther said, and wished her luck. "Hope her daughter's okay."

After she hung up, Maya told Dean what had happened, then showered and dressed in under ten minutes. Over the years, she'd honed her morning routine to its most efficient version, a skill born of necessity. Ten minutes was all she ever had to herself before her pager went off or a child appeared in the bathroom demanding to be attended to. She chose a variation of her work uniform of late—black slacks and a tailored black blazer—and grabbed the maroon leather Kate Spate handbag she'd treated herself to after Madison Smockett's birthday party. It had been out of her budget, but she'd rationalized the purchase by telling herself she needed to look the part of a concierge doctor. She'd also finally gotten a haircut, a smart, angled bob at a high-end salon in Philadelphia that specialized in curly hair. After a cursory glance in the mirror—good enough; better than usual, in fact—she sped to the city.

When she walked into the emergency room at PGH, her stomach momentarily knotted with nostalgia and a bit of dread to be back at what she still thought of as *her* hospital. The building where she spent five years as a resident and four years on staff. The ER where she used to see gynecological emergencies. "Dr. Rao?" The friendly elderly triage nurse at the front desk waved. "I haven't seen you down here in forever! You have a patient here?" The woman evidently hadn't heard that Maya was no longer on staff.

"I do," Maya said, offering no more information than was necessary. "Premrose DeGilles. Can you tell me which bed she's in?"

"We're out of space at the moment—it's been a zoo down here today, let me tell you—so she's in the hallway outside of room twelve," the nurse replied. She waved Maya through to the patient treatment area, calling after her, "Love the new look, Doc! Good seeing you!"

Maya could hear Amelia's voice well before she located her and Prem in a back hallway of the emergency room. "What do you mean, a CAT scan? That's radiation, isn't it? I'm not going to let you irradiate my daughter's brain! Where is your supervisor?"

Prem was seated on a stretcher that had been pushed against the wall. A young man in scrubs and a white coat—an emergency medicine resident, according to his ID tag—was standing cross-armed while Amelia shouted at him. He sighed and said dispassionately, "Ma'am, it's standard procedure in cases of head trauma."

"I don't care about standard procedure!" Amelia said, squinting at him as if his glaring incompetence was physically hurting her eyes. "Why are you treating my daughter like a number?"

Prem, wearing a hospital gown and booties, a gauze bandage affixed to one of her temples, rolled her eyes impatiently. "Mom, he wouldn't be recommending the test if he thought it was dangerous."

"But is it really necessary? You don't want unnecessary X-rays." Amelia turned on the resident with renewed ferocity. "You've already taken five vials of blood from her. Where are the results of those tests?"

"Ma'am, like I told you, the ER is very busy today," the young man replied. "It could be several hours."

As if cued to prove his point, a voice announced on the loudspeaker overhead, "Incoming multiple trauma! Incoming multiple trauma!" and several frantic-looking doctors and nurses went sprinting past. None of this impressed Amelia.

"Do you have any idea how long we've already been waiting? We—" Amelia spotted Maya approaching, and her expression morphed from outrage to relief. She grabbed Maya by the elbow. "This is our private physician. Please update her on what's going on with Prem."

The resident's eyebrows went up. "Oh! Sure. Nice to meet you, Doctor . . . ?"

"Rao." Maya shook his hand.

The resident, accustomed to respecting the hierarchy of medical education that put trainees like himself at the bottom, deferentially reviewed the facts of the case: Prem, according to two friends who rode with her in the ambulance, had climbed over the railing at the top of a flight of steps in front of the Philadelphia Public Library for a picture and fallen six feet into a crowd of women's rights protestors. "When they helped her up, she was confused and disoriented. I've already sent off labs for alcohol and drugs, and a urine pregnancy test," the resident said, proud of himself.

"My daughter fell off a building, and your only concern is whether or not she's a druggie or pregnant?" Amelia threw up her hands. "What kind of circus is this?"

Prem rolled her eyes again. "I didn't fall off a *building*. I don't think it was even six feet. Probably more like four. I feel fine." She looked at Maya hopefully. "Can I just go home?"

Maya indicated the bandage on Prem's temple. "It's very likely, since you hit your head, that you have a concussion. That's what caused the disorientation. But the CAT scan makes sure the injury isn't more serious. I'd recommend getting it."

"But the radiation—" Amelia started.

Maya turned to the resident. "Can you order an MRI instead?" She explained to Prem and Amelia, "There's no radiation with an MRI, it uses magnets instead of X-rays to make the image."

The resident shuffled his feet. "MRIs aren't standard protocol in cases of head trauma."

Maya nodded. "I know."

"They're more expensive and they take much longer to do."

"Neither of those things is a problem," Maya reassured him.

"I'll pay extra for the test without the radiation," Amelia said.

"I'd have to okay it with my attending," the resident said skeptically. "I've never seen them order an MRI in the ER for this sort of injury."

Maya glanced at Prem and Amelia, then back at the resident. "I'm happy to discuss it with them. Lead the way."

The resident hesitated, then showed Maya down a long corridor to a workstation. The attending physician on shift was an elderly woman with white hair and a floral neck scarf. "Dr. Russo!" Maya said, pleasantly surprised to see her former colleague.

"Maya?" The woman peered at her over her bifocals. "It's been ages!" She lowered her voice. "I heard you left. Are you back?"

Maya shook her head. "I'm practicing concierge medicine now."

"Concierge gynecology?" Dr. Russo shook her head and smiled. "Now I've heard everything. What brings you here, then?"

"My client is the seventeen-year-old girl who came in via ambulance after a fall off the steps at the library."

"The one with the head injury and confusion?" Dr. Russo said. "Yes, I saw her when she came in. She was really out of it. We're waiting on blood and urine test results."

"Wait, was she confused when you saw her?" Maya asked. "Not just right after the injury?"

Dr. Russo nodded. "Confused as hell. And paranoid. She thought someone had pushed her off the stairs, but eyewitnesses at the scene—including her friends—told the paramedics she was alone up there. Then she thought one of the nurses had stolen her phone. It was actually pretty entertaining."

Maya shook her head, puzzled. "She seems fine now. I just spoke to her."

"I wouldn't be surprised if she had a seizure after she hit her head," Dr. Russo said. "That can cause prolonged confusion that eventually clears up. The CAT scan will help make sure it's nothing serious."

"But an MRI would be better. No radiation, more detail."

Dr. Russo raised an eyebrow. "You know we don't do those in the ER for head traumas. There's no evidence that an MRI is better in any way for cases like these. The fear of radiation is not based in science. Just like the fear of vaccines or the fear of the boogeyman aren't based in science."

"But you could order it," Maya said. "If you wanted to."

"I could," Dr. Russo conceded. "But why would I want to break protocol and order a more expensive and time-consuming test just to appease your"—she met Maya's eye with a steady, disapproving gaze—"client?"

"Because her mother is Amelia DeGilles, the philanthropist. She's been known to make very large donations to hospitals in the area. And she wants her child to have an MRI, not a CAT scan. She'll pay the difference."

Dr. Russo bristled. "I'm not concerned with securing donations for the hospital. I'm concerned with practicing evidence-based medicine."

Maya took her phone from her handbag. "You're right. I shouldn't be bothering you with this. I'll just give Tad from hospital administration a call. You know how he feels about potential donors. I wouldn't be surprised if he came down here himself."

Dr. Russo adjusted her glasses and cleared her throat. "I remember, Maya, you volunteered in my free clinic at the women's shelter when you were in medical school. I remember thinking you'd do great things in medicine." She clicked a few buttons on her computer, then looked up at Maya again. "Imagine that." She picked up a chart and turned away, saying, "Tell the resident I ordered the MRI."

Unflinching, Maya added, "She's in the hallway."

Dr. Russo sighed and shook her head in defeat. "We'll find her a room."

Prem's blood and urine test results proved she was neither pregnant nor drunk nor high. She was wheeled to the radiology department for the MRI of her brain, and Maya and Amelia were asked to stay in the waiting room until she returned, at which point, they were promised, she would have a private room.

"Maya, I can't thank you enough," Amelia said. They'd been

lucky to find two empty chairs in a corner of the crowded ER waiting room. Amelia rolled an empty foam cup between her hands. She'd started to fill it with coffee, but distractedly sat down with it instead. Her face was drawn, and she'd abandoned her usually perfect posture in favor of slumping forward and resting her forearms on her thighs.

"Don't mention it," Maya said. "But someone from the hospital might call you next week to shake you down for a donation. Sorry if that happens."

Amelia shrugged. "I'm used to it." After a moment she said, "I feel like I owe you an explanation."

"For what?"

"I know you don't believe in some of the things we do at Eunoia. Biophoton therapy and crystals, that sort of thing."

"Well, I mean, I don't believe in them because there's no science behind them," Maya said. "It's not about belief, it's about what's factual and what's not."

Amelia nodded patiently. "I get that. But you have to understand. For me, the way I grew up, it's not so clear cut."

Maya looked at her doubtfully. "I assume you had access to great health care growing up."

"I did," Amelia said. "And I used it. A lot. I was very sick as a child. I was in pain, off and on, for years. I would get these terrible blistering rashes, stomachaches, vomiting. Sometimes I had seizures. I remember weeks where my legs hurt so much I could barely get out of bed. Just all of these crazy symptoms."

Guilt seized Maya's chest. She'd never considered the idea that Amelia had had an unhappy childhood. In her mind, Amelia's life had always been charmed. "I'm so sorry," she said. "What was your diagnosis?"

"There wasn't one, for a long time," Amelia said. "But there were a lot of tests, a lot of really awful, invasive tests."

"How old were you?"

"It started when I was ten, and it lasted until I was sixteen. That's when I moved out of my mother's house to look for other treatments. I lived with my dad and stepmom—my parents were divorced—for a little while, and eventually I went abroad. I traveled through China and India and Vietnam. I tried everything. I thought it was a combination of Chinese herbs and meditation that finally cured me . . . but I'd blocked out a lot of my childhood. There were things I couldn't remember." Her voice trailed off.

"What do you mean?" Maya coaxed.

"They said my diagnosis was a mystery. The doctors. They couldn't understand how I could be fine one month, then back in the hospital the next. They had all sorts of theories. There was a neurologist who was convinced I had MS. He kept sending me for spinal taps, which were absolute torture, but nothing ever came up abnormal on any of them."

"How awful! That must have been so frustrating."

Amelia laughed hollowly. "It was for me. But my mother was never discouraged. She just took me to the next doctor, told me to be strong, that we'd eventually figure it out. She was always so . . . upbeat about it. Everyone talked about how devoted a mother she was. She was a fucking martyr." Tears were streaming down her cheeks now. Maya, alarmed, frantically combed through her purse for tissues. She waited for Amelia to explain. After several long moments, Amelia continued, "Those blocked memories started coming back to me about a year ago. I couldn't be sure they were actual memories and not my imagination, so I started going to a shamanic healer. I've done ayahuasca in Peru every two months for the past year and . . . I've remembered things. Things that I'm sure are real memories."

Maya put a sympathetic hand on Amelia's forearm, but her overarching thought was that a mother of two children going to Peru to take psychedelics was beyond irresponsible. Not to mention ludicrous.

"Have you ever done a shamanic journey?" Amelia asked suddenly. Maya shook her head. "Well, it's really not something I can explain. You just have to try it. And with the ayahuasca it's much more . . . vivid. But suffice it to say, I remembered my mother bringing me my medications in bed. Tylenol and some sort of antibiotic. And a white powder, boric acid."

Maya blinked. "Boric acid?"

Amelia stared at the empty cup between her hands. Slowly, she tightened her grip on it. "Our chef kept a box in the kitchen pantry to kill roaches. She knew it would make me sick."

Maya's eyes were wide with horror. "Your mother?"

"She told me it was good for me. I didn't know. For the longest time I thought it was like castor oil or apple cider vinegar—something that tasted gross but was healthy for you. She'd mix it into applesauce. No one else ever knew." The cup had crumpled and twisted in her hands, splitting apart at the sides.

"Amelia . . ." Maya breathed. "How long have you known?"

"It's hard to say. I always knew something had happened, but I didn't start to have flashbacks until after my mother died last year. We were estranged, mostly. But I went to the funeral and . . . I don't know, seeing her lying there brought something back to me. I just knew. I didn't know what, but I knew she'd done something to me." She finally looked up at Maya. "So you can understand why it's hard for me to trust doctors. No one ever suspected I was being poisoned."

"But why?" Maya asked. "Why would she have done that?"

"She and my father were divorced, and he never came around unless I was sick. I imagine that had something to do with it. My mother used to do things—throw herself down stairs, cut herself on purpose—for, I don't know, his attention, I guess. But after that stopped working . . . as twisted as it is, I think she thought of her and me as kind of the same person. Like hurting me was no different, in her mind, from hurting herself. There was no boundary." Amelia shook her head, as if she still couldn't believe it. "After I left home, I heard she spiraled into a pretty severe depression and was suicidal. I never went back, though. My body knew that home was where I got sick and that leaving saved me."

"Amelia, I can't even imagine."

"Who knows what kind of damage all that poison caused? It might be the reason I developed an autoimmune disorder." Amelia rubbed her forehead. "All I can do is try to be the best mother to Prem and Bodhi that I can be. To protect them. Protect their health, their well-being. You understand?"

Maya nodded. She felt raw, as if Amelia's story had turned her inside out. The thought of a mother poisoning her child for years . . . it was unfathomable, yet here Amelia sat, her childhood proof that even mothers could be monstrous.

"And it's why I feel so strongly about what we do at Eunoia," Amelia said. "Women have been passed over and patronized by Western medicine for years. We're empowering them to take control of their health, to not be passive victims of drugs and tests like I was. We're giving women options, and there's real power in that. And no, not every treatment we offer has years of science behind it, but science couldn't help me when I needed it. There's more out there than just what Western medicine has to offer, and I want women to have access to all of it."

"I understand," Maya said quietly. She meant it. She marveled at the way Amelia not only carried her past trauma but had spun it into a thriving business. She'd gathered the frayed ends of her past—the crippling illness, her mother's betrayal—and woven herself this enviable life.

Maya wondered why she, even after the passage of so many years, the countless sessions of therapy, was still so unable to move forward. Her life had stalled that night in the ER four years ago, but she felt as if she was in constant, frantic motion. As if she was running, head down, arms pumping, away from her mistake and toward absolution, but every time she looked up, she was further and further behind.

TWENTY-SIX

S he's done ayahuasca?" Dean was flossing Niam's teeth at the
sink in the bathroom that evening. "How does she know these
'memories' that suddenly came back to her weren't just hallucina-
tions?"

It was later than usual, and the kids had school in the morning.
Maya had stayed at PGH until Prem's MRI was confirmed negative
and she'd been settled into a private room for overnight observation.
She'd managed to procure, from a unit nurse with whom she was
friendly, a few blankets and a roll-away cot for Amelia, who planned
to spend the night at her daughter's side.

"What's hihooska?" Niam asked, nearly biting into Dean's finger.

"She's more of a kook than I thought," Dean said.

"Munchausen by proxy is a real psychiatric disorder, though,"
Maya said. "It could be true."

"Is that what it's called?"

Maya nodded. "Munchausen syndrome is making yourself sick
for attention. Munchausen by proxy is making someone in your care
sick."

"But her mother is dead, so there's no way to prove that what she thinks she remembers with the boric acid really happened."

"Whose mother is dead?" Diya asked, panicked, toothpaste spilling out of her mouth.

"Is it Auntie Amelia? Did her mommy died again?" Niam asked, then added enthusiastically, "You know my friend Olivia in my class? Her parents are died, too."

"They're divorced, not dead, bud," Dean said. He changed the subject, saying to Maya's reflection in the mirror above the sink, "I got a Venmo request from the new violin teacher. He's twice as expensive as the old teacher."

"He used to perform with Yo-Yo Ma," Maya said.

"What was wrong with the old teacher?"

Maya shrugged. "Nothing. This one is better."

"Maya, we have three kids. We can't spend $200 a month for one of them to take music lessons. Diya doesn't even like the violin."

"She does!" Maya said defensively.

"Can I take electric guitar lessons instead?" Diya asked from atop the toilet.

"Sure. That's much cooler," Dean said, at the same time Maya exclaimed, "No! You agreed to learn violin." She and Dean looked at each other over Niam's head. "We bought her a violin," Maya said pointedly.

"You bought her the violin," Dean corrected. "That was your idea."

This was true, but wholly irrelevant. "The violin will look better on college applications than the electric guitar."

Dean looked perplexed. "She's nine. Why are we talking about college applications?"

"We're already behind!" Maya toweled off Asha's head with frustration.

"Behind?" Dean asked. "Behind what?"

"Everyone else!" Maya handed him the naked baby and ushered Niam into the bath. "We have to be more on top of this stuff. She needs to pick a sport, and I think one of us should start volunteering at the school."

Dean had carried Asha to their bed and was fastening her into an overnight diaper. He called into the bathroom, "I thought you joined Eunoia because you wanted a less-hectic schedule. Now you want to add volunteering? And another after-school activity for Diya?"

Dean's steadfast refusal to grasp the point was exhausting. Maya sighed, and before she knew what she was saying, she'd announced, "No one gets ahead in this world by doing less, Dean."

"Or by spending less, apparently," Dean mumbled.

"What did you say?"

He poked his head back into the bathroom. "I'm just saying we've been spending more. On top of Hamilton tuition, we now have that meal kit service, the organic meat subscription, a math tutor for Niam—which, by the way, I don't think is doing him any good—and now these outrageously expensive violin lessons. We need to take a look at our budget before we end up in the hole."

"We could get rid of cable," Maya suggested. "The kids watch too much TV anyway." She realized immediately what a ridiculous suggestion this was. Without the assortment of cartoons on cable, what would occupy Niam while she tried to wash dishes and do laundry? He'd be constantly underfoot and she'd lose her mind.

"Okay, sure," Dean said. "Except we all enjoy the television. No one but you enjoys the meal kits, the math tutor, or the violin. Maybe you can just stop trying to upgrade the rest of us."

Standing in the tub while shampooing Niam's hair, Maya slowed her movements to a stop. "I'm doing what's best for our family."

"Are you guys in a fight?" Diya asked.

"No," Maya and Dean said in unison, without breaking eye contact with each other.

"Snookus, stop splashing me!" Niam said, slapping at the surface of the water with his palms. "Mommy, look, Snookus is all wet!"

Dean's voice was tired. "As long as I've known you, Maya, you've been leveling up. Or trying to. When will it be enough?"

"What are you talking about?"

"You weren't happy with PGH, you weren't happy with the kids being in public school, you've never been happy with this house, you're dissatisfied with this neighborhood, with our cars, with what I make for dinner, with the *perfectly fine* violin teacher. Is anything in our lives currently up to your standards?"

She held up her hands, and shampoo suds slid down her forearms and dripped off the points of her elbows. "That is incredibly unfair. I do so much around here."

"That's my point! No one *gets ahead* in this world? You have a successful career, and a home, and a happy family. Who are you trying to get ahead of? What do they have that you want? What *more* is there to do?"

Maya thought of her mother working weekends at Macy's and her father running the motel until his health failed. The time he'd almost been shot. She thought of golden, glowing Amelia and the way the women at Madison Smockett's birthday party grew silent with reverence at the mere mention of her name. Then she said, her voice resolute, "There's always more to do."

TWENTY-SEVEN

How are you feeling? Maya texted.

Gynecologically fine, Prem texted back, which made Maya smile. In the two weeks since Prem's discharge from the hospital, they had exchanged a handful of texts. Three dots appeared, and a moment later: I can't believe the only treatment for a concussion is "brain rest." I thought doctors were supposed to be geniuses??

Missing school already? Maya replied.

PREM: Nah. They said I can go back next week.

MAYA: That's good. How's your head?

PREM: Still hurts a little. But I get headaches a lot anyway.

MAYA: Did you see the neurologist?

PREM: Yeah. He said I have post-concussion syndrome.
Basically just a really bad concussion.

MAYA: Makes sense. He told you no screen time, right?

PREM: Yup.

MAYA: So why are you on your phone?

PREM: I'm booored. All I'm allowed to do is paint and take walks.

MAYA: Have you been sleepier than usual? That can happen after a concussion.

PREM: No. I've had insomnia for months. Worse now. Im jittery, like I had 2 much coffee. I don't even drink coffee tho.

Just then, Diya and Niam came thundering down the stairs, demanding breakfast. As she cracked and whisked eggs for an omelet, Maya considered Prem's insomnia and jitteriness. Something about the two symptoms struck her as odd. Both could be caused by a concussion, but Prem said she'd had insomnia for months. And the other complaints: numb hands and feet, trouble concentrating . . . she remembered Prem listing into the paper towel dispenser in the bathroom at the Harvest Concert. Neebles. Imbalance and slurred speech . . . Niam interrupted her thoughts by whining about wanting Lucky Charms.

"We don't have sugary cereals anymore, bud," Maya said.

"We don't have *any* cereals anymore," grumbled Dean, who'd appeared in the kitchen doorway, bleary-eyed and holding Asha like a football. "Are we out of diapers? I thought I just bought a box, but I can't find any."

"They're in the dryer," Maya said. "I just washed them."

Dean, brow furrowed, slowly blinked one eye, then the other. "You washed . . . her diapers," he repeated.

"I thought we'd give cloth diapers a try," Maya explained brightly. "I researched it online. Cloth diapers are better for her skin and better for the environment, and people say they're really easy to use once you get used to them." Dean just stared at her, so she went on. "And in the long run, they actually cost less, because you reuse them."

"How much were they?"

Maya turned the eggs in the pan. "Well, it's a whole diapering system. You have to get the actual cloth diaper itself, which you wrap around the baby, then the cotton liner to put in the diaper, then the diaper cover. And you need multiple sets, obviously. And the detergent."

"They need special detergent?"

Maya nodded. "And you can't wash the diapers with other clothes. The detergent is just for the diapers."

Dean scratched his chin. "So all together that was . . . ?"

"About $600," Maya said.

Had Asha been anything other than a baby, Dean would have dropped her. "Six hundred? For something that's going to make our lives harder? What do we do when she poops?"

Maya plated the eggs. "Oh, we have to rinse the poop off. Some people get a sprayer to attach to the toilet so you can spray the poop directly into the bowl. In the meantime, we can use a spray bottle with water. And they say to put the diaper right into the washing machine after spraying it off."

Diya turned up her nose. "Gross! Can we not talk about this while we're eating?"

"Poop in the bowl!" Niam said to no one, cackling, while Dean spiraled into panic.

"But she poops, like, four times a day!" he said. "You're telling me one of us is going to be standing over the toilet spraying poop off a diaper four times a day and then running this disgusting wet diaper down to the washing machine in the basement? Who's watching Asha while this is happening? And how often are we doing laundry?"

It was Dean's negativity, Maya decided, that was his most unattractive trait. She used to think it was his stubbornness she disliked the most, but the negativity was lately inching ahead. "It'll take a week or two for us to adjust," she said.

"I don't want to adjust!" he said, his stubbornness on full display now, like a child stamping his foot. "I just want you to tell me where the regular diapers are so I can change Asha and go to work."

Maya held out her arms. "I'll take her."

Dean hesitated, then shrugged, kissed the top of Asha's head, and handed her over.

"You'll still be able to take Niam to the pediatrician for his well visit, right?" Maya asked. "It's at 2:30. I have a patient appointment at two, and it's with Skye Hauser, so I doubt I'll get out of there in anything less than an hour. She can talk."

"I don't want to go to the doctor!" Niam squealed in protest, sounding so much like his father. Bits of egg sprayed out of his mouth.

Dean clapped him on the shoulder. "Relax, bud. It's just for a checkup."

"No shots?" Niam whimpered.

Maya shook her head. "Not this time. You got all of them last year, so you're good."

"You got all your vaccines, so now you have a superstrong—what's it called?" Dean asked, his expression goofy and expectant, like a cartoon character.

"Immune system!" Niam yelled, and Dean high-fived him.

"That's right! Immune system!" Dean said, echoing Niam's enthusiasm. "What's dad's job?"

"To learn about bibbibobbies!" Niam shouted.

"Antibodies! But that's close enough!" Dean said.

Maya changed Asha into a cloth diaper, got the older kids ready for school, then dropped off all three of them before heading to the train station to collect Esther.

Their first appointment was an annual checkup for a woman in Bryn Mawr who insisted she didn't need a Pap smear because her new $3,200 "activated charcoal-infused" vibrator was detoxifying her pelvis. After a long discussion during which the woman was surprised to learn that cervical cancer is caused by a virus, not by environmental toxins, and that no amount of vibrating charcoal would protect her from cancer or viruses or, in point of fact, toxins, she agreed to the test. When she asked Maya if she should purchase the Eunoia-recommended brand of immune-boosting vitamin supplements—at a cost of $200 per bottle and available on the Eunoia website—Maya shrugged. "Vitamins can be helpful," she said vaguely.

"Or, you know, just get Centrum for Women and save your money," Esther, who was less concerned about tactfully avoiding the implication that Eunoia was overcharging its clients, added. But their clients were not the type to buy drugstore vitamins, Esther and Maya both knew that. Their clients believed there was always something better to be had, something special and elusive and superior, something at a considerably higher price point. And whatever it was, they wanted it. Maya understood that want. She carried the want in her own bones, felt it in a way she suspected Esther, and certainly Dean, did not.

After completing their morning appointments and stopping for a quick lunch at their favorite pizzeria on Lancaster, Maya and Esther arrived at the Hauser estate just before 2:00 p.m. As usual, they were shown to the examination room in the basement of the pool house. This visit was to be their last with Skye. They'd been seeing her here at the estate every two weeks for the past two months. According to their calculations, she was now measuring about thirty-eight weeks, and the arrival of her child was imminent. Maya had arranged for her to see a local obstetrician, Dr. Liselle, who delivered babies at a posh private hospital on the Main Line that offered every maternity patient a private room and the services of a masseuse twice daily. When Skye went into labor, she would proceed to the hospital to be admitted and cared for by Dr. Liselle, but Skye was Maya's responsibility until then. She and Esther viewed this as the last length of a relay. They were about to hand the baton—the spirited Skye Hauser and her no doubt equally spirited unborn offspring—off to someone else. They were, they had admitted to each other over the pizza, relieved. And mercifully, just as Maya had predicted, Skye had dropped the idea of delivering her baby on a tropical beach. She hadn't mentioned it in several months, and she'd met with Dr. Liselle twice to review her birth plan, which included the stipulations that she not be given an epidural or an episiotomy under any circumstances and that a recording of whale sounds be played during the delivery. With any luck, her baby would arrive in two weeks, right on schedule and according to plan.

The only point of concern was that Skye's baby hadn't turned yet. Its head was still pointed up, away from the birth canal. "If the baby doesn't turn before you go into labor, you'll need to have a C-section," Maya had warned her, and Skye had laughed.

"She'll turn," she said, as if this was something with which she had extensive experience. "Mother Nature does things in her own time."

Now Skye burst into the room, her belly protruding so far out in front of her she had difficulty reaching the doorknob, and squealed, hugging Maya and Esther as if they were all three old friends who hadn't seen each other in years. Late-stage pregnancy suited her. Instead of being winded and worn down like so many other pregnant women Maya had cared for (or like Maya herself with all three of her own pregnancies), Skye was all ebullient, rosy-cheeked vitality. Like a sentient pink party balloon.

"Girls," she announced immediately, "Pack your bags! Belize is back on!"

Maya and Esther stared at her in alarm. "How do you mean?" Maya asked.

"Well, you know how I decided to have the baby here, in the hospital with Dr. Liselle, only because the midwife I wanted in Belize wasn't available?" Maya and Esther had not known this. They'd assumed Maya's lecture about the dangers of an out-of-hospital birth had convinced Skye to change her mind about Belize. "Well, she had a cancellation!" Skye continued. "And I was able to book her for the next three weeks! It's perfect timing. Everything is falling into place, just like Nan told me it would." Beaming, she rubbed her belly in appreciation. "We're taking my dad's plane, so we can leave whenever it's convenient for you two, but not later than Saturday, okay? And I'll take care of booking your flight back home. Figure you'll be gone only like forty-eight hours. I know it's last minute, but whatever childcare or whatever you need, I'll cover it. It's on me." She looked from Maya to Esther and back, taking in their stunned expressions for the first time. Then she smiled with the confident ease of someone who'd consistently been granted everything she'd ever asked for in her life. "Sound good?"

"No!" Maya said, suddenly very dizzy. "No, not good, Skye. Your baby is still breech. I can tell just by looking at you."

Skye waved away her concern. "Oh, don't worry about that. The midwife says we'll do a turning ceremony as soon as I arrive. She says it never fails."

"A turning ceremony? What even is that?" Esther asked.

"It uses sound waves and vibration to turn the baby," Skye said. "I read up on it. They beat a special type of drum and do this, like, rhythmic chanting. The midwife—Clarissa—she's an expert in it. And worst-case scenario, even if the baby doesn't turn, Clarissa has a lot of experience delivering breech babies."

Maya shook her head, the disbelief momentarily rendering her mute. She tried to collect herself. "No, Skye, listen. That is a bad idea. As your doctor, I can't allow you to put your life and your child's life at risk. If something goes wrong, it will be a disaster. You'll be in a foreign country—"

"They have hospitals in Belize, Maya!" Skye said, chucking her gently on the arm as if to suggest she needed to lighten up. "If Nan doesn't turn—as unlikely as that is—and Clarissa doesn't think she can deliver her safely, I'll check myself into a hospital. Worst-case scenario."

Maya could imagine several worst-case scenarios more dire than the one Skye was envisioning. She shook her head again.

"Skye, please listen to Dr. Rao," Esther said.

"Look." Skye had finally grown impatient. "I know you guys don't believe in natural childbirth because, you know, Western medicine and all that. But this is my body and my child, and this is the choice I've made. It's what I believe. I only need you guys for, like, six or seven hours. Just for the flight, just to satisfy my dad and stepmom that I'm not going to be alone on the plane and that I'll make it to Clarissa safely. Once we land, you won't have to worry about me anymore. You guys check into the hotel and fly home the next morning, and you never have to deal with me again. Okay?"

A pit had formed in Maya's stomach. "Skye, we care about you. We want what's best for you and the baby—"

"And I'm telling you what's best for me and the baby," Skye said, suddenly sounding less like a perky sorority sister and more like a stern college professor, the maturity in her voice taking both Maya and Esther by surprise. Maya was reminded of the conversation she'd had with Amelia in the ER waiting room. The way Amelia wanted women to have control over their bodies, the way she wanted to empower them. Skye had made up her mind.

Maya sighed quietly in resignation. "Okay," she said. "I can leave Friday."

Esther's mouth dropped open as Skye squealed and hugged them both again.

No. There is no way. What is happening?" Esther looked on the verge of hyperventilating.

"I'm not asking you to come with me," Maya said, steering the van out of the Hausers' driveway. "I'd never ask you that. But, if I'm being totally honest, I'd feel better about this if you did."

"But why? Why are we even considering this?"

"We've seen her this far. I think we, or at least I, can see her through this last bit," Maya said. "I can just get her safely where she wants to go. I owe her that much."

"No one owes her anything!" Esther cried. "This is a bad idea, you said so yourself."

"And we've given her that information," Maya shot back. "It's up to her to decide what she wants to do with it. All we can do is support her as far as we can."

"Yeah, but getting on a plane with her?" Esther said. "To Belize? I mean, you don't think that's supporting her too far?"

"She's going with or without us. She'll fly coach if she has to."

Esther sighed, admitting the truth of this.

"And, statistically speaking, she's right," Maya continued. "The baby will probably turn in time, and the midwife will probably do a fine job of delivering her. People have babies in worse situations every day."

"And women die during childbirth every day," Esther countered.

"But most of them don't."

Esther shook her head. "This is crazy. This isn't health care! This isn't medicine! What are we even doing here?"

"She needs our help," Maya said.

"Not needs. Wants. She wants our help. There's a difference," Esther said. The words, full of resentment, spilled out of her. "I don't call my doctor and ask him to do outrageous things for me just because I want them. I don't expect him to lie for me. I don't call him and ask him to write me a note to get out of gym just because I want it. That's not the world I live in."

Maya sighed. "Esther, we provide a concierge service—"

"Only to people who can pay." She shook her head again. "I don't want to be a doctor if this is what it's like. What have I been working for? I'm killing myself in school to be part of a system where some people—a LOT of people—literally die because they can't afford to see a doctor, while other people can have their doctor on speed dial and she'll come running. She'll fly to Belize."

"Esther, I know it's not fair, but—"

"Did I tell you—there's a woman with really bad asthma in my parents' building, and I'm basically her medical care right now because the first appointment she can get at the free clinic with a pulmonologist is *eight* months from now. This is happening in *my* community."

"I get it," Maya said. "I grew up brown and poor and—"

"But we're not the same," Esther said impatiently. "I'm not racially ambiguous. I can't just fit in wherever. I can't align myself with white people when it suits me and then unalign myself and say I understand the struggle. When people say you speak well, they're saying they're surprised you *speak English*. They're not saying they expected you to be *uneducated*. And I'd never drive around with a broken side-view mirror for more than six months, because it's literally a danger to my *life*. If someone in one of these fancy neighborhoods saw me driving around in this van, and they called the cops . . . This broken side-view mirror, I'm looking at it right now, and it scares me."

Shame burned Maya's cheeks. She said, under her breath, "Esther, I'm so sorry. I didn't realize."

"Because you don't have to think about it. Because we're not the same," Esther said. She slumped against her seat and sighed, spent. "I'm not holding it against you, I'm saying it's not the world I live in.

I can't do what you do, bounce between one thing, one identity, and another. I belong, forever, to the community that brought me up."

How many years had she spent, Maya wondered, trying to distance herself from the community that had brought *her* up? Trying to prove she was something other than the daughter of a motel manager and a part-time retail clerk. Something other than the child of Indian immigrants. Maya, not Mahalakshmi. She'd been running from her origin story, while Esther, who had no choice in the matter, was leaning into hers.

"I used to think medicine was my calling," Esther continued. "There need to be more Black doctors, that's what everyone says. Diversity will lead to better health care. I thought I'd be doing something important, that I'd be contributing. But what good do more Black doctors do if my parents and their neighbors can't get care when they're sick? If they're shut out of the system? I just don't see the point anymore."

They were in front of the train station. Maya pulled over, and Esther hopped out. "I'm not going," Esther said. "And I don't think you should either. We don't owe Skye anything."

"Esther, the system is unfair, you're right," Maya said. "But this is my career. You can make a different choice, but I'm a lot older than you. I've already spent my entire adult life in this career. I can't just walk away now. I want concierge medicine to work out for me. I need it to."

Esther frowned and shrugged. "Yeah, I get it. Well, good luck in Belize, then, I guess." Before she shut the car door, she said, "Just be careful, Dr. Rao."

In her broken side-view mirror, Maya watched Esther disappear down the steps to the platform, her hands thrust deep into the pockets of her jacket. A heavy weight settled in Maya's chest, the feeling of being utterly alone and the dread that she'd made a terrible mistake. Her phone rang. The voice at the other end was frantic.

"I hope you don't mind me calling you like this, but something's wrong with Prem," Amelia said. Talking fast, she explained that she'd woken up at 3:00 a.m. to find Prem wandering the house, unable to sleep. "She kept saying there were bugs crawling around in her bed, that she could feel them on her skin. And I checked her bed. I turned on all the lights and I checked every inch of it, looked for bedbugs in the corners of the mattress and everything, but there was nothing there. And I told her that. But she wouldn't get back into bed. She kept accusing me of trying to make her sleep in a bed infested with bugs, and she got so angry. She had this look on her face. Maya, it scared me. She was screaming at me. Bodhi woke up and thought she was being attacked. He came running out of his room, and Prem started screaming at him, too."

"Oh my goodness." Maya felt her palms dampen with sweat, and she tightened her grip on the phone.

"She was saying crazy things, Maya. About how we couldn't keep her locked up in the house like this. She's not locked up! She's just off school for a few weeks because of her concussion, and Greg took her car to the shop for a tune-up because she's not supposed to be driving until she's recovered anyway, so she doesn't have her car. But the way she was talking, Maya, it was like she thought she was a prisoner."

"Where is she now?" Maya asked.

"In her art studio. She's been in there all day. She's acting normal again, mostly back to herself, but she doesn't want to talk to me or Bodhi. She says her head hurts and she wants to stay in her studio and paint. She's not eating very much either, which isn't like her. We saw that neurologist you recommended—he only spent ten minutes with us, by the way—and he said she has post-concussion syndrome and she'll eventually get better, but I think she's actually getting worse. And I ran into her friends, the ones that were with her at the women's march when she fell? They said Prem had been acting off all day. They said she kept asking them questions like, 'Where are we?' and 'Who are all these people?' like she didn't know where she was. This was *before* she fell off the stairs at the library."

Maya couldn't tell what Amelia suspected. Drugs? A mental health disorder? "Do you think . . . do you think it would help for her to see a psychiatrist?"

"No! God, no," Amelia said. "They'll just want to put her on medication. That's all they do. I have personal experience with that. No, I want to get to the root of what's wrong. The source. I made her an appointment to see someone I know. A healer."

"A healer?"

"A shaman," Amelia clarified. "She's very good. I'm flying her in from California. And I know shamanism is not really something you believe in, but I'd like it if you joined us."

"If I joined you and the shaman?" Maya asked, and it sounded even more ridiculous when she said it than when Amelia did.

"I spoke to her on the phone," Amelia explained. "The shaman. And she said she thinks something is blocking Prem's feminine energy. Maybe even something from a past life. She thinks Prem has too much masculine energy—she's out of balance—and it's making her angry and irritable. It's like the yin-and-yang thing, where they have to be equal in the body. Anyway, the shaman thought it would be helpful if you, as her gynecologist, were part of the healing journey."

"I'm not sure I understand," Maya said.

"It's like meditation. Like a very deep meditation. Do you meditate, Maya? Have you ever?"

"No."

"Well, there's really nothing to it. The healer does everything. She'll explain it to you. Can you come by the house at noon tomorrow?"

"It's just . . . well, I'm not sure how helpful I'll be," Maya said, stumbling over the words. She wasn't sure how comfortable she felt participating in one of Amelia's pseudomedical treatments. For all she knew, the old man with the rain forest snakes would make an appearance, python in hand. Still, she felt a sense of protectiveness toward Prem.

"Thank you, Maya," Amelia said. "I really appreciate this. I'll pay you for your time."

"Oh, you don't have to—" Maya started to say, but Amelia interrupted her.

"I insist," she said, before hanging up.

Maya stared at her phone and gave a mirthless laugh. Of course Amelia insisted. This was what it meant to be wealthy in the way Amelia was. To make things materialize, to change reality, just by insisting. You insisted, and then it became so. Like a kind of magic, a conjuring. A power. This was, Maya realized, what she'd always wanted. It wasn't the Fendi bag. It was the ability to make it appear as if from thin air.

Growing up poor was a kind of unshakable curse. No matter how much money you eventually had—and Maya had far more than her parents ever did or ever would—you never stopped being poor. In your mind, you were permanently in a state of dearth. In your mind, in your heart, you never stopped wanting.

TWENTY-EIGHT

"What's this?" Dean asked. A glass bottle filled with translucent amber pills had arrived in the mail, decoratively wrapped in blue-and-white tissue paper and nestled within an ornate padded wooden box. "Looks like a gift. Pureganic Ancient Naturals?"

"It's fish oil," Maya said. "I ordered it from this company Amelia uses."

Dean looked at the receipt tucked into a corner of the box. "Eighty dollars for a tiny bottle of fish oil? They sell this at CVS for, like, ten bucks."

"It's organic," she said. She was busy making their latest meal kit. Tonight's recipe was taking far longer than the promised thirty minutes to prepare. "Higher potency."

"Higher potency than what?"

She absentmindedly stirred a pot of simmering jackfruit. She'd been distracted all evening, thinking about Prem. She couldn't decide if Amelia was overreacting to, or maybe exaggerating, her daughter's symptoms. On the other hand, as a mother herself, she knew better than to question a woman's maternal instinct. But Prem was a healthy young woman whose diagnostic tests so far had all come back normal. And a recent concussion could certainly cause some changes in mood. Regardless, if there was something else the matter with Prem, Maya was certain whatever it was would not be cured by a trip to a suburban shaman.

"Higher potency than what?" Dean asked again.

"What?"

"You said these pills are higher potency."

She blinked at him, only now really registering his presence in the kitchen. "They're made from mackerel. It's a better quality, purer fish oil." The older kids were watching television in the living room, and Asha was taking a nap. Maya had hoped for some uninterrupted time to cook dinner.

"So," Dean said, turning the bottle around in his hand, "are they higher potency or better quality?"

She looked at him askance. What was wrong with him? "Both, I guess," she said.

"And you know this how?" he asked.

Maya shook her head. "I don't know . . . the website. And Amelia uses them for Prem, so—"

"So you spent eight times as much on these pills because the Internet and Amelia told you to?"

Dean, she knew, had had a difficult afternoon. After leaving work early and taking Niam to the pediatrician, he'd picked up Asha from day care and was handed a plastic bag full of her soiled cloth diapers. "I was willing to try it for a day," the head teacher told Dean, "but please tell your wife to send Asha in with disposables tomorrow. We don't have the staff to be able to handle cloth diapers." The woman seemed spent and angry. Dean apologized and, while he was driving to Hamilton Hall to pick up Diya, Niam—curious about the contents of the plastic bag—tore it open and spilled the feces-covered cloths all over the back floorboard. The car, even after Dean had spent an hour cleaning it, still smelled like a toilet. So he'd left it parked in the driveway with the windows down, hoping it would air out, but it had unexpectedly started raining a short time later, and by the time he'd realized and shut the windows, the car interior was soaked. Now his beloved sedan smelled like a wet toilet. Somehow, through some immeasurable force of will and self-control and inherent good-naturedness, he'd managed to stay calm through the whole ordeal. Niam and Diya said he'd laughed the whole thing off. Now, however, he was picking a fight with her over this? Over fish oil?

"What is the big deal about these pills?" Maya asked, exasperated.

Dean sat down on a stool at the kitchen island. All he did was sit, but somehow it felt patronizing, like a father kneeling down to look his guilty child in the eye. "Since when do you buy into pseudoscience?"

"I don't."

"Then what is this? What is with you copying whatever Amelia and her rich friends are doing? Like, if you just mimic their every move, maybe you can be one of them someday? It's like you're obsessed with this woman or something."

"That's ridiculous." The pungent smell of jackfruit wafted into her face.

"The fact that you even humored Skye Hauser about Belize—"

"I'm going to Belize." She'd been planning to tell him after dinner.

"What?"

"I'm going to Belize with Skye. It's what she wants to do, and I'm supporting her, even if I don't agree with her. I'm leaving Friday, and I'll be back on Sunday. I just found out this afternoon."

Dean nodded slowly. "And you weren't going to talk that over with me first?"

"It's my practice, Dean," she snapped. "I don't need to consult with you before taking care of my patient."

Dean rubbed his face. "I can't believe I'm having this conversation with you. I don't even know who you are."

"That's a little dramatic," Maya said, gagging a bit at the smell of the jackfruit.

"You're enabling this woman to do something completely irresponsible."

She turned on him. "How am I enabling her?"

"Maya, people like Skye, they think they're special. They know women in other countries—and Black women in this country—die during childbirth on a regular basis, but they think it won't happen to them because, I don't know, the money and privilege makes them delusional. And you're validating her delusion. Don't you see that?"

"I'm not making her decisions for her, Dean. I'm acting as her physician for the flight. That's all."

"Is that what you're telling yourself? That your responsibility to Skye begins and ends with the flight? Is that even ethical?"

"Are you seriously questioning my ethics? Because being a doctor for actual breathing, thinking humans is a lot different than playing with test tubes in the lab, so you are in no position to lecture me about ethics." It was a cheap shot, and they both knew it. The argument was an old one, a greatest hit of their long relationship. Whose work was more important. Whose job was more challenging. Who should call out to watch the sick kid. Whose career mattered more and, by extension, which one of them mattered more.

Dean made some frustrated noises. Then he asked, "Are the sheets for the futon in the hall closet upstairs?"

She stared at him for a moment. She couldn't believe he'd taken it this far and, yet, somehow she'd expected it. In their marriage, one party sleeping on the wiry, ancient futon in the basement was the nuclear option. It had been vaguely threatened a few times over the years, but the last time one of them had followed through with it was nine years ago. "Yeah," she breathed, turning her face back over the pot, gagging again.

"I'll order a pizza," Dean said, before walking out of the room.

The following day, just before noon, Maya sat alone in the van, rolling one of the expensive fish oil pills between her fingers. She held the little amber capsule up to the light, turned it this way and that, as if it held some answer. She'd slipped the bottle into her purse that morning, out of a vague fear that Dean might try to mail it back for a refund when she wasn't looking. Now the thought seemed ridiculous. Yet this harmless little pill might be the thing that unraveled her marriage. She put it in her mouth and swallowed it.

When she arrived at the DeGilles estate, Blake showed her past Prem's art studio and down a sloping path. Maya gasped as another building, twice as large as the art studio, came into view. It was a delicate, conical iron structure with a spired roof, its walls made entirely of glass. It glimmered in the sunlight like a crystal champagne flute turned on end. Blake held the door open for her. "What is this?" Maya asked.

"Amelia converted the greenhouse into a meditation space," Blake explained.

Under her breath, Maya muttered, "Of course she did."

The interior was bright and airy and without furnishings. The entire floor was covered in a painting, a sprawling rendering of the Buddha in bright pastel colors. Growing up, Maya was taught reverence for the Buddha. He wasn't a Hindu god, but in India he was regarded as divine nonetheless. Her mother always found it strange that statues of the holy figure were sold at HomeGoods as garden ornaments. She would have been horrified to see him here, on the floor, reduced to the equivalent of a decorative rug. *No feet on God!* Maya imagined her saying.

Prem and Amelia were seated side by side on jewel-toned velvet floor cushions, and a sinewy, barefoot woman in her fifties with graying hair pulled back in a long braid was seated opposite them. In front of the woman was a large round drum made of what appeared to be some sort of animal hide. As Maya entered, the three women turned their heads to look at her. Six blue-gray eyes.

Prem looked exhausted and on edge, her face sallow. She wore a baggy gray sweat suit, and her hair, matted and unwashed, was held back by mismatched bobby pins. She fidgeted on the floor cushion, avoiding eye contact, folding and unfolding her long legs while picking at her chipping manicure. Amelia smiled up at Maya gratefully and mouthed *thank you.*

"Welcome," the barefoot woman said, her eyes crinkling kindly. "You must be Maya." Maya nodded stiffly, and the woman patted a floor cushion beside her. "Please come, sit. Thank you for being part of this healing journey. I'm Faye. I'm a shaman and metaphysical scientist."

"A metaphysical . . . scientist," Maya repeated, not sure she'd heard correctly.

Faye nodded, then said, "Amelia told me this is your first experience with shamanic journeying. That's perfectly okay. It's Prem's first time, too." She smiled at Prem, whose expression was anxious and distant, her eyes darting about as if she was trying to remember what she was doing here. "Shamanism is the oldest form of healing known to man," Faye continued. "Through journeying, we reach the spirit realm and ask for guidance to restore ourselves to good health."

Maya resisted the urge to roll her eyes. "The spirit realm?" she asked. Were they going to commune with ghosts? Was Faye about to produce a Ouija board?

Faye smiled again. She looked blissful, as if nothing in the world, not even a sudden windstorm that shattered all the windows of this pretentious, culturally appropriative greenhouse yoga studio, could perturb her. "In metaphysics, we believe there is another realm of reality beyond this one," Faye explained. "The unseen world, if you will. As a shaman, I will guide you there, and there you will communicate with your helping spirit, the luminous being, as we call it. We each have a helping spirit in the other realm, you see."

Maya wasn't sure she did see, but she nodded. "Okay," she said. "But how will that help Prem?"

Faye took Maya's hand in her own and, with her other hand, reached for Prem's. Faye's grip was firm and warm. "The four of us will be part of a chain of energy. With our power, we will help Prem reach the spirit realm and commune with her luminous being. There are different points of energy in our bodies, and since I suspect that Prem's female energy, her yoni, is imbalanced"—Prem blushed, but Faye didn't seem to notice—"we will use the power of our own yonis to guide her. Yours is especially strong, Maya, I'm sure, given the work you do." She looked at Maya curiously, as if reading some hidden message in the lines of her face. "It's been your life's work, hasn't it? The female energy?"

This time Maya couldn't help rolling her eyes. This new age obsession with regarding the uterus and ovaries as sacred anatomical entities imbued with some sort of divine power was as laughable as it was medieval. As if your menstrual flow had alchemic powers. As if you could insert a tampon into yourself and, a few short hours later, extract a bar of solid gold. "I just think of them as female internal organs. I'm not sure how much energy they have."

Faye squeezed her hand reassuringly. "Try to keep an open mind." She pulled the drum into her lap. "Let's close our eyes and prepare ourselves," she said. Her voice dropped an octave and slowed, and the effect was slightly comical in how dramatic it was. "Release yourself from care and allow your mind to go blank. I call on Hera, the ancient goddess of feminine energy, to help guide our journey."

Maya watched Amelia, Prem, and Faye close their eyes. Their posture shifted so that their spines were straighter, and their breathing slowed. Maya closed her own eyes and immediately wondered if she should have silenced her phone. It was in her handbag, a few feet away, and she contemplated crawling over to retrieve it, then decided that would be too disruptive. She tried to remember if she'd set the ringer to a quiet volume. Her mind drifted to the children. When was the last time she'd done their laundry? Did Niam have enough clean underwear?

"Once your mind is blank, picture yourself walking out of this beautiful space, walking out through the door," Faye said. She began to beat the drum in a slow rhythm—*dum, dum, da-da-dum*—and the sound echoed and filled the room, pulling Maya's attention back to the present, back to Faye's voice. "In front of you is an ancient forest, silent and still. You can hear birdsong. You can smell the moss on the trees."

Dum, dum, da-da-dum.

Maya could smell nothing but Faye's slightly cloying perfume, but she envisioned a forest, sun dappled and quiet, and she had to admit, it was rather nice.

Faye went on, "You enter the forest, and you find yourself before a giant tree, as wide as you are tall. This tree is ancient, its roots are miles deep, and it is nourished by the water that flows deep within the earth."

Maya pictured the tree, pictured its roots reaching into the earth, and felt oddly comforted by this image. She heard Amelia exhale a long breath.

Dum, dum, da-da-dum.

The tree was hollow, Faye explained, and in one side was an opening just tall enough for a person. "You enter the tree and follow a set of stairs down into the darkness. A cool, quiet darkness. Now you are under the earth, in a cave."

Dum, dum, da-da-dum.

Maya was aware of the hair on her arms rising as she imagined herself descending a set of spiraling stairs. The cave was dim and cold. Vines dangled from above. The ground below her was grassy and damp. Faye's voice seemed increasingly distant, and Maya was aware of being both seated next to her and, at the same time, standing in the subterranean cave. She knew if she opened her eyes the experience would be over, but she didn't want it to end, not just yet.

"This cave is the place your Akashic records are stored," Faye said. "The story of this life and your past lives. Our unresolved emotions can dwell here and make us sick. There is nothing to fear. Call for your helping spirit, reach out to it in your heart, and it will appear."

The drumming intensified and, with it, the beating of Maya's heart. A feeling like adrenaline went through her. In a corner of her mind, she registered this all as fascinating, as something she'd have to read more about later.

"There's something in the darkness, just beyond where you can see," Faye said. "A glowing shape moving toward you. It is your helping spirit in animal form. Allow it to approach, and ask it for guidance for Prem."

Maya watched in wonder as something emerged from the darkness, something about the size of a full-grown beagle. It was a tiger. A very small striped tiger. But why a tiger, of all things? She had no particular affinity for tigers. She didn't even like cats. Her initial confusion was quickly followed by amusement and a tenderness for the adorable animal. It was familiar, as if she'd seen it before somewhere, although she knew she hadn't. *Can you help me with Prem?* she asked it gamely. *I feel like I'm missing something with her.*

The creature didn't answer, but sat back on its haunches, like a dog begging for a treat. It drew its ears flat against its head and pulled apart its lips to show its sharp teeth. It was smiling. A wide, maniacal grin. It tipped its head to one side, eyes crazed and unblinking.

Frightened, Maya drew back. What was going on? The creature dropped back onto all fours. It looked sheepish, as if it hadn't meant to scare her and possibly felt a little guilty about it. Then it spoke without speaking. Maya heard the voice like a whisper in her mind, as if the sound had bypassed her ear canal entirely. *Try again.*

Try what again? she asked silently, desperate to make sense of the apparition.

Try again, the little tiger said, and it gazed at her with an adoration that felt like it would split her in two.

I don't understand. She felt herself growing panicked at her lack of control. Was this how it was supposed to work? What was this bizarre animal, and why was she seeing it?

"Maya?"

She opened her eyes. Faye, Amelia, and Prem were staring at her. "Are you okay?" Faye asked.

Maya put a hand to her face and felt dampness. "Was I crying?"

Faye smiled. "It's very normal to have that reaction. Journeying can take us back to painful memories."

Maya shook her head. "But I didn't have any memories. There was this little tiger and it smiled all weird and then it said something totally cryptic that I didn't understand." She was a little angry with Faye, as if this was all her fault, but Faye seemed delighted.

"You spoke to your spirit animal! That's wonderful," Faye said, clapping her hands together lightly, as if she were at an opera. "Did you ask it to help Prem?" Maya nodded, and Faye turned to Prem. "And you? Did you make contact with your luminous being?"

Prem shrugged. "I think so. I saw a bird. I think it was a duck?"

"Are you sure it wasn't a peacock?" Amelia asked, and Prem

shrugged again, looking bewildered. The easy confidence Prem had displayed the first few times Maya met her was gone, replaced by a twitchy nervousness that made Maya half expect her to stand up and flee at any moment.

Faye nodded solemnly. "I saw a bird, too, Prem. That's a sign of wanting to break free from a toxic energy circle. The good news is, with the help of the spirit, I extracted your negative yoni and set you free." She smiled magnanimously.

"Do you feel any different, honey?" Amelia asked, and the hopefulness in her voice was so desperate it broke Maya's heart.

Prem smiled weakly. "I think so. I think I feel better. I feel like I want to take a nap."

Faye nodded again, pleased. "That's a good sign. A negative energy extraction can leave you worn out. Take a long nap, and you'll wake up feeling rejuvenated."

The afternoon light, streaming in from all around, made Amelia glow. "Thank you so much, Faye," she said, clasping both of Faye's hands in hers. "I wish we'd done this sooner."

Maya felt disoriented as they left the meditation space together, the four of them, and walked back to the main house. Faye was chatting animatedly about past lives and the way we can carry karmic illness from one existence into the next. Maya trailed behind. Surely what had just happened, all of that drumbeating and guided imagery, had had no sanative effect on any of them. Whatever was afflicting Prem, it surely hadn't been cured by Faye's nonsensical "energy extraction." Yet something had brought Maya to tears, and she wasn't, as a rule, a crier. She tried to reach into her purse for a tissue and grabbed at empty air.

"I forgot my handbag," she said.

Amelia looked back at her. They were almost to the house. "I can have Blake go get it for you."

Maya waved away the offer. "Oh, no, it's okay. I'll just run back myself."

Amelia nodded and, as the rest of them headed on to the house, Maya walked the path back toward the yoga studio, the white pea gravel crunching under her feet. She was glad to have a moment away from the others, quiet in which to hear her own thoughts.

Random firings of the brain, she decided. The little tiger, its garish smile, its cryptic advice to "try again." It was like a waking dream and, like a dream, it had no significance or real meaning. Psychology studies had shown that people will read into an inkblot whatever it is they want to see, and this was no different. Faye wanted to see a bird, the symbol for breaking free, and so she did. Maya had probably spotted a tiger . . . where? On a box of Frosted Flakes at the grocery store earlier this week maybe, and it popped back into her head in a quiet moment, for no reason at all. She almost had the matter settled in her mind when it occurred to her again: If it meant nothing, why had it made her cry?

She was going in circles, she thought in frustration. Then she stopped on the path, looked around, and realized she was quite literally going in circles. She must have taken a wrong turn somewhere, and now she wasn't sure which direction the yoga studio was in. The path was lined on either side with tall hedgerows, like one of those garden mazes. She ducked under a trellis overgrown with vines and spotted the roof of Prem's art studio not far away. The yoga studio, she remembered, was just down a hill from there.

She glanced at her watch as she hurried down the path. The ceremony—a soul flight, Faye had called it—had lasted far longer than she'd anticipated, and she had patients to call on that afternoon. Of course Amelia would have a backyard large enough to get lost in.

The art studio's window shades were drawn, its interior dark. After a moment of hesitation, Maya tried the doorknob and found it unlocked. Glancing back toward the house—which was all but hidden behind a row of evergreens—she pushed the door open, stepped inside, and switched on the light.

Whatever was the matter with Prem, perhaps there was a clue here, in the place where she'd been spending most of her time. It was an invasion of privacy, yes, but Prem was still a child, at least until she turned eighteen in a couple of weeks. There were two types of mothers in this world: the kind that respected their children's privacy as if it was sacrosanct, and the kind that went looking for the diary and then unabashedly picked the lock on it. Maya was the latter. Her own mother had been, too, which was why Maya had never dared keep a diary. This anxiety of being found out had persisted into adulthood, and even now, she couldn't easily bring herself to write down her feelings. Her anniversary cards to Dean were always brief and unemotive: It's been ten years! Wow, nice! Love, Maya.

On an easel in the center of the room was a new portrait, one in progress: a woman, perhaps in her forties, wearing an eggplant-colored blouse. She had a round face and green eyes, but her features were hazy. There was an outline of her hair, rendered in pencil. The figure's expression made Maya chuckle: a stern gaze and a tiny, pinched mouth, as if she'd just smelled something unpleasant. Probably one of Prem's teachers, Maya guessed. One whom she didn't particularly like.

On the desk in the corner was a neatly arranged collection of pill bottles. Individual glass vials of Vitamins C, D, E, and A, turmeric, elderberry, magnesium, CoQ10, and the same brand of pricey fish oil Maya had ordered online and then hidden from Dean in her purse. In a drawer were a box of ginger tea sachets, a heating pad, and a few sealed bottles of Fiji water. In another drawer, some tubes of oil paint, the paint-splattered scissors with the sharp steel tip, and a pack of sugar-free gum. Maya wasn't sure what she had expected. Cigarettes? A joint? A hidden flask of gin? Prem appeared to be taking excellent care of herself, even if her self-care routine seemed more suited for a senior citizen than a teenager. Maya could only hope her own children would grow up to be this boring.

She shut off the light and stepped back into the garden, pulling the door closed behind her. She shook the image of the small tiger, its deranged smiling face so vivid still, from her mind. Her imagination was running away with her. Stories. Fiction. A waste of time, clearly, all of it.

TWENTY-NINE

I t was nine years ago that Maya had slept in the basement of their house. As a rule, she avoided going down there at all, if possible. Only partially finished by the home's previous owners, the basement was largely uninsulated and therefore always drafty, damp, and slightly reminiscent of a horror movie. A threadbare orange carpet over the cement floor. A single bare bulb in the middle of the drop ceiling.

Diya was a toddler. It all started when Dean said—well, if he hadn't quite said it, he'd certainly strongly implied—that Maya didn't call his mother enough. On top of everything else Maya had been dealing with at the time—she was in her last year of residency and handling day care drop-off and pickup for Diya, and she was self-administering the weekly fertility shots that would, eventually, result in her second pregnancy (one of the two that would end in miscarriage)—Dean had the gall to expect her to call his mother every Sunday and listen to the singularly self-absorbed woman talk for forty-five minutes about the Anders family farm, about chickens and feed and last season's bumper crop of asparagus. "It's just one phone call a week!" Dean had argued. "I'm not asking for much. It

would mean a lot to her." When Maya asked what Dean's mother—
or father, for that matter—had ever done for them, the argument
escalated to a shouting match about the specifics of what each of
them contributed to the household, a row about everything from
who did the laundry to who changed more diapers that, at its heart,
had nothing to do with laundry or diapers and everything to do with
the loss of the rose-colored glasses with which they used to look at
each other in their before-kids life. It ended with Maya packing her
things into a suitcase and heading for the front door. Realizing she
could never leave Diya behind, not even for a night, she walked past
the door and stomped down the basement steps, the suitcase bump-
ing behind her.

She'd slept down there, alone, for three nights. On the fourth
night, she and Dean sat at the kitchen table, Diya asleep on Dean's
shoulder, and googled "Main Line divorce attorneys." They'd taken
notes, jotted down names and phone numbers. They were being
adults about it, doing what had to be done.

But later that night, Dean had come down to the basement,
blanket and baby monitor in hand. Maya had refused to turn away
from the wall to look at him so, wordlessly, he'd curled up next to
her on the Ikea futon—their first purchase as a couple after Dean
had moved into Maya's tiny apartment in Philadelphia—covered
them both with the blanket, and held her, breathing into the space
between her shoulder blades. "I'm sorry," he said, his voice muffled
against her shirt. "I don't deserve you."

"You don't," she grumbled.

"I'm trash. I'm like the gum on the bottom of your shoe."

"Yup."

"I'm like shower mold. I'm that orange toilet ring that doesn't
come off even after scrubbing."

She chortled in spite of herself.

"I'm like a ham and cheese sandwich that got forgotten at a picnic and sat there in the ninety-degree heat for twelve hours, and now flies are laying eggs on it and—"

"Okay, you know what?" She turned to face him. "That's plenty. Yes, you are the absolute worst." Dean was never one for romantic declarations. Self-deprecating jokes were his love language, but she didn't mind. If there was a time, when she was younger, when she might have preferred an impassioned speech begging her forgiveness, something more reminiscent of a Jane Austen novel than a comedy routine, it had long passed. She'd take good-natured Dean over brooding Mr. Darcy any day.

"You do change more diapers," he'd admitted. "You do more of everything, actually. I'm sorry I let it get this far. I'll help out more. Just tell me what you want me to do. I know you shouldn't have to spell it out for me, but just get me started, okay?" He pulled her closer, and she felt a hot tear fall onto her earlobe, trickling its way into the canal. She'd never seen Dean cry before, hadn't really believed he was capable. "Please," he said.

They'd spent the rest of the night wrapped snugly around each other on the horribly uncomfortable futon mattress and, when he twisted from the bed in the morning, Dean threw his back out. He was useless for the next three days, but once he recovered, he made good on his promise. They'd been a team ever since, a domestic relay team with seamless baton handoffs. Or maybe more like a wrestling duo, outnumbered but united against their three feral offspring.

Maya stood at the top of the basement stairs now. She could hear Dean's phone. He was watching the news, as he always did before bed. She touched her toe to the first step, then drew it back. A few hours on the lumpy futon and he'd forget his anger and come back upstairs. He'd realize he'd been wrong to question her about Skye and Amelia. What right did he have to judge her? To judge her ethics? To judge her ambition? The problem with Dean was that he was perfectly content. He'd always been perfectly content, even when they lived in a shitty one-bedroom walk-up in Philadelphia with a futon for a couch. If she'd left it up to him, they'd probably still be living there now, all five of them, and he'd still wonder why she wanted more.

A voice from upstairs called, "Mommy?" It was Niam, probably out of bed and standing in the doorway of his room, based on how loud he was. "Mommy, I need a glass of water."

"There's a glass of water next to your bed," she hissed up to him, trying not to wake the other children.

"I know, but I need you to get it for me," Niam called back. "My arms are tired."

Maya went upstairs and settled him back into bed. "Can you read me a story?" he asked hopefully.

"It's way past bedtime, bud." She stroked his forehead.

"Are you really leaving tomorrow?"

She nodded.

"I don't want you to go!" He threw himself around her waist, heartsick. "Why do you have to go to Belly?"

"Belize. And I'll only be gone two days. That's so quick."

"Can I go?"

"Why would you want to go to Belize? You're going to stay here with Daddy and have spaghetti and watch movies and have a camp-out in the living room."

"With a tent and everything?" This seemed to satisfy him, at least a little, but still he demanded just one more bedtime story. "Please? Otherwise I'll have bad dreams."

He was persistent, she had to give him that. She opened *Alice in Wonderland* to the mad tea party chapter, held her phone up for the light, and continued reading where she'd left off earlier. She dropped her voice an octave for the Mad Hatter. "'Why is a raven like a writing desk?'" After denying her tea and talking in nonsensical circles, the Hatter revealed to Alice that he didn't know the answer to the riddle either, and Alice replied, "I think you might do something better with the time than waste it in asking riddles that have no answer." Maya glanced over at Niam. He was asleep. She studied the pictures in the dim light. The long, cluttered tea table, the Mad Hatter with a giant polka-dot bow tie and a towering top hat. She smiled ruefully and closed the book. So much of her life felt like that, like she was at a party where everyone else knew the rules and the logic and was having a fabulous time, while she was still trying to make sense of it all, trying to fit in. She kissed Niam's hair.

She stood to return the book to the shelf and there, on the front cover, was an animal. A little tiger. She blinked and held the book in the light from the doorway, heart racing. It was the Cheshire Cat, the wildly grinning creature, Alice's unreliable friend. The image shone in the dim light, the cat limned in black-and-gold foil. She'd loved this cover the moment she first saw it. It was the reason she'd bought the book, so many years ago. Something about the way the cat stared out at her had felt exciting, like a dare, an invitation to open the book and dive headfirst into an upside-down world.

She flipped back to the page she'd been reading and stared at the pencil drawing of the Mad Hatter. He held an overflowing teacup in one hand, blissfully unaware of his own madness. Capricious, forgetful. A riddle with no answer.

Before she could change her mind, Maya went downstairs to the computer in the dining room and sent an email to Diya's science teacher. Then she combed through her purse, dropped two of the expensive fish oil pills into an envelope, and slid the envelope into the homework folder in Diya's backpack.

The next morning, she left for the airport before dawn. She heard Dean in the basement and briefly debated going downstairs to say goodbye. Instead, she sent him a text message from the Uber. Leaving.

Safe flight, he wrote back. Text when you land. Then, a few minutes later: I still think this is a bad idea, but I love you.

She didn't reply.

Neither Maya nor the Uber driver had ever known it, but there was a small private airport not far from the bustling Philadelphia International Airport. When they arrived, they were waved into the complex by a white-gloved, stern-faced security guard. The Uber driver gave a low whistle. Gleaming white jets, maybe thirty in all, were stretched across the tarmac in two neat rows like a mouthful of shiny, jagged teeth.

Maya hadn't traveled internationally since high school, when one summer she and Dak and her parents had flown to India to visit her grandparents and extended family. It had been a long, exhausting journey on Air India in coach from Newark airport to Mumbai with multiple stopovers. An elderly woman in the seat next to Maya for the Heathrow-to-Dubai stretch had a hacking, phlegm-tinged cough and didn't cover her mouth. There weren't enough toothbrushes or blankets to go around. Someone nearby, it was impossible to tell who, suffered from a regrettable bout of flatulence after the dinner service. Once they arrived in Mumbai, the family spent several weeks shuffling from one relative's dark, airless apartment to the next. They were besieged by mosquitoes. They carried their own toilet paper. A beetle came dangerously close to crawling into Dak's ear canal while he slept. Her parents, back in their motherland after nearly twenty years away, had the time of their lives, but when they all finally deplaned in Newark a month later, it was all Maya could do to keep herself from kissing the floor of the international arrivals terminal in gratitude and relief. She'd been a reluctant traveler ever since.

Now, a cheerful attendant took her suitcase and showed her to the Hauser family's plane, and she climbed aboard with a sense of both wonder and trepidation. As she entered the cabin, a phone camera clicked. Esther was taking a selfie in front of one of the wood-trimmed oval windows.

"Esther? What are you doing here?"

"The estate manager sent me an email. She said the plane was taking off at six and to be here early." She looked around the empty plane. "I'm always too early for everything."

Maya shook her head. "No, I mean, I thought you weren't coming."

Esther shrugged. "I still don't think we owe Skye anything, but . . . I've seen *you* this far, I figure I can see you through this last bit. Plus, I managed to score some supplies I thought we might need." She unzipped a large suitcase to reveal a well-organized cache of medical supplies. She said proudly, "IV bags, Pitocin, suture kits, suction bulbs, warming blankets, you name it. We're traveling with a mini hospital here. The only thing we don't have is blood, but hopefully Skye doesn't need a transfusion on the way to Belize." She whispered to herself, "Lord, Jesus."

Maya's eyes went wide. "Where did you get all that stuff? And on such short notice?" She'd packed some supplies in a suitcase, too, but Esther's bag was far better stocked.

"My aunt works in the supply department at Temple. She hooked us up. We just have to return whatever we don't use, which is hopefully all of it, but I wanted us to be prepared."

"Esther, thank you." Maya blinked back tears. The fight with Dean had left her raw, and this unexpected loyalty from Esther threatened to crack her in half. "Really."

Esther smiled. "We've been through a lot together, Doc. And you know I'm expecting the *most* glowing med school recommendation letter, right?"

Maya laughed. "It's going to be the best recommendation letter anyone's ever seen. Promise."

A flight attendant in a trim black skirt suit appeared with two cups of coffee on a tray. Maya and Esther gratefully accepted them.

"I've never been out of the country, so I'm kind of excited, to tell the truth." Esther sipped her coffee. "My aunt said if I didn't go with you, she would. I'm glad I keep my passport up-to-date, just in case. Damn, even Skye's coffee is better than regular-people coffee."

They each had several cups of coffee, followed by a selection of gourmet pastries. By the time Skye finally arrived, late as usual, on this occasion by a full ninety minutes and with her stoned-looking boyfriend in tow, Maya and Esther were on edge, filled with caffeinated, sugar-infused adrenaline. Maya immediately examined Skye's belly, placing her hands on it before Skye had a chance to shrug out of her jacket. The baby was still breech, and Skye, as ever, was unconcerned. "Relax and enjoy the flight, Maya!" she said. "Champagne?" Maya declined on the grounds that she was working and it was 7:00 in the morning. Skye told her she needed to loosen up and "reject time as a man-made construct." As the plane took to the air, Maya leaned her head back against her seat and breathed, reassuring herself that everything was going to be fine.

THIRTY

Skye Hauser had flown on a commercial airline once, to Italy over spring break in third grade when her family's private jet was being refitted with new seats. Andrea Bocelli was performing in the open air in a courtyard in Portofino, and the Hauser family wouldn't have missed it for anything, arduous travel be damned.

"This was years before my parents split, before my dad ran for office," Skye explained as the plane reached cruising altitude. "It was so funny: there were so many of us—five kids, two parents, our nanny, and my dad's secretary, who, now that I think about it, I'm pretty sure he was having an affair with, but whatever—that we took up, like, the entire first-class section. We ran the poor flight attendants off their feet!"

Esther slowly turned the pages of a magazine. "So funny."

"They played I Spy and Twenty Questions with us for, like, six hours straight. One of them brought us warm chocolate chip cookies. I still remember them." Wistfully, she gazed out the window at the passing clouds. "Not their names, obviously, but I remember their kind spirits."

Esther raised the magazine until her face disappeared from view.

Skye shifted her weight and winced. Seated across from her, Maya folded the medical journal she was reading and asked, "Everything okay?"

Skye nodded, then said reverently, "Pregnancy is amazing. I mean, there are so many things happening in my body that I didn't expect. Like the hemorrhoids. I was *not* expecting the hemorrhoids. And they're so painful! But, like, when else in your life will you be able to feel your own anus? It's a miracle. I'm so aware of parts of my body that I never paid attention to before, you know?"

In the seat next to Skye, her boyfriend, a lanky stick insect of a man with a goatee and the remnants of an angry sunburn over his pale cheeks, glanced up from the copy of *Infinite Jest* he'd been reading. "Pain is nature's gift," he said, before returning to his book.

"Exactly, my love." Skye tenderly stroked his arm, and he smiled at her.

"So, how did you guys meet?" Maya asked, desperate to steer the conversation away from the exaltation of anuses.

Skye was delighted to share the story. She and Asher had met on his father's yacht in the Mediterranean a year ago. A charity fundraising concert at sea for leopard seals—or maybe it was sea lions; neither of them quite recalled the details because they had both been fairly high at the time—and were drawn to each other immediately.

"It was, like, even before I first saw him, I sensed his presence," Skye said. "We were like yin and yang, like opposite energies searching for each other, like two spiritual magnets being pulled together from completely different worlds, from completely different ends of the . . ."

"Yacht?" Esther said, at the same time Skye said, "universe."

Asher draped an arm around Skye's shoulders and looked out the window. "My band was performing."

"Oh?" Maya said, gamely trying to make conversation. "My brother's a musician. He plays the guitar in a band."

Asher looked unimpressed. "I play experimental world music. Mostly didgeridoo. Some lute. I'm a multi-instrumentalist."

"He also writes poetry," Skye said proudly.

"About what?" Esther asked Asher, her face fixed in a scowl, her jaw methodically working a piece of gum.

Asher gave a half laugh and returned Esther's scowl. "The spoken word as a weapon to dismantle capitalism. The power of verse to SUBVERT, the systems that keep us enslaved, the systems that make us ENRAGED, the democracies and their HYPOCRACIES and their MONOPOLIES that make us all sleepy sheep. That make us all sleepy SHEEP." He signaled the end of his performance by looking broodingly out the window again.

"Isn't he amazing?" Skye said, beaming. Maya raised her eyebrows and nodded, then returned to her medical journal.

"I mean. Wow." Esther's tone was sweetly earnest. "That's a really powerful piece about the evils of capitalism. Did you write that on your dad's yacht?"

Asher narrowed his eyes at Esther as Skye enthused, "Oh, he just comes up with stuff like that on the spot, off the top of his head. My love, what's that line you came up with that one time? You're the why to my who?"

Asher rubbed his temples, as if her misquotation physically pained him. "You're the *what* to my *why*, I'm the stars to your Skye," he corrected.

Skye clapped her hands with delight. "If we ever decide to get married, I will have that engraved on our wedding bands—*I'm the stars to your Skye.* How romantic is that?" she said. She squirmed in her seat. "Ow. Fuck!"

Maya looked up in concern. "Are you okay?"

"The hemorrhoids again," Skye grumbled, crossing and uncrossing her legs.

"She's fine." Asher laid his hand on Skye's arm protectively. "She doesn't require any 'medical attention,' thanks." He made air quotation marks with the fingers of one hand.

Maya blinked. "I didn't think she did. But for the duration of this flight, she is my patient."

Skye folded her jacket into a cushioning square and sat on it.

"Well, childbirth is a natural process, so I don't see why you're here at all," Asher said.

"My father insisted, Ash," Skye reminded him gently.

Asher kept his gaze fixed on Maya and Esther. "That's not what I mean. I mean I don't see why you guys even exist. Like, what's your purpose?"

"Our purpose?" Esther raised her eyebrows. "We keep women from dying during childbirth. What's your purpose?"

Asher scoffed. It was a throaty sound reminiscent of a dog barking. "You mean you medicalize a natural process, dope women up on drugs to keep them from fully experiencing the most important moment in their lives, for profit."

Esther looked close to lunging out of her seat.

"It may surprise you to know," Maya said, wishing she could fire darts out of her eyes, "that the birthing of children is not the most important moment of many women's lives. I, for example, consider my medical school graduation the most important moment of my life. The birth of my children, I just wanted that to be over with as soon as possible, and as safely as possible."

Asher scoffed again. "Well then, I feel sorry for you. I really do. Because you missed the single most transcendent experience a woman can have."

Esther laughed. "Transcendent? Have you ever had a kidney stone? Childbirth is more painful than passing a kidney stone, and let me tell you, I've seen grown men curled up in the fetal position crying for pain meds in the ER because of a tiny kidney stone. None of them were having a transcendent experience."

"Childbirth isn't painful for women!" Asher cried incredulously, as if he couldn't believe he had to explain such basic biology to them. "The media and pharmaceutical companies gaslight them and tell them it has to be, but it's not naturally painful."

Esther shook her head. "My dude, are you seriously trying to mansplain childbirth to us?"

"Who wants tea?" Skye interrupted cheerily. She waved to an attendant, and a tray of fragrant herbal tea appeared.

Maya cradled a teacup between her hands and, after a moment, said carefully, "Skye, I've been doing some research, and there are several excellent obstetricians in Punta Gorda."

Skye's smile was placid. "Okay."

"We could arrange a consultation once we arrive. Esther and I can go with you."

"That won't be necessary. Besides, we won't have time," Asher said. He sipped his tea loudly. "After we arrive, we're scheduled for a womb blessing."

"We're having a medicine man from one of the local indigenous tribes officiate it for us," Skye added.

Esther pinched the bridge of her nose. "Sorry, what's a womb blessing?"

"We sit in silence on the beach and pay homage to the spirits of the tides that will pull the baby from my womb," Skye said. "It's going to be beautiful. Then Clarissa, my midwife, is going to turn the baby."

Maya nodded, trying unsuccessfully to relax the muscles in her face. "Okay, sure. With the sound waves and the chanting. But what if that doesn't work? You should see an OB just in case. In case the baby stays breech and you need a C-section."

"You mean in case they want to cut the baby out of her?" Asher's jaw went slack. "Yeah, no thanks. Although I'm sure those doctors would love to make some money, there's no way we're letting that happen to Skye or our baby."

Maya briefly considered the repercussions of flinging her hot tea at him.

"The baby isn't going to stay breech, don't worry," Skye said. "She told me—"

"Oh, that's right, her grandma told her," Esther mumbled under her breath.

"And babies can be delivered naturally, even if they're breech," Asher said. "We've done our research, so you can save your fear-mongering."

Maya ignored him. "Skye, yes, breech babies can be delivered vaginally, but there are risks, serious ones, and I—"

"Doc, no offense, but I was hoping this flight would be a chance for me to relax and center myself," Skye said, smiling wanly, as if Maya were a bothersome but lovable child tugging at her sleeve. "Clarissa has a ton of experience with breech babies. She's delivered them naturally before. But after our Zoom consultation, she said she was sure the baby would turn before the dawn of my birthing."

Maya coughed. "The dawn . . . of your birthing?" She wiped a drop of tea off her chin.

"Clarissa doesn't use the word 'labor,'" Skye explained. "It makes a natural process seem like this burden, like work, you know? She likes to think of birth as a beginning, a transition from darkness into life. A dawning. Isn't that beautiful?"

"I'm going to play my didgeridoo during her contractions," Asher said proudly. "The sound vibrations help ease the baby out of the womb naturally."

Maya and Esther exchanged a glance.

"This midwife, you know her well?" Maya asked, suddenly a little nauseous.

"Clarissa?" Skye took a long sip of her tea. "I've followed her on Instagram for years. She's wonderful. I've read everything she's written, and her energy just totally meshes with mine. The baby really likes her, too."

"But you trust her?"

Skye rubbed her belly. "Of course. All three of us do." She gave Maya a kind, pitying look. "This seems to be causing you tension. I'm sorry. It's probably your Western medical training—you doctors are all so blocked in terms of your mindset."

Asher scoffed, this time to signal his agreement.

"But it's not your fault," Skye added. "Have either of you been to Belize before?" The two women shook their heads, and Skye clapped her hands in delight as if she hadn't already known this information. "You're going to love it. Try to relax and enjoy the flight. Everything's going to be great, you'll see."

The attendant brought out scones with rose petal jam on a silver tray, and Maya, Esther, and Asher settled into an uncomfortable silence as Skye closed her eyes, her face taking on an expression of peaceful transcendence.

THIRTY-ONE

As they touched down in Punta Gorda, Maya exhaled in relief. Skye had not gone into labor during the flight, and neither she nor Esther had physically assaulted Asher. Mission accomplished.

A limousine whisked the four of them down dusty roads and past ramshackle roadside fruit stands to a luxury beachfront resort. The long, brick-paved drive was lined with palms and fragrant plumeria and, in the open-air lobby, black volcanic rock steps led down to a serene reflecting pool dotted with pink and white lotus flowers. The turquoise ocean winked just beyond the solid marble check-in desk. As the driver unloaded Maya's and Esther's luggage, the two women climbed out of the car and gaped.

"Told you it was beautiful here," Skye said, pleased with herself. "Wait until you see the infinity pool." She draped an arm out the car window. Next to her, Asher was playing Candy Crush on his phone.

"Skye, this is too much," Maya protested. "We could have stayed somewhere else."

Skye waved her off. "It's the least I could do! You two have been great through this whole pregnancy. It's just my little way of saying thank you."

Asher leaned over her. "Just try not to run up the minibar tab. I know all about how you doctors like your freebies." His didgeridoo stretched from the trunk of the limo, through an opening in one of the seats, across the passenger section, and into the privacy window. The mouthpiece of it sat somewhere behind the driver's right shoulder.

A valet appeared with a tray bearing two elegant glasses of something pink garnished with pineapple. He introduced himself as Hector, took Maya's and Esther's names, and checked them in.

Asher grinned at Hector. "Buenos días!" He said, his put-on accent so cringingly bad Maya almost felt sorry for him. "Take muchos buenos care of my amigos here, okay, jefe?"

"Of course, sir. We strive for every guest to have the most enjoyable stay possible," Hector said in perfect English.

Skye grabbed Maya's hand. "Thanks, Doc! Thanks, Esther! Told you everything would be fine!"

Maya started to protest but stopped herself. Her work was done. She'd seen Skye safely to Belize, and tomorrow she and Esther would fly back home, as planned.

The driver and Hector exchanged several friendly words, the latter clapping the former on the back appreciatively as he climbed back into the driver's seat.

Skye said buoyantly, "Can't wait to introduce you both to Horizon!"

"You decided on a name?" Maya asked as Skye motioned to the driver.

"The baby decided!" Skye said. "Her head will be traveling toward the horizon as she enters this world, since I'll be facing the ocean."

"What if you go into labor—I mean, the dawn of your birthing—overnight?" Maya asked. "You won't be out on the beach in the dark, will you?"

"Don't worry. I have a birthing yurt!" Skye called, waving good-bye as the car pulled away. Maya watched them disappear down the long drive, mute with disbelief. It was like Skye existed on an entirely different plane of reality from anyone she'd ever met, except possibly Amelia. As if the rules of the universe, gravity itself, bent for people like them.

An hour later, after settling into their adjoining suites, Maya and Esther sat on towel-draped lounge chairs overlooking a glittering infinity pool, sipping daiquiris. They were miserable.

"Think she'll die?" Esther asked finally, after they'd been sitting in silence for what seemed like a long time. "Or the baby?"

Maya stared out at the ocean in the distance. "I mean . . . probably not."

Her phone buzzed. She'd texted Dean to let him know she'd arrived safely and, in return, he'd sent a picture of himself and the kids eating spaghetti at the dining table. She'd almost forgotten they owned a dining table. Dean had cleared away all the papers and toys usually piled on it, and the four of them were sitting down to a meal together, Niam and Asha with sauce all over their faces and Diya, notably, without a book. Apparently, the house ran more smoothly when Maya wasn't there.

She and Esther were scheduled to fly back to Philadelphia—via a commercial airline, not Skye's father's jet—the following afternoon. After spending the remainder of the day near the pool, they went to dinner together at the hotel restaurant, drank too much red wine, and fell asleep in their respective four-poster beds. As she sank into the plush bedding, Maya tried to recall the last time she'd slept without a child under one arm, kneading her elbow skin or kicking her from the inside or out. When was the last time she'd slept without Dean snoring in her ear? The valet had left the French doors to the balcony open, and the ocean sparkled in the moonlight. The salty breeze billowed the bed curtains like sails. She imagined herself floating away on the pillows, whisked out to sea, to sleep.

In a dream, she descended the volcanic stone steps in the hotel lobby, looking for Niam, and found herself in a crowded suburban shopping mall. She went frantically from store to store with Asha on her hip, asking if anyone had seen her son, pleading with whomever she passed to call the police, to call mall security, to tell whoever was in charge to lock down the building. But no one she spoke to responded to her at all. A woman in Bed Bath & Beyond told her to stop shouting. "You're getting hysterical," she observed coolly. Finally, Maya stood in the middle of the food court and screamed, again and again, "My son is missing! My son is missing!" while disinterested passersby weaved around her. She cried in frustration at her powerlessness, and the tears stung her eyes as if they were acid.

She awoke to sweat dripping from her forehead into her eyes, her heart pounding. The sun was high, and a chorus of insects buzzed outside. A text from Dean read All good here. How's Belize? He'd sent a picture of the three kids eating French toast at the breakfast table. Now he was just showing off.

She texted back: Haven't seen much of it. But the hotel is really nice. Will text when I board the plane later today. Then she took a quick shower in the marble-tiled bathroom, got dressed, and hurried downstairs to breakfast.

She'd just accepted a glass of orange juice and a menu from the waiter when Esther appeared, bleary-eyed, T-shirt and shorts rumpled, as if she'd just rolled out of bed. She pushed past the host and charged toward Maya, dragging the huge suitcase of medical supplies behind her. "We have a problem." She threw herself into the seat across from Maya, clearly hungover, and drained the glass of orange juice in one long swallow. Then she continued, after a deep breath, "I got curious, so I found Skye's midwife on Instagram this morning." She handed over her phone, and Maya scrolled through the social media page of Clarissa LaRue, Spiritual Midwife, Karmic Counselor, and Zumba Instructor located in San Ignacio, Belize. She was a young, blond, sun-kissed, and freckled woman with dreadlocks who looked like she'd be more comfortable playing beach volleyball than coaching women through labor and delivery. Her feed was filled with photographs of her on seemingly deserted beaches, often mid–yoga pose, as well as shots of her with her clients—smiling, enormously pregnant women with whom she posed with one hand resting on their bellies and a blissful, knowing expression on her face.

Her website listed a menu of services, including a "drum circle karmic cleansing" that could be conducted via Zoom if necessary. Maya clicked on "Belize Ocean-Blessed Birth Package" and scrolled past a photograph of a highly tanned pregnant woman floating on her back in the ocean, her torso supported by a man in swim trunks and sunglasses, Clarissa in a bikini standing between her legs. The next photograph was of a sea turtle swimming underwater past coral. In the final photograph of the series, Clarissa was holding a naked infant, and the pregnant tan woman was holding her bleeding placenta, both women in the water up to their waists. They smiled triumphantly at the camera. The caption read: "Since life itself began in the ocean, an ocean birth is the most natural and gentle way to welcome your baby into the world. Many people don't realize that salt water exactly mimics the water inside a woman's womb in terms of pH and mineral composition. When the baby leaves your body, it transitions to the air via the seawater, thereby easing psychic birth trauma. Call or email for custom birth plan pricing."

A bowl of oatmeal sat on the table in front of Maya, steam rising off its surface and curling into the air. She had no recollection of it arriving, nor of ordering it. She pushed the bowl away. "Wait. Is Skye planning to deliver her baby *into the ocean*?"

Esther began distractedly eating Maya's oatmeal. "I don't know! I mean . . . it's the kind of crazy shit she would do, right? And Skye said this spiritual midwife lady had tons of experience, but she looks like she can't be over, what? Twenty-five? How much experience could she possibly have?"

"She's going to try to deliver a breech baby into the ocean," Maya whispered, afraid to say the words too loudly lest, like a curse, they come to pass. She looked again at the profile picture of smiling, carefree Clarissa LaRue. "Son of a bitch."

Maya, Maya, please calm down. You're getting hysterical, my goodness." From her bedroom window, Amelia had a view of Prem's art studio. She could see the top of her daughter's head, bent over yet another canvas. What was she painting so feverishly in there? She'd have to ask Prem later. "Take a cleansing breath and start again," Amelia suggested. "I want to hear what you're saying, but you're talking too fast."

The doctor started again. Amelia had understood her the first time, but she used the stalling technique to give herself a chance to formulate a response. Her ex-husband had taught her that, one of his negotiating techniques. Once again, the doctor explained that their client, Skye Hauser, Congressman Hauser's daughter, was planning to birth her child not on the beach in Belize, but into the ocean. A seawater birth, which was something Amelia had heard of but had never known anyone to actually do. Amelia didn't know Skye, but she was well acquainted with the congressman. Greg, over Amelia's objections, had contributed to his reelection campaign. The Hausers, she knew with certainty, were a very private family.

Skye had contacted Eunoia, but the congressman had paid the fee for their services. This was how he, a conservative Christian Republican, ensured control over his daughter, over her body. Thinking of this, Amelia felt her pulse start to race, and she closed her eyes and tapped the center of her forehead with her index finger several times to steady herself.

"She's not answering her phone. And the baby, as far as anyone knows, is still in breech position," Maya Rao said, concluding her remarks for the second time. "I need to get to her and talk her out of this insane plan. She and the baby could die. I need you to contact her father or stepmother and get me a phone number and an address for where she's staying, immediately."

"I completely understand your concerns, Maya," Amelia said, her tone soothing. "But we have to respect the wishes of our client. Skye is making an informed choice about what birth plan is best for her, and at Eunoia we look at it as our duty to support her. Sometimes the best thing we can do is take a step back and let the client honor herself." What time must it be in Belize? It was probably very early in the morning. Amelia felt sorry for Maya Rao, jet-lagged and overwrought.

"I don't think you understand," the doctor said, a little breathless now. "This is a matter of life and death. What Skye is planning to do—what I think she's planning to do—is incredibly reckless and dangerous."

"That's just it, isn't it?" Amelia said. "You don't know what she's planning to do. She hasn't told you or us. All we know for sure is that she expressly asked for her privacy to be protected. We have to—we must—honor that."

Maya Rao made a frustrated sound. "And if her baby dies? If she dies?"

First of all, no one really died. Their energy passed from one form to another. But a discussion of the metaphysical was beyond the doctor, clearly. "All births are risky," Amelia said. "Nothing can be sure, except that a woman should be trusted to know her own body. Give Skye the space to listen to her own body, Maya. Can you do that?"

There was a long silence.

"Because if you can't . . . I'm not sure you're as good a fit for Eunoia as I thought you were."

"I see," said Maya Rao, her tone a bit flinty.

"I understand this is hard for you," Amelia said, "given how you're used to practicing. It's how you were trained. To center yourself as the healer. To center *your* needs. But in time, you'll get used to centering the client. You've made so much progress so far. Keep it up."

There was the sound of scuffling in the background, and then another, younger, woman's voice on the line. "Hi, ma'am? You don't know me, but my name is Esther Bernard, and I'm going to have to insist you give us that information, or you're going to be in serious legal jeopardy."

"Are you a lawyer?"

There was a pause on the other end. Then Esther Bernard said, not at all convincingly, "Yes, I am."

"My ex-husband is a lawyer, too," Amelia said. "Perhaps I should give the phone to him and let you two discuss your intent to pursue legal action? He's right here."

"Um . . . no, no, that won't be necessary. If you could just get us the address where Skye is staying—"

"I'm hanging up now," Amelia said. "Tell Maya that I know she'll do the right thing and respect Skye's wishes to not be disturbed."

Amelia hung up, closed her eyes, and breathed deeply. She was grateful she was alone in the house. Greg had taken Bodhi to fencing practice. She fixed herself a gin and tonic. She normally avoided alcohol for the sake of her health, but she'd read somewhere that an ounce of gin a week was sanative. Something about adaptogens in the juniper. She tugged a pack of cigarettes from its hiding place in the liquor cabinet and shook one loose. She normally didn't smoke, either—it had been ages since her last cigarette—but felt the need to urgently now. Had she been wrong about Maya Rao? Amelia preferred to associate herself, in business and in life, with a certain type of person. She had an eye for picking them out of a crowd. They were the rabbits, the elks, the porcupines. The quieter, meeker sort, malleable in personality. Not self-conscious, but lacking in a certain type of conviction. And always, always a little hungry. The hunger was the most important part; it kept them close and loyal. Amelia had noticed it in Maya immediately. The yearning to be heard, to command respect. The yearning to matter. The wanting was an asset, yes. It produced a particularly focused ambition. But it was also a point of control. If you wanted something badly enough and you believed Amelia could give it to you, there was nothing you wouldn't do for her. Was there a limit to Maya Rao's loyalty? No, Amelia thought, filling her lungs with smoke. Some cravings were unshakable, bone deep, in the DNA. Some lives, smaller ones, were made of nothing but pure, unmitigated need.

They found Hector in the lobby, pushing a luggage trolley, and cornered him.

"You need a car, miss? I can call one for you."

Maya shook her head. "We need the driver. The one that brought us here."

"You're friends with him," Esther added, somewhat accusatorily.

Hector looked puzzled. "You left something in the car?"

"No, Hector," Maya said urgently. "I need you to call the same driver we had yesterday. We saw you talking to him. You must know his name."

"I meet many drivers every day, miss."

"We need him to help us find someone, the woman who was in

the car with us yesterday." Maya shook her head in frustration. She knew she must sound unhinged. "A hippie pregnant woman and her lunatic musician boyfriend." She pinched the bridge of her nose. "You know what, never mind."

As she turned away, Hector said, "Mr. Asher?"

A few minutes later, they were speeding along a manicured path on the resort property, Hector steering the clunky golf cart around curves like a downhill skier maneuvering around racing flags. This whole time, Skye had been less than a mile away, in one of the resort's own luxury villa residences. Apparently, Asher had stopped by the hotel bar late last night and treated all the patrons to a round of drinks to celebrate the fact that his girlfriend's water had just broken. Before taking his leave an hour later, he'd given a triumphant trill on the tiny flute he carried in his back pocket. In describing him, Hector had vigorously rubbed his thumb and index finger together in a gesture Maya interpreted to mean that he either ran up quite a tab at the bar or was notably high. She didn't bother getting clarification on which.

If what Asher had claimed about Skye's water breaking was true, Skye had now been in labor for over twelve hours. Like a reflex, Maya's mind shifted into crisis-management mode. Years of practicing obstetrics on the ward had made her chronically anxious, yes, but also primed for emergencies. Silently, she ran through all the possible scenarios that might await them: the baby had turned and had been, or would soon be, successfully delivered (possibly into the ocean); the baby had not turned and Skye was still in labor; both Skye and Asher had drowned; only Asher had drowned and the baby and Skye were perfectly well (better off, in fact).

The villa, a white palace on the sea, was set at the bottom of a long, narrow road overrun with vines. "This is as far as we can go," Hector said, taking the golf cart as close to the end of the path as he could. As they bumped closer, all three of them heard the screams.

THIRTY-TWO

Maya didn't remember leaping from the still-moving golf cart, but she must have, and lost her flip-flops in the process, because now she was running, scrabbling over vines in her bare feet, down the path to the house. She could hear Esther behind her, cursing as the wheels of the medical supply bag caught and tangled in the brush.

The villa was massive, and the screaming sounded far away, impossible to pinpoint. "Skye?" Maya yelled. "Skye?"

An otherworldly sound rose from the direction of the beach. It was deep and resonant, like the call of a moose but more robotic in quality. Maya stopped short on the path. "What was that?"

Esther and Hector, carrying the bag between them, caught up to her. "Fucking didgeridoo!" Esther panted, and the three of them ran toward the beach.

Clarissa LaRue was half dragging Skye out of the water while Asher, who had abandoned his didgeridoo in the sand, complained, "But why? I thought you said it was time? Why is she getting out of the water?"

Skye screamed again.

"You're okay, babe. Childbirth isn't painful," Asher soothed, stroking her hair. "Want me to play the 'doo again?"

"Get the fuck away from me!" Skye, naked and trembling, swung one arm at him wildly and missed.

"Skye!" As Maya sprinted across the sand, she noticed the blood streaming down Skye's legs and was aware of a primal urge to tackle Clarissa LaRue. "What did you do?" she demanded, gasping for breath.

Clarissa LaRue looked offended. "Who are you?"

"She's my doctor!" Skye said, reaching for Maya's hand.

"What did you do?" Maya asked again, and as the two of them carried Skye into the luxuriously appointed birthing yurt that smelled of incense and laid her on the low platform bed covered in flower petals, Clarissa tried to explain.

Skye had been having contractions, irregular ones, and was only a few centimeters dilated as of the previous evening. "She was uncomfortable, so I thought I'd speed up the dilation by releasing the fluid sac," Clarissa said. Maya gaped at her, stunned, and Clarissa added hurriedly, "I've done it before. It's an ancient midwifery technique. I puncture the amniotic fluid sac around the baby. I have a special hook I use for it, made of wood from a Balinese tree and blessed by a dolphin."

"We know what rupturing membranes is," Esther, who hadn't bothered introducing herself, said angrily. She was starting an IV on Skye.

"She doesn't want that! Take that needle out of her arm!" Asher said. Esther ignored him.

"You ruptured membranes on a breech?" Maya's voice caught in her throat. "When?"

"She's not breech. I turned her," Clarissa said defensively. "The baby's head is right at the cervix. I felt it myself." Not only had the turning ceremony gone beautifully, she explained, but she'd further confirmed the head-down position of the baby with a moonstone. She'd dangled the crystal from a string in front of Skye's belly, and it had clearly turned clockwise. "And then I *released* the fluid sac, yes. Last night. I don't use the word 'rupture.' I don't understand why medical terms have to all be so violent, especially when it comes to women's bodies."

Skye screamed again, a contraction taking hold.

"She does seem to be bleeding a lot more than I expected, though," Clarissa said, nervously petting Skye's hair.

Maya put two gloved fingers into Skye's vagina and immediately withdrew them. "It's a foot. That's not a head, it's a foot. And it's stuck."

"Fuck me," Esther whispered.

"But . . . that's not possible. I turned her," Clarissa said.

"Go call an ambulance!" Maya commanded, placing a stethoscope on Skye's belly.

"But I—" Clarissa began.

"Now! Go!" Maya and Esther shouted in unison.

Clarissa nodded and wordlessly fled from the yurt, scrambling up the beach toward the house.

There was still a heartbeat, but it was faint. Maya pulled the stethoscope out of her ears. She placed her hands on Skye's belly and pushed. Skye's scream split the air in two. The baby didn't budge.

Again Maya pushed, and Skye screamed. She tried again and again, every technique she'd learned during her training. The baby wriggled under her hands, but it did not move.

"Is there anything else we can do?" Esther said, panic rising in her voice.

"Skye? How long have you been bleeding?" Maya asked.

Skye moaned. "Awhile."

"Exactly how long?" Maya demanded. She turned to Asher, who had gone boneless at the sight of the blood soaking the mattress and now crouched in a corner of the yurt.

"Should she be bleeding that much? Is that normal?" He pointed. "Should you guys be pushing on her like that?"

Maya grunted in frustration. "Hector! Did you get a car yet?"

Hector, who had been trying to reach the resort on his walkie-talkie, shouted from the beach, "No one is answering, miss! No signal out here! I will go get a car myself! I will run!"

It would take too long. It would all take too long. Just like years ago, in the emergency room. She had been too late. She'd done the C-section too late and the baby had died.

"What's happening?" Skye's voice was a whisper, then louder. "Tell me what's happening, Maya!"

Maya's mouth was dry, and the words stuck to her teeth. She spat them out in a gasp. "Skye, the baby's not going to make it."

"That can't be," Skye said.

"There isn't anything we can do," Maya said. "It's stuck, and I can't get it to move. It's sitting on the umbilical cord, cutting off its own blood supply."

"The ambulance—" Skye started.

"We only have a few minutes. They're not going to make it." She was cool, clinical, stating the facts. She was aware of a firestorm of emotions behind her sternum, but they were safely contained there, deep in her body where they couldn't cloud her thinking.

Skye seized Maya's hand, digging her nails into the flesh. "That can't be. Cut her out."

"I don't have anesthesia. And there's no way to control the bleeding. I could kill you. I would, in all probability, kill you."

Skye tightened her grip on Maya's hand. Her eyes had gone glassy, but her voice was clear, even through gritted teeth. "Cut. Her.

Out. Do it now." She met Maya's stunned gaze, unblinking. She knew what she was asking.

"Skye, are you sure?"

Skye nodded. "Do whatever you have to. Please just save her."

Maya looked at Esther, and Esther's eyes went wide. "We're doing this?"

Maya nodded, her jaw set. "I need Betadine, a scalpel, and something to use as a retractor," she said. "And get Asher over here. We need extra hands."

They cleaned the skin, preparing the surgical site as best they could. Asher paced back and forth with his fingers in his hair, stopping every few steps to squat and take deep breaths. "There has to be something else you can do. Isn't there something else you can do?"

Esther handed Maya a tiny scalpel, the only kind she had in the suture kit she'd packed. Asher clamped a hand over his mouth. "Oohholyshit. Ooohholyshit."

"Dude, you need to hold it together," Esther snapped, at the same time Skye cried, "Asher, shut the fuck up!"

Maya held the scalpel to Skye's taut belly and hesitated. She looked up and met Skye's gaze. Skye nodded her head again, a movement slight but sure.

Maya's heart thundered in her chest. Her vision went spotty, as if a gauze curtain had been dropped before her. It had been years since her last panic attack. *Not now. Please not now.* But of course now. She'd fooled herself into believing that if she were somehow to end up in this exact situation, she could rely on her training to kick in like muscle memory. She'd been reassuring herself for the past nine months of Skye's pregnancy that she was prepared for this possibility, that she was healed from her past trauma, or at least healed enough, despite the evidence to the contrary. Her hands went numb, and she heard the faint clatter of the scalpel against the wooden floor.

"Dr. Rao? Dr. Rao!" Esther's voice sounded far away, faint underneath the beating of blood in her ears. "I don't have another scalpel, and this one's contaminated now. What do we do?"

The beating of her heart was taking on a rhythm. *Dum-dum-da-da-dum. Dum-dum-da-da-dum.*

Maya felt herself sink into the floor. Suddenly she was beneath the earth, in a cave, and a voice was saying, "Try again." Then, just as quickly, the cave wasn't a cave but a dark, cold lecture hall, years ago. Medical school. A white-coated professor was describing a technique for breech delivery. It was controversial, dangerous, and had fallen out of favor a decade ago because it carried a significant risk of breaking one or more of the baby's bones. Maya had never tried it, only read about it. It took three people to perform, one to hold the mother's legs in position, two to turn the baby.

Her eyes flew open, and she gasped as if she were emerging from underwater. "Try again!"

"What?" Esther's hand was on her shoulder.

"We're going to try to turn the baby again," she said. "You and me."

"Is there time for that?" Esther asked, panicked.

A calmness came over Maya, and she said, "Probably not." She positioned Skye's legs and commanded Asher to hold them in place.

"Are you going to be able to get the baby out without cutting her?" he asked hopefully.

Maya ignored him and turned to Esther. "We're going clockwise. On my signal, you push, I pull. Got it?"

"Wait, what's the signal?" Esther asked, at the same time Maya said, "Skye, I'm sorry about this," and, with only that warning, pushed the infant's foot back into the uterus while pulling hard on Skye's belly. Esther pushed clockwise on the soft bulge under Skye's ribs, the baby's head. Skye's scream pierced the layers of the atmosphere, the sound echoing into space. The baby's body turned, just slightly, but it was enough. The child's leg folded up under its body, its pelvis sliding into the birth canal, bottom first. "Push, Skye!" Maya cried.

Skye pushed with all the power in her, with the power of the moon and the earth and the tide, as the call of an ambulance siren, faint in the distance, grew steadily louder.

THIRTY-THREE

The baby—a boy—emerged limp, slightly blue, but breathing. His right thighbone was fractured in two places and his left shoulder was dislocated. The ambulance crew rushed Skye, Asher, and the child to the nearest hospital. The neonatal intensivist there saved the baby's life, and the emergency room team saved Skye's.

Skye spent forty-eight hours in intensive care in Punta Gorda. Then, Congressman Hauser sent a team of two nurses and two doctors—all trained in critical care, one board-certified in neonatology—to collect his daughter and grandson and accompany them back to the United States aboard his jet. He had them both admitted directly to Lenox Hill Hospital in Manhattan, the same place Beyoncé had delivered her first child and where the congressman was a member of the board of advisers. The care was both excellent and discreet.

Maya, Esther, and Clarissa were left behind at the villa. Hector drove Maya and Esther back to the hotel, and they caught the last flight out of Punta Gorda that evening. They flew coach.

Maya leaned her head back against her headrest and looked at Esther, slumped against the window, asleep. It should never have gotten as far as it did. Skye should never have been so misinformed as to have wanted an out-of-hospital birth, a nonmedical birth, a birth in the *ocean*, for God's sake. Eunoia should never have given her the impression that following her own whims and ignoring sound medical advice was anything other than foolish and reckless. Empowering ignorance was no way to empower women. Empowerment had to come through education, not self-indulgence. Carefully, Maya typed out an email to Amelia on her phone and saved it to her drafts folder to send once they landed.

The house was dark by the time she dragged her suitcase up the interminable flight of steps to her front door. Their house, on a cul-de-sac in Wynnewood, with the bay window overlooking the sloped front lawn. The place to which she'd brought all three of her babies home. She'd missed it; she hadn't realized how much until she gently shut the door behind her and, standing still in the tiny foyer, breathed in the smell of it. The smell of school backpacks and Ikea meatballs and Elmer's glue and baby wipes. The smell of a life she'd earned and built herself. She and Dean.

She slipped upstairs and found Dean asleep on the rug in Diya's room. She lay beside him and pressed her face into the space between his shoulder blades. "I'm sorry," she said quietly. "I'm trash, and you're amazing."

He shifted, then murmured sleepily, "I know."

"I'm like the slime inside the garbage disposal, I'm partially disposed food bits that have been sitting there for days, just turning to rot."

Dean laughed. "Okay."

"I'm that green stuff that runs out of the trash can after it rains—"

Dean turned to envelop her in his arms. "Yes, you are all those things. How was your trip?"

"Awful. I'm quitting Eunoia. I'll find something else."

Dean pulled away to look into her face. "You're okay with that? You're sure?"

"Already sent the email. You were right about all of it."

"Is Skye okay? The baby?"

"They made it. Barely." She told him what had happened.

After a moment of stunned silence, he said, "But . . . you did it. You did the delivery." When she didn't reply, he added, "Maya, this is huge."

Her tears stained his T-shirt. Tears of loss and worry. Tears of relief. She nodded.

Dean pulled her into his chest. "It'll be okay." After a moment he asked, "Should we go to bed?"

"Let's stay right here for a minute, okay?"

Dean tightened his grip around her. They found homes for their arms and legs and shoulders and hips, and they drifted off to sleep together. They hadn't slept that way, intertwined, in a very long time, but their tired bodies fell back into embrace without thinking, as if they'd never stopped. As if they'd never forgotten.

The next morning, Maya wrestled one eye open to find herself on the cold, uncomfortable floor tucked under one of Dean's arms. Diya, sound asleep, was folded underneath the other, having abandoned her bed sometime in the night. There was laundry to do and, she'd noticed yesterday, a stack of red-sauce-stained plates piled in the kitchen sink. But that could wait. Right now, with Diya's beatific face pressed against Dean's gently rising and falling chest, there was nothing else to do. She closed her eyes again.

THIRTY-FOUR

Prem bombed the audition for Princeton. "I was having a bad day" was all the explanation she gave her parents. Mercifully, her first round at the Yale School of Music had gone fairly well. The second audition—the callback—was only two weeks away, but that afternoon, when Yuri—the professional harpist, formerly with the Russian National Orchestra, who took the train in from New York every Saturday for her coaching sessions—arrived at the house, Prem screamed at him to get away from her and ran out to her art studio. Amelia tried, but it was Bodhi who finally convinced her to come back to the house, whereupon she locked herself in her room for the rest of the day, refusing to open the door or explain her behavior to anyone.

After several hours of waiting for Prem to reemerge, Amelia finally sent Yuri home. She asked Paloma to take a plate of dinner up to Prem while she called Faye, the shaman, for advice.

"Are there any new items in the house that might be disturbing her energy flow?" Faye wanted to know. "Any items you've recently moved from one place to another?"

Paloma had, just that morning, finished washing and putting away a new set of silverware, Amelia told her. And two days ago, Greg and Blake moved a sofa in the conservatory from one side of the room to the other because Amelia thought it would open up the space. And last week she'd bought a new coffee maker.

"Hmm, could be any of those things," Faye said, and Amelia went to the kitchen immediately and began pulling forks and spoons out of the silverware drawer, much to Paloma's distress. Amelia had cleared the contents of the drawer into a bag and was about to recruit Paloma and Bodhi to help her move the sofa when they heard a crash from upstairs. They ran to Prem's room and found the wall opposite her bedroom door smeared with quinoa and tomato sauce, the hardwood floor littered with bits of food and the broken glass plate. "Stop trying to poison me!" Prem screamed through the door.

"My God," Amelia whispered, clamping one hand over her mouth. She tried to hold back the tears that threatened to spill over her cheeks, not wanting to cry in front of her son.

"What's wrong with her, Mom?" Bodhi asked, his face pale with fear.

"Your sister's not feeling well," Amelia replied. Then she said urgently, "Help me move the sofa."

When even removing the new Keurig from the house didn't produce any change in Prem's behavior, Amelia called her ex-husband. Greg brought over his power drill and took Prem's bedroom door off its hinges. When they finally got inside, she was trying to escape from the window, one leg dangling out, one arm reaching for a tree branch.

"We're two stories up!" Amelia cried. "You'll kill yourself!"

"Leave me alone!" Prem shouted, but she pulled her arm and leg back inside. Terrified, Amelia grabbed her daughter and clutched her tightly. "Oh, my Prem, my love, what's the matter?" Her voice was equal parts soothing coo and screeching reprimand. "Just tell me what's going on!"

Prem's expression went from defiant to helpless, adult to child, in an instant, as if she were aging backward in front of their eyes. "I don't know!" Sobbing, she sank to the floor, pulling her mother down with her. Amelia rocked her back and forth and petted her hair, murmuring in her ear that everything would be okay.

It occurred to Amelia then that perhaps she'd overestimated her daughter. She'd always thought of Prem as so mature, so independent and capable, but maybe she'd been wrong. She was only seventeen, after all, still a child. Prem needed care. She needed mothering. How had she not seen it sooner?

Amelia fed her daughter dinner, even spooning the first few bites into her mouth, stood outside the bathroom while Prem took a shower and changed into her pajamas, and then tucked her into bed. She sat in the dark on a chair in her daughter's room and, when she was sure Prem was asleep, slipped her phone off the bedside table and took it downstairs. She didn't know the code to open it, but Bodhi did. Amelia scrolled through her daughter's text messages for the first time in years. She looked at her emails. She'd heard of children being brainwashed by strangers on the Internet, of predatory men luring young women away from home. She checked for anything suspicious, but she found nothing of concern on Prem's phone. Prem seemed to still text Carter, her ex-boyfriend who broke up with her but wasn't good enough for her anyway, from time to time—friendly, almost flirty messages—but he never replied. Maybe that wasn't considered rude? She could never keep up with the rapidly changing parameters of appropriate online behavior for teenagers. Things she would have considered rude, like not returning a text message, were probably perfectly socially acceptable to Bodhi and Prem.

She turned off the ringer and hid the phone in one of the kitchen drawers. A few days without the device would be good for Prem. She sent Greg back home, went upstairs, and made sure Bodhi was settled for the night. It wasn't until she finally slipped into her own bed that she remembered the conversation she'd had with Maya Rao that morning, when she'd called from Belize hysterical about Skye Hauser. She wondered if Skye had had the baby yet. Then she opened her computer and saw an email with the doctor's letter of resignation. "I can no longer continue to practice in a manner that does not align with my values," Maya Rao had written. Without bothering to finish reading, Amelia went downstairs and poured herself a glass of wine. She drank it in her bed, quickly, trying to numb the stress of it all. Being a working mother could be soul crushing—why did no one ever warn ambitious young women about that? Amelia would have liked to have been warned. *You can absolutely have it all, girls, but you'll trade bits and pieces of your life force for it over the years, just so you know.* She'd been so sure about Maya Rao. Such a disappointment. But the universe had its reasons, and she wouldn't be deterred. First thing Monday, she decided, she'd start looking for a replacement.

Amelia awoke the next morning, Sunday, with a migraine. Despite the headache, however, she felt hopeful. Prem was up already and practicing harp. And though she looked tired and brittle, drained from the prior day's emotion, she seemed otherwise herself. For a moment, out of caution, Amelia considered skipping the Hamilton Hall auction that evening. Then she realized what a ridiculous notion that was. She was the auction chairwoman. The event literally couldn't go off without her.

As if to prove her point, Lainey Smockett called just then, close to tears, to say the balloon arch intended for the main entrance to the gymnasium had been delivered, but half the balloons had popped already. Amelia didn't know Lainey well, but there was no question as to the woman's incompetence. After assuring Lainey that she would take care of the balloon disaster herself, she called Greg to ask him to come over to the house and keep an eye on Prem while she was away that evening at the auction. Greg agreed immediately, then asked, "Babe, do you think there's a chance the kid is on drugs? I looked in her room yesterday and didn't find anything, but—"

Amelia laughed hollowly. "Seriously, Greg?" This was one of the many reasons she'd divorced him: he'd never known their children the way she did. "Whatever is happening with her, it's not of her own doing, I assure you."

"Jesus, Amelia, I'm not blaming her, I just think it's worth considering."

She told him he was welcome to consider whatever he wanted. She'd arranged for a Reiki session at the house for Prem that day and was also starting her on an Ayurvedic cleansing diet of daal and ghee—a Michelin-starred Indian restaurant in Philadelphia would deliver the meals to them starting tomorrow morning.

"Great. But what if that doesn't help?"

"It will." Amelia couldn't bear to consider the alternative. Taking Prem to a traditional doctor and letting them poke and prod her the way they'd done in the emergency room. The way they'd done to Amelia when she was a child. She wouldn't put Prem through what she'd endured. Never. "It will," she said again before ending the conversation and hanging up the phone.

Looking hard at her reflection in the mirror above the bureau, Amelia told herself she was nothing like her own mother. Yes, the nose and lips and eyebrows were similar, but she was nothing like Melinda Spencer DeGilles in any of the ways that mattered. She knew she'd do whatever it took to make Prem well again. She'd dig the herbs from the earth with her bare hands. She'd climb the Himalayas herself and bring home the healing salt. If it took going to the ends of the earth to do right by her daughter, she would, without hesitation. She would be the mother Prem deserved. She would be the mother *she'd* deserved.

THIRTY-FIVE

Maya lay on the carpet in the living room while Diya and Niam watched cartoons. These were their Sunday afternoon plans, ever since Maya had thrown her back out this morning after spending the night on Diya's floor. Dean brought her a hot-water bottle and three ibuprofen, and as she struggled into a seated position, her phone flashed a number from Hamilton Hall.

"Who's that?" Dean asked.

"Diya's school."

"On a Sunday?"

"They probably want to sell us last-minute tickets for the auction tonight," Maya said.

Dean raised his eyebrows, impressed. "Persistent bastards."

As usual, she let the call go to voice mail. It wasn't until several hours later, when she finally felt well enough to peel herself off the carpet, that she listened to the message. It was Diya's science teacher.

"Hi, Mrs. Rao. Dr. Rao. It's Kevin Grove from Hamilton Hall. I got the fish oil tablets you sent in and I was able, like you asked, to run a mass spectrometry on them on our machine and . . . well, I just got the results and there's a really high concentration of mercury in these pills. I think that's what you were curious about, right? It makes perfect sense, depending on what type of fish were used to make these, if they're not regulated or screened properly, they could contain mercury, so . . . no one should take these, obviously. Could be very dangerous. Okay, hope that helps Diya with her science fair project. Any questions, I'll be back here tomorrow, give me a call if—"

Maya hung up the phone and called Amelia. Straight to voice mail. She glanced at the clock. The auction had probably just started. She tried Prem's number. Again, voice mail. She hoisted herself to her feet, grabbed her keys, and called to Dean over her shoulder as she hobbled to the front door. "I'll be back soon. Just order takeout for dinner!"

"Where are you going?" Dean asked, but the door had already shut behind her and, a moment later, she was tearing out of the driveway, the Hotessey's tires squealing.

G reg, perhaps unsurprisingly, had no recollection of who she was. "Are you . . . selling something?" He spoke to her through the security camera in the doorbell.

"Greg, no. It's Maya. I work for Eunoia. I'm the gynecologist." She omitted the part about how she'd just resigned and added, "Prem's my patient."

"Oh! Sorry. Didn't recognize you. Hold on." He swung open the door. "Amelia's at the school auction," he said. "Is there something I can do for you?"

"Is Prem here? Can I talk to her?"

"Sure. Is this about . . . women's stuff?" He waved his hand vaguely, his face pinched in discomfort.

"Well, no. But I ran a test on—"

"Nope! Nope, I'm not the one to talk to about female issues," Greg said, putting his fingers in his ears in a way that was disconcertingly childlike. "Her mother handles that. Prem is in her art studio. Backyard, just follow the path. You can go around and talk to her. Feel free. Go on." And he waved her away and shut the door.

Too distracted to be offended, Maya hurried through the garden to the art studio and knocked urgently on the door. When there was no answer, she pushed the door open and stepped inside, her breath catching at the sight. The studio, once so tidy, was a mess of palettes and brushes and half-eaten plates of food. On the easel was the same portrait she'd seen the last time she was here, now completed. The likeness was unmistakable. The flame-red hair, the emerald green eyes. *The Little Mermaid*. Evelyn Tuttle. There was a jagged tear in the canvas, as if something sharp had been stabbed into it and dragged for several inches. Then Maya noticed them: five other canvases, all with portraits of Evelyn, all with the same jagged slashes through them. Slashes made by an angry hand. They rested on the floor and the desk, strewn about, tossed there after their destruction. A canvas lay facedown on the floor near an upended trash can. Maya knelt and turned it over. Another portrait of Evelyn, this one with a large red dripping line painted across her neck. The paint was still wet. Greg appeared at the door, annoyed. "Hey, my car is gone. The kid took my car without asking." He looked around the studio. "What the hell is all this?"

"Prem has mercury poisoning," Maya said. "From her fish oil pills. It causes paranoia and can make you act irrationally. The hand tingling, the problems concentrating, the loss of balance, mood swings, headaches—they're all symptoms of mercury poisoning." She stared at the portrait. "I think . . . Could she be a danger to herself? Or to her boyfriend's mother?"

"Evelyn?" Greg said, his eyes widening. "Why would she want to hurt Evelyn?"

"She told me Evelyn was trying to break up her and Carter. She said Evelyn was stalking her."

"That's ridiculous," Greg said. "Evelyn hasn't done anything. Carter broke up with Prem at the beginning of the school year, and yeah, she was pretty torn up about it—teenage girls, you know what I mean—but I thought she'd gotten over it."

Maya put a finger to the wet paint. "I don't think so."

They exchanged glances. "We can take your car," Greg said.

They ran for the Hotessey.

THIRTY-SIX

Prem used the back entrance to the campus, the one reserved for maintenance staff. Her father would be angry she'd taken his car. She parked it carefully and locked the doors. The sun had just set, and the asphalt of the lot was cool against her bare feet. In the darkness, she moved swiftly toward the long flight of stairs, toward the sounds of music and voices.

She wore a sleeveless crop top and wide-leg capri pants, and she should have been freezing, but she wasn't. A white-hot anger had been building in her, a feeling like a fever, for weeks. She hadn't slept; she'd barely eaten. She hadn't told anyone, but on her soul flight with Faye, everything had finally come into focus. She'd seen clearly what she needed to do. She'd seen a bird with flame-red feathers, and she'd felt the weight of a weapon, something steel and sharp, clutched in her hand. She'd seen herself stab this sharp steel thing into the fragile animal and felt the relief that immediately followed, the ease.

Carter's mother had stolen her happiness. She'd ruined everything.

Prem curled her fingers around the cold steel in her hand, felt the pleasing heft of it, the dagger-sharp tip against the pad of her thumb. She climbed the steps. Once it was done, she could finally be at peace.

THIRTY-SEVEN

For an old minivan, the Hotessey was impressively fast when it needed to be.

"Circle the parking lot," Greg suggested when they pulled up to the Hamilton Hall campus. "Let's see if she's here."

Maya steered the van under a banner reading *Welcome to Auction Night at Hamilton!* and bypassed the valet stand. Slowly, she circled the parking lot in front of the gymnasium and the nearly completed DeGilles Mindfulness Space, its interior lit by the soft glow of a stained-glass chandelier in the lobby. She and Greg scanned the cars. "I don't see it," Greg said. "I drive a red Maserati. It's hard to miss."

Maya turned onto a narrow road behind the gymnasium. "There's a parking lot behind the dining commons. The auxiliary lot."

"There is?" Greg said, surprised, as they sped down a hill toward the rear of the campus. The little auxiliary lot was empty, except for a bright red sports car parked at an angle across two spaces.

"She's here," Greg said, his voice tight. "What the hell is she doing here?"

Maya turned the car around and, a few seconds later, screeched up to the valet stand and wordlessly threw the stunned attendant her keys. With Greg on her heels, she sprinted into the gymnasium, ducking underneath a perfect balloon arch and past the coat check and the women taking tickets at the door, not stopping when they called urgently, "Ma'am! Sir! We need to see your tickets!"

The gymnasium had been transformed into a warmly lit Moroccan wonderland. A burbling azure-tile fountain marked the center of the room. Ornate woven rugs covered the floor, and a tall golden hookah draped with flowers graced the center of each round banquet table. A troupe of belly dancers weaved among the guests. Waiters in harem pants and fezzes circulated with trays of kebabs. A live band, which included a woman playing the dulcimer, was performing a catchy, Arabic version of a Black Eyed Peas song. Maya and Greg pushed past men in tuxedos and women in evening gowns, scanning the room.

"Let's split up," Greg suggested, before heading in the direction of the band. Maya turned the opposite way and nearly collided with Gill Newall. He was gripping a kabob between his teeth, a glass of beer in one hand, and a plate of appetizers in the other. His eyebrows went up in pleasant surprise, and he made a high-pitched noise in greeting. Maya took the beer from his hand, and he removed the kabob from his mouth. "Hey! Maya! How's it going?" Before she could answer, he added, "Oh, hey, I was disappointed to hear the school board shot down your idea about updating the Health curriculum. I mean, I wasn't surprised, because they're a bunch of old dudes who're afraid of lady parts and whatnot, but I was really bummed for you. I thought it was a great idea." He eyed her baggy sweatsuit, which she hadn't bothered changing out of before she left home. "This isn't a look everyone could pull off, but you're doing it." He gave her a thumbs-up.

"Gill, have you seen Amelia?" Maya asked.

"Amelia? I think I saw her over at the auction table—"

The crowd parted slightly, and Maya dropped the beer. Barefoot and disheveled, clutching a pair of paint-splattered steel-tipped scissors, Prem moved with maniacal purpose from one of the emergency exit doors toward the fountain. Toward a shock of red hair in the crowd.

"Prem!" Maya screamed, but in the cavernous space full of music and laughter, the sound of her voice evaporated as soon as it passed her lips. She ran, shoved past a waiter balancing a silver tray above his head, and lunged for Evelyn, who turned just in time to see a curly-haired Indian woman she vaguely recognized flying through the air, headed straight toward her.

Prem's scissors, aimed at Evelyn's heart, missed their mark. Maya felt it all happen in slow motion. Her full postpartum weight crashing into Evelyn's bone-china frame, which crumpled like paper. The searing of sharp metal piercing the supple skin, then the tough fascia, then the soft muscle of her thigh. The explosion of pain. The crash and gasping of breath as she landed on Evelyn, and Prem landed on her. She let out a cry that, even to her own ears, sounded more animal than human.

Everything went spotty, then momentarily dark. When she became conscious again, Gill and Greg were trying to pull Prem off her, and people were screaming. "Mercury!" Maya tried to say, but she was bleeding quite heavily, the scissors still lodged in her thigh. She looked down at her leg. At first she was fascinated by the anatomy of it, the way the metal blades had just missed the femoral artery, the sheer volume of blood and magnitude of pain. And then she fainted properly.

THIRTY-EIGHT

Amelia heard a woman scream what sounded like "Prem," but immediately knew that was impossible. She was in the middle of a discussion with the head of the school about using some of the evening's proceeds to buy another 3D printer for the science lab when, suddenly, the music stopped and there was a terrible, animalistic sort of screeching from near the fountain. Her first reaction was annoyance. At every school auction she'd ever attended, a student's father—never the same one twice—indulged a little too much, did something inappropriate, and had to be escorted out. That highly accomplished men were powerless in the face of an open bar was a truth she relied on—gourmet Jell-O shots were always distributed just before live bidding began on the slapdash student art and craft creations that no sober person would ever pay money for but that inebriated parents would happily spend hundreds or even thousands of dollars to acquire—but it was also a truth that had its inevitable downside.

She pushed her way through the crowd and saw what appeared to be a scuffle between several people. A brawl? Really? This was a bridge too far. She resolved in that moment never to chair another school auction again.

The she saw the blood. And her daughter.

She must have screamed, but she had no awareness of it. The police were there then, pushing her back into the crowd, clearing space around a pile of bodies, one of them—not Prem, thank God—with a knife or some other metal object in its thigh. And then, somehow, Greg was there, too. And he was telling her Prem had been poisoned. The pills were making her paranoid. There was mercury in the fish oil pills Prem had been taking for the past year and they had been poisoning her. Amelia had been poisoning her.

Prem, struggling ferociously to get free, was being restrained by two police officers. Amelia watched every head in the room swivel toward her. *You did this*, their stunned, judging eyes said. And it was true. She'd done this to her child. She hadn't done it knowingly, but she'd done to her child exactly what her own mother had done to her.

There was no air in the gym. Amelia gasped for breath, tore at the too-tight neck of her beaded evening gown. She realized she was sitting on the floor, Greg's arm around her. She pushed him away, scrambled to her feet, and bolted for the exit, scratching through her handbag for her phone. She could think of nothing but escape. Outside, parents were still arriving, but the valet line had backed up behind the idling police cars. A horn blared. "What's going on?" someone shouted.

With shaking hands, Amelia tried to text Blake. Then she spotted her car, close by in the parking lot, and ran to it. Blake wasn't inside, but the key fob was. Sobbing now, mascara clouding her vision, she climbed into the driver's seat, started the ignition, shifted into what looked like reverse, and pressed hard on what she was fairly sure was the accelerator, the word repeating in her mind: *escape, escape, escape.*

THIRTY-NINE

Witnesses would tell police afterward that they saw a hysterical woman in a beaded evening gown flee the gymnasium, losing one shoe on the sidewalk, and leap into a black Aston Martin SUV with red trim. A moment later, the car burst onto the sidewalk and over the lawn, narrowly missing a Little Free Library box and the school's organic garden, and plowed through the front door of the DeGilles Mindfulness Space before coming to a stop amid a shower of broken glass and twisted metal. "It was like she was either drunk or she'd never driven a car before," a woman remarked. "Or maybe both, I don't know."

"The school is going downhill fast, if you ask me," a man interviewed by the local newspaper said. "They've been letting in more of these scholarship families and, you know, I'm not saying they bring drama and family problems with them . . . but I'm not *not* saying that either."

It took about forty-eight hours for the details of what happened to circulate through the school community. As many people as there were in attendance at the auction, only a few had a clear view of the events as they unfolded. The rest was hearsay. It was generally agreed that the four women involved in the incident were all taken to Lankenau Hospital on the Main Line. The ambulance tried to take them to Mercy, but at least one of the women refused to go there. Amelia DeGilles suffered facial and chest bruising as a result of her airbags deploying, Maya Rao was rushed into surgery to repair a deep stab wound to her thigh, Evelyn Tuttle was treated for a mild wrist sprain and released that night, and Premrose DeGilles was admitted for treatment for mercury poisoning. Rumor was that when her mercury level was tested in the emergency room, it was several times higher than the highest normal value, and that the source of the poisoning was some sort of natural supplement she took. Panicked Hamilton Hall mothers cleared their kitchens of vitamins and immune-boosting powders in the subsequent days, and primary care doctors in the area saw a sharp increase in the number of phone calls requesting blood tests for heavy metals and "other toxins."

The Hamilton Hall community was shaken by the thought that this could have happened to any of them, to any of their children. If Amelia DeGilles was vulnerable, they all were. Suddenly, life seemed even more precarious. In-home water filtration systems were installed up and down the Main Line that summer, and over glasses of chilled prosecco sipped poolside, the parents of Hamilton Hall Academy whispered their gratitude, like prayers into the warm breeze, that despite all of life's stress and uncertainty, at least they still had their health.

FORTY

Maya awoke the morning after surgery in her hospital room, Dean at her bedside gently stroking her hair. "Who's watching the kids?" she asked, still feeling a bit high from the anesthesia.

"Your parents," Dean said. Maya started to protest, but he added reassuringly, "They're fine. Your dad is watching TV with Niam, and Diya is helping your mom with the baby. They're doing great. How do you feel?"

She considered the question. Her leg hurt, but not intolerably. Her shoulder was bruised where it had slammed into the floor of the gym, though the impact had been cushioned—albeit only slightly—by Evelyn's body. She grimaced. "Not bad, considering. How's Prem?"

"Getting chelation therapy for the mercury. Her levels were through the roof, but they said she should be a lot better in a week. How the heck did you figure it out?"

"*Alice in Wonderland,*" Maya said.

Dean raised one eyebrow. "Someone in *Alice in Wonderland* has mercury poisoning?"

She nodded. "It's called Mad Hatter's Disease. We learned about it in medical school. In the 1800s, hatmakers had a reputation for acting weird. Paranoid, delusional. That's what Lewis Carroll based the character on, the saying "mad as a hatter." Eventually, doctors figured out it was exposure to the mercury used in making the felt brim for the hats. They all had chronic mercury poisoning."

"*That's* how you figured it out?" Dean was incredulous. "Some obscure history lesson from med school?"

Maya smiled wanly. "Lucky guess." Even as she said the words, an image of the little tiger flashed through her mind. "Or maybe my subconscious figured it out, I don't know. Anyway, remind me to thank Diya's science teacher for testing the pills."

Dean looked at her with admiration. "You are really good at your job."

"I couldn't agree more," a quiet voice from the doorway said. It was Amelia. She raised one Ace-wrapped arm in greeting. Under the other, she cradled a huge bouquet of orchids and birds of paradise. An angry bruise ringed one eye, and she moved slowly, but she seemed otherwise well. "Hi, Maya. Dean. Sorry to interrupt." They said nothing in reply, just looked at her, so she continued, "Ah . . . I'm being discharged today. I just wanted to bring you these. I was hoping I could talk to you for a minute . . . see how you were feeling . . . if you have time."

Maya nodded, and Dean excused himself to get a cup of coffee from the cafeteria downstairs. As he passed Amelia on his way out, he glared at her.

Amelia approached cautiously, and it seemed to Maya that, for the first time, Amelia was actually looking at her, seeing *her* instead of what role she could play in Amelia's life.

"How's Prem?" Maya asked.

Amelia nodded. "Much better, actually. Clearer. I'm not sure she fully grasps what she's done yet," Amelia said, gesturing vaguely to Maya's leg. "And they have her in a room with a nurse keeping an eye on her all the time so she can't try to get away. They at least took those awful restraints off her wrists, thank goodness. They literally had her tied to the bed, can you believe that? The psychiatrist says it'll take several weeks before she's back to herself. At least he thinks so. Mercury poisoning is, apparently, extremely rare." She sighed, sat on a chair at the foot of the bed, and carefully placed the flowers on the windowsill. "I heard about Skye Hauser. Her father, Congressman Hauser, called me. Wanted me to convey his family's thanks to you and Esther. She and the baby almost died, they said. They would have, if you hadn't ignored me and gone to find her." She looked down at her hands. They were covered with tiny cuts from the broken glass of the Aston Martin's windshield. "I should . . ." She swallowed and started again. "I never should have made you feel like you had to choose between doing what you knew was medically right and working for Eunoia. I should never have put you in that position. I should have helped you, gotten you the address. I've been so foolish about so many things." She covered her mouth with one hand and sobbed. "I've been giving Prem those pills."

"Amelia, you can't blame yourself for that," Maya said kindly.

"I'm the only one I *can* blame," Amelia replied, wiping her eyes with her fingertips. "Although I'm suing the company that makes those pills, believe me. They've already heard from the FDA, and their website has been shut down. Other customers will be warned. That's at least a silver lining, if there is one."

Maya nodded. "I'm sure Prem will be fine, now that she's being treated. It'll just take some time."

Amelia looked into her lap. "I'm so sorry for what happened to her, what happened to you. I want you to know, Maya, that Eunoia will be different from now on. I'm going to hire doctors—MDs—and I'm going to be more careful where I get my information, who I trust."

Maya nodded again. "That's good."

"I was hoping," Amelia said, "that you'd reconsider your resignation. I was hoping you'd stay on and help me remake the practice as our new medical director."

"But Gretchen—"

"Has decided to relocate to Boca permanently. To pursue other opportunities," Amelia said, her gaze momentarily drifting to the window. Then she smiled at Maya hopefully. "But you and I, we can work together to make Eunoia a premier women's health concierge service. We can offer clients a whole range of scientifically proven medical care. I talked it over with Greg, and basically you could name your salary. Or we could offer you a buy-in, if that's something you want."

Maya's eyebrows went up. Amelia was offering her the chance to own—or at least co-own—her own practice. It was something she'd never dared to consider, something that had always seemed so far out of her reach that it might as well have been a fantasy.

"You don't have to answer now, of course," Amelia said. "But just think about it, please."

Maya shook her head and, though disappointment clouded Amelia's face, said without regret, "Thank you for the offer, Amelia, but I have to decline."

Dean came back with two cups of coffee in time to catch this bit of the conversation. He smiled at Maya from the doorway.

"Of course." Amelia looked crestfallen, but not surprised. "You've found something else?"

"Not just yet," Maya said. "But I think I know what I'm looking for, finally. I know what I need."

Amelia nodded reluctantly. "Good for you, Maya. It's important to honor yourself." She smiled. "They'll be lucky to have you, whoever they are."

Amelia looked slight and sallow in the chair, her golden glow having dissipated under the harsh fluorescent hospital lights. "Goodbye, Amelia," Maya said.

Amelia looked at her for a long moment. Then she said, with a sad but resigned shrug of her shoulders, "Goodbye, Maya Rao."

It was the last time the two women saw each other. Amelia returned to Villanova, tucked herself back into the rarefied shadows, behind the tall, tangled trees and the dense green hedgerows. And Maya Rao stepped fully into the light.

FORTY-ONE

One Year Later

How has meditation been going?"

"Good. I try to make time for it two or three times a week. I know that's not as much as you suggested, but I've been trying—"

"Ah, be careful. There you go again, right? Are we shooting for perfection here, Maya?"

"No."

"Right. And what's the thing I always say?"

"Life is not a competitive sport."

"Are you any closer to believing that?"

As Maya considered the question, she let her eyes drift from the computer screen and wander around her cramped office. There was the splintered bulletin board where she tacked up the thank-you and Christmas cards from patients. There was the ratty couch left here by the office's former inhabitant, above which hung, slightly askance, her medical school diploma on the circa-1970 wood-paneled wall. There was the pile of yellowed obstetrics-and-gynecology textbooks that made the room smell vaguely like an attic. There, on the desk before her, were the framed photographs of her family. Asha taking her first steps. Niam cuddling their new labradoodle puppy, Snookus. Diya playing the electric guitar. Her and Dean on their wedding day, that dress she still loved.

"I think I am, yes," she said, returning her attention to the Zoom call.

Her therapist smiled. "Wonderful. How is Diya?"

"Good. I can't believe she's almost done with fifth grade. She and her friends have all started writing their first novels. I've read some of Diya's. It's actually not bad."

"So you're keeping her in the public school next year?"

"Yeah. All her friends are there, and she's doing great. Making all A's and B's," Maya said proudly. "She's even trying out for the school musical."

"Does she seem happy and well adjusted to you?" the therapist asked.

"Definitely," Maya said. "Much happier than last year."

"Then you're doing a fabulous job, Mom," the therapist said, peering at Maya over her reading glasses to drive home the point. Lately they'd been working through Maya's maternal guilt issues. "Tell me, how is work? Did you do any deliveries since we spoke last week?"

Maya nodded. "Two. One we had to convert to an emergency C-section, but it went fine."

The therapist consulted her notes. "You're still having one of your colleagues, one of the other doctors, shadow you as backup, just in case?"

Maya nodded again. "Yeah. I'm not quite ready to be in the OR or delivery room by myself. But I haven't had any further flashbacks. I mean, in the moment, during the delivery, I feel good. I feel like I'm in the zone, you know?"

"But afterward?"

"It's still a little rough afterward. I have trouble sleeping, I lose my appetite, feel anxious."

"That's all very normal, Maya," the therapist said, removing her glasses. "Recovery from PTSD, as you know, is a slow process. One step forward, two back, and all that. But you're doing great." She folded her hands on her desk. "Do you appreciate the progress you've made over the past year?"

"I do. I see that I've moved forward for sure."

The therapist wagged a finger. "Don't just tell me what I want to hear, Doctor."

Maya smiled. "No, really. I mean it. I feel like I'm getting there, one step at a time."

"Good. So, I'll see you same time next week?"

Maya agreed and signed off, just as her assistant knocked and poked her head around the door. "Your last patient is here, Dr. Rao. She's thirty minutes late. Do you still want to see her, or should I have her reschedule?"

Maya smiled. "She's always late. I'll see her."

A few months after the Hamilton Hall auction, Cooper Medical School in Camden, New Jersey, had a job opening in its ob-gyn teaching clinic. One of Esther's aunts had worked there for years, and she'd recommended Maya for the position. With her therapist's blessing, Maya had applied for the job. In the interview, she was forthright with the department head about her mental health issues. She told the story of the little blue boy in the emergency room. The department head, a slight, silver-haired woman, sighed sympathetically and shared her own story of a delivery gone wrong early in her career. "Do you want to get back into delivering?" she asked Maya.

"Yes," Maya replied. Then she added, "I'm in therapy."

The woman nodded in approval. "Good. What do you need from us? How can we support you?"

"I'd like to be part-time. With a flexible schedule. And I'd like to shadow some of the doctors until I'm comfortable doing deliveries on my own again."

The department head had been having trouble keeping the clinic staffed. Three doctors had left the practice earlier that year, citing the low pay and the clinic's shoestring budget. More lucrative opportunities were available just a short drive away in the affluent suburbs of southern New Jersey, where the clinics were housed in sparkling, modern office buildings, not in a crumbling hospital tower in one of Camden's poorest neighborhoods.

"I can't give you part time," the woman said, "but I can give you flexible hours and all the shadowing you need. Are you willing to teach medical students in return?"

Maya nodded, and the two women shook hands and agreed that she would start as soon as possible. As she left, Maya stopped and turned in the doorway.

"One more question," she said. "Would you be open to the idea of my doing house calls?"

The department head raised her eyebrows.

Maya knocked and entered the exam room.

What a difference a year, and a baby, made. Skye Hauser had let her hair fade back to its natural dark brown. She had broken up with Asher. She had moved out of her father's mansion, gotten a job volunteering with a women's shelter, and used her substantial trust fund to buy her own apartment in Philadelphia, where she lived next door to an elderly woman named Bunny Foster who had recently developed a serious problem with blood clots due to excessive use of estrogen tablets prescribed by some quack in Arizona. "It's, like, the saddest story," Skye had told Maya. "She's looking for a new doctor. Of course I gave her your name."

Skye had had a difficult postnatal course. She'd dealt with depression and what was ultimately diagnosed as post-traumatic stress disorder related to the birth of the baby. She'd been to counseling and was doing better now, but the experience, Maya knew, had taken a toll. Still, now three months into her second pregnancy, she was taking excellent care of herself.

"Hi, Maya! Sorry I was late," Skye said. She was lifting her son, a cherubic butterball with a permanent string of drool down his chin, out of his car seat. "How are you, Doc?"

"Fine, Skye." Maya smiled warmly. "How are you and Horizon doing? Hi, bud!" She tickled the baby's chubby toes, and he giggled and waved his right hand in her direction. His left arm hung limply by his side, partially paralyzed due to the shoulder dislocation he'd suffered at birth. He was getting physical therapy, but it was unlikely he'd ever have full use of the arm.

"Awesome. I got the ultrasound. Guess what?" Skye beamed. "It's a girl! We are so excited." She bounced Horizon on her hip. "Aren't we so excited for your baby sister?"

"That's wonderful news! Congratulations, Skye."

Skye was adhering strictly to all of the American College of Obstetrics and Gynecology–recommended prenatal testing, and she planned to deliver, this time, in the hospital with Maya and one of her colleagues. Skye had tracked down Maya in Camden as soon as she discovered she was pregnant again. "I don't care where I have this baby, or who else helps you deliver it, as long as you're the one seeing me through this," she'd said. "We have, like, history now, you and me."

"Based on what happened last time, there's a good chance you'll need a C-section this time around," Maya had explained. "Are you okay with not having a natural birth?"

"Every birth is natural, Doc," Skye had replied, smiling at the irony. "Whatever gets the baby out as safely as possible is fine by me. I'm not going to love it, but I've made my peace with it."

Maya completed her examination. Thus far, the baby, whom Skye had already named Sunrise, was thriving. The two women agreed that Skye would come back for another appointment in a month. Then Skye said, "There's one more thing. A request. From me and my family."

The Hauser Family Foundation, a nonprofit now headed by Skye, wanted to fund a health-outreach program for children and adults in Philadelphia. "Hauser's of Manchester is getting some flak because potato chips aren't the healthiest snack option, and our biggest customer is the company that makes and distributes public school lunches," Skye explained. "So now we have $5 million, and we don't know what to do with it, basically. I wanted to do something focusing on women and children, but I'm not sure what. Something to do with education, but beyond just, like, you know, 'eat healthy and exercise.' I know you teach the medical students, so I was wondering if you had any ideas?"

Maya left the room and returned a moment later with the laminated grant proposal she'd written at PGH the previous year. The one Tad had dismissed as mere "community outreach." She explained the idea to Skye, who, leafing through the proposal, said, "This is perfect. This is something the foundation could really get on board with."

"But what about Congressman Hauser?" Maya asked. "His conservative base? Will they let us teach about contraception and sexual education?"

"I'm the head of the foundation, so you can teach whatever you want," Skye said. "And my father is starting to come around on this stuff. I mean, don't get me wrong, he's appalled I'm not married, but at least he thinks science shouldn't be, like, political. And he respects the hell out of you. I could bring you on as a paid consultant for the foundation. What do you say? Can we count you in?" She extended her hand.

It felt like fate, though Maya didn't believe in fate; that was the wrong word. It felt like—she laughed to herself—cause and effect. Like karma. She shook Skye's hand firmly.

"Count me in."

FORTY-TWO

The Cooper medical students were an eager bunch. Once a week on Tuesday evening, five of them (not always the same five) piled into the Hotessey, chattering about board exams and ZDoggMD's latest YouTube offering and the way the smell of formaldehyde in the gross anatomy lab always made them hungry. They ensured the van was stocked with supplies and argued over which one of them got to carry the examination table for the doctor.

Esther, who was due back this summer to work at the clinic, was finishing her first year of medical school at Johns Hopkins. Maya had written her a glowing letter of recommendation for her application, but as it turned out, Esther hadn't needed it. She scored in the 99th percentile on her MCATs and received a nearly full tuition scholarship. She hadn't decided on a specialty yet, but she had ruled out ob-gyn. "I've seen too much," she said. At the moment, she was considering neurosurgery.

Before she left for school, Esther put Maya in contact with a community group she volunteered with in West Philadelphia called the Love League. The group supported disadvantaged new and expectant mothers by helping them find affordable childcare and arranging free transportation to and from doctor's appointments. They had a sister organization in Camden doing similar work. The community there was mostly Black and Latino, the working and unemployed poor. Maya met with the group's director and asked how she could be of help. What did women in the community need to be able to optimize their gynecological health? Time, she was told. Women were busy working multiple jobs or caring for young children or grandchildren, and taking time out to travel to and from a routine doctor's appointment—never mind arranging and paying for transportation and childcare—was a luxury many could not afford. "What if I went to them?" Maya had asked, and after several months of logistical planning and preparing, the Camden Love League Mobile Gyn Clinic was born.

The medical students volunteered their time—answering phones, making appointment schedules, and triaging patients based on symptoms—in exchange for an education they could never get inside a classroom or within the halls of the hospital. They visited patients in their homes, saw firsthand the multitude of nonmedical challenges their patients navigated on a daily basis to try to keep themselves and their families healthy. The broken refrigerator, the drafty apartment, the water tap that only ran in the mornings. What was the point in encouraging a new mother to pump breast milk, in reassuring her the cost of pump supplies and the time spent pumping were worth it, if her freezer wouldn't get cold enough to store the milk safely?

The students, most of whom were themselves from privileged backgrounds, were there to help and observe and learn. Maya made that clear when they signed up to volunteer. She did the examinations herself, in a private space in the home or behind a drape, chaperoned by a female volunteer from the Love League. It wasn't charity care, she reminded the students. It was a house call. It was bringing health care—the same quality health care they provided in their clinic—to the patient, with the dignity and respect for the patient that implied. Once, a particularly earnest and interested medical student, a young white man, asked Maya if he could perform one of the patient examinations, under Maya's supervision. "I need more practice with my speculum exams," he'd explained. "I can never quite visualize the cervix. Maybe you can tell me what I'm doing wrong."

"Do you know who James Marion Sims was?" Maya asked, looking over her shoulder at him from the driver's seat. He was sitting where Niam usually sat, a carpet of pulverized Goldfish crackers under his feet.

The young man shook his head.

"I was never taught about him either," Maya said. "Not in med school, not in residency."

As she maneuvered the van out of the parking garage, she explained that Dr. Sims, the father of gynecological surgery, perfected his techniques in the late 1800s by experimenting on enslaved Black women. He routinely did multiple surgeries on the same woman, usually without anesthesia. In the rearview mirror, she saw the faces of the five students go slack with horror.

"You and me, we aren't personally responsible for what Dr. Sims did, or for what medicine has historically done to Black people, women, the LGBTQ community, or the mentally ill," Maya said. "But we are responsible for the legacy that has left us with. The mistrust that some communities, rightly so, have of doctors. When we're caring for a community that's different from our own, it's on us to make sure we're educated about their history. The oath says to 'do no harm,' right? We can inadvertently do harm if we don't know the context in which we're practicing." She addressed the young man. "Instead of perfecting your speculum exam, it would be a better use of your time with me to talk to the patients and learn about their lives. Try to find out how you can be useful to them, not how this experience can benefit you. Center the patient, not yourself. Does that make sense?"

The young man nodded solemnly.

Maya glanced into the van's side-view mirror—long since repaired—and merged into traffic. "You know, I used to practice in a suburb where everyone was privileged. And it was all about giving the patients what they wanted. This is so much better. This is about trying to give patients what they need. Not what I think they need, but what they are telling me they need to stay healthy. When I can do that, when I can really be helpful, it's the best high, you know? I can't get enough of it."

The students nodded in agreement, but of course they did. They were still so young and altruistic. For Maya, it was the replacing of one type of ambition for another. A reimagining of what it meant to have *more*.

This wasn't the life her mother had wanted for her. The life she herself had once yearned for. She didn't have the power to command a room, the instant admiration of people like Amelia DeGilles or Evelyn Tuttle, or the trappings of status and respectability. What she had was this aging van filled with medical students and gynecological supplies, a schedule of house calls to complete before heading home to her three children and Swedish Meatball Tuesday, and nothing more to prove.

What she had, in fact, was everything.

EPILOGUE

On a sunny morning the following September, at Little Creek Elementary School, Maya stood in front of a white screen onto which a simple color diagram of the female reproductive system—the uterus, fallopian tubes, and ovaries—was being projected. A class of twenty-six inquisitive first graders, Niam front and center, sat before her on a multicolored alphabet rug in rapt silence. Their teacher looked on, smiling.

"So the ovary releases the egg, and the egg floats down the fallopian tube and ends up in the uterus."

A boy raised his hand, and Maya nodded to him. "Are the eggs like chicken eggs?" he asked.

"Kind of like chicken eggs. But much, much smaller. The size of a grain of sand. And there's no shell."

The boy nodded as if to say *isn't that something?*

Maya glanced at her watch. "Okay, that's it for this session. I'll see you all next week. We'll be learning about our kidneys! Does anyone have any other questions?"

Every hand in the room enthusiastically shot into the air.

ACKNOWLEDGMENTS

First, thank you to the mothers.

Thank you to my mother, and to her mother, and to all the mothers who came before them. Thank you to the mothers of yesteryear who did the laundry by hand and cared for children with polio and took their toddlers to visit other toddlers with chicken pox because that is what good mothers did. To the immigrant mothers, like mine and like my mother-in-law, who, when they were scarcely more than children themselves, said goodbye to their mothers and flew or sailed or fled to a strange land in the loving hope that their future babies could live a better life. To the mothers of today, who have seen their worth and their work discussed and debated and dismissed by people who are not and will never be mothers. To the mothers fiercely holding on to dreams of who they want to be and what they want to do in this world, dreams that perhaps have nothing to do with being a mother, or perhaps have everything to do with being a mother. Thank you for quietly holding the universe together at the seams so the rest of humanity can go to work, make art, sleep, write books, and otherwise go about its business without worrying about how the kids are getting fed or who is taking them to the dentist. I am proud to be one of you.

Thank you to my editor, Kristine Swartz, and my agent, Jessica Watterson, for suggesting that I write a book about a doctor with young children and then letting me run with the idea in whatever direction I chose. I am forever grateful for your steadfast support and guidance.

To my team at Berkley: Christine Legon, Fareeda Bullert, Tara O'Connor, Megha Jain, Rakhee Bhatt, and Mary Baker. My deepest thanks for your care and dedication.

Thank you to Vikki Chu for creating the beautiful cover for this book.

Many thanks also to the team at SDLA, especially the wonderful Andrea Cavallaro.

Thank you, as always, to Katie McCoach for her consistently brilliant insight and advice.

Thank you to Dr. Stephanie Pearson for speaking to me about the practice of obstetrics and gynecology.

For their support, I am grateful to Kristan Higgins, Samuel Shem, Maiken Scott, and Saloni Sharma. Many thanks also to the Cherry Hill Public Library in Cherry Hill, New Jersey, and Blue Willow Bookshop in Houston, Texas.

To my family, thank you for your unwavering support despite the fact that, if we're being honest, some of you really don't like fiction.

To my husband, thank you for making dinner while listening to me vent about the patriarchy. I continue to be exceedingly pleased that I decided to marry you. You are the best person I know.

Most of all, to L and K, my sparkling, clever, irrepressible girls. Being your mom is the greatest privilege of my life. You infuse everything, even eating spaghetti on a Tuesday night, with meaning and purpose and joy, and there does not exist yet a word in any language that can capture how utterly and completely I love you both.

AT LEAST YOU HAVE YOUR HEALTH

MADI SINHA

DISCUSSION QUESTIONS

1. In an early scene, Maya is accosted by a white parent at Hamilton Hall who mistakes her for her children's nanny/babysitter. How does this scene set the tone for the intersecting themes of race, class, and gender that play out in the rest of the book?

2. Maya is Indian, and her medical assistant, Esther, is Black. Discuss how these two characters interact with each other and with the white characters in the book. In what ways is the manifestation of racism the same in the two women's lives? In what ways is it different?

3. Amelia tells Maya she founded Eunoia to empower women and offer them choices regarding their health care, but only wealthy women can afford to pay the yearly subscription fee Eunoia charges. Consider the idea that both health and choice are commodities in our society and that they are only truly accessible to the wealthy/privileged—do you agree? Why or why not?

4. Reflect on Maya's relationship with her mother. How does Lalita's dissatisfaction with her life affect Maya? How does it influence the way Maya is raising Diya?

5. What do you think of the book's title? Does it capture the content and theme of the book for you? If not, what title would you have given to this novel?

6. Dean is content with his situation in life, while Maya is ambitious and desperate for more. What do you think accounts for this difference in their personalities/attitudes?

7. Which of the three Anders-Rao children is your favorite?

8. Amelia has a Ganesh fountain in the foyer of her home, despite the fact that she's not Hindu. Is there a difference between cultural appropriation and cultural appreciation? Who gets to decide this?

Keep reading for an excerpt from

THE WHITE COAT DIARIES

Available now!

I just want to help people, I just want to help people, I just want to help people. . . .

I crouch on the floor in an Emergency Department supply closet, wedged in between boxes of adult diapers and pregnancy tests. The door swings open, and a nurse pokes her head in.

"Are there any linens left in here?" she asks.

"I'm not sure." I stare into my lap, letting my hair fall across my face like a curtain. Hopefully she doesn't notice my puffy eyes.

"Are you the intern that just stuck herself?"

"Yes." I discreetly wipe my nose with the back of my hand. I try to sound less panicked than I feel. "Yup, that was me. I just took the needle out of the patient and accidentally stuck myself in the hand with it. Like an idiot." I attempt to laugh ironically, but it comes out sounding more like a desperate whimper.

"Well, when you're done doing whatever it is you're doing, you need to report to Employee Health. They'll test you and give you medication." She peers down at me through her tiny bifocals. Her voice sympathetic, she asks, "Have you ever had a needle stick before?"

My chest is so tight I can barely get the word out. "No."

"Well, I've had four in my career, and it's not that big a deal."

"Really?" I'm buoyed by a surge of hope. "Did you—"

"Make sure to get yourself together before coming back out here. It's unprofessional to cry in front of the patients." She closes the door abruptly.

The motion-sensor light goes off, and I am left in near–pitch darkness.

I just want to help peo— Oh fuck everyone!

I spend probably fifteen minutes sitting in the dark supply closet, too exhausted and depleted to move. I've been awake for more than twenty-four hours. During that time, I've peed twice, eaten once, and asked myself, *How did it come to this?* eighteen times. I thought I'd be good at this. Why am I not good at this? I reach into the pocket of my white coat for my inhaler, and the lights flick back on. From the corner of my eye, I see something tiny and brown scurry across the floor and dive behind a box of gauze pads. I spring to my feet, and my head strikes the shelf above me. Pain sears through the back of my skull. I yelp, and as my hand flies up to my scalp to check for bleeding, I knock over a box, causing a million little Band-Aids to come fluttering down all around me like ticker tape, as if to say, *Congratulations! You're a twenty-six-year-old loser hiding in a closet.*

It wasn't supposed to be like this. I graduated at the top of my class—Alpha Omega Alpha honor society, in fact—from medical school. I beat out hundreds of other applicants for a coveted internal medicine residency spot at Philadelphia General Hospital. *The* Philadelphia General, my first choice. I could have easily gone to the Cleveland Clinic or Mass General or Mayo, but I chose to go where I knew the training was rigorous and unmatched because I was certain, beyond a doubt, that I could handle it, probably with one arm tied behind my back.

I can recite the name of every bone, muscle, and nerve in the adult human body the way other people can recite song lyrics (and, just for reference, there are 206 bones in the human body). I can diagram, from memory, the biochemical pathway by which the liver converts squalene into cholesterol. I can list the top twenty medications for hypertension *and* the side effects of each, without using a mnemonic device. I've studied. My God, have I studied. I've studied to the point of self-imposed social isolation. To the point of obsession. I've prepared for this for years, decades, my whole life. I wrote an essay in third grade titled "Why Tendons Are Awesome!" that not only earned me an A, but was prominently displayed for months on the classroom bulletin board. I mean, I was *meant* for this.

I've been an intern for twenty-four hours, and that arm that's tied behind my back? I'm ready to rip it off this instant.

Sighing, I crouch down, pick up all the Band-Aids, and cram them back into their box. Then I emerge from the closet sheepishly, expecting to find at least one of the several ED nurses waiting for me, ready to comfort me in that stern-but-understanding, maternal way of theirs. The only person at the nurses' station is a disinterested janitor on his cell phone.

A balding man wearing large, square, wire-rimmed glasses and an angry expression barks at me from the hallway. "Excuse me! Miss, do you work here?"

I nod, and he approaches. "My wife is still waiting for a bed." He indicates a woman in a hospital gown lying on a stretcher that's been pushed to one side of the bustling ED hallway. "When is she going to be moved to her room?"

"I'm not sure . . ." I say, uncertain if I can help him but desperately wanting to do something, anything, right. "Has she been admitted?"

"Obviously, yes. She's being admitted for observation for pneumonia. Her name is Tally. Lenore Tally. Do you have any information on her?"

The name means nothing to me. "I'm sorry, she's not one of my patients, but I can try to find her nurse for you," I offer. The few nurses in sight look busy, drawing blood and taking vital signs. "It might take a few minutes, but—"

The man throws up his hands in frustration. "None of you people have any answers! Oh, for God's sake, I'll find her nurse myself!" He storms off, and I can hear his voice echoing down the hall: "Excuse me? Do you work here?"

My shoulders sag. So much for doing something right. At this point, it's clear: the gaping black hole of despair that has consumed my being can be filled by only one thing. I need baked goods, and I need them *stat*. I hurry to the vending machine in the ED waiting room, eat two and a half bags of mini chocolate chip cookies while waiting for the elevator, and find, to my great disappointment, that my mood is only marginally brightened.

It had never occurred to me—until the moment I drew the needle out of my patient's vein, popped off the test tube full of his blood, crossed my hands to reach for the gauze pad, and jabbed the end of the needle into the back of my hand—that I might be putting myself at risk by spending my days and nights tending to sick people. Well, then again, that's not true. It *had* occurred to me, but before it became an actual possibility, the idea of contracting a potentially lethal disease from a patient had a noble, romantic, Victorian sort of feel to it: the selfless, waistcoated doctor carrying a leather satchel and a jar full of leeches, sacrificing herself at the bedside of her patient—that sort of thing.

I know the chances of actually getting sick are extremely slim, especially if I take prophylactic antiviral medication, but I worry nonetheless. I worry with a fervor that I both recognize as irrational and embrace as inevitable. Worry out of proportion with reality is kind of my *thing*.

"Is this your first needle stick?" The nurse at the tiny Employee Health office next to the hospital pharmacy—her name tag identifies her as "Rhonda"—looks irked and preoccupied. When I walked in a moment ago, she was engaged in a heated phone conversation with someone named Hank about getting his lazy ass off the couch and maybe, for once in his worthless life, cleaning up the cat's vomit. It was quite a few minutes of this sort of thing before she turned around and realized I was sitting right in front of her desk, awkwardly trying to decide whether to wait for her to notice me or just interrupt her. When she hung up the phone, it was with one eye fixed suspiciously on me. "Can I help you?"

I told her what had happened and, in doing so, triggered another bout of panicky tears. Rhonda kindly, if impatiently, handed me a box of Kleenex. Then she proceeded to fish out from a filing cabinet no less than eight different questionnaires, each of which she now seems determined to methodically complete in its entirety.

"No. This is my first needle stick," I answer, twisting the damp Kleenex around my fingers.

"Do you have any risk factors for HIV or hepatitis C?" Rhonda asks.

"No."

"Have you ever been tested for either?"

"No."

"Are you currently sexually active?"

"Nope."

"When was the last time you were sexually active without barrier protection?"

"Um . . . never."

"As in you've never had unprotected intercourse?"

"As in . . . I've never had intercourse."

Rhonda pauses, her pen hovering above the paper.

"It's cultural," I add quickly. "I'm Indian. Premarital sex is frowned upon. Like, a lot. You've seen *Bend It Like Beckham*, right?"

"That's . . . fine," Rhonda says, scratching one raised eyebrow.

I sigh inwardly. *Whatever, Rhonda.*

She asks me for my medical history (*None, except a mild case of asthma*), list of allergies (*None, except cats*), and social history (Do I smoke? *No.* Drink? *No.* Do I use illicit drugs? *Obviously not.*). Then she asks me to put my arm on her desk, ties a tourniquet around my biceps, and draws four vials of blood.

As she tapes a wad of gauze over my skin, she says, "You'll need to come in for another blood test in six weeks and again in three months." She hands me a slip of paper. "And this is for the antiviral tablets. Pick them up at the pharmacy next door. You'll take them three times a day for the next six weeks."

I look at the prescription. "Lamivudine? A nucleoside reverse transcriptase inhibitor?" I say, aghast.

Rhonda stares at me. "That's the protocol."

"But the potential side effects of this are nausea, diarrhea, abdominal pain, headaches, pancreatitis, and liver failure."

She regards me skeptically. "If you say so."

"Isn't there anything else I could take instead?" I plead. "I'm an intern. I can't afford to have headaches and go into liver failure. I have patients to round on. I have a lot to do."

"That's the protocol." She enunciates each word in a way that indicates that she has fulfilled the duties laid out in her job description and, therefore, our interaction must come to an immediate close.

I turn toward the door. "You don't think didanosine or even efavirenz would be a better—"

Rhonda puts her phone to her ear. "Have a nice day, Doctor!"

'm sitting at one of a cluster of long tables near a picture window. A curt little sign in a metal stand nearby reads: RESERVED FOR PGH DOCTORS AND STAFF. It's early, a half-moon still visible in the dawn sky, and the only other patron in the cafeteria dining room is an elderly man connected to an oxygen tank that he carries in a cloth duffel bag. He shuffles in my direction, notices the sign, then shuffles away. A plastic tray appears across the table from me, and a slender young man with round glasses says, "Hi. Stuart Ness, Harvard Med." He begins to vigorously dissect a grapefruit.

"Yes, I remember. We met at orientation." Where you introduced yourself as Stuart Ness from Harvard Med. Twice.

"Being on call is great!" he enthuses without prompting. "I admitted eleven patients, started fourteen IV lines, and still had time to watch a movie. I'm not even tired. I think I'll go for a run when our shift is over."

I wonder if it's possible that I'm so fatigued I'm hallucinating this entire interaction with this gratingly peppy Harry Potter lookalike. "That's dynamite," I say.

"I'm so psyched to finally be here. I can't wait to meet Dr. Portnoy. The man, the legend, am I right?"

"Yup."

"And *the* Dr. V. Did you hear that we get to work with him? Like, actually round with him and everything?" His eyes gleam. "So awesome!"

"It's pretty awesome." I manage a thin smile.

"What was your name again?"

"Norah Kapadia."

"Hey, any relation to Dr. Kapadia, the head of Pediatrics at UPenn? The one that came up with the Kapadia criteria for Kawasaki disease? I mean, I don't know how common the last name of Kapadia is, but—"

I blow a puff of air through my pursed lips. I've lost track of how many times I've answered this question over the years, but it always comes from someone eager to show off that they're well-versed in rare pediatric disorders. "That's my father."

"No way! Is he still practicing?"

"He passed away." I tuck a strand of hair behind my ear.

Stuart shifts in his seat. "Oh, wow. I'm really sorry."

I nod tersely and shrug. "It's fine. It was a long time ago."

"His paper on the diagnosis of Kawasaki is epic. It's practically biblical."

I smile at the compliment.

Having finished dismembering his grapefruit, Stuart starts in on an enormous bowl of oatmeal. "He must have been an amazing doctor."

"That's what I've heard." And I'm sure he never spent a night on call crying in a supply closet. I stare at my plate and silently count exactly twenty-three little sugarcoated doughnut crumbs.

Stuart clears his throat. His tone is forcefully bright. "So, how was your night?"

"I got a needle stick."

His eyes widen in a way so cartoonish I almost expect a honking sound to accompany his stunned facial expression. "Seriously? Yikes. Did the patient have any . . . you know . . . communicable diseases?"

"HIV."

"Oh, boy. Well, the rate of HIV infection from a needle stick is like one in one hundred thousand. I wouldn't even worry about it. Now, hep C, that's the scary one. That's more like one in forty."

I jab my index finger at the crumbs. "He had hepatitis C, too."

He takes this in. "Wow. You were that kid in elementary school who ran with scissors, right?"

A tray slams onto the table, silverware rattling. Clark, an acquaintance of mine from medical school who has the soulful eyes and determined jawline of a young Ernest Hemingway—as well as the tendency to crack each of his ten knuckles one at a time, loudly and repetitively—drops into a chair. Wearing a faded white T-shirt over bloodstained green scrub pants, he looks as if he's narrowly survived some sort of natural disaster. Sections of his black hair project from his head at varying sharp angles. "Good morning." His voice is a low growl that reminds me of a lawn mower. "This place should be burned to the ground."

Stuart puts out his hand, grinning. "Whoa! Another rough first night. Hi! I'm Stuart Ness, Harvard Med."

Clark glances at Stuart's hand and takes a slow breath. A vein bulges in his left temple. "Norah," he says without looking at me, "I'm going to put my head down on the table. I want you to take this fork and jam it into my carotid."

"Ha! I like this guy!" Stuart laughs, clapping him on the back.

I smile sympathetically at Clark, though I'm fairly sure my night was worse than his.

"Let me ask you," Clark says. "Is it too late to get off this crazy train? What if we quit now, before it gets any worse?"

I sigh and rub my forehead, the beginnings of a migraine coalescing somewhere deep in the frontal cortex of my brain. "I can't quit. I've put too much time and work into getting *on* this crazy train. I can't bail out now. What about student loan debt?"

"Sallie Mae. That heartless bitch," Clark grumbles, rubbing his eyes with the heels of his hands.

"Easy there, buddy. It's only the first day," Stuart says, smiling encouragingly. He's about to clap Clark on the back again when Clark shoots him a look so menacing that Stuart's hand freezes in midair.

A moment passes before I realize that a female voice is commenting, dispassionately, from the loudspeaker overhead: "Code blue, room 512. Code blue, room 512."

A fork clatters to the floor.

We run.

Photo by Ashley Walsh Photography

MADI SINHA is a physician and writer. She lives in New Jersey with her husband and two children.

CONNECT ONLINE

MadiSinha.com
🐦 MadiSinha
📷 MadiSinha

Ready to find
your next great read?

Let us help.

Visit prh.com/nextread

Penguin
Random
House